THE AIR RAID GIRLS

Jenny Holmes

CORGI BOOKS

TRANSWORLD PUBLISHERS
Penguin Random House, One Embassy Gardens,
8 Viaduct Gardens, London SW11 7BW
www.penguin.co.uk

Transworld is part of the Penguin Random House group of companies
whose addresses can be found at global.penguinrandomhouse.com

Penguin
Random House
UK

First published in Great Britain in 2021 by Bantam Press
an imprint of Transworld Publishers
Corgi edition published 2021

A CIP catalogue record for this book
is available from the British Library.

ISBN
9780552177078

Typeset in   of New Baskerville   n Keynes
Printe   and bound in Great   .p.A.

The auth   House
Ireland   YH68.

P
futur   ook
is n   r.

For Gill and Nuala

CHAPTER ONE

April 1941

'Come on, slowcoach!' Connie Bailey emerged from her cubicle in her new two-piece swimming costume. It clung to her curves and showed an expanse of bare midriff that was bound to invite a chorus of approving whistles and envious gasps from fellow bathers at the mixed session at Kelthorpe's baths. It was six o'clock in the evening; still daylight as a war-torn England crept out of winter hibernation and spring took hold. Connie rattled the metal door of the neighbouring cubicle. 'I'll catch my death if you don't get a move on.'

'You go ahead without me,' her sister, Lizzie Harrison, instructed as she struggled with her zip. 'I won't be long.'

'No, I'll wait.' Connie peered over the top of the swing door. 'Here, let me do that.'

So Lizzie unbolted the door and stepped out on to the cold concrete floor. Once the back zip of her green one-piece was fastened, she reached for her white rubber bathing cap. 'All set!' she announced with a smile.

The sisters paused by the mirror to pull on their

1

tight regulation caps, pushing stray strands of dark hair out of sight and grimacing at their less-than-glamorous reflections. Then they waded through the ice-cold footbath and stepped out into the iron-and-glass cathedral of the municipal baths – a raucous, echoing, tiled monument to health and cleanliness that had been built at the end of the Victorian period and was still going strong.

The girls paused briefly at the shallow end to take in the sights and smells: bare limbs scything through chlorinated water, children kicking and squealing. They glanced towards the deep end at twin spring-boards, where lithe youths dived into the water with scarcely a splash.

'I will if you will,' Connie challenged Lizzie with a raised eyebrow and a grin. Let the men ogle and whistle and wink – what did she care?

'You're on!' Lizzie agreed.

So they set off at an elegant, hip-swinging trot along the side of the pool – two tall, loose-limbed figures weaving through other swimmers who were taking a breather, taking care not to slip on the wet tiles, smiling eagerly as they reached the diving boards. Stepping up – Connie on the left and Lizzie on the right – they inspected the dozens of dark heads bobbing in the water below. Then, when a space appeared, they nodded and gave a little skip before running along the boards in perfect unison, arms above their heads, anticipating the headlong dive. One last skip and the twin boards dipped violently as the girls sprang and flung themselves forward. An instant in mid-air, a curve downwards, then the shock of entering cold water and a plunge to the bottom and up again through a cloud of bubbles to surface with a gasp.

Connie laughed and spluttered as she adjusted her shoulder straps and then the bottom section of her costume. 'These two-pieces weren't designed for diving,' she admitted. 'I'll remember that in future.'

'That'll teach you!' Lizzie grinned as she swam to the side then trod water. What a joy to feel buoyed up and fully alive after her wearying day spent delivering bread and teacakes up and down the terraced streets of old Kelthorpe then along the quayside past Anderson's timber yard. From there she'd driven around the harbour's edge, with its fishy, salty reek, and on under the towering headland into the new, more fashionable part of town to deliver loaves to hotels and shops lining the seafront. The familiar sight of her green van proudly emblazoned with the words 'Harrison Family Bakers, Est. 1923' had brought cheery waves from passers-by as seagulls had soared overhead.

Having adjusted her swimsuit, Connie completed a couple of swift lengths of front crawl. It was a pity that the pool was so crowded, but what could you expect? When the good folk of Kelthorpe needed a break from rationing and make do and mend, it cost only a couple of pennies to pass through the swimming baths' turnstile into a world of frolics and fun. It was a choice between that or a Saturday matinee at the Savoy and Lord knew, Connie had had more than her fill of ushering cinemagoers up and down those dimly lit aisles.

'Blimey, Connie; knock a chap out, why don't you!' George Bachelor thrashed his arms and legs in an exaggerated display of getting out of her way. They'd

3

almost collided in the deep end and now they turned together and swam at a more leisurely breaststroke pace back towards the shallow end. 'It was full steam ahead as usual for Air Raid Warden Connie Bailey.'

'Well, there's no point doing things by halves.' Connie had been coming to the Elliot Street baths for years – ever since her family had moved into a house opposite, a small two-up two-down in a terraced row. She and Lizzie had both been able to swim almost as soon as they could walk. In fact, Connie had learned to dive even before she could swim, encouraged by her father, who would stand up to his waist in the shallow end, arms spread wide, calling out, 'That's it, Con – head first. Ready, steady, dive!' She could hear his deep, gravelly voice now and see his smiling face as she'd flung herself into the breathtakingly cold water then bobbed up into his strong arms. 'Talking of air raids – are you on duty later tonight?' she asked George as they finished their length.

'You bet,' he promised as he hauled himself up on to the side and perched with legs akimbo then ran a hand through his fair, wavy hair – a movement that showed his glistening torso to full advantage. 'I'll be ready to show the new girl the ropes,' he added jauntily.

Connie had lately arrived back on Elliot Street and was a recent recruit to the Civil Defence lark. 'Serve to Save', as the old poster went at the start of the war, when it wanted to attract new volunteers to become wardens. 'A responsible job for responsible men'. *And women, too*, Connie had thought at the time. But back then she'd had a different life, away from family and friends.

In Connie's opinion – and in the opinion of all the girls she knew – George ('Bachelor by name, bachelor by nature') needed taking down a peg or two. 'Just because you've been wearing a tin hat and a boiler suit for two months longer than me doesn't mean that you can lord it over me.' Her reminder was accompanied by a playful splash, which showered cold water over him and his offer.

'Point taken.' Kicking his feet vigorously, George splashed back.

Laughing, Connie pushed away from the side and resumed her swim. 'Blooming cheek!' she said as she rejoined Lizzie in the deep end and gestured towards the exit.

'Who? What?' Lizzie caught sight of George's muscular back view as he paddled through the footbath towards the men's changing room. 'Oh, him,' she said dismissively.

'God's gift,' Connie grumbled. George Bachelor was the foreman at Anderson's timber yard; a natty dresser, teller of tall stories and renowned maker of false promises. 'Come on, Liz; what say we climb up on those boards again?'

'You're on!' Lizzie said for a second time as they raised themselves on to the side of the pool – water babies, synchronized divers, best friends, sisters-in-arms.

Never one to stick to the rules, Connie had opted for the battledress uniform more normally issued to male air raid wardens since February that year. 'What good is a skirt when you're clambering through rubble?' she'd asked her father, Bert Harrison, who'd

5

volunteered for the service at the start of the war and had served non-stop ever since. If anyone was qualified to show her the ropes it would be her conscientious, unflappable father, not Johnny-come-lately George Bachelor.

In fact, there was no military-style discipline, no ranks, no saluting in Civil Defence, so what you wore to rescue people from bombed buildings was up to you.

Obviously the tin hat and gas mask were obligatory, and Connie wore her silver ARP lapel badge with pride – as she had throughout her basic Air Raid Precautions training, when she'd been taught first aid, anti-gas measures and how to deal with incendiaries and high explosives. Now she could use a stirrup pump and assist with casualties alongside the best of them. On top of which, Connie knew the location of every public and privately built shelter between the gasworks and St Stephen's dock, where the River Kell flowed out into the North Sea. She knew exactly who lived in which house, together with the routine of each inhabitant, and she could tell you, if required, the location of stopcocks and electrical main switches, telephone boxes, builders' stores and breakdown lorries within a half-mile radius of her sector post on the corner of Park Road and Gas Street.

So that evening she set out confidently from number 12, having rinsed the chlorine from her hair and hung her two-piece swimming costume on the washing line at the back of the house to drip-dry overnight. She waved at her young cousin Arnold, who was squatting on his front doorstep six doors along from them, his skinny white legs and knobbly knees protruding from grey flannel shorts, his school blazer unbuttoned and his gas mask slung across his chest. 'What are you up to?' she called to him.

'Waiting for Mam.' His glum face brightened at the sight of Connie.

'Are you off trekking again?' she checked.

Arnold nodded then his face fell back into a scowl. 'Worse luck.'

'What's up? Is it too cold to sleep out under the stars?' She sympathized with the lad; there was nothing romantic about kipping under a hedgerow in the middle of the North York Moors at this time of year. But Arnold's mother, Connie's Aunty Vera, insisted that it was better to be safe than sorry. 'You never know when a nuisance raider might attack Kelthorpe,' she would say with a shiver of apprehension. 'We could be fast asleep in our beds and Firebomb Fritz could blow us all to smithereens.'

So trekking was the order of the day for many residents with young families – out into the windswept wilds then back again in the morning, pinched with cold, yawning and yearning for a good night's sleep.

Connie reached her wardens' station as the light began to fade. It had been set up in a disused cobbler's shop and still retained the smell of old leather and shoe polish as well as a shoe mender's last and two unclaimed pairs of working men's boots gathering dust on the shelves behind the counter. The entrance was heavily sandbagged and the windows boarded up so that the interior was gloomy and stuffy even during the day.

Bert glanced up as Connie entered. 'Look what

the cat dragged in,' he said with a wink, one hand pressed over the telephone receiver. He was on the line to the town hall Report and Control Centre, phoning in a situation report and updating them on an unexploded bomb on the corner of Maypole Street. 'Top priority,' he told the telephonist in his brisk, alert way, though his thin face looked lined and tired. He was fifty years old, and two decades of waking at half three in the morning to cycle to the baker's shop on College Road in order to fire up the ovens and bake the day's first batch of bread had taken their toll. These days, the stint of bread-making would be followed by a long afternoon shift at the wardens' post and so home to an early bed before the gruelling routine started again at the crack of dawn.

'Ta, Dad. It's nice to see you, too.' Connie took off her natty ski cap and reached for her helmet, stashed behind the counter. She planted a kiss on the top of her father's white helmet, the metal cold on her lips. Then she went through into a smaller, even dingier back room to pick up her first-aid haversack, then her warden's torch and rattle, which she tucked into small slings attached to her wide canvas belt. Everything in its place, she mounted the creaky stairs to the wardens' restroom, where she found George playing darts with their colleague, Tom Rose.

The two men didn't break off their game, so she settled into one of the two armchairs and began flicking through a magazine, accompanied by the soft thud of darts hitting the cork board. The air was thick with cigarette smoke and the blackout blind was already pulled down to set a good example to the rest of the street. As soon as the daytime shift clocked off and the paperwork was completed, it would be time for George, Tom and Connie, along with the rest of their team, to set off on their dusk patrol.

The sound of voices below warned Connie that the handover was under way. Maypole Street was mentioned again, together with a necessary update to the Household Register (two extra persons at number 11 Gas Street: a Molly Stevens and her brother, Lionel) and a check through the list of residents who had chosen to trek out into the countryside overnight. Then she heard her father mention a new messenger, whose job it was to carry information between wardens' posts, control centres and first-aid posts.

'Colin Strong is the lad's name – he's a Boy Scout; lives with his family in one of the new bungalows over on Musgrave Street.' Bert's voice grew louder as he came to the bottom of the stairs. 'Are you there, Con?' he called.

Connie put down the magazine and went out on to the landing.

'Come and say goodnight to your old pa,' he invited. 'But before that, tell me; how was your swim?'

Connie happily obliged by skipping downstairs and giving her father a peck on the cheek. 'The swim was a real pick-me-up. Lizzie came too. She's at home now, cooking you a nice supper of bangers and mash.'

Bert gave her hand a quick squeeze. 'And you're – you know – you're . . . ?'

'I'm tickety-boo, Dad. Don't you worry about me.' He would, though – worry was part of Bert's make-up – so she steered him off in a brighter, breezier direction. 'You should have seen Lizzie and me dive in at the deep end earlier – no splash, clean as a whistle.'

Her father's face brightened immediately. 'I'll bet you gave the boys something to look at.'

George leaned over the banister. 'You can say that again, Bert. I saw those dives with my own eyes and gave the girls a well-deserved ten out of ten.'

'Did you, now?' Bert hung up his helmet and replaced it with his shapeless flat cap. It was ingrained with flour dust from the bakery, as was the overcoat that he pulled on over his battledress. 'Right, I'm off. I've put two fire watchers up on the roof of the corporation baths overnight,' he mentioned to Kenneth Browning, the senior night warden, on his way out. 'And Connie, remember to keep an eye on the new lad, Colin. Between you and me, he's a bit wet behind the ears, bless him.'

Connie pushed her father out on to the street with a good-natured shove. 'Goodnight, Dad!' His bicycle was propped against the sandbags and she watched him bend to attach his bicycle clips then mount and cycle off down Gas Street, a hunched figure swerving to avoid manhole covers and the unexpected obstacle of salvaged metal piled up by the kerb. Light was fading fast and dusk fell like a grey blanket over stone-flagged pavement and cobbled street. Doors were closed, blackout blinds were down. Another long night of keeping watch had begun.

'You and Connie did what?' Bob Waterhouse sat in his usual seat across the table from Lizzie in the kitchen at number 12. The sight of two swimming costumes hanging limply from the washing line in

10

the backyard left him in no doubt that his fiancée's account of their adventures at the swimming baths was true.

'We did running dives off the springboards, no hanging about – just like the lads. One, two, three, and in we went!' Lizzie secretly enjoyed Bob's grunt of disapproval. 'Twice.'

'Just like the lads,' he repeated. 'Your Connie's a bad influence, if you ask me.' Drumming his fingers quietly on the table, Bob's displeasure showed itself in a downward curve of the mouth.

'What do you mean? Why shouldn't we girls have as much fun as anyone else?' Lizzie put down her sewing and rocked back on her chair. 'Who cares if people stare?'

'And did they?' Bob knew he was being teased but he couldn't let it go. It was one thing to fling yourself about at the baths when you were seven or eight years old – doing underwater somersaults and cartwheels from the side into the pool – no one cared. But in his opinion women in their twenties ought to show more decorum.

'Some did,' Lizzie admitted mischievously. 'But it was Connie they were staring at, not me.'

'That's what I mean; ever since she came back home she's been leading you astray. I take it that skimpy maroon thing is the reason that the men were gawping at her.' He gestured towards the items on the clothes line.

'In what way, leading me astray?' Bob could be a stick-in-the-mud at times. He was twenty-three going on fifty. Lizzie studied him carefully as he stumbled towards a reply. His dark hair was neatly parted to

11

the side, his features symmetrical and attractive and his skin was smooth with no trace of five o'clock shadow.

'You used not to lark about so much,' he explained uncomfortably. Lizzie and he had known each other since he was thirteen and she was twelve and they'd been walking out together since she was fifteen – textbook childhood sweethearts. 'I like it better when you're serious.'

'And quiet?' she prompted.

Bob nodded. 'Connie can be a bit loud at times. And let's be honest, after what she went through last autumn, you'd think she'd have calmed down – for a little while, at least.'

There was a movement upstairs in the back bed-room and the faint sound of her father coughing. 'You mean losing John so early in the marriage?' Lizzie murmured.

Bob nodded. 'I think the poor bloke deserves to be shown more respect.'

They were heading into deep waters, Lizzie realized. 'Connie does respect John's memory,' she insisted. 'But her way of dealing with things is different – she looks forward, not back.'

There was another cough from upstairs, which led to a long pause before Bob continued. 'Granted, Connie is doing her bit for Civil Defence,' he conceded. 'I know she tackled the training course head-on – the gas van rigmarole and learning first aid and suchlike. She's no doubt a dab hand with the stirrup pump.'

'Don't be so mean,' Lizzie objected to his sarcasm. 'Honestly, Bob – it's as if you blame her for what

12

happened to John, which – as you know better than anyone because you were there – was an accident, pure and simple.' A careless moment at work on St Stephen's dock; a crane swinging its heavy timber load from quayside to storage yard while John's back had been turned, followed by tragedy.

'I don't blame Connie,' he snapped back. 'I'm only saying that to look at your sister now, you'd never think she was a widow. And it only happened six months back.'

Lizzie sighed and stood up, turning from Bob to stare out at the gathering dusk. Was there any justification for his complaints? she wondered. Had she gone off the rails a little since Connie came back? 'I'm sorry,' she said, without turning towards him. 'But scratch the surface and I'm still me – the same person I've always been.' The shy sister waiting patiently in the wings; the one you could depend on.

Bob approached from behind and slid his arms around her waist then kissed her softly on the back of the neck, her dark curls brushing his face as he did so. 'I'm sorry, too. You know I don't like us arguing.'

Lizzie turned and put her arms around his neck. He hadn't changed one iota; not since he'd left school at fourteen and gone to work at the timber yard – always the same steady-as-a-rock, reliable Bob in an unstable world that was often hard for her to make sense of. 'So we won't,' she decided in her sweet, low voice. 'No more arguments from now on.'

After a quick, light kiss, Lizzie returned to her sewing (turning the frayed collar on one of her father's shirts) while Bob scanned the newspaper headlines then tuned in to listen to music on the wireless. There was no more noise from upstairs, which meant that Bert was at last getting his much-needed sleep.

Lizzie sewed and listened, pushing her needle through stiff white fabric discoloured by years of wear, her foot tapping gently to the rhythm of big-band tunes until the evening ended as it always did with lingering kisses on the front doorstep.

'Tomorrow?' Bob stepped shyly back as a group of trekkers, mainly women and children, filed silently by, making their exodus in semi-darkness without torches to guide them. They were bundled up in winter coats and scarves, heads down, some carrying flasks of tea and tins of biscuits in knapsacks to help them through a cold, dark night.

'Tomorrow,' Lizzie agreed.

Unless Jerry saw fit to drop his incendiaries on the dockside and set the skyline ablaze. Unless high explosives fell on the gasworks or the town hall, reducing all to rubble.

Bob blew her a kiss as he sat astride his bicycle. 'Goodnight, sweetheart.'

'Goodnight, God bless.' With a small sigh Lizzie watched him weave his way between trekkers; the man she was to marry, the man whose diamond-and-sapphire ring fitted snugly on the third finger of her left hand.

Connie and George's nightly patrol began as usual with a thorough check of the blackout. Not a chink of light from houses and shops was permissible, and the few cars that were out and about after dark had to be fitted with headlamp hoods that allowed only a narrow beam to be directed down on to the road.

14

'Put that light out!' was the warden's cry from the street to anyone failing to comply with regulations. Disgruntled residents would chunter to each other as they rearranged blinds or flicked a switch, complaining about the little Hitlers in Air Raid Precautions uniform who loved to throw their weight around.

'Careless beggars,' George muttered, having turned a corner on to Tennyson Street, where he'd yelled the curt, four-word order at the occupants of number 5. Light from a bare electric bulb was shining brightly from a downstairs window but his barked command had been ignored. 'Telephone Luftwaffe HQ and tell Jerry you're here while you're at it.'

'That's old Mr Ward's house. He's lived alone since his wife died.' Connie thought it was worth a closer look. 'Wait here,' she told George as she went to investigate.

There was no answer to her knock on the front door, which hung slightly ajar. 'Mr Ward?' She knocked again.

'Just tell him to put the bloody light out!' George shouted impatiently from the pavement.

Hearing a movement, Connie peered cautiously down the narrow hallway but it was too dark to make anything out. 'Mr Ward, are you there?'

As her eyes got used to the gloom, she saw the old man sitting on the floor, legs stretched straight out, back propped against the wall. His walking stick had slid beyond his reach and he seemed unable to get up.

'I'm stuck,' he confirmed crossly. 'Come in, whoever you are, and help me back on my feet.'

'It's me, Connie Bailey – Connie Harrison as was. I used to deliver your bread – you remember me?' She

15

turned on her torch and hurried to the rescue, easily able to take the old man's weight and haul him up from the floor. Poor old thing; there was hardly any flesh on his bones and he smelled of stale tobacco and Brylcreem. 'Here, Mr Ward; here's your stick. How long have you been sitting there in the cold?'

Grasping the walking stick with a trembling hand, he made light of what had happened. 'Not long. I was setting off for the shelter as per usual but I tripped and fell – I was stone-cold sober before you ask.'

'You left your front-room light on,' Connie told him gently. 'Let me turn it off then I'll be ready to guide you to the shelter.'

'That's too much trouble,' he protested more meekly as he tottered towards the door.

'Not at all – it's my job.' She took out her torch and used the yellow beam to get the old man safely out of the house and down two steps then along the short path. 'We have to take him to the Gas Street shelter,' she explained to George. 'He's not very steady on his feet. What's the best thing to do?'

Her fellow warden came up with a solution. 'We're in luck: my car happens to be parked down the next side street. Do you think you can walk that far?' he asked Mr Ward in a loud, deliberate voice.

'Yes, yes, no need to shout. My legs may be jig-gered but I'm not deaf. Your car, you say?'

'That's right – better still; you wait here with Connie while I run and fetch it.'

So that was what happened – Connie and the old man stood outside his house while George disap-peared into the pitch-black night.

'You're Bert Harrison's lass?' Ward looked her up

16

and down, taking in her uniform as he tried to place her. 'The one that got married?'

'I am,' she agreed.

'And is that your hubby?' He jerked his thumb in the direction of George's departing figure.

'Oh no.' Connie's answer came with a quick, light laugh. 'We work together, that's all. My husband was John Bailey.'

While Mr Ward pondered her reply, she thought ahead to the rest of the night's tasks. She would have to take a register of all those seeking refuge in the Gas Street shelter, then she would check the barriers around the unexploded mine on Maypole Street. With luck there would be no sightings of enemy bombers intent on one of their deadly tip-and-run raids and so no need to sound the yellow alert. At the end of the shift she would report back to her post and take part in the handover to the morning team.

'John Bailey – the name rings a bell,' the old man recalled. 'Didn't he . . . wasn't there . . . ?'

'An accident, yes.' Connie was relieved to see George's black Ford emerge from the side street. Then, as he pulled up to the kerb where they stood, she spotted a boy pushing a bike and looking around uncertainly.

'Which street am I on?' the lad asked as he approached. He wore a black helmet, a respirator and an armband sporting the words 'Civil Defence' in bright yellow letters. His uniform showed that he was a member of the Boy Scouts.

'You must be Colin,' Connie realized. 'What's the matter – are you lost?'

The worried messenger nodded. His face looked

achingly young under the tin hat. 'I'm meant to take this letter to the first-aid post on King Edward Street.'

Connie turned to George, who was bundling Mr Ward into the back seat of his car. 'You go ahead,' she suggested. 'I'll give directions to Colin then join you at the shelter.'

'Right you are.' With the new arrangement in place, George didn't waste time before driving off.

'Now, Colin – this is Tennyson Street.' Connie spoke slowly. 'You have to turn around and follow it down the hill until you come to the very bottom. Then you'll be able to see the harbour straight ahead – with fishing boats and Anderson's timber yard; you know where I mean?'

He nodded eagerly.

'Turn left there and you come on to King Edward Street. The first-aid post is halfway along, just past the telephone box.'

Memorizing her directions by whispering them to himself, Colin turned his bike around, ready to cycle back the way he'd come.

'And watch out for potholes,' Connie warned, her heart fluttering with apprehension. What were the authorities thinking, putting kids not much older than her cousin Arnold in harm's way? Colin Strong ought to be safe in a shelter or holed up in his family's cellar, complete with bunk beds and an electric fire – not wobbling down the hill not knowing if or when a Messerschmitt would fly low and lean, straight off the North Sea – machine guns blazing, bombs dropping and exploding with great whooshes of air that would lift Colin clean out of his saddle and throw him backwards across the harbour to kingdom come. Connie knew – she'd seen it with her own eyes when she lived with John on the hill overlooking the new part of town. She'd had a bird's-eye view of death and destruction all along the seafront: houses turned to rubble in an instant, the sea wall collapsing, the majestic Royal Hotel going up in flames.

'Good luck,' she called after Colin, cupping her hands around her lips. 'And mind how you go.'

CHAPTER TWO

Nothing could beat the smell of baking bread. Lizzie breathed in the warm, yeasty scent as she stacked fresh wholemeal loaves on to a wooden tray that she would carry out to the Harrison Family Bakers' van, which was parked outside the College Road shop. Her father had already set off for the wardens' post while Connie continued to serve behind the counter. It was twelve o'clock on Saturday afternoon – a half-day – and the last customers trickled in to see what was left of the morning's batches: a couple of currant tea-cakes, some finger rolls and a solitary cottage loaf.

'Why not think about it?' Connie asked Lizzie, who bustled through the shop with the final tray for delivery.

Lizzie's face was flushed from the heat of the ovens, and wisps of damp, curly hair stuck to her forehead. She was dressed in practical corduroy slacks and a lightweight, short-sleeved jumper. 'Think about what?' she asked.

'You know – what we were talking about earlier.' Connie popped a teacake into a brown paper bag then accepted money from the hairdresser's appren- tice working in Cynthia's Salon two doors along.

'When – earlier?' Lizzie stashed the tray in the van then asked her question through the open shop door.

Connie wiped her hands on her patterned cotton apron – blue with white daisies – which she wore over a pale-blue blouse and navy-blue skirt. Her glossy, shoulder-length hair was swept back from her forehead and pinned into place with kirby grips. She, too, was warm from the morning's work. 'Before breakfast. I said: why not train as an ambulance driver?'

'Ah, yes – and do my bit for king and country?' Lizzie leaned against the door jamb, arms folded, and staring up at a clear blue sky. She remembered the conversation well enough but wasn't keen on pursuing the subject.

But Connie was like a dog with a bone. 'Yes; why not? You know these streets like the back of your hand and you know a bit about car engines, too. The ambulance service needs people like you.'

Lizzie shook her head. 'Bob wouldn't be keen.'

'Why not?'

'He'd rather I stayed in the shelters out of harm's way.'

'Has he said so?'

'Not in so many words. But I know how his mind works.'

'And is that a good enough reason not to volunteer?'

Frowning, Lizzie came back into the shop. 'Don't badger me, Con. You know I already do my bit, driving for the WVS. Anyway, I don't know any first aid. What use would I be driving a flipping ambulance?'

Connie recognized the dogged tone and the glint of stubbornness in her younger sister's brown eyes.

End of conversation. 'I'm just saying think about it, that's all.' She untied her apron and hung it on a hook behind the counter. 'Put up the "Closed" sign on your way out, will you?'

Lizzie obliged then jumped in the van to begin her third delivery round of the day – following a route that would take her from College Road through the town square with its soot-stained statue of Queen Victoria, down Tennyson Street towards the harbour and then on around the headland to the new part of town. Her sister certainly knew how to make a girl feel guilty – not once but twice in a single day.

Of course Lizzie had thought about volunteering – who hadn't? But she wasn't convinced that putting on a tin hat and a uniform then ordering people around would come naturally to her.

She sighed as she drove and wound down the window for some fresh air. *I'm not like Connie,* she thought, bumping along the cobbles and trying to ignore the heap of rubble that had once been number 30 King Edward Street. A high explosive had scored a direct hit and blown off the entire front of the large terrace, leaving the innards of the house on display – flowered wallpaper hanging in strips, a bedroom door swaying in the wind, a claw-foot bath tilting at an angle of forty-five degrees over a dangerous abyss. *I hang back and try to work out what to do for the best. I never see things in black and white the way she does.*

At the bottom of the steep hill Lizzie came to the harbour, where a breeze blew off the sea, carrying with it the familiar salty tang and the cry of gulls. Today the brownish water was calm, making only a low slapping sound as lazy waves hit the stone jetty.

Half a dozen small fishing boats bobbed cheerfully nearby; three larger trawlers were anchored further out, with men on board scrubbing down decks and making everything shipshape after a morning at sea.

Lizzie stopped the van and took in the scene. She watched the grey-and-white gulls swoop and land on the jetty, ever on the lookout for scraps from the trawlers. Then her eye was caught by one that soared high overhead, riding an air current that carried it over the squat row of harbourside cottages and on over the headland with scarcely a beat of its wings, upwards and out of sight. She sighed again, envying the bird its freedom.

One day, she thought. *One day this miserable war will come to an end. There will be no more bombs, no dreary trekking out into the countryside or huddling in damp, dark shelters. We won't be cramped and clipped by circumstance and plagued by fear. We'll be free to spread our wings.*

So far Kelthorpe Leisure Gardens had escaped Jerry's attention. Crocuses had already come and gone, and daffodils were past their best as Connie made her way across the smooth green lawns and past the boating pond, deserted except for silent flotillas of ducks and swans. She was en route to work a matinee shift at the Savoy cinema, its sleek white outline already visible at the far end of the park; a stuccoed, flat-roofed edifice built in the 1930s that exuded Hollywood glamour and offered war-weary residents an afternoon or evening of welcome escape.

'It's all right for some,' she grumbled to the ducks as she flung scraps of stale bread into the water and they flapped and fought over every crumb. 'They pay their money and settle in for two hours of cowboys and Indians. Me, I have to stand around and watch dratted Deadwood Dick shoot the villain for the hundredth time.' *Bang-bang; you're dead!* Being an usherette at the Savoy definitely had its downsides.

Connie scattered the last of the bread then picked up her pace. Leaving the park, she crossed the wide pavement and entered the cinema through a curved entrance flanked by life-sized posters. Across a sea of blue carpet she waved to Pamela Carr in the ticket office. 'Ready for the invading hordes?' she yelled.

'As I'll ever be.' Pamela was perched on her upholstered stool behind a sheet of plate glass. The young ticket seller called her answer then slid back the glass partition and beckoned Connie across. 'Mr Penrose is on the warpath,' she warned in a conspiratorial whisper. 'He found toffee wrappers under the seats in Row E.'

'And he's looking for someone to blame.' Connie had no doubt she would be in the firing line. 'Thanks, Pamela. I'll make sure to keep out of his way. I like your hair, by the way. Where did you get it cut?'

'At Cynthia's Salon on College Road.' Pamela felt the colour rise to her cheeks as she patted her light brown, newly shorn locks. 'I wasn't sure about the length.'

'It suits you.' Pamela had a heart-shaped face and big grey-green eyes. Connie thought that her small Cupid's-bow lips gave her the look of a young Claudette Colbert. 'I've been wondering about having my own mane lopped off. What do you think?'

'No, keep it long.' Pamela blushed several shades deeper at being asked for advice. She lived in awe of

Connie Bailey, who always looked as if she'd stepped out of the pages of a women's magazine. 'I mean, I'm sure you'd look lovely with it short, too.'

Connie tilted her head to one side so that she could examine her reflection in the glass partition. 'How's your mother, by the way?'

'She's fine, ta.'

'Still giving piano lessons?'

'Yes.' Spotting the first young customers forming a queue outside the door, Pamela checked that her ticket machine was loaded and ready to go.

'And your pa?' Until last autumn Connie had lived next door to the Carrs on Musgrave Street. Edith Carr, Pamela's mother, was a neat, slim woman approaching fifty, with pinched features and dyed black hair. Her father, Harold, was a few years older than his wife. A mild-mannered clerk at Anderson's, he rarely spoke when you passed him on the street. In fact, the whole family had a reputation for keeping themselves to themselves.

'He's fine, thanks.' With one eye still on the length-ening queue, Pamela confirmed that her till was in working order. 'Yours too, I hope?'

'Yes, but he's working too hard, as usual.' Running out of things to say, Connie was about to drift on until she spied their manager, Mr Penrose, heading their way. She stepped back, hoping that she wouldn't be spotted. But no such luck – he saw her duck out of sight and made a beeline for her.

'Mrs Bailey,' he began in his officious way, 'toffee papers – on the floor in Row E.'

Connie bit her tongue and prepared for a wave of criticism to break over her head.

The cinema manager puffed out his chest. Short of limb and round of belly, sporting two double chins and a short grey moustache, he mustered his scant authority. 'My rota tells me that you were responsible for rows A to E last night and that includes checking under the seats for rubbish, as you well know. But lo; what do I find?' Penrose opened his palm to show the offending wrappers.

'I'm sorry. It won't happen again.' *Oh dearie, dearie me! People are getting blown to pieces every night of the week and I have to listen to this drivel.*

'Make sure it doesn't if you want to hang on to your job.' Despite Connie's apology, the fussy manager found her manner less than satisfactory. 'Remember, there are plenty of other girls willing to step into your shoes.'

Connie pressed her lips together and nodded.

Inside her ticket office Pamela shuffled a sheaf of papers, cleared her throat then leaned forward. 'Mr Penrose, it's dead on half past two.'

'Quite right, Miss Carr.' With a glance at his wrist-watch and an impatient shake of his head, Penrose went to unlock the revolving door.

'Thanks, Pam – you saved my bacon.' Connie breathed again. 'Another second of him wittering on and I'd have given him a mouthful. And I need to hang on to this job, worse luck.' She worked three nights a week when she wasn't volunteering plus Saturday matinees; the wages allowed her to pay her father some rent money, with a little left over for the odd pair of nylons and an occasional treat.

'Think nothing of it.' Pamela smiled back sweetly. As Connie ran to change into her usherette's uniform and Deadwood Dick's followers burst through the doors, she prepared herself for a steady stream of copper coins released from hot little palms; for excited, freckled faces and sharp elbows jostling towards a world of heroes on horseback. Meanwhile, she smiled as she ran through her conversation with Connie – *I like your hair . . . It suits you . . . No, keep it long* – exchanging compliments as girls did, making small talk and experiencing how the everyday world jogged along.

After her breather on the harbourside, Lizzie decided it was time to get on with her deliveries. But when she turned the key in the ignition all she got out of the engine was a cough and a splutter. She tried again – this time there was nothing more than a high whine.

'Drat!' The van had been playing up lately – probably dirty spark plugs, which she ought to have seen to before now. So she got out and was in the process of raising the bonnet when a voice interrupted her.

'What's wrong? Has she given up the ghost?'

Lizzie turned to see that Bill Evans had emerged from his cottage and was strolling towards her, still dressed in the oilskin trousers and rubber boots that he wore when he and Tom Rose took their fishing trawler out to sea. 'Yes, and I'm in a rush to finish my deliveries.'

'Need any help?' Bill had been standing at his open door, winding down after the morning's activities, when he'd noticed Lizzie daydreaming on the quayside.

'No, I can manage, thanks.' She went to fetch the toolbox that she carried in the back of the van.

He studied the engine with an expert eye. 'Is it the spark plugs?'

'Probably.' There really was no need for Bill to get involved – still, Lizzie appreciated his friendly offer of help. Selecting a spanner from the metal box, she set to work.

He watched with interest. Lizzie's slim hands with their sparkly engagement ring worked expertly to remove the ceramic tops of the plugs one by one. Then she examined the metal contact points before wiping them carefully with a clean rag, blowing on them for luck before replacing them in their sockets. 'I see you've done this before,' he commented.

'Once or twice,' she replied modestly. The sun was directly behind Bill so Lizzie squinted as she looked up at him. All she saw was the outline of his broad shoulders and the silhouette of his head with its mass of dark curly hair. 'How's life treating you, Bill? Are you still getting out to sea each day?'

'Yes, thank God, but only between sunrise and sunset and we're not allowed to go beyond the thirty-mile limit.' Bill didn't admit how hard this made it for the Kelthorpe fishermen to make a living. In fact, only four of the original twelve trawlers working out of the port were still in action, the rest having been requisitioned by the Royal Navy Patrol Service as minesweepers. Besides which, fish prices had soared, putting cod well beyond the means of many of their customers.

Lizzie finished work on the spark plugs and straightened up. Now she could make out Bill's face – those grey eyes set off against a tanned complexion were certainly something. And he was always smiling, as if he didn't have a care in the world. 'Let's see what happens when I switch her on,' she said as she lowered the bonnet.

Bill crossed the fingers of his right hand and held them up for her to see.

She turned the key and – hallelujah – the engine sprang into life.

'Sweet as a nut.' Bill's smile broadened.

Lizzie was about to drive off when he stooped to pick up her toolbox. 'You forgot this.'

So she jumped out to open up the back doors and when she turned to take the box from Bill he stood nearer than she'd expected and she brushed against him. 'Sorry,' she mumbled shyly.

'No; my fault.' The box was exchanged and he took an awkward step back. 'Have you ever thought of putting those mechanicking skills of yours to good use with Civil Defence?'

Lizzie blushed. 'Not you as well,' she groaned. 'Connie's already been on at me to join the ambulance service.'

Bill nodded his approval. 'I've been roped in as a first-aider four nights a week. We could definitely do with more drivers to take casualties to the hospital; I know that for a fact.'

Returning to the driving seat and aware of time ticking on, Lizzie put the van into gear and edged forward. 'Maybe I'll think about it,' she said vaguely.

'You do that.' Bill watched her drive away, window wound down, hair blowing in the breeze. There was something striking about Lizzie Harrison. How old must she be now – twenty-one or twenty-two? She'd been in the class below him at St Joseph's and was one of those skinny tomboys who always joined in with kicking a ball around in the playground. He hadn't noticed her much back then but, boy, did he notice her now.

Yellow alert. At five minutes to midnight that night Kenneth Browning sounded the warning siren. German bombers had been spotted by fire watchers on the roof of the Elliot Street swimming baths. Enemy planes were flying in low, the distant drone of their engines audible. How many was not yet known.

Browning went calmly through the routine – telephone Control, report briefly and precisely the information, request that all services were on standby. Sit tight, take a deep breath and wait.

The alert spread to all sectors. A chief warden on Musgrave Street sent out three underlings with rattles to make sure that all residents took to their shelters.

At number 30, Pamela sprang out of bed. With the siren wailing and rattles rattling, she flung on a mackintosh over her nightdress and slipped her feet into her shoes. By the time she emerged, her father had shepherded her mother into the kitchen.

'Quick as you can – both of you,' he instructed, keeping them close and herding them forward. 'Pamela, you lead the way.'

Edith clung to the cuff of his jacket. Her face was deathly pale, her dark eyes glittered with fear.

'Let go, dear,' Harold cajoled. 'Go with Pamela.' He promised he would follow immediately with provisions.

So Pamela guided her terrified mother out into the small, sloping garden and found her way by moonlight to the entrance of their shelter. A cat shot out from behind a water barrel and disappeared into the night. A dog howled. Yellow alert – how many planes and from which direction? Pamela's heart raced as she looked up at the stars but found no answers.

Short of breath and trembling from head to foot, Edith followed Pamela into the brick-and-concrete shelter. Pamela switched on the electric light then sat her mother down on the lowest tier of a bunk bed. 'Where's your father?' Edith wailed. 'Go and fetch him this minute. Tell him to hurry.'

The intermittent yellow alert siren changed to continuous red. Now it was a case of not if but when.

Bombers approached in deadly formation, loaded with high explosives and incendiaries. The walls of the Carrs' shelter were two feet thick and the flat roof was made out of eighteen inches of reinforced concrete. Harold had insisted on building the safest refuge possible for his small, precious family. Now he entered the shelter with blankets and flasks of tea that he'd brewed before he went to bed. Closing the door with a firm thud, the yellow light made him blink as he set the flasks on a low table beside cups and saucers left permanently in the shelter for just such emergencies. 'There,' he murmured, handing one grey blanket to Pamela and one to Edith. 'No need to worry. We'll be perfectly safe in here.'

There were two bunk beds with comfortable mattresses, even an electric fire to keep them warm in the windowless box that was six feet wide and ten feet long. There were books and magazines on the table next to the cups and saucers.

Pamela withdrew quietly to the top left-hand bunk, leaving her father to reassure her highly strung mother. Distant explosions from the outside world could be heard – there was no way of telling where the bombs dropped and she knew it might be morning before they could emerge to see whether or not their bungalow had been flattened overnight. Fear encased her heart and threatened to crush her lungs. Her ribs ached as she tried to take several deep breaths.

'There, there,' Harold murmured as he patted his wife's hand. 'Relax, dear. There's nothing any of us can do now except pray.'

Pamela lay still under her blanket. The silence seemed to hiss with static. Outside the shelter, for all she knew, the whole town could be on fire, the sea ablaze with burning oil, the streets choking with brick dust and the smell of cordite.

'Try to get some sleep,' Harold told Edith, before switching off the light.

Sealed inside the shelter, Pamela lay awake. *Breathe in, breathe out. Pray.*

On Elliot Street there was no panic. As soon as the alert sounded, Bert was out of bed. Always a light sleeper, he was up and dressed in less than a minute and knocking on Lizzie's bedroom door.

She emerged, rubbing sleep from her eyes, wearing dark-blue pyjamas and bedroom slippers.

'It's all right – we're on yellow so we've got time,' Bert assured her calmly. Yellow ought to mean that there was still ten minutes to go before a possible attack.

But yellow changed unexpectedly to red as they went downstairs. The mood altered in an instant. At any moment a deadly parachute mine could float down and blow up the whole street, as had happened in Raby only the week before – fifteen killed, including a newly married couple, and forty-one injured. Bert and Lizzie must get down to the cellar double quick before Jerry released his bombs.

'I hope Connie copes all right.' Bert voiced what they were both thinking. At that very moment she would be swinging her rattle and ushering people into shelters, reporting back to her post, waiting for all hell to break loose.

'She will.' Lizzie tried to imagine what it must be like: sizing up a situation, venturing into bombed houses and deciding who was alive and who was dead before calling for fire services, ambulances and demolition teams. Connie always refused to go into detail when she returned home after a serious incident, but her ashen, exhausted face said it all.

Down in the stone-flagged cellar, Bert and Lizzie settled in for a long wait. There was a dank, musty smell despite the whitewashed walls and attempts to brighten things up with posters and pictures cut from magazines. Three beds – little more than makeshift wooden platforms – lined the walls and in the centre of the room was a big stone keeping table once used to store perishables such as milk, cheese and vegetables. Six large meat hooks hung from the flaking ceiling.

'I worry about her,' Bert confessed, his face etched with lines to form a deep frown. He sat on the edge of one of the beds, quietly drumming his fingers against the frame. 'I've no idea how she feels about being back in Elliot Street, let alone being out on

33

patrol at night. Connie never lets on what she's feeling – not to me, at least.'

'Or to me,' Lizzie added in response to his questioning glance.

'I suppose doing the voluntary work keeps her mind off what she's been through.'

'Perhaps.'

'Being widowed at the age of twenty-three . . . It can't have been easy.'

'Dad, I don't know.' Now was not the time. All Lizzie knew was that Connie was one of the brave ones whose courage didn't waver as the bombs fell. She picked up a pamphlet lying on her sister's empty bed – *Notes for the Guidance of Wardens at Rescue Incidents*. 'Remove as much debris as possible by hand rather than by the use of tools,' she read as she flicked through. 'Where it is necessary to employ shovels they should be used with care . . . Do not smoke or strike matches in case coal gas is escaping . . .' Lizzie closed the pamphlet with a sigh. 'I'm proud of her – aren't you?'

'Of course I am,' Bert agreed. 'She's always had plenty of get-up-and-go – just like her mother.'

His remark took them both back to the days when his wife Rhoda had ruled the roost at number 12. A stickler for housework, she'd cleaned and polished with a will – Monday was washing day; Tuesday was for ironing; Wednesday for sweeping, scrubbing and mopping, and so on through the week – until she'd fallen ill with a stomach tumour and grown too weak to continue. Connie had been ten, Lizzie eight. Rhoda had died within the year, leaving a hole at the heart of family life that had never been filled.

Father and daughter fell silent, lost in their memories and straining to hear what was happening at street level. Red alert – at any minute there could be a direct hit on timber yard, school, hospital or gasworks – any target that Jerry chose, regardless of loss of life and the heartache that must follow.

CHAPTER THREE

The fire watchers on the roof of Elliot Street baths identified the first planes through their binoculars – Messerschmitts and Junkers; at least fifteen flying in deadly formation towards Kelthorpe. They watched helplessly as bomb doors slid open to release parachute mines – white mushrooms against a black sky, floating silently to earth. The men on the roof recoiled from the nearest blast, which exploded like the lash of a whip, ripping out the windows and doors of a house on nearby Gas Street.

Then came the rattle of machine-gun fire from the vanguard – Junkers bullets ricocheted from the walls of the town hall, the fish market and the jetty, while giant searchlights lit up the sky and anti-aircraft guns retaliated from the beaches. They brought down a Messerschmitt, which exploded into flaming fragments over the headland. But Jerry kept on coming and bombs continued to fall.

Behind the sandbagged entrance of the Gas Street post, Kenneth Browning sized up the situation.

'George, see what's what on Tennyson Street,' he ordered. 'Tom and Connie, check Elliot Street. Mind how you go and report back here double quick.'

Protected only by helmets, the three wardens set out. They followed their training: keeping to the middle of the deserted streets to avoid possible falling masonry, steeling themselves to ignore the planes still thundering in from the sea. The task in hand was what mattered – to assess any incident on their designated patch then convey the information straight back to their chief warden by whatever means possible.

'Good luck,' George shouted to Tom and Connie above the roars, blasts, rattles and dull thuds all around. Their faces were lit up by pinpricks of bright light from an incendiary exploding on Park Road, the fierce white glare quickly turning to red as fire took hold.

'You too,' Tom called back. 'Most likely a one-kilo Electron,' he muttered to Connie as he judged the force of the latest blast. 'It's a Luftwaffe favourite.'

He and Connie darted, heads down and shoulders hunched, towards their destination. 'You check the left side of the street,' he told her. 'I'll take the right.'

She followed Tom's crouching figure. Her mouth was dry, her chest tight with fear. Every time the sky lit up with a fresh explosion, her heart thudded at her ribs. Yet she must seem cool and steady as they approached Elliot Street, must follow orders and try not to think of Lizzie and her father less than a hundred yards away, taking refuge in their cellar.

They proceeded methodically down the street. 'So far so good.' Tom stopped by the entrance to the baths to check with Connie. 'And Fritz seems to be easing off, thank goodness.'

Connie risked a glance at the sky and saw that her

fellow warden was right – there were no more planes approaching from the east, though several Messerschmitts still circled overhead to release the last of their load.

She paused beside Tom, gaining strength from his apparent calmness. Tom Rose was the silent, steady type; he was not the sort to draw attention to himself, though his height – head and shoulders taller than average – made him automatically stand out in a crowd. Connie would watch him methodically checking supplies in the back room at the wardens' post and had admired his thoroughness. 'No damage to report?' she asked.

'Not so far.' Tom looked up and down the street, considering what to do next. There was always the danger of unexploded bombs but they could be dealt with later. 'It seems Park Road wasn't so lucky, but at least Fritz didn't score a direct hit on the gasworks – we'd have known about it if he had.'

'You report back to Kenneth,' Connie decided. 'Tell him we don't need any support here. I'll stick around until we get the all-clear, to be on the safe side.'

'You're sure?'

'Certain.' She took a deep breath and set off again – past the baths and her own house opposite, on along the street, reminding herself that those she loved were safe and sound. Thank the Lord there was no need for the fire service or ambulance on Elliot Street. There would be no dodging blasts and falling debris, no picking through rubble and counting casualties tonight, at least. However, returning the way she'd come and still waiting for the all-clear, she heard a whimpering sound and sensed an unexpected movement in the entrance to the baths.

'Who's there?' Connie felt the hairs on the back of her neck prickle. Maybe it was a dog or a cat. There was certainly something or someone hiding there. She advanced warily in case the frightened creature sprang out at her.

'Go away!' a child's voice sobbed.

What on earth? Connie paused then ventured up the broad steps towards the double doors. 'Don't be scared,' she began then thought better of the advice – it was obviously nonsensical, for who wouldn't be scared on a night like tonight? The deep shadow of the entrance porch still concealed whoever had taken refuge.

'Didn't you hear me? I said shove off!' A boy's figure leaped from the shadow and rushed straight at her.

She grabbed him by the arm and held tight. Taking her torch from its sling, she aimed the beam at the boy's tear-stained face. 'Arnold!' she gasped.

He pulled away with surprising strength, forcing her to let go.

'Oh no you don't!' Grabbing her young cousin for a second time, she swung him back towards the entrance then firmly sat him down on the top step. 'What are you doing here? Where's Aunty Vera?'

Squirming until he almost wriggled out of his school blazer, Arnold at last gave in and slumped sideways. 'She's up on the moor, sleeping out.'

Connie sat down beside him. 'And why aren't you with her?'

There was no answer; only a sob that Arnold tried in vain to hold back.

Connie waited for him to wipe his face with his sleeve and calm himself. 'Listen,' she told him. 'Do you hear that? Silence. No more planes. Jerry's gone.'

'Good riddance – I hate him!' Arnold's voice was high pitched and vehement. 'It's his fault I have to go trekking every night. I hate trekking and leaving Scruffy at home!'

'The dog.' Connie began to understand. 'Does Aunty Vera say you can't take him with you?'

'Yes and it's not fair. He's scared in the house with nobody there.'

'And that's why you came back.' She eased an arm around Arnold's shoulders. 'Does your mum know where you are?'

'Mam don't care! She's always telling me off and giving me the belt.' The slight shoulders shook with rage. 'She says she'll tell Dad on me.'

Connie knew that Arnold's father was currently sailing the Atlantic with the Merchant Navy, leaving Vera to cope with three kids and a yappy, long-haired Jack Russell as best she could. 'So, Arnie, how did you get back home all by yourself?'

'I waited till Mam was asleep.' Telling Connie the tale seemed to raise the lad's spirits. He grew conspiratorial, sneaking glances up and down the dark street. 'We were bedded down in a ditch near the folly.'

'I know where you mean,' she said with an encouraging nod. Raynard's Folly was a well-known local landmark; a tall, round tower built on an exposed hilltop by an eighteenth-century landowner during a period when his labourers had nothing better to do. As Connie and Arnold sat and talked, the sound of the all-clear gave them both a reason to breathe deep sighs of relief. 'Well?' she prompted.

'I planned it – I knew I couldn't leave until they were all asleep, then I ran back home to stay with Scruffy so he wouldn't be frightened. I don't care if I get the belt cos of it.'

'But you were banking on Jerry not attacking this night of all nights?'

Arnold nodded. 'I hate the bangs.'

'Me too,' Connie admitted. 'But listen, Arnie, we have to let your mum know where you are.' Quite how they would do this she didn't know. 'She'll be worried sick.'

His lip quivered and his voice grew faint. 'What about Scruffy?'

'We'll go and get him.' A plan formed in Connie's mind. It had to be done quickly so she could report back to her post. 'Then we'll dash to my house and fetch Lizzie. She can drive you and Scruffy up to the folly and put your mum's mind at rest. How does that sound?'

'Like I'll get the belt,' he answered miserably.

'Not if Lizzie puts in a good word for you.' *Come on, Arnold; cooperate!* 'Scruffy will be pleased to see you,' she promised, by way of enticement.

Eventually she talked him into it and within five minutes they'd collected the terrier and roped Lizzie in.

'You're a godsend – thanks for doing this,' Connie told her sister at the door of number 12. Their father hovered anxiously in the background. 'I have to get back to the post.'

'Off you go,' Bert urged. 'We'll take over from

here. Come inside, Arnold, and bring that dratted terrier with you.'

Thrusting both boy and dog over the threshold, Connie smiled wanly at Lizzie. 'An incendiary landed on Park Road,' she warned. 'You'll have to make a detour. And watch out for the UXB on Maypole Street.'

'Will do,' Lizzie promised. She gazed up at the eerily quiet sky and the thin silver clouds drifting across the moon. A pall of smoke hung low over the town, pierced by red glows that flared yellow and then died to red once more. 'And you be careful, you hear?'

'I will.' Kenneth would be waiting impatiently for Connie's report; then after that it would be back out to check the streets and shelters and to lend a hand with stirrup pumps and sand buckets, dousing fires and joining the demolition teams that shifted rubble by hand. 'No rest for the wicked,' she quipped as she adjusted her haversack and returned her torch to its sling. 'So long, Lizzie – I'll see you in the morning, all being well.'

Second only to her precious Bechstein piano, Edith Carr loved her garden. Come June she would plant purple and white petunias in her borders and line up pots of bold red geraniums along the top of the air raid shelter. In the meantime, she kept the tender plants in a small greenhouse close to the bungalow.

She was there, potting on and watering, when Pamela sought her out on the morning after the latest raid.

'I brought you a cup of tea,' Pamela told her mother,

who must have heard the glass door slide open but had gone on watering nevertheless. She put the cup down next to a tray of seedlings then hovered.

'Do you want something, Pamela?' Edith pricked out a tiny petunia, ready to transfer it to a small clay pot. 'I'm rather busy, as you can see.'

Pamela studied her mother's back view – her permanently raised shoulders told of unrelenting anxiety, as did the stiff, jerky movements of her thin arms and hands. Her dyed hair looked unnaturally dark in the bright daylight. Even in gardening clothes – a flowered overall over a blue day dress – she insisted on keeping up appearances: not a hair out of place, face carefully powdered, nylons with straight seams, slip-on shoes with a small heel. 'I came to see if you were all right.'

'Of course I'm all right – why wouldn't I be?'

Pamela thought back to the night before, when her mother had sat bolt upright on her bunk with Harold quietly holding her hand. The dull sound of explosions over the town and quayside had continued for a whole hour, during which time Edith's face had been frozen in an expression of sheer terror. That morning she'd refused breakfast, pleading a delicate stomach, and had retreated to her greenhouse so that she didn't have to listen to the wireless when Harold had turned on the news.

'That's good.' Still Pamela hovered, trying to find the right tone. 'I thought I might go for a swim,' she said as casually as she could.

Edith's hands fluttered over the clay pot then came to a standstill. 'You can't – the beach is cordoned off. There are landmines everywhere.'

43

'Not in the sea – in the corporation baths.' Pamela felt a flush creep up her neck and suffuse her cheeks as her mother turned deliberately and stared at her aghast.

'The swimming baths?'

'Yes. They have a ladies-only session on a Sunday morning.'

'Ladies only,' Edith repeated faintly. 'Even so.'

Pamela had been prepared for this reaction, knowing her mother's long-held objections to chlorinated water and unhygienic changing rooms, to the rowdiness of the public baths and the calibre of the clientele who frequented such places. 'It'll be quite all right, Mum – I'll make sure to use the shower and the footbath.'

'Yes, but will other people bother to do that?' Edith's distaste was clear. 'You know my rule; it's not yourself you have to worry about – it's the people who ignore instructions and do as they please.'

'The sea's not exactly clean, Mum.' Pamela argued her case. 'But you used to let me swim in it when I was little.'

'Paddle, not swim,' Edith corrected. 'And only during the week when it was less busy.'

Pamela thought back to weekdays during the school holidays when, bucket and spade in hand and dressed in sun hat and red polka-dot swimming costume, she would hold her mother's hand and walk the short distance down to the beach. The stiff poplin of her mother's summer skirt had rustled as they walked and her canvas sandals had been freshly whitened. As the only child of older parents, Pamela had never played with anyone during these rare expeditions.

She'd been the solitary girl building sandcastles then watching the tide rise and wash them away. 'I came to tell you where I was going,' she said with an edge to her voice. 'Not to discuss the ins and outs.'

'And why the sudden urge, pray?' The mask of disapproval remained – sour as lemons – a look with which Pamela was all too familiar.

'Just because,' she muttered. *Because it's a normal thing to do on a Sunday morning, because I'm tired of being seen as stand-offish, because I might run into Connie there and maybe we will chat again.*

All her life Pamela had been a loner – the brainy and serious type with her mind set on going to college in Leeds to train as a teacher until the outbreak of war had put paid to that. So she'd remained at home, enduring her mother's stranglehold and her much more easy-going father's resignation to the status quo.

But taking the job at the cinema had opened her eyes to other, more relaxed ways of living. Pamela had started to think about the way she looked, painstakingly altering her drab skirts and blouses – an extra dart and a raised hemline here, an elaborate bow or a frill there – to make them more fashionable, and only last week taking the rash decision to have her hair stylishly cut and curled. That had been a big move, all right; to risk her mother's waspish comments and to do as she'd pleased for once. And now the swimming baths.

Edith gave up and returned to her plants – dib the soil then pop a seedling into the hole, firm in and water. 'Dinner's at one o'clock,' she said pointedly.

Her mother's back view said it all: *Don't expect me to approve. Just don't be late.*

45

Stepping out of the greenhouse, Pamela picked up the duffel bag containing her swimming costume and towel. The bus stopped a hundred yards down the street. She must hurry if she wanted to catch it and reach the swimming baths in time.

'So what did Aunty Vera say when you drove Arnie back up to the folly?' Connie walked along Park Road with Lizzie, taking in the damage from the night before. Civil Defence rescue teams were still at work, clambering over the remains of yet another house whose front had been blown clean off. A crane had been brought in to lift heavy timbers, and a knot of people stood next to a car almost completely buried by rubble. 'Did the poor lad get it in the neck?'

'Not too bad.' Lizzie stepped to one side to allow access for the Fire Service crew with their trailer. Smoke still issued from the ruined building and the men had arrived with their pumps and hoses to put paid to any fire that remained. 'Aunty Vera had a fair idea where Arnie must have run off to and of course she was at her wits' end once the bombing started. But she couldn't leave the two little'uns, so she had to sit tight and hope for the best.'

'I bet he got a thick ear once she got him back home.' Vera was known as a strict disciplinarian; but who was Connie to pass judgement? Putting herself in her aunt's shoes, she suspected she might well have dished out a clout or two. 'Doesn't it strike you as odd?' she went on after a pause for thought. 'It's a Sunday and everyone is going about their business – going to church and so on – as if the bombing never happened.'

Women had put on their best hats; men wore collars and ties. St Joseph's doors stood open just the same.

'A bit.' Lizzie felt for the people who had emerged from their shelters to find their homes in ruins; nothing left of their lives except dust and rubble. She nodded towards the smouldering remains. 'Did they find anyone in there?'

'No, thank goodness.' Connie shook her head. 'George was first on the scene. He knew who lived in the house and sent a messenger to check that the family was safe in the communal shelter on College Road.'

'Imagine coming back to this.' Watching the fire team ordering everyone to stand clear before directing their hoses, Lizzie shuddered then linked arms with Connie before walking on. 'I've been thinking . . .'

'What?' When Lizzie hesitated like this it usually meant an important announcement was on the cards.

'I finally made up my mind last night during the raid.' On they walked towards the Leisure Gardens, heading for a bench that overlooked the pond from where they would watch the ducks. Connie was an inch taller than Lizzie and more eye-catching in her cherry-coloured jacket and black slacks, while Lizzie wore a loose-fitting cornflower-blue jacket over tartan trousers. Both wore felt hats with narrow brims to complete their outfits.

Connie studied Lizzie's animated expression. 'I think I know what you're about to say—'

'Yes, but let me get the words out for myself,' Lizzie interrupted, her eyes sparkling. 'It came to me in a flash – I decided that I can't sit on the sidelines any longer. I have to do my bit.'

'Guilty conscience, eh?' Connie ran through the implications as they strolled through the park gates then along an avenue of copper beech trees budding into vivid new life. 'Have you told Bob?'

'Not yet. You're the first person I've spoken to since you were the one who nagged me half to death in the first place.'

'I knew you'd do it sooner or later.' The pond lay straight ahead, shining like glass in the sunlight. 'But will it be the ambulance service or something else?'

'It doesn't matter,' Lizzie declared, jutting out her chin and breaking free, pirouetting on the spot then challenging her sister to a race along the path. 'First thing tomorrow morning I'm off to the town hall to volunteer. Stretcher party, rescue services, messenger, first-aider, ambulance driver – I'll do whatever they ask me to.'

CHAPTER FOUR

Bob had picked bluebells for Lizzie on his three-mile walk through the woods from his home in the neighbouring village of Easby. He stood on the doorstep of number 12 and presented them to her with a broad smile.

She took the bunch and raised them to her face. 'Mmm; smell that.'

'I knew you'd like them.' Bob sniffed the flowers then took off his cap and followed Lizzie down the narrow corridor into the kitchen, where he watched her take an empty jam jar from the shelf above the sink.

'I do. Bluebell time is my favourite time of the year.' Lizzie filled the jar with water and arranged the flowers. 'Pride of place,' she beamed as she put them in the centre of the table then stepped back to admire them.

'Where's your dad and Connie?' Bob perched on a stool by the window, glancing round the somewhat ramshackle kitchen, noticing that the broken door handle on the cupboard under the sink still hadn't been mended. Pots and pans from the Sunday dinner were stacked on the draining board waiting to be dried.

'Out,' Lizzie replied. 'Dad's gone to have a chat with Aunty Vera about Arnold and guess who came calling for Con? No, never mind; you won't guess. It was your boss down at the timber yard, George Bachelor.'

'Did he now?' Bob worked at Anderson's yard as a crane driver and kept his opinion of his brash, over-pushy foreman to himself. 'Was Connie expecting him?'

'No, George turned up out of the blue; all dapper in blazer and cravat, asking if she fancied a stroll along the prom. So off they went.' In fact, Connie had hesitated but George had seemingly sweet-talked her into it. 'You and Bob can have the place to your-selves,' she'd whispered knowingly to Lizzie on her way out in her cherry-red jacket. 'I know you'll have plenty to talk about.'

'There's no harm in that, I suppose.' Bob waited for Lizzie to finish admiring the bluebells then drew her to the window and put his arms around her waist. 'So, my luck's in – we have the house to ourselves?'

She nodded then sat in his lap, her arms around his neck, resting cheek to cheek. 'This is nice,' she sighed.

They kissed, with the sun on their backs and the scent of bluebells filling the room. Kisses led to stroking – her fingers on his freshly shaven cheek, his hand roaming across the small of her back as he pulled her closer. Lizzie sank against him, eager to respond, but after seven chaste years together each knew how far they should go and when to stop.

'Not until after we're married,' Bob had promised from the start. 'However much I want to, we won't do anything we shouldn't.'

It was the respectable way and innocent Lizzie had trusted him to keep his word. In all their years as sweethearts they'd walked hand in hand along the beach and sat side by side in the dark at the Savoy with Bob stealing a kiss before the lights came on. On big nights out they waltzed together in the Royal Hotel ballroom beneath glittering lights – the perfect picture of young love.

The sun through the glass was warm on Lizzie's neck as she drew away. 'There's something I want to tell you,' she began softly.

Bob pulled her back and kissed her throat. 'Ssh! This is better than talking.'

She tilted her head away from him. 'I'm serious. And I want you to think before you say anything.'

'Uh-oh.' He sat up straight and looked at her carefully. 'I get the feeling I'm not going to like this.'

'It's nothing bad.' She clasped his hands in hers, trying to ignore the flicker of doubt in his hazel eyes. 'The long and the short of it is this: I intend to volunteer.' His eyes narrowed and a frown appeared. 'No, listen. I've made up my mind; it's something I want to do.'

'Volunteer for what, exactly?' Images flashed through his mind of rescue squads armed with nothing more than stirrup pumps and buckets of sand dashing to put out infernos or pull bodies from rubble. He twisted his hands free to pull out a packet of cigarettes. 'Connie's put this into your head, hasn't she?'

'Why must you always blame her?' Lizzie stood up to stare out of the window at the small yard and outside privy. 'I can think for myself, you know.'

'But it's not your style, Lizzie – I can't picture you

51

in bluette overalls and a helmet, patrolling the streets with bombs falling willy-nilly.'

'Why not?' When Bob didn't reply she twisted his words around to their true meaning. 'You mean you don't *want* to see me doing it because it's dangerous – and I understand that, honestly I do.'

'Well then . . .' He spoke through a cloud of blue smoke.

'We're all in danger anyway,' she pointed out. 'People die in the shelters if there's a direct hit – it happens all the time. Remember those poor beggars in Raby.'

Bob inhaled deeply. 'What does your dad think?'

'I haven't told him yet; only Connie.'

'So it *was* her idea?' He turned his head to the side and blew a disgruntled plume of smoke across the room.

'Don't go on, for goodness' sake!' If Bob was going to behave like a petulant child she would rather he went away and came back once he'd cooled down. 'The plain fact is I want to make myself useful in any way I can. I don't know how that will be, exactly – not until after I've done my basic training. Then they'll decide what suits me best. It could be decontamination work or they could send me to join a stretcher party. They could even get me delivering leaflets or arranging public meetings – who knows?'

'I'm only saying I hope you know what you're letting yourself in for.' This was not at all what Bob wanted to say. If he'd spoken from the heart he would have told Lizzie how much he hated the idea of her deliberately putting herself in harm's way, how he loved her more than anything in the world and couldn't bear to live without her. But those words wouldn't come and the ones he spoke sounded peevish even to him.

'I have a fair idea of what it involves,' she said steadily. 'Dad's been doing the warden's job for long enough and I've seen the pamphlets he brings home to study.'

'How many hours will they want out of you?' Raising the sash window, Bob stubbed out his cigarette on the sill and admitted defeat. 'Will it mean we won't see as much of each other?'

'It'll be part-time,' she promised, watching his features like a hawk. His face gave little away – his straight, dark eyebrows shielded his eyes and he kept his gaze fixed firmly on the floor. 'Dad will still need me to do the bread deliveries during the day but there will be some evenings when I'm free.'

'I can't stop you doing what you want,' he mumbled. 'But I'll be worried stiff about you.' *I love you; don't you know that? I want to build a nest and line it with feathers, to look after you and keep you safe – but you won't let me.* Thrusting his hands deep into his trouser pockets, Bob scuffed the skirting board with the toe of his boot.

Lizzie saw how he was suffering and her eyes filled with tears. 'I do love you,' she murmured softly.

The words melted the last icy crystals of resentment that had frozen his heart and he opened his arms to embrace her, to breathe her in and hold her close. She was his Lizzie, his sweetheart.

'I love you too,' he whispered back.

'Is that a new blouse?' Connie stood beside Pamela in front of the mirror in the ladies' cloakroom at the

Savoy, putting finishing touches to her make-up before she started her shift.

Pamela ran a comb through her hair. 'No, it's an old one that I altered. I changed the collar and added this bow.'

'It suits you.' Appraising the cream rayon garment with a practised eye, Connie stooped to tug at the hem of her maroon usherette's uniform. 'Lucky you, being able to wear your own clothes at work. This thing hangs off me like a sack.'

A dimple appeared in Pamela's left cheek when she smiled. 'You're lucky – you can get away with anything,' she insisted as she put the comb into her handbag then snapped the bag shut.

'Sweet of you to say so.'

'I mean it.' Connie was one of those girls admired by men and women alike. The former were drawn like bees to honey by her trim figure, dark wavy hair and vivacious manner, while the latter envied her confidence and flamboyance. As Pamela picked up her bag, she ventured another shy comment. 'I used to try to copy your look when you lived next door.'

'You're kidding!' Taken by surprise, Connie turned her head to look directly at a blushing Pamela.

'No, but I could never quite pull it off. Anyway, I was sorry when you moved away and I had no one to copy.'

'I never knew that.' Connie had always had Pamela down as the studious type; quiet and lacking in confidence, with no idea how pretty she was with those arched eyebrows, long lashes and grey-green eyes. As a result, Connie had made little effort to get to know her. On top of that she'd been put off by her mother's fussy nature and snootiness.

'You should get to know the neighbours,' John had told Connie soon after they'd moved into the rented bungalow on Musgrave Street. 'You realize that Edith Carr is old Cyril Anderson's daughter? He's dead now and his son, Hugh, has stepped into his shoes.'

Mention of the wealthy owner of the timber yard where John was employed had surprised Connie.

'Edith fell out with her dad years ago. It was over her wanting to marry Harold Carr, who was only a junior clerk at the timber yard. By all accounts, the old man didn't fancy the idea of Harold marrying into the family firm.'

'He thought she was marrying beneath her?' Connie hadn't found this hard to believe.

'More like Cyril suspected Harold was after her money. She went ahead and got spliced anyway and they say old Anderson never spoke to her again. When he died he left everything to Hugh. Edith didn't inherit a penny. All she got was an old piano from the big family house next to the Royal. Apparently, she was always keen on tinkling the ivories.'

Connie had listened to John's account and formed the conclusion that it had been an act of spite on the old man's part to leave his estranged daughter the piano as a reminder of what she'd lost – a bit like twisting the knife every time she sat down to play.

Recalling these details now, Connie saw Pamela in a new light. 'We never really got to know each other properly when we were neighbours, did we?'

Pamela shook her head. 'I was very sorry about John.' She remembered the evening the previous autumn when her father had come home and described the tragic event at work. He'd seen it from the office window; John Bailey had been standing in a forbidden area of the timber yard with his back turned, having a heated discussion with George Bachelor. The arm of the crane had swung round and Keith Nelson, the crane driver, had spotted John too late to prevent the accident.

'We all have crosses to bear,' Connie said in a low voice and she was glad when they were interrupted by a tap on the door.

'Miss Carr, are you in there?' Mr Penrose called sharply.

'Coming!' Pamela pulled an exasperated face then hurried to the door. She opened it to find the manager huffing and puffing about the queue of customers at the door, all champing at the bit to see Edward G. Robinson navigate his way to a sticky end as the cruel captain of a seal-hunting ship in *The Sea Wolf*, the Warner Brothers' latest action yarn.

Alone in the cloakroom, Connie sighed and dabbed lipstick on to her lips. Everyone was sorry about the tragic way John had died – and rightly; no one would wish that on anyone. But the manner in which he'd lived had been far from blameless. However, Connie had kept her mouth firmly shut about her husband's bad moods and his sailing close to the wind as far as the law was concerned. She'd never talked about it when he was alive, not even to Lizzie, and it didn't seem fair now that he was dead. *That'll do*, she said to herself as she pressed her lips together and gave one last glance in the mirror.

She went out into the foyer and stationed herself at the entrance to the auditorium. 'Tickets please,' she said cheerily to Tom Rose and his pal Bill Evans, the first customers through the revolving door.

The two handsome trawlermen, spruced up in neat pullovers and slacks, handed Connie the tickets they'd just bought from Pamela, who was perched on her stool inside her booth.

'Nice to have a night off from warden duties,' Tom mentioned to Connie as she showed them to their seats. The dimly lit interior of the picture palace, with its ruched gold curtain and the curved, sleek lines of an ocean-going liner, tricked cinemagoers into believing that life was more glamorous than it actually was.

'It is.' Connie stopped to shine her torch on their seats. 'Enjoy the film,' she said as they squeezed sideways along the row. 'By the way, Tom – my sister Lizzie is set to join us in the ARP as soon as she's finished her basic training.'

Bill cocked an ear at the news and smiled as he sat down.

'What are you grinning at?' Tom asked him as Connie went off to continue her ushering.

The shoulders of the two burly men brushed against each other as they settled into their plush seats. 'Nothing,' Bill replied. 'Well, all right; if you must know, it was me who gave Lizzie Harrison a nudge about volunteering for the ambulance service. I bumped into her on the quayside on Saturday and told her that's what she should do.'

'Did you, now?' Tom offered his friend a cigarette. 'Admit it; you've always had a soft spot for Lizzie.'

'Not guilty – the girl's already been snapped up,' Bill protested unconvincingly. 'Anyway, you've got no room to talk. What about you and Connie?'

'What are you on about?' The glow from Tom's lighter illuminated his guarded expression.

'Come off it. I've seen the way you look at her.' Bill's seat clicked and swung up as he stood to let other customers shuffle by. 'Not that I blame you. She's single now, so what are you waiting for?'

'Don't be daft,' Tom said with a laugh. Bill might have the confidence to proposition either of the good-looking Harrison girls if he felt like it, but it wasn't so easy if you were on the quiet, shy side. 'Just pipe down and watch the damned film.'

But first the Pathé News. As the curtain glided up and the lights dimmed, Tom and Bill stubbed out their cigarettes, preparing to listen to the crow of the Pathé cockerel before they learned how that very day the Royal Navy had bombarded Tripoli. A submarine had been damaged and six Italian freighters sunk.

While Connie ushered cinemagoers into their seats at the Savoy, Lizzie was back in the schoolroom at St Joseph's with seven other volunteers. It turned out there was a lot to learn.

'Defence against air raids falls into two divisions,' her father instructed from the front of the room. He stood in front of a blackboard to which he'd pinned a chart, pointing with a cane to various items on a list. 'First we have active defence, which consists of fighter aircraft, searchlights, anti-aircraft guns, barrage balloons and radar. These branches fall under the responsibility of our military services, namely the Army, the RAF and the Royal Navy.'

The classroom was stuffy and it had to be admitted that her dad wasn't the most inspiring of teachers.

Lizzie failed to suppress a yawn, which was spotted by Bert and prompted a frown.

'Someone open a window,' he ordered. If Lizzie was serious about volunteering she would have to learn the basics. 'The second division is passive defence in three separate sections, namely police, fire brigade and, finally, us – the ARP.' He tapped each name in turn. 'We're currently officially being renamed as the Civil Defence but personally I prefer the old moniker. As ARP wardens our job is to report and control any air raid incident that may occur, including the organization of rescue services, repair, demolition, anti-gas, decontamination and gas identification.'

As he paused for them to jot down notes, Lizzie glanced around a room she remembered from her schooldays. It had high windows and rows of wooden desks in which inky initials and dates were carved. At the front was the teacher's podium and the walls were lined with children's paintings, maps of the world and a framed reproduction of a famous painting of a water mill.

'Casualty services . . . first aid . . . stretcher parties . . . shelter wardens . . .' Her father's voice droned on and it was hard to relate his dry-as-dust information to the chaos of alarms, enemy aircraft, parachute bombs and incendiaries that the inhabitants of Kelthorpe knew all too well.

'Teamwork,' Bert insisted. 'And I can't stress enough the importance of keeping civilians at bay in the event of an incident.'

A hand shot up at the front of the class. 'Who exactly do you mean by civilians?'

Bert acknowledged the question with a nod. 'There

will always be untrained people who are willing to lend a hand,' he explained. 'Often they don't know how to do the job and they can do more harm than good. For instance, as a warden you have to ask them to stand back and explain to them that removal of debris after a bomb has dropped is best left to the rescue service.'

Lizzie glanced again at her pupil cohort. Four were middle-aged men who were too old to join the forces, one was a well-dressed woman in her thirties and the rest were Boy Scouts in uniform. She imagined that the four men would have little trouble getting gung-ho civilians to cooperate in the event of an emergency. As for the woman, the three boys and herself, she was less certain.

Her confidence dwindled as her finger traced initials on her desk lid. How would she react if she was confronted by tumbling masonry and fleeing residents, not to mention the dead or dying?

'After tonight's introductory talk your training will include first-aid classes and local exercises,' Bert informed his students. 'This will involve a mock-up of the real thing, with volunteers acting as casualties. That's when your training in first aid will be put to the test, with you deciding on the level of treatment – whether it's on-the-spot or in need of an ambulance, et cetera. But before that we expect you to have decided which of the services you want to join, depending on what you think you'll be most useful doing.' His attention flicked back to Lizzie and he saw that she was looking worried. He decided he would have to have a word with her as they walked home.

After half an hour he rounded off the first training session by standing at the door to hand out leaflets, shake hands and thank each individual for volunteering. 'Don't look so het up,' he told Lizzie, who was last out of the room. 'You'll do a grand job when the time comes.'

'I only hope I don't let you down,' she said as they set off for home. Outside on the chilly streets all was quiet, with the eerie silence that they'd all grown used to. The town was deserted except for the occasional messenger pedalling furiously between a wardens' post and the control centre and junior wardens patrolling their beats.

'You never let me down,' Bert assured her, plodding along with rolled-up charts under his arm, his threadbare overcoat buttoned up against the cold. 'Or anyone else, for that matter.'

'Thanks, Dad.' She slipped her arm through his and they walked in step.

'I mean it, Lizzie. You may not be the one people notice straight away – that's our Connie – but you get things done in your own quiet way and I'm proud of you.'

Lizzie absorbed the compliment in silence as they turned on to Elliot Street. Her confidence blossomed again under her father's praise. 'Con says I'll be put to best use as an ambulance driver and I agree with her,' she informed him as they reached number 12.

Bert turned the key in the lock. 'Ambulance driver it is, then,' he said, stepping aside to let her go first into the empty house. 'They'll train you in the old laundry van from Morrison's and teach you how to drive wearing a gas mask and how to look after your equipment – stretchers and suchlike. You'll learn how to apply splints and bandages.'

'Champion,' she told him with a bright smile as she flicked on the light. 'I don't know about you, Dad, but I could eat a horse. What shall we have for our supper – tinned sardines or cheese on toast?'

Neither Tom nor Bill reckoned the film they'd just seen was up to much.

'Too far-fetched by half.' Tom volunteered his opinion to Connie and Pamela when they encountered the girls in hats and coats on their way out of the cinema.

'He means it was a load of old codswallop,' Bill elaborated. 'If it had been me I'd never have gone within a mile of that dodgy Wolf Larsen chap and his rust bucket of a boat.'

Connie grinned at their disgruntled faces then she and Pamela stepped through the revolving doors. 'Bad luck; it's too late to ask for your money back,' she quipped when they all stood on the pavement, where knots of departing cinemagoers still lingered. It was a chilly night, with a stiff breeze – pitch dark, as usual, so it was a second or two before she noticed George Bachelor loitering beside the blue-and-red poster advertising the week's main feature.

'Fancy meeting you here.' George smiled at Connie's obvious bemusement. He acknowledged Tom with a cursory nod.

Connie didn't know whether to be pleased or annoyed. After their walk on the prom the previous day they'd made no firm arrangement to meet again. 'You're not following me, by any chance?'

'No, I happen to be going your way, though.' In fact, he'd spent the evening playing cards at a friend's house and had carefully timed his departure to co-incide with Connie's likely exit from the Savoy. 'Shall we?' He offered her his arm, keeping his elbow extravagantly crooked while she made up her mind.

'Why not?' Connie had her reasons for going along with George's offer and so she slipped her arm through his.

'That's the ticket. We can't let these young ladies walk home alone, can we, lads?' George said to Tom and Bill before whisking Connie off towards the Leisure Gardens.

'Quite right.' A gallant Bill stepped forward to offer Pamela his arm. 'You live past the headland, don't you?'

'Yes, on Musgrave Street; but there's no need to go out of your way.' Pamela felt her face flame bright red in spite of the cold. She was sure that neither Bill nor Tom would have given her a second thought had it not been for George's heavy hint.

'Don't be daft; Tom and I will be glad to see you home.' Her startled look reminded Bill of a shy bird – a sparrow or a wren. 'Won't we, Tom?'

'Of course we will,' Tom assured her, and the three fell into step together. He would leave it to his more sociable pal to put Pamela at her ease. Meanwhile, he kicked himself for letting George rush Connie away. It was the old story, though; you had to be quick off the mark when Bachelor was around.

'How do you find working at the Savoy? Do you usually catch the bus to and from Musgrave Street? How long have you and Connie known each other?' Bill's steel-tipped heels clicked along the pavement as he fed Pamela some casual questions. He could feel her hand shaking against his arm as they walked.

Her brief answers came quietly and hesitantly. 'It's all right, I suppose . . . Yes, the bus . . . I don't really know her that well. We used to be neighbours.'

After ten minutes of stilted conversation the trio passed the gaping hole in Tennyson Street where Saturday night's bomb had exploded, observing that the rubble had been partly cleared. Sandbags shored up what remained of the mid-terraced house.

'Were you on duty when Fritz let rip?' Bill asked Tom as they walked on.

'Yes, but not down by the harbour. Connie and I were sent out to Elliot Street. How about you?'

'I was called out to Gas Street – only minor injuries to deal with, as it happened.'

Pamela risked a quick glance at Bill's face. 'Are you a warden too?' she ventured.

'No, a first-aider – four nights a week. It's better than sitting at home twiddling my thumbs, what with fishing going down the drain the way it is.' Bill launched into the rights and wrongs of converting the trawlers into minesweepers. He got carried away on wartime restrictions and how the remaining fishing boats often found they were sitting ducks. 'Only last month Tom and I had to cut our nets loose when a Focke-Wulf 190 came straight at us in broad daylight. Our hull and bridge are the old-fashioned wooden type so we'd have been blown out of the

64

water if we'd been hit. We went full steam ahead, weaving to and fro like a bloody eel – excuse the language. Ask Tom; he'll tell you.'

'That's awful.' It was the first time Pamela had heard a member of the fishing community express his opinions with such force. Strange to say, though she'd lived in the port all her life, she had never considered the extra dangers the trawlermen currently faced every time they went to sea.

'Fritz won't stop us, though.' Bill released her arm so they could negotiate their way around the cramped quay, past nets and creels, then on towards the harbourside cottages where he lived. 'I was born to this life and I love it. Nothing beats being miles out to sea without a care in the world; just me and the waves and the sky.'

'You get yourself off to bed; I'll take over from here,' Tom suggested to Bill as they reached the cottages. 'If that's all right with you, Pamela?'

Blown sideways by strong gusts of wind and with the sound of the waves crashing against the jetty, she protested that Tom had already done more than enough. 'My house isn't far from here. I can make my own way.'

But he wouldn't hear of it. 'It's blowing a gale on the headland – you could get swept clean off your feet.'

'Do as you're told,' Bill said with a laugh and a knowing wink as he turned the key in his front door. 'You'll be safe with Tom, I promise.'

'Take no notice.' Tom held her firmly by the arm and they carried on, heads down, battling the wind, along the narrow footpath that took them around the massive bulk of the dark headland until the path opened out into a wide, railed promenade that curved along the neighbouring bay. To their left stood Sunrise, the Andersons' magnificent family home, adorned with gables and with mock turrets at each corner and with extensive grounds. Next to it was the burnt-out shell of The Royal, once the most expensive and luxurious hotel in town but now a blackened, derelict ruin.

'It's quite a hike from the Savoy,' Tom said as they turned off the prom up Musgrave Street. 'No wonder you normally get the bus.'

Pamela paused to catch her breath. They were less than a hundred yards from her house, which was out of sight around the next bend. 'Honestly, there's no need for you to come any further,' she told Tom with a touch of desperation.

'Are you sure?' He caught her uneasy tone and thought of making a joke about her not wanting to be seen with a trawlerman; all brawn and no brains. But Pamela Carr wasn't the sort you teased.

'I'm quite sure,' she insisted. 'But thank you.'

She walked on up the hill alone, aware that Tom watched her until she rounded the bend.

Crikey, I thought I was shy and retiring but I'm nothing compared to Pamela Carr. He stood, hands in pockets, watching the slight figure disappear into the gloom.

Pamela held on to her hat as a sudden gust threatened to blow it away. No man had ever walked her home before and she didn't want the novel experience to be soured by her mother's sharp, scornful questions or by her father's worried cross-examination. *A new haircut, a visit to the swimming baths and now this – talk about entering the fray!* There was a bounce in her step as she approached the garden gate then slipped quietly into the house without being noticed.

CHAPTER FIVE

For the rest of that week Lizzie juggled her duties at the College Road bakery with her training as an emergency ambulance driver. She learned the different layouts in ambulances: from those that had been converted from delivery vans to those that had once been smaller, privately owned cars, adapted to carry a stretcher on the roof; and lastly something they called sitting-case cars, which were used for transporting casualties who were able to sit up.

'How about lending our bread van to the King Edward Street ambulance depot?' she asked Bert on the Thursday morning as she stacked fresh loaves on to trays. He was dressed in his bakery whites, putting the morning's last batch into the oven, and Lizzie had caught him at what she hoped was a good moment when his work there was almost done. 'I reckon we could fit at least two stretchers in the back – three at a pinch.'

Bert grumbled and dithered. 'It's about time they supplied us with the real thing like they have in Raby, then we wouldn't have to use our own vehicles; you know – the proper ambulances with the Red Cross insignia painted on the sides.'

'But in the meantime, why not?' she wheedled. 'There's plenty of room in the back of the van for blankets and first-aid equipment.'

'But what about sandbags?' Bert was aware that they were used by the first-aid parties to keep broken limbs immobilized during transport. 'If any sand escaped from the bags and got into the bread we'd soon hear about it.'

'It won't – I'll clean the van out properly every single time. Please, Dad!'

One glance at his daughter's eager face softened Bert's resistance. 'All right, but on your own head be it.'

'Thanks, Dad. I'll let the depot know.' Rushing out with the loaded trays before he could change his mind, Lizzie looked ahead to the evening, when she would receive her tin hat along with an attractive ski cap with its Civil Defence badge and a yellow armband with the word 'Ambulance' painted on it – the only uniform that would be provided for the time being. As yet she had had little practice in putting on splints and applying bandages, and the promised mock-up of a major incident hadn't materialized.

'The instructors go on and on about decontamination squads,' she mentioned to her father as she came back for another tray. 'Anti-gas this and anti-gas that. They showed us the oilskin suits and hoods they have to wear. But I've never heard of Jerry using gas against us, have you?'

'No, not this time around and touch wood it stays that way.' Memories of men gassed to death in the trenches during the Great War haunted anyone over the age of thirty. 'Mind you, do as you're told and wear your gas mask on duty – without fail.'

'Yes, sir, cross my heart!' Still delighted by his permission to use the bread van, Lizzie hurried off. She spent the rest of the day rehearsing in her head the drills she'd been taught by first-aid specialist Bill Evans at the previous night's training session and looking forward to tonight's class. In fact, she was so caught up in the excitement of it all that she forgot she'd arranged to see Bob for half an hour after work. She found him sitting on the doorstep of number 12 watching Vera's two girls play hopscotch on the pavement.

'There you are!' Bob jumped up to greet her with a peck on the cheek. 'I've been here ages.'

'Come in and put the kettle on for us,' she said hurriedly. 'I've just got time to get changed and have a bite to eat before I have to rush out again.'

Then it was upstairs to put on a fresh blouse and slacks, down to tea and a salmon-paste sandwich, a quick catch-up with Bob's news – there was a new clerk called Fred Miller in the office at Anderson's and Bob's mother had twisted her ankle hanging out washing in the backyard – before Lizzie said she was sorry but she had to dash.

Connie came in from an after-work swimming session just as Lizzie was leaving.

'There's no need for you to make a move just because I am,' Lizzie told Bob. 'Con can give you the lowdown on George Bachelor's latest attempt to woo her – can't you, Con? They had a walk home in the moonlight on Monday night, no less.'

'Pooh; it was nothing.' Connie played down the occasion as she dumped her swimming togs on the kitchen table.

'No, I'll head home.' Bob's deflated air was obvious to Connie but not to Lizzie, who blew him a kiss then dashed off.

'Don't take it to heart; she's been like a cat on hot bricks all week.' Connie offered Bob a crumb of comfort. 'It's the excitement of tackling something new.'

'And I'm old hat,' he grumbled, picking up his cap and making for the door. 'Tell Lizzie I'll see her at the weekend if she can find the time to squeeze me in.'

'There will be two drivers per vehicle.' Bill stood at the front of the classroom in St Joseph's school, instructing the new ambulance volunteers in their final desk-bound session of the week. His manner was easy, his voice rich and slow. Though he was new to teaching and he seemed too big and brawny for the confined, inky, Victorian schoolroom setting, he spoke with natural authority, paring down the information to the essentials and giving his pupils plenty of time to jot down notes. 'As ambulance drivers you'll carry a metal water bottle at all times and a haversack with small, medium and large bandages – six of each. There'll be rubber gloves and six of these . . .' He held up a small brown label of the sort you might attach to a parcel. 'These are to write the names of casualties on before you drive them to hospital.'

Lizzie disliked the idea that you must treat an injured person like a package for posting. Apparently an indelible pencil came as part of the first-aid kit, too. If there wasn't a label to hand you could write an initial on the casualty's forehead – 'X' for internal injuries, 'T' for tourniquet fitted.

'All right, Lizzie – have you got that?' Bill noticed her distracted expression.

'Yes, thanks.' She scribbled down some more notes, copying from the woman sitting next to her.

At the end of the lesson the woman introduced herself as Moira Shilling. 'It's a lot to take in,' she said in an educated voice as she packed away her things. 'But I hear we'll have a dummy run tomorrow night.'

'You two can drive the Morrison's van,' Bill suggested as he waited by the door. 'I'll be in charge. Come to the depot at the old brewery on King Edward Street – eight o'clock sharp.' As Moira went off with a promise that she would be on time, Bill waited for Lizzie. 'Did you come in your van?' he asked.

'No, I used Shanks's pony.'

'I'll give you a lift home if you like.'

Her heartbeat quickened as she gave him a brief smile. 'No, ta. The fresh air will do me good.'

'As you like.' They walked down the corridor together, chatting about the old days at St Joseph's. 'They say school is the best time of your life but I couldn't wait to leave. A life at sea is all I wanted, ever since I can remember.'

'You're lucky – I've never really known what I wanted to do.' Lizzie's heart skipped and jumped again as Bill held open the door. What on earth was the matter with her; feeling this flustered at his gallantry? 'Not much was expected of girls in those days except for learning to sew and cook and then getting married and having babies. It's different now that most of the men have been called up. Suddenly they need us women to drive tractors and work in the munitions factories.'

71

'And why not?' Bill followed her on to the pavement, where his motorbike was parked. 'Are you sure about the lift?'

'On that thing?' Lizzie raised her eyebrows in mock horror.

He grinned – a flash of genuine amusement across his handsome features. 'Where's your sense of adventure, Miss Harrison?'

'Right, you're on!' A modern girl could change her mind and rise to a challenge if she felt like it. She strode alongside Bill towards the bike and waited for him to kick-start the engine.

'Ever ridden pillion before?' he checked.

'No, never – but there's a first time for everything.' A thrill of anticipation ran through Lizzie as she swung her leg over the saddle.

'Hold tight,' he ordered, anchoring her hands around his middle. 'I'll take you on a nice little detour, along the prom and around the headland.'

And off they went – slowly at first then gathering speed along the straight, broad promenade, with the salt wind blowing off the sea and Lizzie gripping Bill tight around the waist.

The office at Anderson's was a plain, two-storey brick building overlooking a vast yard next to St Stephen's dock. Timber was piled high in every direction: logs and planed planks of various lengths placed there by two tall cranes that swung huge loads from ship to quay then from quayside to storage yard. The largest building on the site was a vast cutting shed containing noisy mechanical saws and a long conveyor belt.

Harold Carr's job, tucked away in a corner of the

upper storey of the office block, was to enter each new shipment into the appropriate ledger – a task that he undertook in his immaculate handwriting and with meticulous attention to detail. However, he knew that the days of relying on this old-fashioned method were numbered. Only last week Hugh Anderson had employed a new clerk called Fred Miller – a somewhat taciturn type in his mid twenties – and had put him in the opposite corner of Harold's office then set him the task of transferring a backlog of information on to typed sheets, which Fred then stored in alphabetical order in a smart new ring binder.

'This is quicker once you get the hang of it,' Fred informed Harold from behind his typewriter on one of the rare occasions when he chose to break his silence. *Clickety-clack, ching, clickety-clack.*

'For you, maybe.' Harold looked at the new man over the top of his glasses. Clean-cut and with not a dark hair on his close-cropped head out of place, his fingers darted over the keys at breakneck speed. 'But I'm an old dog, remember. It's hard for me to learn new tricks.'

It was late afternoon on the last Friday in April and Harold was busily bringing accounts up to date when Pamela popped her head around the door with a message from Edith.

'I'm sorry to be a nuisance,' she began, casting a glance in Fred's direction then quickly looking away again. 'Mum asked me to remind you to pick up the sheet music she needs for Sunday's service from the music shop on College Road.'

'I hadn't forgotten,' Harold assured her, putting down his fountain pen and turning towards the new clerk. 'Pamela, meet Fred Miller. Fred, this is my daughter, Pamela.'

Once the awkward formalities were done with and Pamela's usual embarrassment overcome, Harold drew his daughter out of the office on to the small landing. 'You're wearing lipstick.'

She resisted the urge to draw the back of her hand across her lips to wipe away the make-up. 'I'm on my way to work.'

Harold tilted his bald head to one side and scrutinized the effect. 'It suits you,' he conceded. 'My little girl is growing up,' he added fondly.

'About time too,' Pamela countered with a shy smile. 'I'll be an old maid before you know it.'

'Get away with you.' He nudged her towards the stairs then sighed wearily as he watched her descend quickly and smoothly. *Sheet music from Benson's for Edith.* He made a mental note as he went back to work. 'I'll be leaving the office fifteen minutes early today,' he informed Fred – *clickety-click, ching!* Clean white collar, perfectly knotted tie, a look of total concentration on his chiselled young features – *clickety-click, clickety-click, ching.*

Moira Shilling's cautious driving carried Lizzie, Bill and two trainee first-aiders sedately around the dark headland – Lizzie in the front passenger seat and the first-aid party in the rear.

'This weighs a ton.' One of the young first-aiders dragged a large haversack from under a ledge as the Morrison's van crawled past Sunrise and the burned-down Royal Hotel. It was a clear night, with a bright moon reflecting off the restless waves.

'That one has spare equipment in it,' Bill explained. Opening up the haversack by torchlight he pulled out a device made up of four webbing straps with a metal handle at each end. 'This is a Trigg lift and this here is a King's harness.' He showed them some loose, buckled straps for fixing a casualty to a stretcher.

Up in the front Lizzie was itching to take a turn at the wheel. The dummy run was meant to end in an emergency dash to the far end of town, where another team of first-aiders had been strategically laid out in the North Street bus station to act as mock casualties, complete with fake blood and broken limbs. They were due there by half past nine but at this rate it would be more like ten o'clock.

'Why don't I take it from here?' she offered on a straight stretch of road.

Well-brought-up Moira obligingly stopped the van and changed places with Lizzie, who was about to take off the handbrake when, out of nowhere, sirens sounded around the town.

'Yellow alarm!' Bill warned, every inch of him suddenly alert.

'Oh no; not again!' Instinctively Lizzie checked the sky for approaching planes. Nothing yet, but right this second every resident in every street in town would be preparing to head for shelters, wardens would swarm out to sound their rattles, and phones at the control centre would be red-hot with the exchange of vital information.

'Forget about our dummy run,' Bill decided. 'Turn around, Lizzie. Let's head back to the depot quick as we can.'

She followed the order by backing into the hotel entrance and turning the van in the direction they'd just come. Still sirens blared and bright searchlights raked the sky. Soldiers from the 39th Brigade scrambled towards cement pillboxes lining the beach. Their job was to man the anti-aircraft guns concealed there. Everyone held their breath – perhaps Jerry would pass overhead without incident as sometimes happened.

With the accelerator pedal flat on the floor of the old van, Lizzie picked up speed. Minutes flashed by. Yellow alert turned to red.

Then came the dreaded drone of approaching aircraft – not from the east but from the west, where the last glimmer of red sunlight remained. With luck it would be a tip-and-run raid that would be over in a few minutes. Feeling the twist of sheer panic deep in her gut, Lizzie approached the headland as the first incendiaries fell. Next to her Moira gripped the door handle until her knuckles turned white. Unable to see anything from the back, Bill climbed into the front to perch between Moira and Lizzie.

In the rapid flashes of light caused by a series of incendiaries, he was able to identify the planes in the vanguard of the attack. 'Dornier Do 17s – ten of them.' He flinched as several parachute mines floated out of the black sky to land on the headland just ahead. 'Turn around again if you can,' he told Lizzie as a dozen high explosives detonated directly ahead of them, ripping up trees and destroying a row of shops and boarding houses on the seafront. 'It looks like Fritz is gunning for the timber yard and the old town.'

More planes, more heavy bombing. A searingly bright searchlight raked the sky and caught one of the Dorniers in its full glare. Gunfire from the beach brought it blazing down into the sea.

Lizzie spun the steering wheel and turned the van with a screech of tyres. Once more the outline of Sunrise and the ruins of the Royal came into view, illuminated by a hundred flaring lights from falling incendiaries. The two trainees in the back crouched silently and were thrown back and forth by the violent swaying of the vehicle.

In the passenger seat, a fearful Moira wound down her window and leaned out. Behind them the whole of the old town seemed to be ablaze. Thick black smoke from the incendiaries on the headland billowed towards them.

'Close the window,' Bill ordered as fumes filled the interior. 'Lizzie, try to make it as far as the end of the prom – we can pull in at a sector post there and phone the depot for instructions.'

She gripped the wheel tightly and drove as fast as she dared until suddenly the road fifty yards ahead suffered a direct hit from a high explosive. Her foot slammed down on the brake pedal and they screeched to a halt as a shower of debris – chunks of concrete, tarmac and paving slabs – fell all around. Moira jerked forward out of her seat but managed to brace herself against the dashboard while Bill gripped the back of Lizzie's seat to stay upright. He turned around to check on the state of the passengers in the back. One of the first-aiders had been flung against the front seats while the other rolled on the floor, groaning.

'What shall we do now?' Driven out of her wits by the thud of more bombs hitting the ground and the rattle of falling debris on the roof of the van, Moira seemed to be about to abandon the vehicle and make a desperate run for it. She appealed to Lizzie as Bill crawled into the back to assess injuries.

There was a hole ten feet deep in the road ahead and a blazing town behind. Their only logical escape route was to the left, up Musgrave Street. Once more Lizzie wrenched at the steering wheel with all her might and turned up the hill. The engine whined and strained at the steep gradient. 'Don't give up on me, damn you,' she said through gritted teeth.

Dorniers and now Junkers – dozens of them, returning from a failed raid on Manchester or Liverpool – were now intent on dropping their deadly cargo on unlucky Kelthorpe before heading for home. They attacked relentlessly until the final incendiary slid from its metal cradle in the rear aircraft's belly.

Silence followed the roar of enemy planes. The raid was over before Lizzie's van reached the brow of the hill and the worn, overheated engine finally gave out. She gazed down on a wall of flame along the seafront and harbour, with individual fires dotted across the headland. Musgrave Street had not escaped. An incendiary had fallen on two bungalows that had collapsed like houses built of playing cards – flimsy wall panels were scattered, furniture had been blown into the air. A grand piano stood crookedly on two legs in someone's front garden, blazing fiercely, never to be played again.

*

At the sound of the yellow alert Connie set out with George from her Gas Street post. Other wardens in their dark battledress and white helmets spread out across the sector, using their rattles to usher residents to shelters and checking that no one was left behind. Every door was knocked on and soon the dark streets were crowded with silent, huddled figures clutching blankets and supplies to see them through the night, all hurrying to what they prayed would be safety.

Connie's specific task was to double-check residences occupied by those most in need of assistance – the old and infirm, like Mr Ward at the top of Tennyson Street, and little Neville Shaw on Gas Street, stricken with polio and so unable to trek out to the countryside like many of the families with young children chose to do. She began with Elliot Street and her Aunty Vera's house – 'In case that little tyke Arnold has taken it into his head to stay behind with Scruffy again,' she explained to George as they parted company. A knock on the door followed by a sharp volley of yapping barks confirmed that the dog was there but of Arnold there was no sign. Satisfied, Connie hurried on, darting down an alleyway and using a short cut to the Shaws' house, where she found Janet Shaw struggling to ease Neville's wheelchair down the steps on to the pavement.

'How long have we got?' Janet asked Connie, who had seized the front end of the chair. She was a tiny woman with prematurely grey hair scraped back into a bun, wearing a winter coat that had been hastily flung on over her nightdress.

'We're still on yellow,' Connie assured her. The nearest shelter was on College Road – a five-minute dash from where they stood. So Connie took charge of the boy's wheelchair and they sprinted towards the town centre, with Janet struggling to keep up and six-year-old Neville gripping the arms of his wheelchair and yelling out at the excitement of going so fast. 'It's a chariot race, like in olden times,' Connie told him as yellow changed to red and actual planes could now be heard – distant and threatening. 'Hold tight, Neville!' A hundred yards, fifty, twenty and at last she could spy Tom standing steadfast at the sandbagged entrance to the shelter, chiding stragglers and hurrying them down the steps into what had until recently been one of Kelthorpe's underground public toilets.

Seeing Connie with the wheelchair, he strode to meet her and together they carried the boy and his wheelchair down the steps to join thirty-five other refugees. Then he ran up to ground level to help a breathless Janet.

Knowing the Shaws were in safe hands, Connie hurried on under the red alert. The first incendiaries lit up the night sky in a sinister version of Guy Fawkes Night. Volleys of ack-ack fire vied with the roar of approaching aircraft. From College Road she backtracked towards Tennyson Street, relieved to find that Tom soon joined her.

'Everyone on the College Road list is accounted for,' he informed her, 'except for the Thomsons on Tennyson Street.'

'Rightio – number 7.' Connie knew the family he meant. Eric Thomson was reputed to be a heavy drinker who often mistreated his wife and two daughters. 'Eric might be lying dead drunk on the floor, for all we know.'

'Let's wait and see.' Tom's long stride outpaced Connie's and he arrived at the top of the street before her. At that moment a deafening blast from a high explosive tore through the air. A fountain of earth and bricks erupted at their feet, creating a crater that was twenty feet wide and six deep. Hands pressed over their ears, Connie and Tom staggered backwards then fell to their knees and crouched forward as earth spattered down. Then there was another thud of a second bomb followed by deathly silence.

'Gas masks on,' Connie muttered. It was possible that the first bomb had fractured a gas main, so she fumbled to lift her mask out of its canvas case and strap it around her face while Tom did the same. They waited in dread for a second blast but when it didn't come, Tom gave a signal for them to venture forward, cautiously skirting the crater then heading on towards the fourth house on the left-hand side of the street – number 7, where the Thomsons lived.

The tight-fitting mask pressed into Connie's cheekbones, making her want to rip it off. *Damn Eric Thomson for not getting his family to safety!* She glanced sideways to check their next move. Tom gestured them forward and then stopped, his right foot hovering directly above a slim metal cylinder about eighteen inches long, lying dormant on the pavement. *Incendiary!*

Tom's foot had almost made contact and the disturbance caused by his approach was enough to set the sluggish device alight. A white flame flared from the cylinder – small enough to be extinguished if only there was a sand bucket to hand.

Connie spotted one stationed under a lamp post some ten yards away. 'Don't move!' She gestured for

Tom to stay where he was while she ran for the bucket. Any small vibration could cause the incendiary to explode into a terrifying ball of orange flame. She lifted the bucket and sprinted back, flinging its contents on to the bomb and dousing the fire.

They were both still in one piece, thank the Lord. Now they must check for residents inside number 7.

Once more Tom went ahead, seemingly unshaken by the near miss. He knocked then tried the door and found it was locked but when Connie glanced at an upstairs window she made out three terrified faces pressed to the glass – Nancy Thomson and her two small girls.

Connie raised her hands to her face. 'Open the door!'

Nancy shook her head then struggled to slide up the sash window. She managed it at last and leaned out to speak to Connie. 'Eric locked us in the bedroom!' she cried, her long hair falling loose across her pale face.

Tom hammered harder on the door.

'Is he in there with you?' Connie shouted.

The wailing girls clung to their distraught mother. 'No – he went out to the pub and left us.'

'We'll have to break down the door,' Connie told Tom between several more blasts. Planes droned relentlessly overhead, laying waste to Kelthorpe old town.

So Tom stepped back then kicked at the lock with all his might. The jamb was splintered and the door hung askew on its hinges. 'You go and fetch them,' he told Connie.

She ran up the stairs two at a time then along a

short landing, sliding back a strong bolt before flinging open the bedroom door. *Damn Eric Thomson twice and three times over for abandoning his defenceless family and putting them in mortal danger!* Standing in the doorway, she took in Nancy Thomson's dishevelled appearance. Her dress was torn, her face and arms covered in bruises. 'Quickly, come with me!'

The children shrank back at the sight of Connie's grotesque rubber and canvas mask, clinging to their mother and hiding their faces in her skirt. So Connie removed the mask and let it hang loose around her neck. 'Don't worry, we'll get you to the shelter in a jiffy,' she told Nancy calmly as pandemonium crept to their very door. Another incendiary fell to earth in a cloud of sparks, crashing through the roof of the house opposite then flaring up in a sheet of white light.

But the instinct to survive was strong even in a woman beaten into submission by a violent husband and terrified out of her wits by the bombs. Nancy thrust the bigger girl at Connie and scooped up the smaller. Together they stumbled downstairs to where Tom was waiting. He led them out on to the street, past the gaping black crater, on down an alley towards College Road.

The girls clung to the women and mewled like kittens as the small group picked their way through the chaos of blackened rubble and choking smoke. *Not far now. Soon, soon!*

At last they reached the sandbagged entrance and descended the steps. An electric light illuminated their surroundings – tiled green walls in a large, windowless room lined with bunk beds, where people lay under grey blankets. There was the smell of disinfectant, the sounds of a tap dripping and a man softly playing a tune on a mouth organ.

'You see – I promised we'd look after you.' Connie comforted the child clinging like a limpet around her neck until a kindly elderly woman rose from her bed and took the girl and cradled her in her arms. A lad of thirteen or so offered Nancy and her other daughter space in his bunk.

Tears of relief pricked Connie's eyes as she took off her helmet. Tom brushed plaster dust from her shoulder. 'Take a deep breath,' he advised, unscrewing the top of his water bottle and making her drink. 'A pity it's not something stronger to take the edge off things, eh?'

'Whisky would do it,' she agreed, gulping back the cool liquid.

'You'll have to let me buy you a drink, then,' he offered on the spur of the moment. 'Tomorrow lunchtime, if you happen to be free.'

CHAPTER SIX

'Bang – our whole lives went up in smoke.' Harold stood in the living room of his sister Lilian's house in the fishing village of Raby, coming to terms with what had happened the night before. 'Edith and I waited for the all-clear then when we came out of the shelter we saw straight away how bad it was.'

Nothing was left of their bungalow except for burning timbers and a heap of broken roof tiles. The fire had consumed all.

Edith sat silently in a corner of the room, still wearing her dressing gown and slippers. She had shrunk into herself – her head hung low, seemingly too heavy for her fragile frame to support. Pamela sat next to her, offering what little comfort she could.

'Thank God you weren't hurt.' Lilian had reacted quickly when she received a telephone call from the wardens' control centre first thing that morning, informing her that her brother and his wife and daughter had been made homeless during last night's air raid. Harold had named Lilian as his next of kin.

She hadn't hesitated – Harold, Edith and Pamela must come to stay in her house in Raby. It would be a tight squeeze in her two-bedroomed cottage, but she would do her best to find space for them. She'd driven to Kelthorpe and picked them up from the Boy Scouts' hut where the family had been housed by the WVS for the night.

'But we've lost everything.' Until now Harold's life had consisted wholly of work and duty. He and Edith had saved hard all their married lives, trying not to dwell on the Anderson wealth that she'd forfeited by marrying him. But Edith's tastes had proved irredeemably refined and she'd wanted only the best china for her table. She must have a cut-glass fruit bowl, a set of silver cutlery; and, of course, the Bechstein stood in the bay window overlooking the sea, a reminder of past glory. 'Everything,' he repeated with a defeated sigh.

'They say it was a parachute mine that did the damage,' Pamela explained to her practically minded aunt. 'I was at work at the time so I didn't see it for myself. I only knew about it after the all-clear when I was allowed to head for home.' She remembered the anxious knot in her stomach as she'd left the shelter on Park Road then run through town before climbing Musgrave Street in the dark, the shiver of fear as she saw fires smouldering on the hillside, the shock like a hammer blow to her chest as she rounded the bend and discovered what had happened to her home. 'But like you say, Aunty Lilian, no one was hurt and that's a blessing.'

Resenting Pamela's attempt to make the best of things, Edith took a deep, jagged breath but didn't look up. She didn't express what she felt – that she would rather be dead and buried than face a future without a home and all her precious possessions to shore up her spirits. She couldn't face starting all over again. It was simply too hard.

'You and Edith can have the back bedroom,' Lilian said to her brother. There was no point including Edith in arrangements – her sister-in-law was in no state to take anything in. 'Pamela, come and help me make up the spare beds. Harold, you stay here and make us another pot of tea.'

Glad to be given a task, Pamela followed her unflappable aunt up the stairs. They took starched white sheets smelling of lavender from the airing cupboard then worked together in silence. Once the beds were tidily made, Lilian sat on the edge of the one nearest the door and invited Pamela to perch next to her.

'It's hit your mother hard,' Lilian began. 'Don't get me wrong, but I'm not surprised. After all, Edith is not one of life's copers.'

'She'll miss her piano the most.' Pamela's voice was choked with sadness. 'And her garden.'

Lilian rested a work-worn hand over Pamela's slim one. She was everything that Edith wasn't – broad-featured, sturdy of limb and spirit. 'I'll do my best to look after her. And there's room for you here, too, for as long as you like. We can make up a bed for you on the front-room sofa – you're young so you can prob-ably fall asleep on a pinhead.'

Pamela's attempt at a smile failed miserably. Her lip trembled as she murmured her thanks. 'But it'll only be for a day or two.'

Lilian peered at her over the top of her glasses – a gesture of concern that she shared with her brother. 'Then what?'

'I'll start looking for lodgings back in town,' Pamela decided. 'My job at the Savoy means I have to work evenings and there are no buses out to Raby after eight o'clock.'

Lilian squeezed her hand. 'Time to spread your wings?'

'Yes. I only hope Dad sees it that way.' She would seek out a room on a major bus route or within walking distance of the cinema. Of course, she'd lost all of her clothes in last night's fire and only had what she stood up in. She would have to go to the bank and draw out some of her savings, buy material to make new dresses, borrow a sewing machine. There was an awful lot she would have to do to set up on her own.

'And your mother,' Lilian reminded her gently. 'Will she object?'

Pamela was brought down to earth with a bump. 'Probably.' *She objects to me breathing without her permission, if the truth be known.*

'Never mind – you start looking for a place to rent.' Lilian stood up with a determined jut of her chin and smoothed over the dent in the candlewick counterpane where she'd been sitting. 'Leave Edith to me.'

A rescue party was still hard at work when Lizzie and Connie walked through the old town to assess the damage from the previous night. The squad's task was to shore up or demolish damaged buildings – a job undertaken by men in the building trade and by council workers using specially equipped lorries carrying jacks, blocks and tackles and oxyacetylene cutting tools.

Connie pointed to the gang of five men in bluette overalls and black helmets marked with an 'R'. 'Like ants on an ant heap,' she remarked as they scrambled over mountains of rubble until they uncovered a burst main that was gushing water into nearby cellars.

'Rather them than me.' Lizzie gave a shudder as she imagined the possibility of residents being trapped in their cellar and having to watch the water steadily rise. 'Lord knows what they might find.'

Connie thought back to the tense moment when Tom had narrowly missed stepping on the incendiary. She quickly pushed the memory to the back of her mind, only for it to be replaced by a vision of three desperate faces at an upstairs window, imprisoned there by a heartless husband. 'Men!' she said with venom as she and Lizzie turned their backs on the rescue party and made for the relative peace of the Leisure Gardens. She described to Lizzie the drunken actions of Eric Thomson. 'Everyone in town knows he's a rotten layabout, but now it turns out he beats his wife and locks her and his two daughters in the house during air raids.' Connie shook with rage.

'Did you report him to the police?'

'You bet your life we did.' Fury propelled Connie at high speed towards the pond. 'They promised to arrest the rotter.'

'And what about Thomson's wife and kids?'

'The WVS have stepped in. They'll find a safe place for them to live and make sure they have proper food and clothes. Honestly, Lizzie, all three were skin and bone. And you should have seen Nancy Thomson's face and arms – covered in bruises.'

Lizzie shivered again. 'Not all husbands are as bad as him, thank heavens. So you can hardly say "Men!" and lump them all together.'

'You mean your Bob is different?' Connie gave her sister a shrewd glance.

'Chalk and cheese,' Lizzie assured her. She and Bob had made an arrangement to meet at the end of the prom to take an afternoon stroll. 'He's not a drinker, for a start.'

'And he doesn't have a bad bone in his body.' Connie had always been fond of her sister's fiancé, though he was a stick-in-the-mud at times. 'That's worth remembering,' she added as they stopped at the edge of the pond for her to scatter the bag of breadcrumbs that she'd brought from the bakery.

'Look who's dishing out advice all of a sudden,' Lizzie objected. She made a fresh knot in the patterned silk scarf tied around her head. 'Only the girl who dashed headlong into marriage at the age of eighteen.'

'And why not?' Connie shot back. 'John was a catch, there's no denying it.'

'Tall, dark . . .'

'And handsome.' She finished Lizzie's sentence for her. 'What girl wouldn't fall hook, line and sinker for looks like that, especially when the man in question whispers sweet nothings into her ear? So no more of the "dashing headlong" remarks, if you please.' As usual, Connie swerved the issue of her hasty marriage. 'Anyway, why so testy all of a sudden?'

'I'm not testy.'

'Yes you are.'

'All right then, I am.' Lizzie pouted and sighed.

'To tell you the truth, I'm still getting over last night. It was the first time I've been out in an air raid and it scared me to death – not that I let it show.'

'Join the club.' Connie crumpled the empty paper bag and shoved it in her coat pocket.

'Really?'

'Yes, really. You'd be mad not to be scared.'

The sisters linked arms amicably and walked along the side of the pond. April meant cherry blossom and white petals floating in the air like confetti. It meant the zing of red tulips in green grass and clouds of blue forget-me-nots by the park gates.

'By the way, I'm meeting Tom at The Anchor in twenty minutes,' Connie mentioned to Lizzie.

'Tom?' For a second, Lizzie thought that her sister had made a slip of the tongue. 'You mean George, surely?'

'No; I mean Tom – Tom Rose.'

'Tom has asked you out?' Lizzie ran quickly through the things she knew about Bill's fisherman pal: Tom was reputed to have a decent singing voice, he was a junior warden under their dad, he didn't hog the limelight (something he and Lizzie had in common) . . . Oh, and he wasn't bad-looking, though rather on the tall, lanky side.

'Yes. Don't look so surprised. It's only for a drink.'

'So that's why it took you a whole hour to get ready.' New bluebird-patterned dress, best cherry-red jacket, matching wedge-heeled sandals, straw hat set at a jaunty angle.

'Cheek!' Connie shot back. But yes, she'd wanted to look her best. 'Not too much?' she asked, touching the brim of her summer hat.

'No, just right,' Lizzie assured her. 'You look a million dollars, as always.'

The tide came in and went out again regardless. The sun rose high in the sky. Certain rhythms of life never altered. Young mothers pushed prams along the windswept promenade. Seagulls fought over scraps of stale bread.

'I'm not late, am I?' Bob was waiting on the wrought-iron bench where he and Lizzie had arranged to meet so she ran the last few yards to join him.

'No, you're bang on time.' Bob greeted her with a warm smile, looking relaxed in an open-necked shirt and sports jacket. He took her hand and they set off along the prom. 'I was five minutes early.'

Up on the headland fires smouldered. On the beach, to a background wash of waves reaching the shore and pulling back again, a team of soldiers worked to set up barriers around a UXB. 'Poor old Kelthorpe,' Lizzie murmured. 'Did Fritz get Easby, too?'

'No, he gave us a miss, thank heavens.' Bob swung Lizzie's arm in an easy manner. 'What about your lot on Elliot Street – any harm done?'

'Not a scratch. Con was on duty – they had a busy night at the Gas Street post.'

A lad kicked a football sky high. When a gust of wind caught it and blew it on to the beach, a soldier on patrol swore angrily at the culprit.

'What about you?' Bob's pace slowed and his expression tightened into a frown. 'Don't tell me you were out in the thick of it too?'

Lizzie hesitated then decided it was best to tailor

the truth. 'Not in the old town. I was on a dummy run in the Morrison's van, heading for the bus station on North Street – with Bill Evans and his first-aiders. We kept well clear of the worst of the raid.'

Bob let go of her hand, broke his stride and pulled a packet of cigarettes from his jacket pocket – his customary refuge at tense moments. He attempted to strike a match, but the wind extinguished the flame. He tried three times before he succeeded.

'Say something,' Lizzie pleaded.

Bob shook his head. 'You already know what I think.'

'All right then, we'll change the subject. How's your mum coping with her sprained ankle?'

'It's swelled up like a balloon.'

'I'm sorry to hear that.'

'Lizzie . . .' he began then faltered. He had a sour taste in his mouth and a tight knot had formed in the pit of his stomach.

She linked her arm through his and made him walk on past the Royal and the row of newly bombed-out shops, waiting for him to continue.

'How am I meant to stop worrying about you?'

'You can't; it's only natural. But try to understand that driving an ambulance is my way of not letting Hitler win. I want to fight for my country – it's as simple as that.'

'And you think I don't?' A worm of guilt burrowed into Bob's brain and made him sulk and pull away again.

'I didn't say that.'

'No, but you thought it.'

'I did not.' Lord, he was exasperating!

'Keeping the timber yard going is helping to win the war, just as much as fighting in Italy or driving a bloody ambulance.'

'I never said it wasn't.'

Bob talked himself into an even worse mood. 'The country needs timber for rebuilding the houses and factories that Jerry bombs, just like it needs fish for people to eat. I bet you don't have a go at Bill for not joining the navy.'

'I'm not having a go at anyone.' A raw nerve had been hit at the mention of Bill's name but she tried to disguise it by gazing out to sea.

'He's your new hero, isn't he?' Bob goaded. 'Bill Evans teaches you all about first aid. He dashes into bombed buildings and saves people's lives. Me? I just drive a crane.'

'Why are you being so mean?' Lizzie challenged him with a defiant, unblinking stare. 'I thought we were meant to be having a peaceful stroll, not pecking away at each other like a pair of seagulls.'

'Because!' Bob flicked his cigarette to the ground.

'Because what?'

He blinked and ground the stub underfoot. 'Let's leave it at that for now, shall we?' he muttered before striding away.

Tom had been surprised by Connie's agreement to meet up at The Anchor. In fact, the first shock had been when the impromptu suggestion had popped out of his mouth in the first place.

She'll probably change her mind, he'd told himself as he shaved and put on a clean shirt. *I'll be left in the lurch like the idiot that I am.* But then, nothing ventured, nothing gained.

'It's a bit early in the day, isn't it?' Bill called out across the harbour as Tom propped his bicycle against a lamp post outside the pub. Bill was still in his oilskins after a morning's fishing and badly in need of some shut-eye after thirty-six hours without sleep.

Tom brushed off his friend with a throwaway remark. 'You know me – it's never too early for a pint.' He disappeared into the snug without a backward glance.

Connie won't show up, he predicted. *She'll have better things to do.* Feeling a tap on his shoulder, he turned around.

'Don't look so surprised.' Connie had, in fact, got there before him. Since parting from Lizzie at the park gates, she'd had time to grow nervous but was determined to bring her butterflies under control and by the time she'd reached the pub she was her usual chirpy self.

'Sorry, I . . . er, what can I get you to drink?' Tom asked.

'How about that whisky?'

'Right you are.' Three strides across the dark, cluttered interior took him to the bar, where he ordered a pint of bitter for himself and a whisky for Connie.

Finding a table close to the small, mullioned window overlooking the harbour, Connie took off her hat and sat down, absorbing the details of her surroundings. The Anchor was a typical fishermen's watering hole, with amateurish paintings of sailing ships hanging askew on the roughly plastered walls and faded sepia photographs of bearded men in sou'westers ranged along the stone mantelpiece.

'I should've suggested somewhere else.' Tom joined her with the drinks then apologized for his choice of venue. 'This place is a bit basic.'

'Basic suits me fine,' she assured him.

'Thanks for coming.' As he sat down opposite Connie, his knee brushed hers under the small round table. 'Sorry.'

She dismissed the apology with a smile. 'Thanks for asking me.'

'Did you hear that Anderson's took a direct hit?'

'Anderson's caught it last night.'

They spoke over each other then laughed. 'Great minds think alike,' Connie said.

Their talk wandered over events of the night before – the near misses as well as the damage done to the timber yard and to St Stephen's dock – then turned to more cheerful matters. Tom told Connie about the choir he belonged to and suggested she should join, too. She informed him that she couldn't sing.

'Everyone can sing,' he argued.

'You haven't heard me,' she contradicted. 'I was seven when the music teacher at St Joseph's decided I had a tin ear and threw me out of the junior choir.' The whisky was warm on her tongue and throat – a delicious sensation that she savoured as Tom tried to convince her that singing was as natural as breathing.

'You should give it another try – never mind what Miss Thingummy said.'

'Miss Lister-Smith. Remember her? Skinny and wizened like the wicked witch of the west.'

'Let me think – was she the teacher with a green face?'

Connie leaned across the table and pushed playfully at Tom's hand. 'You know what I mean. Anyway, what type of thing does your choir sing?'

'Gilbert and Sullivan – *The Pirates of Penzance*. "Away, away! My heart's on fire!"' Tom kept a straight face and enjoyed Connie's look of disbelief. 'Not really. We go in more for the traditional sea shanty.'

She still didn't know whether or not he was serious. 'Do you all stand there with your fingers in your ears?'

He laughed then winked. 'Why not come along and find out?'

Connie didn't answer but there was a comfortable pause while they finished their drinks.

'Do you mind if I say something?' Tom leaned forward. 'In my opinion you've done a good job picking yourself up the way you have these past few months. I admire you for that.'

Connie's eyes widened in surprise at the sudden change of gear. 'I couldn't have done it without Dad and Lizzie,' she confessed. 'It was that pair who persuaded me to move in with them. I wasn't keen at first – it felt like a backward step. But I was too young to qualify for a widow's pension so I was strapped for cash. Moving back home was the only way forward and now I'm glad I did it.'

'I hope I haven't spoken out of turn.'

'No, you haven't.' In fact, she was touched by Tom's concern. 'John's death came as a terrible shock, as you can imagine. Especially since they never got to the bottom of what went on – why he was in a part of the yard where he wasn't supposed to be, and so on.' Connie stared into her empty glass. 'Not that it came as a complete surprise.'

'How come?'

She smiled ruefully. 'Everyone knows what John was like – there wasn't a rule that he wasn't prepared to bend.'

'Right.' True enough; John Bailey had got into scrapes as far back as Tom could remember, from pinching sweets in the school tuck shop to nicking petrol from Brearly's garage. More recent rumours, never proved, had him involved in dodgy black-market deals. 'He got away with it, though.'

'Most of the time.' She ran a finger around the rim of her glass. 'Anyway, that's in the past.' It had been a different life crammed with a few ups and many downs. 'What about you, Tom – have you got a sweetheart tucked away somewhere?'

'Not guilty.' He ducked his head and examined his fingernails.

'Too busy fishing and patrolling the streets in your warden's uniform?'

'That's it.' *Too shy and backwards in coming forwards, more like.* He'd been sweet on one or two girls over the years but it had never led to anything. 'Let's say I haven't met the right girl.'

'Not yet.'

He glanced up at Connie to see if she was making fun and saw a gleam in her eye and an upward curve of her lips. God, the woman could knock your socks off with a look like that. 'I'm picky,' he said with a retaliatory grin.

'Well,' Connie pushed her stool back from the table,

'it's time I made a move – I'm working at the Savoy tonight and I've got a hundred things to do before then.'

'So soon?' Tom stood up with her. 'It's been nice, anyway.'

'Very,' she agreed.

They left the pub to find that the fine weather had changed to a brisk April shower. Rain had darkened the cobbles and formed a puddle by the kerb that Connie had to leap over before she could be on her way.

'We could go back inside and have another drink until it eases off,' Tom suggested.

'No, I don't care about getting wet.' Better to leave on a high note. 'Thanks for the whisky. Maybe we can do it again some time?'

'We can,' he agreed. 'Whenever you like.'

But Connie didn't stop to arrange another time. She jumped over puddles and ran through the rain in her red jacket. Tom watched her dash along King Edward Street – a bright figure in grey surroundings – and his heart beat fast enough to jump clean out of his chest. What a woman, what a catch! A bright-eyed, silvery creature slippery enough to wriggle through any man's net.

The main feature at the Savoy was under way when Connie went to commiserate with Pamela, who was cashing up in the ticket office.

'It's too bad about your house,' she began, aware through talking to Lizzie that the Carr family home had been bombed during the previous night's raid. 'I was very sorry to hear it.'

Pamela looked pale but composed, arranging shillings and sixpences in neat columns before tipping them into a blue cotton bag then tugging the draw-string tight. She'd come into work as usual, determined to soldier on. 'There are people worse off than us. Luckily we came out of it without a scratch.'

'Still, it's a shock. So if there's anything I can do . . .'

'We'll be fine, thanks.' Fine as long as Pamela didn't dwell on the memory of the smouldering heap that had once been her home. Fine as long as people didn't offer too much sympathy, in which case she was certain that the tears would begin to flow and never stop.

'I could lend you some clothes, for a start.' Connie supposed – rightly – that everything inside the house had been destroyed. 'I reckon we're more or less the same size, you and I. Why not come to my house and borrow what you need – just to tide you over?'

'I couldn't possibly.' Pamela shook her head. She placed several small bags of coins on a weighing scale then jotted down figures.

'Why not? I have far too many dresses hanging up in my wardrobe – Lizzie is always nagging me to get rid of some.'

'No, I'll manage – thank you anyway.' Taking a hankie from her pocket, Pamela dabbed at her treacherous eyes.

Connie refused to take no for an answer. 'My things might not be your style – maybe a bit too – what's the word – flamboyant? But you could always tone them down with a plain cardigan or a dark jacket.'

Now Pamela started to cry in earnest. Tears trick-led down her cheeks then fell on to her desk. 'This is all I have to my name,' she admitted, brushing her hands over her demure cream blouse and black skirt. This and my blue coat and hat. Apart from that, I lost every single thing I own.'

'Which is why you should come to my house and borrow what you need.' Gently Connie drew Pamela out of the ticket office then led her across the foyer to the ladies' cloakroom, where she ran her own hankie under the cold tap. 'Here – dab your face with this.'

Pamela sobbed all the harder, saying sorry through her tears.

'No need to apologize. Have a good cry – let it all out.'

So she leaned on the washbasin and cried her eyes out – tears for the bald and much loved teddy bear she'd had since she was three that she still kept on the end of her bed and for the postcards that her father had sent during a work trip to Canada when she was eight and for all her childhood memories gone up in smoke. She cried until her ribs ached and she could cry no more.

'Here.' Connie handed her a clean, dry handkerchief. 'Where are you going to live, out of interest?'

Pamela sniffed and dabbed at her face. 'I have an aunt in Raby. She's offered to take in all three of us – Mum, Dad and me.'

'But . . . ?' Connie sensed there was a definite catch in there somewhere.

'It's a small house.' Catching sight of her blotchy face in the mirror above the sink, Pamela splashed her cheeks with cold water. 'So I've decided that I'll look for lodgings here in Kelthorpe.'

'I see.' Connie stood with her head to one side. 'Do you have somewhere in mind?'

'Not yet. I haven't had a chance to look.' Seeing Connie's thoughtful reflection, she turned to face her. 'Why – do you know of somewhere?'

'It just so happens . . .' Connie waited for Pamela to pat her face dry. 'I have heard of a room that's free opposite me on Elliot Street – at number 21, next to the swimming baths.'

'I know it.' Pamela had noticed the vacancy sign in the window when she'd defied her mother to go for a swim. The house was shabby and the windows had needed a good clean, but so what? But realistically, could she manage to pay the rent and would the room be furnished or unfurnished? A dozen questions buzzed around her head.

'We'd be neighbours again,' Connie pointed out.

'We would.' Pressure eased from around Pamela's chest. She took a deep breath and got ready to face the world. 'I'll ask to look at the room tomorrow morning, first thing.'

CHAPTER SEVEN

Connie and Lizzie carried a pile of small sewing jobs into the front room at number 12 and settled down for a Sunday morning of darning socks and sewing hems. There was better light there than in the back kitchen and two comfortable chairs to sit in while they worked. It was a room in which time had stood still – photographs of their parents' wedding in 1916 were arranged on the marble mantelpiece, alternating with delicate china ornaments that their mother Rhoda had chosen. The antimacassars on the backs of the chairs had been embroidered by her, and each Friday she'd methodically polished the brass fender framing the fireplace until it gleamed. Now rain beat against the window panes, obscuring the girls' view of the outside world, while in the kitchen their father took his time to prepare a rare fry-up of bacon and egg on his day off from the bakery.

'The smell of that bacon is making my mouth water.' Lizzie had made do with a breakfast of porridge. She was intending to take up the hem of her blue summer skirt and was trying it on to judge the new, shorter length. 'I want it to skim my knees,' she explained to Connie. 'Can you pop in a couple of pins at the right level? Not too short, though.'

Connie quickly obliged. 'The latest fashion is for just above the knee,' she pointed out. 'Are you sure you don't want it an inch shorter?'

'I'm certain. I don't want to be the talk of Elliot Street.' Lizzie slipped out of the skirt and back into her slacks. 'To be honest, I'm happier wearing trousers these days. It saves the fiddle of suspender belts and stockings.'

'But you have such good legs – you ought to show them off more.' Connie returned to the ancient pair of socks that their father refused to consign to the rag-and-bone cart. 'This is the third time I've mended this pair,' she complained. 'Dad never throws anything out, bless him.'

'Old habits.' The girls worked on for a while in companionable silence, their dark heads bent in concentration and their fingers working deftly with needle and thread. The April shower eased and sun soon broke through the clouds. 'Don't tell Dad, but Bob and I had a tiff yesterday afternoon,' Lizzie confessed.

Connie's hand hovered over the half-darned sock. 'What about, pray?'

'What do you think? He still doesn't approve of me volunteering. He says he's worried sick about me.'

'And what did you tell him?'

'I made it clear that he couldn't change my mind – driving an ambulance is what I want to do.'

'And that didn't go down well?'

'No – he stormed off. I haven't heard from him since.'

Connie sewed on. 'Bob is in the wrong,' she said with

conviction. 'He ought not to object. Turn it around: think of the millions of women up and down the length of this country – wives and mothers who watch their men go off to fight. Do any of them try to stop their husbands from doing their bit? No, of course not. And what would we think of them if they did? We'd say those women were putting their own needs before their country and that it was a selfish and short-sighted way of going on.'

'It's true,' Lizzie agreed. 'And Friday night proved that I can keep my head when the sirens sound. I promise you, I carried on driving that old Morrison's ambulance through thick and thin.'

'Of course you did.' Connie had never had any doubts that Lizzie was up to the job. 'We Harrison girls are made of stern stuff.'

'Bill was cool as a cucumber. He was the one who kept us all in order,' Lizzie explained.

Connie raised a knowing eyebrow. 'Did you sing Bill's praises to Bob?'

'No, of course not – give me some credit.'

'But his name was mentioned?'

'Only in passing,' Lizzie protested. 'Bob was nasty about Bill without good reason and then he stormed off.'

In and out went Connie's needle to reinforce the heel of her father's sock. 'I rest my case.'

A deep flush crept up Lizzie's neck and across her cheeks. She didn't want to believe what Connie was implying – that Bob was suffering from jealousy. 'It's not as if I've done anything wrong. I only accepted a lift on the back of Bill's motorbike – just the once, that's all. And Bob doesn't even know about that.'

Connie gave a long, cool stare that said more than words. Then she broke her silence with, 'Your fiancé may be many things – finicky, careful with his money, slow to see a joke sometimes – but he's not stupid.'

'I know he's not.' Pushing her sewing from her lap, Lizzie stood up and paced the room. 'I love Bob; you know I do. And I would never do anything to hurt him.'

'He loves you too.' But Connie knew better than most that young love sometimes wore out and couldn't be mended.

'It's just that I feel tied down by him.' A glance at the ring sparkling on her finger made Lizzie sigh. 'Not all the time – only sometimes.'

Lizzie's candid assessment prompted a halting confession from Connie, who lowered her voice to make sure that their father couldn't overhear. 'I recognize that feeling of not being free to be yourself. It was like that with John right from the start. He had strong views on how a woman should behave and he wanted me to fit in with them.'

Lizzie was distracted from her own problem by Connie's troubled tone. 'Such as?'

'Such as what I should wear and how I should do my hair – everyday things. And I had to hand over my wage at the end of each week – all except for two shillings, which I was allowed to keep to spend on items that women need; that's how John put it.'

'I never knew that.' Lizzie was truly shocked. As far as she'd been aware, Connie's husband had been the genial, generous type, never slow to put his hand in his pocket when it came to buying a round of drinks. 'He didn't come across like that. Why didn't you put your foot down?'

'You didn't argue with John,' was all that Connie would say on that topic before she became tight-lipped. It wasn't the done thing to divulge details, good or bad, about married life so she had never spoken about John's occasional lashing out with his fists. The first time had been a terrific and shameful shock; a Jekyll-and-Hyde moment that she'd hoped would never be repeated. It had been, of course – especially after a few drinks. But still, the least said the better was the motto she'd chosen to live by. 'Never mind about me; what are you going to do about Bob?' She joined Lizzie at the window. 'When are you two going to kiss and make up?'

Outside the pavements gleamed from the recent rain. A trickle of swimmers with towels and swimsuits tucked under their arms began to form a queue for a Sunday morning session at the municipal pool. Connie recognized Pamela in her blue coat and hat as she walked up the street and knocked at the door of number 21.

'That's up to Bob,' Lizzie decided. 'He was the one who walked off in a huff, not me.'

Thora Mason took her time to respond to Pamela's knock. Once a handsome, well-built woman with striking dark eyes, thick black eyebrows and copper-coloured hair, she was now in her sixties and had let herself go to seed. Her figure was slack, the vibrant hair dull grey, the eyes sunken. Only the eyebrows remained as a reminder of her former glory. As for clothes: a faded floral apron covered a threadbare brown dress and the slippers that the landlady wore were a pair of cast-offs belonging to a previous lodger.

'Yes?' Thora eyed Pamela keenly, taking in the slight figure and nervous air.

'You have a vacancy sign in your window,' Pamela began. She clutched her handbag tightly in front of her in an attempt to stop her hands from shaking.

'Yes.'

'Is the room still free?'

'It is.' But did Thora want to let it to this youngster – that was the question. Pamela's smooth, pale skin and wide-eyed stare gave her a childlike, defenceless air; Thora preferred her lodgers to be self-sufficient and able to stand up for themselves if necessary. 'I only take gentlemen as a rule,' she informed her.

'Oh, I see.' Pamela's hopes plummeted. About to step back from the door, she glanced over her shoulder to see Connie on the doorstep of number 12.

'I'll vouch for her,' Connie called to the stern landlady. 'Pamela works at the Savoy with me – a totally reliable sort, I can assure you.'

Thora harrumphed then studied the caller more closely. No doubt she would be quiet – not flighty like some of the young ones these days. And it seemed she had a steady wage coming in. 'I do make exceptions now that so many of the young men have been called up,' she conceded stiffly, though still blocking the door with her considerable frame.

'I would be no trouble,' Pamela promised. 'And I would be able to pay a deposit if required.'

'You'd best come in.' Thora held the door open, leaving Pamela just enough space to sidle past then down the narrow corridor with two doors to the left and one straight ahead. 'The room that's vacant is up two flights of stairs, right at the top of the house. Go on up – I'll follow you.'

Pamela breathed in an odour she couldn't identify – perhaps a mixture of mothballs, musty stair carpet and stale cooking. The striped wallpaper on the stairs was badly faded and some of the brass stair rods were missing.

'There's a shared bathroom and toilet on the first floor.' Thora's heavy tread followed close behind. 'Lodgers fill in a rota and stick to it, no ifs or buts.'

Pamela hesitated on the small landing at the top of the second flight of stairs.

'It's the door on your left,' Thora instructed.

The door opened on to an attic room with sloping ceilings and two small skylights. There was an iron bedstead in one corner, a washstand with ewer and pitcher (both cracked), a chest of drawers and a wooden chair in front of a card table with folding legs and a green baize top. The whitewashed walls were clean enough and there was an old-fashioned Turkish rug (worn in places) in front of a tiny cast-iron fireplace.

'You'll take your meals – breakfast and dinner – with Mr Fielding and Mr Miller in the downstairs dining room, half seven and six o'clock sharp. Meals are an extra five shillings a week, on top of rent.'

'And how much is the rent?' The reality of launching out on her own was more daunting than Pamela had expected. How could she live with so little daylight, no view and so few creature comforts? She experienced a strong urge to retreat to Raby and the hospitable arms of Aunty Lilian.

'Twelve shillings and sixpence, payable in advance.' If Thora had been a betting person she'd have wagered that Pamela was about to beat a hasty retreat. The girl was too refined and nervy to accept what was on offer.

Pamela gulped back her doubts. 'I'll take it,' she declared with new resolution. 'Room and breakfast only, please. I work as a cashier at the cinema so it won't be necessary to provide me with an evening meal.'

Connie waited on her doorstep for Pamela to emerge from Thora's den. 'Well?' She hailed her from across the street.

Pamela felt weak at the knees as she joined Connie on the opposite pavement. 'It's done – I move in later today,' she replied as if scarcely able to believe what had happened.

'By Jove, that was quick.'

'The room was vacant so I grabbed my chance.' All that remained was for Pamela to tell her parents.

'Well done, you. Now, how about a little pick-me-up – a cup of tea and a biscuit?' Connie was insistent, ushering Pamela into the house and showing her into the front room. 'You remember my sister Lizzie from school? Liz, Pamela here has just rented a room at number 21.'

Lizzie quickly put two and two together. 'I witnessed what happened to your poor house on Musgrave Street. How are your mum and dad coping?'

Leaving Pamela in her sister's capable hands for a moment, Connie organized refreshments. 'Dad, we have a visitor. Put the kettle on and make us a good, strong pot of tea, would you?'

'Coming up,' he called from the kitchen.

110

'Dad will cope,' Pamela replied to Lizzie as Connie came back into the room. 'But Mum has taken it very hard.'

'It must have been a terrible shock,' Lizzie sympathized. She hadn't seen much of Pamela since they'd left St Joseph's but she remembered her back then as a tidy girl with neat pigtails and well-ironed clothes. Her braininess had made her a target for bullying on occasion – Pamela had suffered the taunts without retaliating, merely retreating to a quiet corner of the classroom and burying her head in a book. Looking at her now, in her demure coat and hat, still with the same naive, shy air, Lizzie wondered how on earth she would fit in at Thora Mason's rough-and-ready establishment.

'Excuse the mess.' Connie gestured towards the pile of mending perched on the arm of a chair and to Lizzie's unfinished skirt. 'Now, since you're here, I want you to look at a couple of dresses that I set to one side.' She picked out from the pile a pink-and-white cotton frock with a floral pattern and held it up for Pamela to inspect. 'It's missing a top button but that's easily remedied and I reckon it would suit you to a T. And this green one with white piping and a pretty sweetheart neckline; all it needs is a couple of stitches in the hem.'

Pamela smiled and blushed. 'It's very good of you, but—'

'No buts!' Connie declared as Bert came in with a tray of tea things. She held the green dress against Pamela to check the fit.

'Eh up, I didn't know we were having a fashion show.' Bert put down the tray then made a quick exit.

'It suits you.' Lizzie joined Connie in persuading

111

Pamela to borrow the clothes. 'And if it needs alter-ing we have a Singer sewing machine tucked away in a corner – it'll just be a case of a quick dart here and a raised hem there.'

'What else can we lend you?' Connie imagined her-self in Pamela's position. 'I bet you don't even have a hairbrush to your name, do you? Or a stick of make-up, let alone a spare pair of stockings.'

Seeing that it was useless to resist, Pamela accepted her new neighbours' help. Tea was poured, biscuits eaten. Arrangements were made for Pamela to call back later to collect the borrowed items.

'I can't thank you enough,' Pamela told the sisters as she made her exit and tears of gratitude welled up. 'You've been so very kind.'

Connie squeezed her arm affectionately. 'You'd do the same if the shoe was on the other foot.'

'Drop in for a chat any time,' Lizzie urged. 'Our door's always open.'

Bolstered by their support, Pamela made her way down the street towards the bus stop with a fresh sense of purpose. She discovered from the notice inside the shelter that Sunday service was limited but that a bus to Raby was due in fifteen minutes. So she sat and waited, watching the comings and goings from the swimming baths and noticing the door to her new lodgings house open. A man she recognized but couldn't place stepped on to the pavement and looked both ways before crossing the street. As he walked towards the bus stop, Pamela did place him – it was the smart new clerk in her father's office. He stopped six feet from her to read the timetable then acknowledged her presence with a polite nod.

Pamela nodded back then watched him walk on without saying a word – tall, straight-backed, unsmiling. *Mr Fielding and Mr Miller!* She remembered her new landlady's mention of two fellow lodgers. Fred Miller – the very same!

It seemed he hadn't recognized her out of context; after all, they'd only been briefly introduced. In any case, she probably wasn't of much interest to the young, go-getting addition to Anderson's payroll. Pamela dismissed Fred Miller from her mind; she had more important things to concentrate on. The bus turned the corner on to Elliot Street and she stepped out of the shelter to flag it down. *Dad, Mum . . .* She got on the half-empty bus and sat down in a seat directly behind the driver, rehearsing the speech she would make when she reached Aunty Lilian's house. *Please don't be upset. I've made up my mind and I've found myself lodgings in town. Twelve and sixpence per week, with breakfast extra.*

Keep it simple, she told herself. *Expect Mum to wail and cry.*

'Tickets, anyone?' the conductor said as he approached Pamela. The bus lurched to a stop to let passengers alight. The bell rang and on they went. 'Tickets please.'

Before the start of her night shift on the following Wednesday, Lizzie stood outside the King Edward Street ambulance depot, mulling over her situation with Bob, who hadn't been in touch since the weekend. He was obviously waiting for her to make the first move. On a less personal front there had been no raids on Kelthorpe since the previous disastrous

Friday and inhabitants were beginning to hope against hope that the Luftwaffe had decided to concentrate future attacks on the poor beggars in ports and cities further south.

'Mr Churchill won't admit it but Hull took a dreadful battering through the whole of March and April,' Bill remarked as he waited with Lizzie at the gate of the old brewery. Both had arrived fifteen minutes early and were enjoying the cool, clear night air while other first-aiders and ambulance drivers came and went. 'Worse than us?' Lizzie asked.

'Far worse,' he confirmed. 'The docks were flattened along with the Shell Mex building. It's the parachute mines that do the worst damage. It turns out the government has slapped a D-notice on the whole city.'

'What does that mean?' She was curious to learn more.

'It's a request – more of an order, really – to keep the name of the town out of the papers, in the interests of security, so they say. More likely it's because they don't want us to know what a hammering we're taking – they reckon it would be bad for morale.'

As Lizzie considered the pros and cons of the propaganda move, a young messenger cycled furiously towards them. He dropped his bike at their feet and gabbled at them.

'Parachute ... headland ... not one of ours ... man injured.'

'Slow down,' Lizzie said. 'Do you mean a German pilot has parachuted down on to the headland?'

As the boy nodded and gasped for air Bill and Lizzie sprang into action. 'Run inside and tell the

man in charge that Lizzie and I will answer the call –
he's the chap with the white helmet and three red
stripes on his arm. Tell him to telephone for the
police.'

The messenger did as he was told while Lizzie
jumped into her newly equipped bakery van and Bill
joined her.

'The headland covers a big area,' she reminded
him, a knot of fear forming under her ribs.

'Yes, but Musgrave Street is the only road up. Once
we get to the top of the hill we should have more of a
clue where he came down. It's a clear night so it
shouldn't be hard to spot a white parachute against
the dark rock.'

'I wonder what happened to his plane?' Lizzie set
off as fast as she dared along the darkened street.

'Who knows? He probably took a direct hit from
one of our lads during a dogfight. Maybe he was
hoping to limp back to France but his luck ran out.'
Such stories were so common these days that they
scarcely reached the newspapers.

'What will the police do?' she wanted to know.

'They'll take Fritz into custody unless he's too
badly injured – in which case, we'll drive him to
hospital.'

Not knowing exactly what she and Bill would find
filled Lizzie with dread. She continued to drive at
speed through narrow, crooked streets, around the
quayside and into the new town, then swinging left
up an eerily quiet Musgrave Street. What if the German pilot were dead when they found him? It would
be her first experience of seeing a lifeless body. How
would she feel and what would she do?

She was glad that Bill was sitting beside her, scanning the dark hillside as she drove on. He knew the ropes and would guide her every step of the way.

When they reached the top of the hill and could drive no further, their dim headlights shone on a solitary figure flagging them down with a white handkerchief. Bill was first out of the van. He strode towards an elderly man who gave his name as Jack Scott then explained that he was a resident at number 52 and had seen the stricken Dornier descend over the headland and into the drink. The pilot had ejected at the last minute and his parachute had drifted to earth.

'I got straight on the blower to the wardens' control centre,' he told Bill, chest puffed out with pride and obviously basking in the importance of his role. 'My nephew Frank works there so he knew what to do.'

Lizzie parked the van, hitched her haversack over her shoulder and joined them. 'Did you see where the pilot landed?'

'This way.' Their wiry informant led them sure-footedly down a rough, steep track with heather and gorse to either side. 'I walk the dog here so I know this area well,' he assured them. 'He came down a hundred yards to our left, by that big boulder over there. I didn't go too close but I could hear him moaning and groaning from a distance.'

Scanning the hillside in the direction in which Jack pointed, Lizzie and Bill made out a white patch against the dark scrub.

'You stay put,' Bill instructed the old man. 'Lizzie and I will take it from here.'

She removed her torch from its sling and they strode away from the track through the rough heather towards the landmark boulder and the tell-tale parachute.

'Go carefully – he could be armed,' Bill warned her before cupping his hands around his mouth. 'Hello there – we're first-aiders!' he yelled into the murky distance. 'Ambulance! We're on our way.'

With her heart in her mouth and wondering if the Luftwaffe pilot knew any English, Lizzie continued, stumbling over heather bushes and struggling to keep her balance. 'Can you hear anything?' she muttered to Bill.

'Not a dicky bird.' The boulder loomed over them as they reached the torn parachute, only to find that the enemy airman had unclasped his harness and abandoned it. A strong wind caught the flimsy silk and the parachute, entangled in the shrubs, billowed high in the air.

'He can't be that badly injured,' Lizzie concluded. Her chest was tight as she scanned the area for signs of life.

'No, but on the other hand he can't have got far.' Bill set off to search behind the boulder while Lizzie shone her torch along the horizon.

She listened intently, trying to detect signs of life. Then she followed a sound to her left and saw a movement among a thicket of prickly gorse, quickly followed by a groan. 'Bill!' she called. 'Over here!'

Creeping closer, she made out the figure of a man on his belly, attempting to slither into the bushes but giving it up and lying inert, face down, some five paces from where she stood. She crouched down on her haunches and shone the torch on his face. His eyes were open and scared, his cheek was gashed. And he was young – scarcely twenty years old, she guessed – his hair concealed beneath a leather helmet, his flying suit torn at the shoulder to reveal another deep wound.

Bill arrived at her side and they advanced together. The pilot made one last effort to slide out of reach but groaned again, turned on to his back and lay helplessly, arms spreadeagled.

'Lie still,' Bill insisted as he lowered his haversack to the ground.

Lizzie unscrewed the top of her water bottle and attempted to trickle liquid into the wounded man's mouth. She took a lint pad from her own haversack and pressed it hard against the man's shoulder wound to reduce the bleeding. Then she secured the pad with sticking plaster.

'The left ankle seems to be broken,' Bill concluded after a quick examination. He took two small splints from his bag and Lizzie helped him to strap the ankle in place with bandages. Then she sprinted as fast as she could towards the van to fetch a stretcher.

'Is he still in the land of the living?' Jack Scott stood guard beside the makeshift ambulance, warding off neighbours whose curiosity had drawn them to the scene. Half a dozen people had gathered on the windy hilltop, demanding to know what had happened.

'Alive and conscious,' Lizzie confirmed. As yet there was no sign of the police.

'Has he said anything?'

She shook her head. 'He's bleeding heavily. I expect he's in a lot of pain.'

118

'That'll teach him.' A bitter bystander voiced what others might be feeling.

But Lizzie was stuck with the stricken, helpless, despairing look she'd witnessed on the young man's face. She slid the rolled-up stretcher from the back of the van, tucked it under her arm and hurried back to Bill and the patient.

Bill motioned to the pilot that they intended to ease him on to the stretcher. The young German seemed to understand – his panic had given way to resignation and he raised himself on to his elbows so they could slide the top half of the canvas contraption under his upper body. With the broken ankle splinted, he gritted his teeth and allowed Bill and Lizzie to raise his legs and gently lower them on to the stretcher.

'That's the spirit.' Lizzie laid a comforting hand on his chest.

'Ready?' Bill asked as he prepared to take the man's weight.

Lizzie took the strain at the top end of the stretcher. 'Yes. Go ahead.'

It was hard going across the heather, even though the pilot was slightly built. By the time they reached the ambulance, staggering a little and stopping once to draw breath, the crowd of onlookers had swelled to a dozen or more and a policeman wheeling a bicycle had arrived. Seeing his uniform, the pilot panicked and attempted to sit up.

'Lie down – you're not going anywhere,' Bill told him. 'You took your time,' he grumbled to the constable.

The seasoned, moustachioed officer took in the

blood, the bandages and the splinted ankle. 'So what? Like you say, Jerry's not about to make a run for it.'

'It's all right.' Lizzie soothed her patient and removed his helmet. His hair was blond and cut very short. 'Can you speak English?'

His light brown eyes widened and he nodded. 'A little.'

'Good. We'll take you to a doctor. Understand?'

He nodded again, one wary eye still on the constable.

'Are you going to arrest him on the spot or wait until we get him to the first-aid post to set the ankle?' Bill asked as he and Lizzie slid the stretcher into the van.

The policeman didn't seem to care. 'Either way this lad's going to sit out the rest of the war in a POW camp.' He agreed to follow the ambulance down to King Edward Street. 'That's it, everyone,' he told the knot of onlookers. 'The show's over.'

'Relax,' Lizzie told the pilot, climbing into the van and crouching beside him. 'Bill will look after you while I drive the van to the first-aid post.' She mimed what she intended to do. 'Then a doctor will fix you up.'

'Ich verstehe.' I understand. His eyes followed her as she clambered into the driver's seat and Bill closed the doors behind him.

Bill bent over the patient. 'Name?' he asked as he used cotton wool to clean the blood from his face.

'Kurt.' Talking was obviously an effort as Lizzie turned the van to face downhill, making him groan anew.

'I'm Bill Evans.'

'Kurt Braun.' The injured man closed his eyes, exhausted.

Lizzie checked in her overhead mirror. 'All set?'

'Drive on,' Bill confirmed.

In the moonlight she saw the curve of the bay below and the white fringe of breaking waves. She pictured Kurt Braun's Dornier plunging into the dark sea, imagined a mother at home in Germany receiving a telegram to say that her son was missing presumed dead. For Lizzie it was the first time that the enemy had a human face and she realized with a shock that it was no different to that of any eager young man queuing to sign up outside Kelthorpe town hall. German or British; airman, sailor or soldier – all indistinguishable except for their uniforms. Kill or be killed. Live or die.

CHAPTER EIGHT

The start of May saw Pamela nicely settled in her new surroundings. Though the room on Elliot Street was far from luxurious, she had brightened it up with cushions, pictures and ornaments on loan from her aunt.

Lilian had driven over with Pamela from Raby late on Sunday afternoon, taken one look at the dingy lodgings and rolled up her sleeves. 'You'll be surprised what a bit of spit and polish will do,' she'd promised.

Together they'd pummelled lumps out of the horse-hair mattress and swept cobwebs from every corner and crevice. They'd shifted furniture under Thora Mason's eagle eye – 'Anything you break you'll have to pay for' – and taken the rug down to the backyard to sling it over the washing line and beat out every mote of dust. It had been almost dark by the time they'd finished.

'That'll do for now,' Lilian had decided, standing back with her sturdy arms crossed to judge the results of their efforts. A small table lamp cast a cosy glow across fresh bed linen and newly plumped-up red velvet cushions. A crisp linen cloth covered the green baize table and garishly glazed figurines of a shepherd and shepherdess decorated the narrow mantelpiece.

Pamela had experienced a small surge of pride – she had her very own place for the first time in her life. The dresses that Connie had given her lay on the bed, together with some underthings and a pair of Lizzie's wedge-heeled sandals. ('I hardly ever wear them,' Lizzie had offered. 'If they fit you, they're yours for keeps.') 'Tell Mum that there's no need for her to worry about me,' Pamela had urged her aunt.

'She won't take a blind bit of notice,' Lilian had predicted phlegmatically.

Earlier that afternoon they'd left a bereft Edith in the Raby cottage. All the disasters in the world had been imagined by Pamela's weeping mother when she'd learned of her daughter's plans to rent a room; from violent intruders to burst water pipes, from stray incendiaries falling through the roof to rowdy neighbours and miserable penury and starvation.

'I'll call in and see Mum and Dad next Saturday,' Pamela had promised as Lilian had buttoned her coat and descended the stairs of the lodging house.

Then she'd closed her door with a satisfied sigh and revelled in her new-found freedom. She'd re-arranged the cushions and guiltily hidden the shiny shepherd and his coy lass in a drawer, resolving to buy more modern ornaments in due course. Then she'd lain on the bed fully clothed, staring at cracks in the sloping ceiling. She owned nothing, yet she had everything – a tiny attic room and the whole world. And best of all, she had new friends in Connie Bailey and Lizzie Harrison.

*

Three days later no pipes had burst or bombs fallen on number 21. Pamela had entered her name on the rota for the bathroom and gone quietly about her business, alert to every creak of the timbers in the roof and every hollow footfall on the stairs. She'd quickly established her routine, waking at seven each morning to use the facilities before either Fred Miller or the mysterious Mr Fielding was up. At half past seven she went down to Thora Mason's breakfast of porridge – 'with a pinch of salt, not sugar' – followed by toast – 'I'll need part of your sugar ration if you want marmalade on that.' On the Monday morning Pamela ate alone. On Tuesday she sat in the break-fast room with Fred, who chose the far corner and exchanged only basic pleasantries – 'He's not a great talker, that one.' Wednesday came and went without her seeing either of her fellow lodgers.

'Mr Fielding is indisposed,' Thora informed Pamela breathily as she served up the porridge the following morning. 'I expect he'll keep to his room today.'

Fred glanced across at her but said nothing. For a moment Pamela considered entering into small talk about the weather but thought better of it. Instead, she wondered, not for the first time, whether the new clerk at Anderson's was afflicted by an intense shyness or whether he simply thought her unworthy of his notice. He left the breakfast room before her and when she made her way upstairs he emerged from his first-floor room and their paths crossed on the landing.

Dressed in a fawn raincoat and carrying a trilby hat, Fred's face was expressionless as he politely stepped aside to let Pamela pass.

She thanked him then went up to her attic room

to plan her day. First she would walk to the haberdasher's on College Road and buy a new trim for her cream blouse and a few sewing items – needles and thread, pins, small scissors, et cetera. She made a careful list. Then she would pop in to Cynthia's Salon to make an appointment for a trim. After that she would go to the library and explain that two of their books on loan to her had been lost in a direct hit. She would happily pay for them and renew her membership, giving her new address. The afternoon would be free for reading or sewing, whatever caught her fancy.

The haberdashery was a small piece of heaven as far as Pamela was concerned. Ribbons of every conceivable colour festooned the display racks behind the counter while boxes of shiny buttons – pearly white, lemon yellow, sky blue and rose pink – were ranged along the shelves. Zips, elastic, embroidery threads, lace trim, dress patterns, collars, cotton gloves; in every corner there was something that attracted her attention. 'I could spend a fortune in here,' she confessed to the girl behind the counter, restricting herself to a blue zigzag trim that would brighten up her blouse, together with the essentials on her list.

Even the ping of the bell as she left the shop had a cheerful ring.

She headed across the street to the hairdresser's.

'We can fit you in for a trim two weeks from today.' Cynthia's assistant consulted the diary and put Pamela's name down for half past three.

Then, back out on College Road, who should Pamela bump into but Lizzie, coming out of the bakery shop with a tray of bread buns and teacakes?

'I'm in a rush,' Lizzie apologized as she loaded the tray into the back of the van, 'but Connie's at a loose end in there. Why not pop in and have a natter?'

There was plenty for Pamela and Connie to gossip about, starting with Mr Penrose's latest petty ruling that all employees at the Savoy must refrain from smoking on the premises, moving on to the damage done to Anderson's during the last air raid – part of the highly combustible timber yard had gone up in flames before the fire services could reach it – then on to how Pamela was settling in at number 21.

'Who's that good-looking young chap I see coming in and out?' Connie wanted to know. 'You know – the one who looks like William Holden.'

For a second or two Pamela was thrown.

'You know William Holden – he starred in *Our Town*.' It had proved a popular film at the Savoy, thanks to the new young star's appeal. 'I take it the handsome mystery man lodges with Thora?'

Pamela blushed and nodded. 'He's called Fred. He doesn't seem keen on getting to know me, though.'

'What's wrong with the fellow – does he need his eyes tested?'

Connie's expression of exaggerated disbelief made Pamela giggle. 'I'm not bothered. Anyway, I'd better let you get on.' A customer had come into the shop so Pamela went on her way.

She left College Road and crossed the town square then ascended the broad steps to the library and entered the building to talk to a librarian about the burned books. It was early afternoon by the time she got back home and caught her first glimpse of Mr Fielding as he went into the bathroom on the first floor. From his back view she made out that he was a short, stout man in braces and shirtsleeves who moved slowly due to his weight. She could tell no more about him and there was no opportunity to introduce herself so she went on up to her room, where she spent the afternoon sewing. Once, at around three o'clock, she thought she heard noises from the room below: a heavy thud followed by the slow scraping of furniture across floorboards. Then later, as she got ready to leave for work, she heard the front door open and close then lively footsteps running upstairs.

Picking up her handbag, she came out of her room a few minutes later to see Mr Fielding holding fast to the banister on the first-floor landing. He swayed forward then lurched a few steps, grabbing the door handle to his left to steady himself.

Pamela hesitated outside her door. Mr Fielding was plainly drunk. His thin grey hair was dishevelled and his collarless shirt unbuttoned at the neck. Perhaps it would be best if she waited for him to retreat into his room.

But Fielding tilted his head back and spotted Pamela. Through his blurred vision he made out a girl with shapely legs, wearing a green summer dress, with her hat in her hand and her coat folded neatly over her arm. He extended his right hand and tottered again. 'Cyril Fielding,' he slurred, before overbalancing and falling heavily against the banister.

Pamela's heart jumped. She pictured the banister breaking under the man's weight and him tumbling down the stairwell. Fortunately it held. But her fellow lodger still seemed intent on introducing himself.

'Fielding,' he repeated as he pushed himself upright then leered at her.

She swallowed back her disgust. If this was what Thora had meant by 'indisposed', it was a very poor show. She decided she had two choices – to disappear back into her room as she'd first thought and wait for the drunken man to stagger away, which would make her late for work and incur Mr Penrose's wrath, or to carry on down and attempt to pass him on the landing, a prospect that made her shudder. So when Fred came out of his room she breathed a sigh of relief.

'I say, old chap.' Glancing up at Pamela, Fred approached Fielding in an emphatically chummy way. 'Why not come with me?' He steered him by the elbow, along the landing towards a door at the far end.

But Fielding resisted. 'Don't "old chap" me. And leave off, if you know what's good for you.' He shoved Fred sideways, losing his own balance as he did so. He landed on his broad backside with his legs spread-eagled.

Fred motioned for Pamela to make her exit. 'Quick as you can,' he advised.

So, as Fred helped Fielding to his feet, Pamela ran down the stairs, mouthing a thank you and scarcely breathing, deeply ashamed on Fielding's behalf. *What a state to be in*, she thought with a shiver as she stepped out on to the street.

She'd walked past the swimming baths and was trying her best to push the incident to the back of her mind when Fred caught up with her, carrying his gas mask under his arm and wearing his raincoat unbuttoned to reveal a dark-blue uniform underneath.

'Are you all right?' he checked without preliminaries. 'I managed to get Fielding back into his room. I'm afraid he was very drunk.'

'You don't say.' Pamela walked on but then stopped at the end of the street. 'Thank you, Mr Miller.'

'Fred; please.'

'Thank you, Fred. I was considering retreating into my room and barricading the door.'

'I'll have a word with Mrs Mason for you if you like. Fielding can be a nuisance when he's the worse for wear. In fact, he's on his final warning; one more incident of this sort and she's sworn to turf him out.' Fred's offer was sincere and he made it clear that it was one he was willing to follow through.

'Oh no, please; not on my account.' Pamela preferred to give Fielding the benefit of the doubt.

'Are you sure?'

'Quite sure.' Curious about Fred's uniform, she suggested that they walk on together. 'You're with the Civil Defence?' she asked.

'Yes. I work at the Report and Control Centre at the town hall, collating then forwarding damage and situation reports to the Ministry of Home Security. I started there three weeks ago.'

'Then you're at the heart of things.' She imagined him sitting at a desk with a telephone and a typewriter, surrounded by charts and maps, efficiently gathering rapidly changing information during and after each raid.

'You could say that.' His answer was modest and he quickly changed the subject. 'I haven't told your father that we share the same lodging house; I wasn't sure of the situation.'

'You mean, did he and I have an almighty row before I left?' Pamela picked up on Fred's meaning. 'No, I'm glad to say we didn't. It was my own decision.'

'Then I might mention it tomorrow.'

'Please do.' She paused again by the gates to the Leisure Gardens. 'This is where we go our separate ways. And thank you again.'

Fred bowed his head in acknowledgement then hesitated before continuing in a more confiding way. 'I hear your family lost everything in the latest raid?'

'Unfortunately, yes.' In her mind's eye she saw smoke spiralling into the night sky, the wind tearing it away. The vivid flashback to the previous Friday made Pamela clutch her collar tight around her throat.

'I'm sorry – I do know how hard that is.'

'You've been through it?'

'Yes; in London's Hatton Garden. We were hit hard by incendiaries last year.'

'I'm sorry, I had no idea.' So Fred was a long way from home. Pamela guessed that he might have been in London for Black Saturday: the notorious German retaliation for the Luftwaffe's humiliation at the hands of the RAF.

'How could you?' He shrugged his shoulders. 'I decided to head north; I supposed I might be in less danger, but it turns out I was wrong.'

'Yes, the whole country is in the same boat.' It seemed that she and Fred had something in common. As they parted ways, Pamela went over the events of the previous half hour. It was true what Connie had said: when Fred smiled he did have a touch of the Hollywood star about him. There was a suggestion of a wave in his short, dark hair and he had a direct,

130

disarming way of looking straight at you with those clear grey eyes. And his neat, even features undeniably appealed.

He should smile more often, Pamela thought as she walked by the pond in the late-afternoon light. A boy and a girl sailed a toy yacht and a brown dog chased after a ball. As always, the gulls wheeled over the grey water then swooped down to scavenge from the litter bins by the park gate. When Pamela reached the cinema she decided to mention to Connie that Fred had rescued her from Mr Fielding's lecherous gaze. Connie would no doubt give a mischievous, told-you-so grin. *Fred has a nice smile*, Pamela would confide. *And from a certain angle he does look a little like William Holden, just as you said*.

Waiting at Anderson's gate for Bob to finish work, Lizzie saw for herself the damage that had been done to the yard by the latest German bombs. One of the two huge steel cranes was twisted and leaning at an angle, and heaps of useless, blackened timber had been bulldozed against a high brick wall. Beyond the yard the normally busy dockside was practically deserted.

A hooter sounded and workmen came out of the vast cutting shed then filed out through the gates, their boots crunching over the loose cinder surface. They cast curious glances in Lizzie's direction. Some recognized her and said hello. When George Bachelor spotted her he made a special detour across the yard to speak with her.

'If you're waiting for Bob he might be a little while,' he informed her as workers passed by on either side. 'The boss called him into the office.'

'What for?' Alarm bells rang in Lizzie's head.

'I have no idea. I'm only the messenger.' George offered her a cigarette, which she refused. 'No doubt Mr Anderson has his reasons.'

'Is he laying people off?' It stood to reason that this might happen now that the timber yard wasn't running at full capacity.

'Not yet.' George lit up and inhaled deeply. 'Anyway, Miss Lizzie, how's tricks?'

She was immediately affronted. How was it that men like George had the brazen habit of undressing you with their eyes? Right now he looked her up and down with that harsh glint of appraisal. 'I'm fine, thanks. How are you?' She stared back at him with a hint of defiance.

'Never better. And how's that big sister of yours?'

'Connie's fine, too.'

George flicked ash on to the ground then moved a step closer to allow a fellow worker to cycle by. 'As it happens, I'll find out for myself later on.'

'Are you on duty tonight?'

He nodded. 'And how are you enjoying life as an ambulance driver? I hear you had to drive that Jerry pilot to hospital. If it had been me I'd have been tempted to break the bastard's other leg and have done with it.'

Lizzie suppressed a gasp. 'I just did my job, that's all.' Seeing Bob emerge from the office building, she eased past George. 'I'm sorry, I have to go.'

The foreman glanced over his shoulder and spied her fiancé. 'Here he comes, love's young dream.'

Hateful so-and-so! Lizzie thought. *I pity Connie for having to work with him.* Advancing slowly, she waited for Bob to spot her and when he did she hesitated. Would he be pleased to see her or would he still be holding a grudge?

'Go and make it up,' Connie had nagged Lizzie several times. 'Clear the air; the longer you leave it the more awkward things will be.'

The well-hidden stubborn streak had made Lizzie resist until now. But by the end of the week she saw that it was time. However it turned out, she and Bob must talk.

'What are you doing here?' He approached uncertainly.

'I came to sort things out.' Suddenly the timber yard didn't seem the ideal place for a heart-to-heart. It was hardly private and Bob's workmates would probably tease him when they got the chance. 'Can we go somewhere else?'

He nodded then led the way down the side of the yard on to the dockside.

'Why did Mr Anderson want to see you?' Lizzie asked.

'Who told you about that?' Bob rolled his cap and stuffed it in his jacket pocket then ran a hand through his hair.

'George did.'

'Trust him to poke his nose in.' He walked along the dock to the point where concrete and stone gave way to the wide estuary's natural bank; an area of reeds and marshy grass with a clear view of the open sea.

'I'm not here to talk about George.' Lizzie tugged at Bob's sleeve and brought him to a standstill. 'Don't you want to say why your boss called you in?'

'To dock my wages, if you must know.' The admission hurt. Bob prided himself in doing his work well and being paid a decent wage. Besides, this would affect his and Lizzie's plans. 'I won't be able to save as much for the wedding.'

'Why has he cut your money?' Lizzie was so incensed on Bob's behalf that she ignored his comment about their wedding.

'He's taken me off driving the crane and put me on to general labouring.' Inwardly he seethed but outwardly he tried not to show it. 'Keith Nelson stays on the one crane that's left in working order. I can see why Mr Anderson had to do it – only half the yard is operating.'

'I see.' She took his hand and they walked on. 'You've been loyal to Hugh Anderson through thick and thin – it's a rotten thing to do to you,' she commiserated.

'Maybe I should give up the job altogether and join the navy instead.' The idea had crept up on Bob during the week of separation from Lizzie but it was the first time he'd voiced it. Now it sounded as if he was merely getting his own back – she had joined the Civil Defence so he would show that he too could make an independent decision.

'Is that what you want?' she said slowly. Her heart fluttered then struggled to regain its steady beat.

He pulled away. 'I don't know what I want,' he said crossly. 'What do *you* want me to do, Lizzie? Tell me truly.'

'I want us not to argue.' The wind plucked at her simple words and scattered them across the marshes. 'Why are we fighting? We need to talk properly; that's why I'm here.'

But Bob was too far gone to listen. 'I had it all worked out; I'd carry on at Anderson's and you'd work for your dad until the war finished. Then we'd get married. We'd have saved up enough to pay a deposit on a house of our own. That's my dream. I thought it was yours, too.'

'It was,' she whispered. Again her heart faltered. Marriage, a house, children – this was the map of her life, with its inevitable route marked out.

Through his anger he saw her fatal hesitation. It was as if she'd picked up one of the dark rocks that lay at his feet and used it to smash his shiny glass dream to smithereens. 'Not any more?' he groaned.

She froze, unable in that moment to gather the pieces back together. 'I never said that.'

'You didn't have to.' A bitter taste filled Bob's mouth. All he'd ever wanted was to have Lizzie at his side. When he was away from her – at work, at home with his mother – he would wonder where his sweetheart was and what she was doing. They had never been apart for longer than the few days last October, when Lizzie had gone with Connie to the Lake District, soon after John's death. 'This is Connie's doing.' He flung the usual complaint at Lizzie. 'She thinks I cramp your style.'

Lizzie denied it. 'Connie likes you – she was the one who wanted us to make up.'

'That means you didn't!' Another flash of anger seared his soul, drawing from him a hasty challenge that gave voice to a suspicion he'd harboured for some time. 'You want us to call it a day – that's why you're here.'

She shivered in defeat. There seemed no point in reaching out; not until his anger had cooled.

'You see; I'm right.' Her silence said it all. Bob couldn't even look at Lizzie, could only turn his back and walk on towards the horizon where sea met sky and all was grey and empty.

When Connie arrived at the sector post that evening Kenneth Browning had already taken over from her father. Like most of the head wardens, he was well past the age of conscription, a veteran of the Great War – a small, slight man with an upright bearing and a clipped moustache, who wore his Civil Defence beret at a natty angle.

Spotting the new arrival, he cupped his hand over the mouthpiece of his telephone to pass on a message from Bert. 'Your dad says you can use his bike to cycle home at the end of your shift. He's left it in the back-yard for you.'

This meant that her father had taken the bus home for a change. Connie thanked Kenneth then went into the cramped back room to sort out her equipment, along with three fellow wardens all preparing for the night ahead.

'Here's hoping we won't need this tonight,' one said as he tucked his warning rattle into the sling on his belt.

'Yes; fingers crossed.' Connie slung her gas mask over her shoulder then climbed the stairs to the rest-room, where she found George and Tom engaged in their usual desultory game of darts. 'Who's winning?' she asked as she picked up a magazine.

'Even-stevens.' George landed a double twenty with his final dart.

Tom gave her a quick, friendly grin before taking George's place and launching a dart at the board.

George came close and pretended to read the magazine over Connie's shoulder. 'Is that a picture of Hollywood's latest heart-throb?'

'No – this is Cary Grant – he's old hat.' Connie moved away into a better light. 'You know: *Blonde Venus* with Marlene Dietrich and *She Done Him Wrong* with Mae West.'

George gave a low whistle. 'Mae West – my favourite. I'd take her over Katharine Hepburn any day.'

'Yes, but would she take you?' Connie shot back.

It was George's turn to throw again and this time he began with a bull's-eye. Tom shrugged his shoulders at Connie. 'I'm up against an expert,' he conceded with his usual equanimity.

She put her magazine to one side to give Tom her full attention. 'Have you sung any sea shanties lately?'

'Yes, the night before last. I expected to see you there.'

George threw again.

Connie laughed. 'I don't remember when or where your choir meets.'

'Every Wednesday in the assembly hall at St Joseph's – we start at seven o'clock sharp.'

Removing his darts from the board, George chalked up his score. 'So you warble a bit, do you?' he said to Tom. 'Boney was a warrior, Way, hey, ya!'

'I sing in a choir now and then, if that's what you mean.' Tom realized that his leg was about to be viciously pulled.

'What shall we do with the drunken sailor, more like.' George winked at Connie. 'Come on, don't deny it, you trawlermen are fond of a tipple or two.' Instead of carrying on with the game, he swayed then slung his arm around Tom's shoulder. 'Sling him in the long boat till he's sober . . . Pull out the plug and wet him all over . . . Eh, boy?'

Colouring bright red, Tom shoved him away. 'Wednesday nights at St Joseph's,' he repeated to Connie as he cut the game short by putting away his darts and going downstairs.

'Uh-oh, someone can't take a joke,' George said with a grin. 'But Tom Rose is sweet on you, Connie – anyone can see that.' The grin developed into a scornful laugh as he aimed for the board, threw with unnerving accuracy then did a little jig. 'He'd love to do the sailor's hornpipe with you, if you know what I mean.'

'Message received loud and clear,' she retorted as she prepared to follow Tom downstairs. 'But not everyone's mind works the way yours does, George.' She went down two steps then stopped. 'Oh, and by the way, I was thinking about you earlier.'

'Should I be flattered?'

'I don't know; should you? Actually, I was wondering if you could put your hands on a few pairs of nylon stockings if a girl were to ask nicely.'

George stiffened and his face grew suspicious. 'What makes you ask that?'

Connie gave a conspiratorial wink. 'John wasn't the best at keeping secrets, if *you* know what *I* mean.'

'Lies – all lies.' George's expression remained serious despite the jokey tone. He turned his back to reclaim his darts and stow them away in a leather pouch. When he prepared to face Connie again the devil-may-care smile was back in place but Connie was already out of sight.

CHAPTER NINE

At eight o'clock the next morning the last of the over-night trekkers trickled past the bakery on College Road. They were in good spirits as they made their way home, for despite the discomfort of sleeping rough they returned with the knowledge that Kel-thorpe had been spared another attack.

One elderly man wearing a heavy overcoat and a thick scarf stopped to talk to Lizzie, who was loading bread into the van. 'We live to fight another day,' he said cheerfully as he dug into his pockets and found some stray coppers. 'Can I buy one of those brown loaves off you?'

Lizzie obliged with a smile and the man carried on. Then she spotted her cousin Arnold playing a game of hide-and-seek with his sisters while their mother trudged behind, loaded down with bags and blankets. The kids nipped in and out of doorways, calling 'Coming, ready or not!' but when Arnold spied the bread van he left off playing and shot across the road.

'Have you got any of them titchy little loaves?' he demanded, peering into the aromatic interior of the van and breathing in the heady scent.

'You mean the penny buns?' Reckoning rightly

that he and his sisters would be starving after a night on the moors, generous Lizzie scooped three miniature Hovis loaves into a paper bag and handed them over. 'Hush,' she said with a wink. 'One for you and one each for the girls. And don't say I never give you anything.'

Clutching the bag, Arnold grinned then shot back across the road.

'I saw that.' Vera stopped to ease her burden. She bore a strong family resemblance to her brother, with the same thin, lined features, and this morning she looked especially weary and worn down. 'How much do I owe you?'

'Nothing.' Lizzie closed the van doors. 'You get yourself home, Aunty Vera. You look done in.'

'Aren't we all?' Vera sighed then walked on.

'I saw what you did as well,' Connie mentioned when Lizzie went into the shop for a fresh tray. 'You're a soft touch, our Lizzie.'

'Come off it – you'd have done the same.' Checking with their dad in the bakery at the back of the shop and finding that the last batch of loaves was still in the oven, Lizzie perched on a stool behind the counter. 'Do you fancy a swim later on?' she asked.

'Maybe.' Connie arranged loaves on a rack. 'What time did you have in mind?'

'I should be finished with deliveries around one. We could catch the two o'clock session.'

'That suits me,' Connie agreed. 'I'm not due at the Savoy until half six.'

'No matinee today?'

'No. Penrose has cut back my hours this week. I think he's gone off me.'

'The feeling's mutual, from what I gather.'

It was too early for customers so the sisters chatted on. 'How's your love life?' Connie asked as she set more of the penny loaves in neat rows.

The question caught Lizzie off guard. 'You mean Bob?'

'Who else?' Connie looked up sharply.

Lizzie blushed under her gaze. 'I saw him yesterday.'

'And?'

'We had another barney,' Lizzie admitted. 'A big one, this time. He said he was thinking about joining the navy.'

'Did he now?' For once Connie didn't push the matter.

Lizzie slid from the stool and went to stand at the open door. 'I'll probably cycle over to Easby tonight to sort things out.' She gazed along the quiet street towards the town square, where the imposing statue of Queen Victoria surveyed the sandbagged entrances to the library and the town hall. 'Why does life have to be so hard all of a sudden?' she said with a sigh.

'You tell me.'

'No; you're the expert on men.'

'If you say so.' Connie gave a wry chuckle.

'Let me ask you one thing, though.' Now that they'd broached the thorny subject of the opposite sex, Lizzie ploughed on. 'What on earth do you see in George Bachelor? I wouldn't have thought he's your type.'

'Mr Love-'em and leave-'em?' Connie's good humour drained away and she grew cautious. 'I don't see any-thing in him, since you ask.'

141

'So why let him pester you?' Lizzie recalled with a slight shudder the foreman's insolent way of stripping a woman naked with a look. 'To my mind, he's a nasty piece of work.'

Connie turned her back to carry on arranging loaves on racks. 'He's not so bad.'

'Come off it, Con. He thinks he's God's gift to women. Connie, are you listening to me?'

Connie turned slowly and deliberately. 'George isn't pestering me,' she insisted. 'And if he did, I'd soon put him in his place.'

'So what's going on? Why do you encourage him?'

'I have to work with him, don't I?' Connie fell back on her usual evasive reply, using her apron to dust flour from her hands. 'Besides, there are other reasons for me to keep him sweet.'

'Such as?'

Connie tapped the side of her nose.

'Don't fob me off.' Lizzie hated it when Connie grew secretive. 'I'm your sister – you're supposed to tell me everything.'

'Reasons,' Connie repeated darkly.

'Lizzie,' Bert called from the back room. 'The last batch is ready for you.'

'You heard what the man said.' Connie stood to one side to let Lizzie pass. When Lizzie came back out with the tray her expression had altered. 'You don't have to worry about George,' Connie assured her softly. 'Trust me; I know what I'm doing.'

Pamela woke in her attic room to the sound of gulls shrieking. It was Saturday: the day of her planned visit to Raby to see her mum and dad. But before that she intended to do her usual good deed for the WVS. This would entail a visit to the library followed by a walk across town to the Queen Alexandra Hospital, where she would hand out the borrowed books to patients.

First, though, there was the matter of Mrs Mason's porridge – tasteless and with the consistency of wallpaper paste – followed by toast and marmalade – sugar coupons having been donated. Down in the small breakfast room, Mr Fielding's bulk occupied much of the available space so Pamela ate quickly, without exchanging many words, and only breathed freely again when she was out on Elliot Street and ready to begin her errands.

The day was fine but blustery. Already there was a queue outside the swimming baths and a general bustle of women with baskets hurrying towards the fish market by the harbour, men tinkering with motorbikes at the kerbside and children playing with go-karts cobbled together out of pram wheels and planks of wood. Pamela found that she liked the busy feel of living close to the centre of town, so different to Musgrave Street's cul-de-sac remoteness.

Hatless and dressed in the pale green frock that Connie had given her, with her blue coat unbuttoned, she strode out and was soon crossing the town square towards the library, one of her favourite buildings in Kelthorpe. She entered through its revolving doors to be greeted by the familiar musty scent of leather-bound reference volumes mixed with lavender furniture polish and by the soft thud and click of librarians checking out books at the counter with their rubber stamps. Straight ahead was History and Biography, to her left was Geography and Art. Ignoring these, she made a beeline for Fiction – shelf upon shelf of Dickens and Thackeray, H. G. Wells and H. Rider Haggard. She gave her selection some thought; many of the hospital patients were men – casualties from the armed forces sent back to Blighty for treatment – so Pamela avoided the shelf containing romances and went for crime fiction instead. She followed the alphabetical system, rounding a corner to browse through Fs and Gs, and was too caught up in her examination of various titles to notice Fred Miller engaged in an identical activity. They practically brushed shoulders before glancing up.

Fred was a fraction ahead in his greeting. 'Why, hello. I'm sorry; I didn't see you there.'

Pamela snapped her book shut and stepped back, refraining from making the obvious remarks but failing to find something more original. Instead, she ducked her head and was about to sidle by.

'Are you looking for a particular title?' he asked in his precise, detached way.

'Not specifically. Perhaps crime or science fiction.'

'Have you tried Dashiell Hammett?' Fred pulled a book from the shelf. '*The Maltese Falcon* is a good one if you like crime. Or Raymond Chandler's *The Big Sleep*.'

'The books are not for me.' Pamela grew more flustered by the second.

'Or Aldous Huxley.' Fred pulled out a second volume. '*Brave New World* is science fiction, as I expect you know.'

'They're for patients at the Queen Alexandra.'

'Ah.' Fred replaced the books. 'That's quite a co-incidence. I happen to be engaged in the very same task – choosing reading material for patients at the hospital.'

Glad to find common ground, Pamela grew more talkative. 'The problem is that it's hard to know what to choose. Nevil Shute is popular. I generally avoid the classics, though.'

'Too demanding,' Fred agreed. 'And far too long, with the exception of Jane Austen, perhaps.'

For a while they browsed in silence.

'I hope Fielding hasn't bothered you again,' Fred remarked once the books were selected and they were on their way to the counter.

'No. As a matter of fact, I hardly ever see him.'

Fred stepped aside to let Pamela go first. 'It's the alcohol, I'm afraid. When he's sober he's a perfectly nice fellow.'

The assistant stamped Pamela's books. 'Shall I wait for you in the vestibule then we can walk to the hospital together?' The boldness of her suggestion made her blush anew.

'Good idea.' He waited for his books to be stamped then joined her. The revolving doors took them out into the breezy square. 'What is it, a ten-minute walk from here?'

The wind caught the hem of her dress and made it flutter. 'Yes, about ten minutes.'

'And how do you like living on Elliot Street?' Fred continued the conversation with the same detachment as before. 'Not too noisy for you, I hope?'

'Not at all. I have no complaints.'

'Not even about Mrs Mason's porridge?' The first glimpse of a sense of humour showed as a half-smile. 'You're very tolerant, to be sure.'

'I don't suppose her evening meals are much better.' Under Queen Victoria's stony stare Pamela responded with a small smile of her own. It turned out that her decision to rely on food on the hoof – fish and chips or a quick sandwich – had been a wise one.

'You're right about that.' He waited at the kerb for a delivery wagon to drive by. 'One good thing about moving to Kelthorpe,' he continued as they crossed the road, 'is that the traffic is much less busy.'

'Than London? You lived in Hatton Garden, I remember.'

'Yes, in Holborn. My father had a small jewellery business – imports from Holland, in the main. Of course, that came to an end when the war started.'

Pamela pictured exquisitely cut diamonds glittering on black velvet cushions, fashioned into earrings and necklaces for rich ladies in the West End. 'It sounds glamorous,' she said wistfully. 'Compared with fishing for cod or importing timber, anyway. Kelthorpe can't compete with diamonds, I'm afraid.'

'As I say, that's all in the past.'

She glanced at his face with undisguised curiosity. 'And where are your mother and father now? Still in Holborn?'

Fred shook his head. 'They both died in an air raid,' he told her.

Pamela was startled by his matter-of-fact tone. 'I'm very sorry. Forgive me.'

'Don't apologize. You weren't to know.' On they went, up the hill towards the Queen Alexandra, each lost in thought.

I've said too much, Fred decided. *Now she'll feel sorry for me and the last thing I want is pity.*

Pamela clutched her library books close to her chest. She felt her heart beat hard against her ribs. *He can't bear to dwell on it,* she thought. *And I don't blame him. We must look forward. It's the only way to get through this dreadful war, with a stiff upper lip, putting one foot firmly in front of another.*

There was nothing like cycling to blow away the cobwebs. Lizzie set off from Elliot Street soon after tea on the hilly five-mile ride to Easby.

'Is Bob expecting you?' Connie had asked as she set off for work at the Savoy.

'No, it'll be a surprise.' Lizzie's reply had been terse. However, the butterflies in her stomach had gone by the time she'd left town and she began to take an interest in the fresh green growth in the hawthorn hedges and busy blackbirds building nests in the branches of elm trees by the side of the road. She slogged up the hill in bottom gear towards Raynard's Folly then free-wheeled into the next valley, with the rocky coastline to her right and brown moorland stretching as far as the eye could see to her left. By the time the small port of Easby was within sight, nestled into a narrow inlet that opened out on to the bracing North Sea, Lizzie felt a surge of fresh hope that the current problems between her and Bob could be resolved.

She cycled into her fiancé's village, past its eighteenth-century church at the top of a steep hill overlooking a narrow main street. The ancient stone cottages to either side had small mullioned windows and narrow doorways – seemingly built to accommodate owners of somewhat lower stature than their present-day counterparts. Could it be true that people were smaller several centuries ago? Lizzie wondered. She dismounted then turned down an alleyway leading to a courtyard where Bob's house stood in a terraced row opposite a blacksmith's forge and next to a butcher's shop.

Bob's mother, Kathleen, sat outside her door knitting and making the most of the warm spring evening. The Waterhouses' tabby cat was curled at her feet and together they made a timeless picture: a stout older woman with her shoulders wrapped in a woollen shawl and her skirt covered by a calico apron almost down to the ground. Her grey hair was worn in a tight bun and her dextrous fingers clicked the needles with effortless speed. Looking up at the sound of Lizzie's approach, she immediately put down her knitting and stepped inside the house to call Bob's name.

'Hello, Lizzie love. Is he expecting you?' Kathleen's smile was warm as she came back out.

'No. This is spur-of-the-moment.' Lizzie leaned her bike against the butcher's shop wall. Her forehead was damp with sweat and she patted her windswept hair into place as she waited for Bob to appear. 'How's your ankle? Better, I hope.'

'Much better, ta. Where's he got to?' Kathleen tutted. 'I know he's in there. Bob, can you hear me?'

Looking up, Lizzie glimpsed a movement of the net curtain in the upstairs window. Seconds later there were footsteps on the stairs then Bob appeared in shirtsleeves and navy-blue serge trousers with braces dangling. His hands were thrust deep into his pockets and his brows knitted together.

'Come inside.' Remembering her manners, Kathleen ushered Lizzie into the tiny sitting room. 'Lizzie's cycled all the way here,' she told her son. 'I'll put the kettle on. The poor girl must be parched.'

Left alone with Bob, who was still scowling, Lizzie's confidence wavered. 'Would you rather I hadn't come?' she began.

'That depends.' He took a packet of cigarettes from his pocket, thought better of it then tossed the pack on to the windowsill.

'On what?'

'On why you're here.'

In the background Lizzie heard the sounds of a tap being run and a kettle set on the hob to boil. 'To sort things out with you, of course.'

'So you don't want to call it a day?' Bob took up where they'd left off, with the same dark looks and angry tone. He paced the small room, tapping the mantelpiece as he came to rest in front of the fireplace.

Lizzie was disappointed that Bob's resentment hadn't yet worked its way through his system. 'I wish you wouldn't keep on saying that,' she said with an exasperated sigh. 'If you must know, I couldn't sleep last night for worrying about us. I went through and through it in my head, trying to think of what I could do to make things better.'

'You know what you could do.' From tapping the mantelpiece he took to kicking the fender with the toe of his boot. 'But you won't.'

'No, and I won't go round in circles either. It's not fair, Bob. And it's not like you to bear a grudge.' Lizzie's heartbeat grew rapid as she fought to control her temper. 'I understand that the problem at work hasn't helped; no one likes to see his wages cut and it must have been a dent to your pride.'

'That's got nothing to do with it.'

'If you say so.'

'It hasn't, Lizzie.' He sank into an armchair then leaned forward with his elbows on his knees, staring down at the rug. 'This is you and me we're talking about; nothing else.'

From the kitchen Kathleen had heard her son's raised voice and now she hovered outside the sitting-room door, tea tray in hand.

'It's not even really about this ambulance-driving business. It goes deeper than that.'

Fear squeezed Lizzie's heart and made it race harder. 'I don't understand.'

'It's about whether you really love me, deep down. Christ, I need a cigarette.' Bob stood up abruptly to retrieve the packet and light up. 'Why do I have this feeling that you've changed? I can't put my finger on it but you definitely act differently from how you used to.'

'It's wartime. Everyone acts differently,' she pointed out, her voice shaky and quiet. 'We stagger on from one day to another, not knowing when the next raid will happen or whether we'll have a roof over our heads come morning. It's bound to affect us, like it or not.'

Bob lifted the cigarette to his lips with nicotine-stained fingers. 'I'd have thought that would make you want to spend every spare minute with me. I know it does me.'

'Because you want to look after me and make sure I'm safe?'

'Yes. What's wrong with that?'

'Nothing. But we can't wrap each other up in cotton wool. We have to do what we can to help Mr Churchill put Hitler in his place. All right, I'm sorry.' Lizzie put up her hands in a gesture of defeat. 'We've been through that and I know we're never going to agree.'

'You're wrong there.' Through clouds of blue smoke, he decided to call her bluff. 'I agree that I ought to do my bit; that's why I plan to follow up the Royal Navy idea. I reckon they'll have me if I show up at the town hall and take the King's shilling. What do you think?'

A sudden vision of him sailing in a convoy across the Atlantic or through the Strait of Gibraltar, a prey to U-boats and aerial attacks, made her draw a sharp intake of breath. She steadied herself before replying. 'I'm sure they're crying out for men like you.'

'So you think I should enlist?'

Lizzie was trapped: a proven hypocrite if she said no. 'If it's really and truly what you want,' she murmured reluctantly. Tears came to her eyes. 'I can't say otherwise, can I?'

Bob marked his hollow victory by flicking his cigarette butt into the empty grate. 'Monday morning, then,' he said through gritted teeth. 'I'll join the queue at the town hall.'

Kathleen turned the knob and opened the door. 'What's this I hear?' she demanded as she put down the tray with a no-nonsense rattle then took Lizzie to one side. 'He's always hated the sea. He can't even swim.'

Lizzie quickly wiped away her tears. 'It's my fault,' she confessed. 'He's proving a point, that's all.'

'I am bloody here, you know!' Bob stood up and

began pacing again. 'Mother, tell Lizzie she should drop this Civil Defence lark – it's too dangerous by half.'

'Ah, I see.' Kathleen pulled herself up to her full height of five feet one inch to deliver her verdict. 'I know for a fact that some of those wardens are three-quid-a-week army dodgers who don't know one end of a stirrup pump from another.'

'I'm not a warden, I'm an ambulance driver. And I'm not paid a penny.' Finding herself on the back foot, Lizzie put Kathleen straight.

'It's only what I read.' The older woman quickly backed down. 'But that's not to say I side with Bob. You have to do what's right for you, love. And he has to respect that and back you up.'

'I am here in the room,' he reminded them again, but this time with less force.

'Rightio; I'll leave you to kiss and make up.' Bob's mother gave him a stern look then beat a retreat.

'Can you really not swim?' Lizzie had never thought to ask her fiancé why he stayed away from the Elliot Street baths, simply assuming that the football field and cricket pitch had always been stronger draws. The absurdity made her lips twitch and she had to repress a smile.

'Not a stroke. I sink like a stone,' he admitted bashfully. 'Like a lot of the blokes round here.'

'That's like me joining the ambulance service without being able to drive,' she pointed out.

Bob had the grace to concede the point. 'I could still join the army, though,' he said without conviction.

'Or you could carry on working at Anderson's.' The smile broke free and spread to her eyes. This was

152

better – it had been like chipping away at reinforced concrete but now she could see that Bob's resistance was softening and the scowl was beginning to fade.

'I suppose I could.' Bloody hell, when Lizzie gave him that special smile he was as helpless as a kitten.

'And we can carry on as we are?'

He let her approach and put her arms around his neck. 'You're flipping annoying sometimes; you know that?'

'Ditto,' she whispered, kissing his cheek. 'Stubborn as a mule.'

'Pot and kettle,' Bob reminded her. He drew her towards him and held her close, felt her body give way and accept his embrace.

They agreed to differ. There was a sweetness to it that carried them along and when it was time to break apart and for Lizzie to cycle back to Kelthorpe, a truce was signed with a dozen lingering kisses. Promises were made afresh and Kathleen watched with satisfaction from the upstairs window as Bob walked Lizzie across the courtyard and gave her one last kiss goodbye.

Connie's star sign was Leo. Not that she believed in astrology – it was too much like end-of-the-pier fortune-telling for her liking – but nevertheless some of the Leo characteristics fitted her. She was a fire sign, a natural born leader, according to the magazine left behind on a seat in Row C. Her strengths were that she was passionate and warm-hearted but her weaknesses included arrogance and stubbornness. *I don't like the sound of that,* Connie thought, tucking the magazine into her handbag before putting on her coat. She'd finished her shift and was almost the last to leave the building, save for Mr Penrose, who hovered by the door jangling a large set of keys. *I wonder what his star sign is.* Connie amused herself by running through various options. Scorpio with a sting in its tail was a possibility, or else bull-in-a-china-shop Taurus.

'Goodnight, Mrs Bailey,' he said in a pompous, long-suffering manner that was meant to hurry her out on to the pavement. 'You've kept your gentleman waiting quite long enough.'

My gentleman? She had little time to wonder, for there was George standing on the pavement, dapper as ever in a Harris tweed jacket and dark brown trousers with matching brogues, with a rolled-up newspaper stuffed into his pocket. He took a step towards Connie, ostentatiously offering her his arm.

'Don't tell me – you've lost your shirt on cards again.' She took his arm and they walked together towards the park.

'Who says I've lost?' Actually, George had been nowhere near a pack of cards – he'd had other fish to fry. But the idea of rounding off a somewhat tense evening with a stroll through the Leisure Gardens with Connie was one he hadn't been able to resist. He padded the thick wallet poking out of his breast pocket. 'And there's plenty more where this came from,' he assured her.

'You're not a Leo, by any chance?'

George gave her a quizzical look. 'Why do you ask?'

'Leos like to blow their own trumpets, that's all. I read about it in my magazine.'

Amused, he pursed his lips and mimed blowing a trumpet with accompanying sound effects.

'On the plus side, Leos are very generous.' Connie batted her lashes and swung her hips as they walked. She banked on George being too vain to realize that there was a hidden purpose behind her flirtatiousness.

'You're not still on about those stockings, are you?'

'Maybe. Actually, I'm surprised you remembered.'

'I never forget. Is that a Leo characteristic, too?'

'No, that's an elephant. So George – about these nylons . . .'

He slid his arm around her waist. 'You have to ask nicely, remember?'

She ignored the arm and the hand that wandered downwards and steeled herself to plant a kiss on his smooth cheek, catching the sharp smell of cologne as she did so. 'A bottle of perfume wouldn't go amiss, either. And perhaps a bar or two of Cadbury's chocolate.'

'Whoa!' He reined back an imaginary horse with his free hand. 'Steady on, Mrs Bailey. How do I get hold of perfume and chocolate?'

'The same way you can get hold of stockings.' Connie raised her eyebrows and gave him a knowing look. 'The same way that John used to do it – straight off St Stephen's dock. He was good to me in that way.'

George laughed and returned the look. 'You wicked, wicked girl!' The straying hand pinched her backside. 'And what did you give John in return?'

'Mind your own business.' She lifted the hand with firm deliberation. By now they'd reached the boating pond and there was enough moonlight to see that the path wound to the left, past an ornate wrought-iron bandstand. 'As a matter of fact, I might be interested in picking up where John left off.'

He laughed again. 'You have plenty of nerve; I'll give you that.'

'Oh come on, George – I'm not a simpleton. I saw what used to come through my house on Musgrave Street; mysterious crates and packages. John never made much effort to hide them from me.'

George stopped by the bandstand. A partner in crime as glamorous as Connie was certainly a temptation. But ought a man to mix business with pleasure? 'It's an interesting proposition – let me think about it.'

'Don't think for too long,' she urged as he led her up the steps into the bandstand and waltzed her around its circumference. At close quarters she got another whiff of cologne.

George whirled her round and came to a stop next to an iron pillar. He pressed her against it and kissed her hard on the mouth. She didn't resist, so he reckoned she'd enjoyed it. 'Tomorrow night,' he promised. 'We're both on night shift. I'll have made my decision by then.'

CHAPTER TEN

Lizzie took it upon herself to teach Pamela how to swim more than a few frantic strokes, which was all she'd been able to achieve on her previous solo visit. She and Connie arranged to meet her outside the baths at ten on Sunday morning and before long they were through the turnstile and changing into their swimming costumes, emerging just as the whistle went to signal the end of one session and the start of the next.

'No need to feel nervous,' Lizzie assured Pamela as dripping swimmers filed into the changing room, their towels around their shoulders. 'We'll stay in the shallow end and I'll show you how to do the breaststroke.'

Pamela hitched up the strap of her new turquoise costume. 'I find that I can float on my back all right but when I try to turn on to my stomach I sink to the bottom. I don't understand what I'm doing wrong.'

'It's easy – just copy Lizzie.' Connie waded through the footbath ahead of the others. The empty pool beckoned so she trotted nimbly along its length and was up on the springboard ready to dive in before Pamela and Lizzie had eased themselves into the water.

Pamela shivered. 'Brrr – it's cold.'

'Not when you get used to it.' Lizzie pushed off from the side. 'Think of how a frog kicks its back legs,' she instructed, demonstrating as she talked. 'Forget about your arms for the moment – just stretch them out in front. Chin up. Kick-kick-kick – see!'

Taking a deep breath, Pamela made her first tentative attempt and to her surprise found that she stayed afloat. She smiled and kept on kicking until a couple of reckless lads jumped in with a mighty splash. With stinging eyes and a mouth full of chlorinated water, she grasped the side rail and spluttered.

'Ignore them,' Lizzie insisted. 'Now watch what my arms do – push them forward close together then separate them and pull them back to your sides – see?'

Pamela nodded then copied the circular motion, feeling the resistance as she pulled. Before long she'd got the hang of what to do with both arms and legs and was able to put them together to create a decent stroke.

Satisfied by her rapid progress, Lizzie encouraged her into deeper water. 'You're a quick learner – you'll be fine.'

With Lizzie on hand to rescue her if she disappeared beneath the surface, Pamela bravely ventured out of her depth.

'Kick-kick-kick!' Lizzie urged.

Pamela navigated between other swimmers, staying close to the side just in case. She swallowed more water. But she was swimming – actually swimming!

Lizzie stayed by her side until Pamela had swum the whole length of the pool. 'Enough?' she asked.

Pamela nodded. She was panting as she hauled

herself up the rungs of a steel ladder on to the side, where she sat to catch her breath and watch Lizzie do a length of front crawl.

'You're a proper little water baby.' Connie came to sit beside Pamela, legs dangling. 'How come you didn't learn to swim before now?'

'Mother was against it.'

'Against you having fun?' Connie raised her eyebrows.

'Against sharing the water with unwashed bodies, I suppose.'

'That's what the chlorine's for. Anyway, I hope you're having fun now?'

Both girls shied away from another splash made by an inexpert diver. 'Lizzie's an excellent teacher,' Pamela said. 'And yes, I am.'

'That's all that matters.' Connie gazed down at her scarlet toenails. 'What's the latest on this Fred Miller chap? How are you two getting along?'

'He's nice.' Pamela swished her feet through the water to hide her bashfulness. 'Not at all stand-offish as I thought at first.'

'Ah-ha!' Connie's rich, low voice developed into a chuckle. 'Tell me more.'

'He's very polite.'

'And?'

'Clever.' Pamela chose the word carefully. 'He reads the classics and he has interesting opinions.'

'And?' Connie nudged Pamela with her elbow. 'Besides him being extremely good-looking and well educated, is he charming and funny as well?'

Pamela gave the question serious consideration. 'I wouldn't say he was funny, exactly.'

Connie suppressed a smile. 'But charming?'

'Yes, in his own way.'

'And is our friend Mr Miller starting to appreciate sharing lodgings with one of the best-looking girls in Kelthorpe?' As Lizzie swam by, Connie beckoned for her to join them.

Pamela took Connie's teasing in her stride. 'He'd better be,' she joked back. 'I made a good deal of effort to look nice for him when I went down to breakfast this morning.'

'And what did he say?'

'He wasn't there.' Pamela giggled.

'Oh.' Connie looked deflated.

'But I'm visiting the Leisure Gardens with him later on today.'

Connie perked up again. 'Oh! You hear that, Lizzie? Pam and Fred Miller are walking out; it's official.'

Lizzie joined them at the side of the pool. Shrieks of laughter from excited children echoed to the roof and swimmers ploughed determinedly through the clear water. 'Who's walking out with who?' she asked above the racket.

'Pamela and Fred too-handsome-to-be-true Miller.'

Pamela laughed and blushed then pushed Connie off balance and into the water. Then she slid from the side to join her, followed soon after by Lizzie. Still smiling and laughing, the three girls surfaced and swam side by side towards the shallow end.

'We have a treat – lamb chops for lunch,' Lizzie told Bert. 'If you go out into the yard and pick some mint I'll make mint sauce.'

Lizzie peeled potatoes at the kitchen sink. The

meat had come via Bob from Geoff West's shop in Easby (an under-the-counter perk of living next door to a butcher, Kathleen always said). Bob had dropped off the chops while Lizzie and Connie were at the baths and Bert was visiting his sister Vera. Finding no one at home, Bob had scribbled a note then left the unexpected gift on the windowsill, trusting that no passing mongrel would jump up and seize it between its ravenous jaws. Then he'd cycled back home.

'Let's hope the government never rations bread,' Lizzie commented as she chopped the spuds then placed the pan on the hob. 'We'd find it hard to make ends meet in the bakery if they did.'

Connie agreed. 'No one is living in the lap of luxury while the war is on.'

'Except for dodgy black-market types.' Without realizing that she'd hit a raw nerve, Lizzie took down a tin of peas from the shelf above the sink.

Connie set the chops sizzling in the frying pan then got busy with gravy powder and boiling water.

'Everyone's at it if they get half a chance,' Lizzie went on. 'I expect Bob slipped Geoff a bob or two for those chops. And Bill mentioned it to me the other night – he said you wouldn't believe what comes through St Stephen's dock on the sly. Cigarettes, oranges; you name it.'

As bad conscience wormed its way to the front of Connie's brain, Bert reappeared with a handful of fresh mint then ambled off again. 'I do believe it,' she contradicted. 'I know for a fact it's true.'

Placing a lid on the pan of potatoes, Lizzie waited to hear more.

'John used to tell me what went on down there at

the dock. He didn't say much at first – just a hint or two that he was involved. But then he got careless. He hid items in our air raid shelter thinking I wouldn't see them.'

'John?' Lizzie echoed uncertainly.

'Don't look so shocked. Like you say, everyone's at it if they think they can get away with it.' Now that Connie had broken her silence the words tumbled out. 'There's plenty of money to be made from smuggling rationed goods through every port in the country. John knew that when he took the job at Anderson's.'

'You don't say.' Lizzie picked up a sharp knife and chopped the mint finely.

'You're wondering why I didn't say anything at the time?' Connie's stomach twisted and churned as she recalled events that she'd previously kept hidden. 'But consider this: I knew what John's temper was like when he was crossed. I soon found it was in my best interest to ignore the packages stashed away in the shelter.'

'Weren't you scared of being found out?' Lizzie's knife hovered over the chopping board as she waited for an answer.

Connie nodded. 'In a strange way so was John. I think he was in too deep and he couldn't get out of whatever racket he was caught up in – him and George both.'

'George Bachelor was part of it?' Astonishment made Lizzie open her eyes wide and hold her breath.

'He still is,' Connie confirmed. Lunch was almost ready and she could hear their father's feet slip-slopping down the stairs. 'On top of which, he was there when John had his "accident".'

162

'Which you're implying wasn't an accident at all?' Lizzie scarcely noticed what she was doing as she scraped the mint into a bowl and mixed it with sugar and vinegar.

'Quite right. John shouldn't have been in that part of the yard,' Connie reminded her. 'There were plenty of witnesses, including Bob, who said that George was close by, yelling at John. Maybe they'd had a fight – the inquest didn't go into it – but that's what I intend to find out.'

'Oh, Connie.' Lizzie gave a quiet groan. 'Take my advice and steer well clear.'

Connie shook her head and sighed. 'Don't say anything,' she whispered as their father came into the kitchen.

Bert sat at the table and watched his daughters dish out Sunday dinner. 'Something smells good,' he said with relish, tucking a napkin into his shirt collar and picking up his knife and fork.

Pamela chose the pale green dress for her walk with Fred. It contrasted prettily with her brown hair and she felt that its nipped-in waist and panelled skirt showed off her willowy figure to advantage. She was less sure about the sweetheart neckline; perhaps it dipped an inch too low? But after studying her reflection in the small mirror above the mantelpiece, she gave a satisfied nod then set sail down the narrow stairs.

Fred was waiting for her by the front door as arranged.

'Will I need a coat?' she wondered as they stepped out on to the pavement.

'The weather forecast is for sun all afternoon.' He offered his arm and she took it.

'In that case . . .' As they set off past the swimming baths arm in arm, Pamela felt as if she were treading on air. She scarcely noticed the children playing ball and skipping or the women standing at their front doors in the spring sunshine.

Fred, too, felt buoyed up and full of happy expectation. He'd gleaned enough information about Pamela during their visit to the Queen Alexandra to pluck up the courage to suggest this outing – it had taken a fair amount of nerve as they'd walked back through town because she was exceptionally shy and hard to read; was she interested in him or not? They hadn't strayed far from safe ground – favourite books and authors, the type of music they enjoyed. She'd asked him about his work at Anderson's and he'd drawn her out on the subject of hobbies. 'Besides reading, how do you spend your spare time?' She'd said that she liked to sew and play the piano, though that was impossible now that the family instrument had gone up in smoke. She'd answered earnestly, without any of the flirtatious games that women often played. He'd appreciated this about her.

So when they'd arrived back on Elliot Street he'd taken the plunge. 'Would you care to come to the Leisure Gardens with me tomorrow?'

'Yes,' she'd said in less than a heartbeat. 'Please,' she'd added as an afterthought and with the shy smile that he was beginning to like a lot.

And now here they were, entering the Leisure Gardens on a sunny Sunday afternoon, choosing the shade of a broad colonnade that ran the length of the park.

'We could sit for a while and watch the world go by,' Fred suggested as they came to a bench at the end of the covered path.

They sat and looked down on a peaceful scene of couples strolling hand in hand and families clustered around the edge of the boating pond. Children waded knee-deep into the brown water to rescue becalmed yachts, mothers distributed sandwiches from picnic baskets while fathers flapped newspapers to fend off the inevitable gulls.

'You'd never guess that we were in the middle of a war.' Pamela gave a wistful sigh. 'Sometimes I think that these last couple of years haven't really happened and that one morning I'll wake up and it will all have been a bad dream.'

A dream in which whole convoys were destroyed and cities brought to their knees, in which thousands died in Europe, Northern Africa and the Far East every day. Fred stayed silent on the subject.

'I love my country,' she went on, 'but I don't find it in my heart to hate the enemy because I know they suffer as much as we do. Is it wrong to say that?'

'It's not wrong,' he reasoned. 'But families on both sides are losing husbands and sons. They're bound to blame someone – it's only natural.'

Fred's comment reminded Pamela of his own sad loss. 'Ought we to talk about something more cheerful?' she asked with delicate consideration.

'If you like. Books are always a safe topic.' They stood up and linked arms again. 'I've just started reading Jerome K. Jerome's *Three Men in a Boat*. Do you know it?'

'I've heard of it but I haven't read it. What's it about?'

'Three men in a boat,' Fred answered with a straight face.

Pamela laughed – Fred was funny after all. A small boy on a tricycle veered off-track towards them so Fred steered Pamela quickly out of harm's way and her heartbeat quickened at the strong, decisive movement – his hand clasping her elbow, his body shielding hers.

'Jerome's tale is very English – the author takes delight in small, humorous details from everyday life.'

'Like Jane Austen?'

'If you like – but without the romance.'

'She's my favourite writer.' Pamela had learned passages from *Pride and Prejudice* by heart. She identified with Elizabeth Bennet's fastidious dislike of pretentiousness and scorned the silliness of poor Lydia. 'It's always been my ambition to train as a schoolteacher then share my love of Austen with my pupils. The Brontës, too.'

'I can see you in that role.' Fred felt she would be the rare sort of teacher who cared and inspired in equal measure, whose lessons would be crammed with interesting facts and infectious enthusiasm. 'I remember an excellent history teacher during my last year at grammar school who taught us about the English Civil War. I was firmly on the side of Oliver Cromwell's Roundheads and against the Royalists.'

By now they'd done a full circuit of the Leisure Gardens, strolling past the pond and the bandstand and up the hill to the shady colonnade. It was late afternoon and the park was starting to empty. Their time together was coming to an end.

'Thank you.' Pamela smiled up at him. 'This has been lovely.'

'Then we must do it again.' She had no idea how

pretty she was or the effect she had on him. Her innocence brought out an urge to protect but it also inhibited him. He must go slowly and not scare her away. 'Soon,' he added.

'I'd like that.' Pamela held on to his arm, imagining that she would float away if she were to let go. 'Very much.' Would he kiss her? she wondered. Was this the moment or would he wait until next time?

Her face was like a flower with its petals slowly opening. The grey-green eyes were soft and shining, the pale skin miraculously smooth. And those lips – curved and full – were irresistible. So Fred leaned in and kissed her after all.

Sunday night saw all hands on deck. Lizzie was on standby at the King Edward Street ambulance depot, playing gin rummy with Bill and other members of his first-aid team, while Connie clocked on at the Gas Street post. She did her best to put last night's bandstand encounter with George to the back of her mind and to concentrate on the task in hand, but reminders kept on shoving their way to the forefront – not least when George reported for duty at Kenneth's desk then crept up behind Connie in the storeroom and patted her on the backside.

'Now then, Mrs Bailey, may I say how much that battledress uniform suits you?' It was tight over the hips as she leaned forward; a revealing sight.

'No, you may not.' Swiping his hand away, she slung her gas mask over her shoulder and picked up the rest of her equipment. The big unresolved question stood between them but it would probably have to wait until later.

'Connie, I'll put you and Tom on Elliot Street tonight,' Kenneth called through the open door. 'I'll have two fire watchers on the swimming-baths roof as usual and two extra at Anderson's – George, you can patrol the dock area with Brian Bellamy from the Tennyson Street post.'

Hearing his name, Tom came clattering down the stairs from the restroom.

'We're on Elliot Street together,' Connie informed him as she put on her helmet.

George grinned toothily at Tom. 'Look after her for me, there's a good lad.'

Tom frowned and went out on to the pavement. Why did Connie let the rotten so-and-so get away with sly digs like that? he wondered. Had he got her all wrong after all? 'Time for me to have a quick cigarette before we set off,' he muttered to the chief warden.

'What do you mean, "Look after her for me"?' Back in the cramped storeroom Connie was incensed. 'I'm not your property.'

'Tsk, tsk; why so touchy all of a sudden?' George enjoyed upsetting Connie – he liked the way her eyes flashed and how she stood with defiant hands on shapely hips. He cornered her to whisper into her ear. 'I thought you'd want to talk about our little arrangement.' A walk, a kiss, a proposition that he had yet to respond to – which, if handled correctly, would give him the whip hand for the foreseeable future. 'I don't want my new business partner ending up in the Queen Alexandra, do I?'

'So you've decided?' Connie's stomach twisted itself into a knot. Of course, she'd known that she was on the right track as far as George's black-market

168

dealings were concerned, but Lizzie's warning to steer clear was still fresh in her mind. What if, like John, she got in too deep to get out? Then again, she'd convinced herself that George held answers to the mystery surrounding her husband's death – namely, why on earth John had stumbled into a prohibited area.

'What do you say we give our partnership a trial run?' He continued to whisper, his cheek against hers. 'For a week or two – see how it goes.'

George's breath was hot on her neck. 'That's fine by me. You won't regret it,' she assured him as she fought to hide her distaste.

'Promise?' he said with the same insulting familiarity.

'Connie, get a move on,' Kenneth growled. 'Tom's waiting for you.'

Her face was flushed as she hurried outside and apologized.

Tom jerked his head towards the storeroom. 'He's not bothering you, is he?'

'Who – George?' She affected a brittle cheerfulness. 'No, don't worry – he's full of hot air, that's all.'

'Because if he is—'

'He's not.' Connie interrupted briskly.

So they set off in the direction of Elliot Street, with torches and rattles at the ready and carrying a list of trekkers for the immediate neighbourhood.

'Numbers 9, 13, 25, 2, 18 and 30 will be empty tonight,' Connie read from her list, which as usual included Aunty Vera and her brood. It wasn't long before they reached the top end of the street and began their inspection. To the right, the row of terraced houses was interrupted by the large, square bulk of the municipal baths, but the left side consisted entirely of small domestic dwellings running as far as the eye could see.

'Do you see what I see?' Tom spotted a light in an upstairs window of number 21.

'That's Thora Mason's boarding house.' Connie identified the culprit and together they hurried along the deserted pavement.

'Put that light out!' Tom cupped his hands around his mouth then gave the familiar cry and waited for a response.

Nothing happened so Connie tried again. 'I say, put that light out!'

There was another delay but this time the message got through. The light was switched off then Thora appeared on the doorstep in her dressing gown. 'Mr Fielding nodded off in front of his fire,' she explained with a bullish air. 'Mr Miller sorted him out.'

'She means that Fielding was dead drunk,' Connie interpreted as the door closed and she and Tom walked on.

A fire watcher on the roof of the swimming baths heard their footsteps and called down. 'We've had a telephone report of a lone raider stooging around over Raby,' he reported.

'Any damage?' Tom yelled back from across the street.

'None that we know of.'

'I don't like the sound of that.' The fire watcher's report sent a shiver down Connie's spine. It was the second such incident she'd heard of in the past week; nothing had come of the previous one, though, which had happened in daylight and had involved a fast, low-level fly-over by one of the newest Messerschmitts – most likely on a reconnaissance mission.

Tom stopped to check that six sand buckets stationed beside a lamp post were full to the brim and that three Redhill containers stored down an alleyway were in working order. The Redhills were ingenious devices to deal with incendiaries – consisting of a small bucket with a handle and a long scoop like a hoe. The idea was to whisk the lethal metal cylinder into the container then bury it in the nearest sand bucket before it had time to explode.

'All present and correct,' Tom told Connie. Now that they were away from George's sly presence he felt more relaxed. It had been a while since he'd spent the cosy hour with Connie at The Anchor and, typical of him, he'd failed to follow it up with a second invitation. Now he intended to put that right. 'I'm sorry we haven't organized another get-together.'

'I've had a lot on my mind.' Not meaning to sound so offhand, she decided to elaborate. 'It's not long since I moved back to Elliot Street and I'm not used to the single life. Besides, I'm still uneasy about John's accident.'

'In spite of the inquest?'

'Yes, because the coroner only skimmed the surface. There are questions that I still need answers to.'

'I see.' Tom said little but thought a good deal. He had no idea whether or not Connie's doubts about the inquest were justified but he could see why she found it hard to let the matter drop. He imagined the shock of her husband's death and the grief that must surely have followed.

Connie sighed. 'Someone must know why John went

into the section where the crane was unloading timber. He wasn't daft – he would have known that the area was out of bounds.'

'Yes, but you could drive yourself round the bend trying to puzzle it out.' They continued their patrol cloaked in darkness, unable to see each other's faces. 'Wouldn't it be better to try to forget?'

Lost in the maze of her own thoughts, Connie ignored the question. 'It's funny; I haven't missed him exactly – not once I got over the shock.'

Colin Strong, the eager Boy Scout messenger, cycled around the corner and carried on at top speed towards the Gas Street post. At the end of the street Connie and Tom turned back on themselves to patrol the other side.

'That sounds awful, doesn't it? But John wasn't easy to live with, let's say.'

Tom was surprised and flattered that Connie had chosen to confide in him. It could hardly have been a picnic to be married to a man who 'wasn't easy to live with'. Then another collection of sand buckets drew his attention, while Connie went to check on the front door of number 30, which had been left wide open. Her list showed her that the residents – the Gardiner family – had joined in the trek to Raynard's Folly, and so she closed the door then rejoined Tom.

It was at that precise moment that the siren sounded. There was no yellow warning – simply the ear-splitting, uninterrupted blare of red. In an instant, dozens of searchlights raked across the dark sky and the air was filled with the menacing roar of approaching engines. There was no time to take cover, no time to do anything but stand open-mouthed in the middle of the street and wait for the worst to happen.

The siren woke Pamela from a deep sleep. She sat up in bed and her heart lurched. Her throat was dry.

Fred pounded at her door. 'Get up! Get up!'

She flew to join him on the top landing, felt him grab her hand and pull her down the stairs.

'No time to lose,' he told her. 'We're on red alert.'

Fielding flung open his door and staggered out in his pyjamas. Thora appeared at the end of the landing, her face grim and determined.

'Go with Mrs Mason into the cellar.' Fred saw in a moment that Fielding was incapable of getting downstairs unaided, so he pushed Pamela towards the landlady and together the two women did as he said.

With the sirens going full blast and the sound of explosions in every direction, Thora led the way. Pamela looked back as Fielding tried to push Fred to one side. Why on earth didn't Fred leave the drunken man to his fate and save himself?

'Hurry,' Thora urged. Her grip on Pamela's arm was strong as iron. The cellar steps smelled of damp and mould, but the room itself was adequately kitted out with an electric light and several sturdy benches. A large heap of coal stood beneath a sloping chute that opened out on to the street and an empty beer barrel lay on its side. Rusty tools hung from hooks on the wall.

Pamela sank on to the nearest bench with her heart hammering inside her chest. She heard Fielding swear loudly, held her breath and prayed.

*

173

At the Gas Street post Kenneth telephoned the casualty services. Five incendiaries had fallen on the dockside area. Two had failed to go off but three had started fires – small at present but close enough to the timber yard to cause concern. George and Brian Bellamy had been present and had requested the AFS and a trailer pump. 'Quick as you can,' George had shouted down the phone. In the background there had been the deafening sound of a high explosive going off, soon followed by bricks and rubble showering down. The line had gone dead so Kenneth sent a rescue party to the spot.

Then came a call from the fire watchers on Elliot Street. Apparently, the entire horizon was ablaze, from the far side of the headland to Maypole Street, including College Road and Tennyson Street. Anti-aircraft guns were having little effect – Jerry just kept on coming.

'Which services do you need?' Kenneth yelled down the phone to make himself heard.

'Send the whole bloody lot!' the fire watcher yelled. 'Rescue, fire, ambulance, engineers – anything you've got.'

CHAPTER ELEVEN

'We've been called out to your neck of the woods.' Bill sprinted across the depot yard with two first-aiders to where Lizzie sat in her ambulance.

'Right you are.' Once her passengers were in the van she set off at high speed along King Edward Street. She didn't have time to be frightened, though incendiaries had already started fires in the immediate area and a high explosive had torn out the front of Cynthia's Salon on College Road. The bakery was untouched, thank heavens. Lizzie swerved to avoid a heap of smoking rubble close to Benson's music shop then drove on through a stream of water that gushed from a burst water main. A rescue party was already on the scene – four men in gas masks working to cut off gas and electricity supplies.

Approaching Elliot Street, a sight greeted Lizzie that made her heart jump with fear – it was an unexploded parachute mine dangling from a lamp post, clearly visible in the red glare of flames all around. She slammed on the brakes. 'What do we do?' she asked Bill, who sat beside her.

The mine swung dangerously towards the post then away again. Without doubt the smallest touch and the resulting vibration would cause the bomb to explode.

'Let's risk it.' Bill told Lizzie to drive on. 'Not too fast,' he warned as the parachute billowed across the street.

Lizzie held her breath and inched forward. The mine swung within inches of the lamp post. Two hundred yards down Elliot Street incendiaries tore holes in the roof of the swimming baths and burst into flames.

Connie and Tom watched in horror from the middle of the street. As yet they were the only ones on the scene. The squat Victorian building was alight and there was no sign of the two fire watchers on the roof. Flames roared, sending up clouds of red sparks and briefly illuminating the lifeless body of one of the fire watchers draped across a burning timber. For him there was no hope. But what of the other man?

'He might still be alive.' Connie was in favour of entering what remained of the building.

Tom agreed. To the sound of rafters cracking and crashing down, they strapped on their masks and entered through the main doors, groping their way forward through thick black smoke.

Tom's weak torch beam didn't penetrate the smoke – they would have to feel their way through the turn-stile then on into the main part of the building.

After what seemed like an age, Connie grabbed Tom's arm and pointed towards a metal staircase that would have been the means by which the fire watchers had gained access to the roof.

He signalled for her not to touch the hot metal.

Looking up, he wondered if a rescue attempt was worth the risk. Perhaps the man had died instantly alongside his companion.

Feeling the intense heat through her uniform and through the soles of her rubber boots, Connie watched as a large section of the glass roof above the swimming pool splintered then crashed into the water. Red-hot debris hissed then sank. Should they go on or should they retreat?

'There's still a chance of finding him alive – let's carry on.' Connie's muffled voice delivered the difficult decision. Tom followed her up the metal steps to the first landing. More beams collapsed and yet more of the roof caved in. The heat was becoming unbearable. They were on the point of turning back when the smoke cleared briefly and Tom made out the shape of the second fire watcher sprawled across the stairs directly above. In less than a minute they reached the man and discovered that he was unconscious but still breathing. Carefully they raised him to a sitting position but failed to rouse him. Realizing that a fireman's lift was the only way to carry him to safety, Tom slung the insensible victim over his shoulder. He staggered under the weight then steadied himself and gestured to Connie that she should lead the way. No time to lose – the heat was getting worse, if anything, and the smoke was thicker.

They made their way down the stairs one agonizingly slow step at a time until at last they reached ground level, where Connie took part of the burden and together she and Tom dragged the fire watcher towards the door. They emerged on to the street as the fire service arrived and yet another incendiary fell on to the pavement close enough for Connie to kick it away. It exploded in a hundred white sparks before one of the AFS crew dropped a sandbag on it and others rushed to help Tom with the injured fire watcher.

Tom handed over the man then tore off his mask and helmet. His face ran with sweat and the back of his uniform was soaked through.

Exhausted, Connie sank down on the wide steps. This was a vision of hell; one that still hadn't ended as she sat and gasped for air. She leaned forward and coughed. Her scorched throat hurt and every muscle ached.

Tom took off his haversack and sat down beside her as the ambulance arrived. 'Take it easy – we've done our bit,' he said wearily.

Connie's eyes smarted as she watched Bill Evans approach with two stretcher carriers, who lifted the unconscious man into the ambulance. She saw Lizzie sitting in the driver's cab but lacked the strength even to wave. 'Not "we",' she corrected in a low whisper. '*You* were the one who carried him out. You saved his life.'

Gone; all gone. From the ambulance, Lizzie watched the entire roof of the municipal baths collapse. Directing her gaze down to ground level, she made out her sister and Tom huddled together on the steps, safe but obviously exhausted.

'Did you speak to Connie?' she asked Bill as he rejoined her.

He nodded. 'She's all right and so is Tom. We have to get this fire-watcher chap to hospital – he's inhaled a lot of smoke.'

At the sound of the back doors slamming shut, Lizzie started the engine. A glance in her overhead mirror told her that a bomb squad had erected barriers to deal with the unexploded parachute mine at the top of the street, which meant that her only option was to drive carefully past the AFS team scrambling to set up hoses and pumps in front of the baths then wind through back streets towards the Queen Alexandra. It wasn't ideal because many other roads were partially blocked by rescue parties and by rubble, but eventually they reached the town square from where it ought to be a straight run up the hill to the hospital.

However, the Luftwaffe had other ideas.

Out of nowhere a lone Dornier flew low over the square, machine-gunning everything in sight. Bullets ripped chunks out of Queen Victoria's plinth and the library steps and still the plane kept on coming, straight at Lizzie's ambulance, its Plexiglas hood reflecting orange flames, its guns spitting a chain of fast-moving, red and yellow sparks. Lizzie froze and closed her eyes in terror.

'Duck!' As the windscreen shattered, Bill jerked her sideways across his lap, where she lay prone until the shooting stopped.

In the eerily quiet aftermath she sat up and brushed splinters of glass from her shoulders before turning in her seat to check with the two stretcher carriers that they and their patient were safe. Then she glanced sideways at Bill. He sat in the passenger seat, staring straight ahead and pressing one hand to his chest. Lizzie waited for him to tell her to drive on but then she saw that his face was drained of colour and his breathing was rapid and shallow.

'What's wrong?' A sharp stab of dread shot through her.

Bill turned his head, unable to speak.

She looked more closely to see blood seeping between his fingers. It trickled down the back of his hand and soaked into the sleeve of his dark jacket.

Lizzie controlled her panic. 'Bill's been hit. What do I do?' she asked the first-aiders in the back.

One scrambled forward to assess the injury. 'Drive on,' he ordered. 'Quick as you can.'

So Lizzie used her elbow to knock loose shards of glass from the shattered windscreen then slammed the van into gear while the first-aider took a pair of scissors to Bill's uniform then applied pressure directly to the wound. The van's clutch made a grinding noise and there was little response as she tried to move off. *Forget first gear – try second.* This time they moved sluggishly forward. 'How is he?' she demanded of the first-aider.

'He's losing too much blood. Can't you go any faster?'

Lizzie put her foot down hard on the accelerator. Lord only knew what damage the hail of bullets had done to the engine because all she could get out of it was a high-pitched whine and a slow crawl forward. She tried third gear and they lurched on under moving beams of white light cast by the searchlights on the beach, to the dull sound of explosions on the headland and beyond.

'Stay awake,' the first-aider urged Bill. 'That's right – keep your eyes open.'

Fear had formed a tight band around Lizzie's chest, making it hard to breathe. She forced herself

180

to look straight ahead and to coax the van up another gear.

'Talk to him,' the first-aider said. 'You know him better than I do – perhaps he'll respond to your voice.'

'Listen to me, Bill.' She gripped the steering wheel and struggled on up the hill. 'We're nearly at the hospital. You have to hang on until we get there, you hear?'

'That's right, love – keep talking.' The first-aider applied more pressure.

'You're not to give up,' Lizzie insisted. 'Think of sailing that fishing boat of yours, doing what you love best – out on the open sea, free as a bird.'

Bill turned his head and fixed his gaze on her.

The engine faltered on the incline and she was forced to change down to second gear. 'You hear me, Bill? I fancy another ride on that bike of yours. You can take me all the way up the coast with the wind in our hair and the whole world spread out before us. How does that sound?'

He stretched his lips into a smile then closed his eyes.

Oh God, don't go to sleep! 'We're almost there,' she promised frantically.

The hospital gateway was in sight. Another ambulance sped past and entered the drive ahead of them. There were two others at the door, damn it, and it seemed they must wait their turn. But Lizzie parked haphazardly and sprinted inside. 'Man bleeding to death,' she gasped to the first nurse she saw. 'Emergency – come quickly.'

It was done at top speed. The first-aiders stretchered the unconscious fire watcher in through the doors while porters from the hospital brought a trolley to transfer Bill from the van. Lizzie ran beside them, holding Bill's hand. As they rolled him through the doors she felt his weak grasp fade to nothing.

'You must stay here.' A nurse came forward and advised Lizzie gently. 'There's nothing more you can do.'

Distraught, Lizzie glanced down at her bloodstained hand then at the trolley disappearing through a wide door. If Bill hadn't grabbed her and pulled her down as the Dornier flew at them this might never have happened. He could have saved himself instead.

'Please don't die,' she murmured with quiet desperation. The door had closed. New patients had arrived. Calm nurses in blue-and-white uniforms and serious doctors in white coats hurried to tend to the injured and the dying, leaving Lizzie stranded on an island of misery. 'Please, Bill – I want you to live.' Tears trickled down her cheeks and she walked out into the night.

CHAPTER TWELVE

In the calm after the storm of the night before, Pamela decided to walk to Anderson's to see her father. As she stepped out of the front door she was dismayed to see that little was left of the municipal baths except blackened girders and piles of rubble. The twisted remains of a metal staircase rose from the ruins. More shocking still, when she turned into Tennyson Street, was the sight of an iron bed frame thrown from the first floor of a bombed house. It stood in the middle of the road, complete with its mattress, for all the world as if it had been placed there on purpose rather than blown clear of someone's bedroom by the force of an explosion. Pamela looked up to see a chimney stack silhouetted precariously against a grey sky and the arm of a crane swinging towards it with a wrecking ball. A woman in overalls and a flat cap warned Pamela to stand clear.

So she quickly backtracked and found another route down to St Stephen's dock, past a horse and cart piled high with furniture rescued from wrecked buildings. At the end of an alleyway she caught a glimpse of her old school with its front railings mangled and a deep crater in the playground – she guessed there would be no lessons there today. And yet life went on. Housewives carried shopping baskets to the fish market at the harbourside, men cycled to work, buses ran to the normal timetable – all intended to show Herr Hitler that England would not be beaten. Pamela raised her head high and walked with the women in the direction of the dock.

When she came to the entrance to the timber yard she stated her business to a man in a booth by the gate. 'I'm Harold Carr's daughter. Is it all right if I go in for five minutes?'

The gatekeeper eyed her with unabashed curiosity then nodded her through. She crossed an open area, her feet crunching over the cinder surface, then she entered the two-storey office block, still under scrutiny from passing workers.

'Yes?' A well-dressed secretary with a string of cultured pearls and matching earrings spoke tartly from behind a desk.

'I'm here to see Harold Carr,' Pamela explained.

'Is he expecting you?'

Before Pamela could reply, Fred rushed down the stairs to greet her. 'It's all right, Betty. I expect that Miss Carr is here to see Harold. Am I right?' As he ushered her up to the first floor he told her that he'd spied her through the window. 'Your father's in the middle of a telephone call so I offered to fetch you. How are you? Have you recovered from last night's drama?'

She and Fred had spent three hours cooped up in their landlady's cellar until the all-clear siren had sounded and it had been safe to return to their rooms. Fielding had been the only one to get any decent sleep, stretched out on a bench and snoring to high heaven while Thora, resplendent in crimson dressing gown and hair curlers, had occupied a second bench and the two young ones had sat up and played games of draughts on a board kept on a shelf beside a pile of tattered magazines.

'Not quite,' she confessed. 'I have no idea how you persuaded Mr Fielding down into the cellar. My heart was in my mouth.'

'It wasn't the first time and it won't be the last we'll find him in that state, unfortunately.' Fred showed Pamela into the office – a long, light room that had filing cabinets along one wall opposite a row of metal-framed windows overlooking the yard.

Harold was at his desk, finishing off the call. Seeing Pamela, he quickly put down the receiver and came to greet her with the broadest of smiles. 'My, my; it's lovely to see you. Fred assured me that you were all right but I'm so pleased to see it with my own eyes.' To satisfy himself he turned her around on the spot. 'Yes; all in one piece and none the worse for wear, thank the Lord.'

Pamela set down her handbag on his desk. 'I'm absolutely fine, thanks to Fred waking me the moment the siren sounded,' she assured him. 'And how's Mummy?'

'She's worried about you,' Harold reported as Fred discreetly withdrew to his own desk. 'Otherwise she's coping. Raby was spared last night – there were no direct hits.'

Pamela studied her father's face. His florid complexion was unchanged and his standard workwear of a fawn cardigan beneath a tweed jacket with neat collar and tie suggested that the loss of the house on

Musgrave Street and the move to Aunty Lilian's cottage hadn't upset his routine.

'As a matter of fact, that was your mother on the telephone,' Harold went on. 'It seems she's had a most surprising visit from Hugh – from Mr Anderson.'

'I don't understand.' How could this be? As far as Pamela was aware, there'd been no contact with the Andersons since her mother had married her father. 'How did he know where to find her?'

Harold drew up a chair and invited her to sit down before resuming his place at his desk. 'That's due to your Aunty Lilian. Apparently she thought it was high time Edith and Hugh made up, so she took it upon herself to bring your Uncle Hugh up to date with recent events.'

'You hadn't said anything to him?' Still bewildered, Pamela leaned forward and spoke in a whisper.

Harold shook his head. 'No one was more astonished than me; I make sure to keep work and family life quite separate. It's for the best, or at least it has been until now.'

'And what was behind . . . Mr Anderson's visit?' It seemed unnatural to refer to her father's employer as her uncle so she stuck to the formal address.

'That's precisely what I asked Edith.' Clasping his hands in front of him, Harold adopted an equally confidential tone. 'It seems bridges are being built between the two of them – Hugh was concerned about us losing the house and everything in it. And he has troubles of his own to contend with.'

'Business troubles?' Pamela cast a quick glance over her shoulder to make sure that they weren't being overheard.

'No, that's not really a problem – the demand for timber is as high as ever. But Hugh told Edith that his wife, Peggy, has gone into a home for invalids. You've never met her, of course. She's been ill for some time and isn't expected to get better.'

With the revelations coming thick and fast, it took Pamela some time to work out the implications of what she was hearing. 'Is Mummy ready to forgive Uncle Hugh?'

Harold drew a deep breath. 'It's early days, dear. But Edith has always known that it was her father, not Hugh, who made the original decision to cut her out of his will.'

All this – the unreasonable anger of her grandfather and the lasting resentment on her mother's side – had begun before Pamela was even born. And now it was impossible for her to imagine the passion that must have brought her parents together and driven them apart from the rest of Edith's family. Look at them now – no star-crossed lovers but two ordinary, careworn people drifting uneasily through middle age. 'What will happen next?' she wondered aloud.

'Time will tell.' Harold reached across the desk to pat her hand. 'The main thing is that we're all safe and well.'

'But aren't you . . . don't you . . . ?'

'Hope that Edith and Hugh call a truce?'

'Yes; surely it would make a big difference.'

'Would it?' Harold looked doubtfully over the rim of his glasses. 'Would we be any happier?'

The question set Pamela back in her chair. A reconciliation could lead to many improvements – perhaps fewer money worries and a chance for her father to retire from the drudgery of office work, not to mention the opportunity for her mother to re-enter the social circles she'd known as a child. Her mind jumped ahead through various possibilities.

Harold seemed unconvinced. 'Naturally, I'm pleased for your mother if this is what she wants.'

Pamela acknowledged his doubts but didn't pursue them. 'Tell her I'll come to see her tomorrow afternoon if I can.' The wall clock above Fred's desk reminded her that she'd taken up enough of her father's time so she stood up and put her handbag over her arm. Harold showed her to the door. 'Don't get your hopes up too high,' he warned. 'As I say, it's early days.'

Pamela kissed his cheek then squeezed his hand. 'The first move is always the hardest.'

'Yes; especially after all these years.' His round face looked unexpectedly sad as he closed the glass-panelled door.

Pamela glanced across the room to wave at Fred, who waved back. Then she went downstairs to face Betty's lofty scrutiny and the keen appraisal of the man on the gate. Who knew what each day would bring? On Sunday disaster for Kelthorpe, on Monday a healing of old family wounds; it turned out that fate could spin you about and turn you in any direction it pleased.

The Harrisons' damaged van was in for repair.

'We'll have to manage without it,' Bert had told Connie as soon as they'd received the news via Kenneth Browning. 'A replacement windscreen won't be cheap; neither will a new clutch. Still, Lizzie wasn't harmed and that's the main thing.'

'I wasn't hurt,' Lizzie confirmed to Connie on the Monday morning after she'd delivered the vehicle to Brearly's workshop then returned to the bakery, 'but Bill was.'

Seeing that she was pale and shaking from head to toe, Connie sat her down on a stool behind the counter. 'Badly?'

Lizzie nodded. 'It's touch-and-go. He was shot in the upper part of his chest.'

Connie drew up another stool. 'Of course I want to know how it happened, but only if you feel able. Don't try to talk if it's too upsetting.'

'He lost a lot of blood,' Lizzie managed in short bursts. 'He might die.'

'Hush then; no need to say any more.' Connie took Lizzie's hand. 'Take some deep breaths. Do you need to go home and rest?'

Lizzie shook her head. 'What about the deliveries?'

'Dad and I will cope.'

'No; it's best if I keep busy.' Lizzie was still in her grimy ambulance driver's uniform and her hair was dull with brick dust, her face smeared with soot. She hadn't had a wink of sleep. 'I can deliver everything by bike.'

'You cannot,' Connie told her firmly. 'I never heard such rubbish. What you need is a good hot bath then a lie-down.'

'But who'll do the deliveries?' Lizzie was on the verge of tears.

'I will. Dad can keep an eye on the shop while I'm gone.' Brooking no argument, Connie called through the door into the bakery. 'Dad, Lizzie is going home to tidy herself up. That's all right, isn't it?'

'Course it is,' was the muffled reply.

'See.' Connie guided Lizzie on to the street, where rescue teams worked to shore up the front of the hairdresser's. 'Go straight home and do as I say.'

Lizzie lacked the strength to argue. She set off for Elliot Street and hardly took in her surroundings; simply reaching home by instinct and shutting the door behind her. She only got halfway up the stairs before her legs gave way and she slumped against the wall. Bill might already be dead, for all she knew. What if the doctors hadn't been able to save him? Cold dread ran through her veins, soon replaced by a new, gritty determination. She must find the strength to go to the hospital and find out.

But first, she would wash her face, brush her hair and change her clothes. By giving herself strict orders, she accomplished these simple tasks. A cup of tea would help to revive her. Then a bite to eat . . . Slowly but surely Lizzie pulled herself together.

It was eleven o'clock before she set out again in a clean white blouse, black slacks and her cornflower-blue jacket; once again ignoring the havoc wreaked by the German bombers, her mind fixed on one thing only.

Please let Bill be alive, she repeated to herself as she walked through the town square.

The library was sealed off behind barriers and Queen Victoria had been toppled from her plinth. Remnants of the stone statue – a hand holding the empress's orb and part of the crowned head – lay scattered on the surrounding flower beds.

He will be alive! The power of positive thinking carried Lizzie up the hill towards the Queen Alexandra. As she passed between the gates she ignored the comings and goings of ambulances and made her way, head down and fists clenched, towards the main entrance.

'Lizzie?'

A tentative voice stopped her outside the wide doors. She almost ignored it and walked on, but a hand was laid lightly on her arm.

'Lizzie.' Tom saw from her face that she was in a daze.

She blinked as her brain clicked slowly into the here and now. 'Hello, Tom.'

'Are you here to visit Bill?'

'Yes – why?' She fought the impulse to cover her ears to block out any bad news. 'Have you seen him?' *He's dead, he's dead!* Hammer blows struck at her heart.

'I have.' Tom's face was grave. Poor girl; it seemed she'd been driving the ambulance when the plane attacked. 'The doctors are doing everything they can,' he assured her.

'Are doing', not 'did'. She clung to those two precious little words with renewed hope.

'He's still unconscious. They say he was lucky – the bullet missed his heart by half an inch.'

Alive then. 'Thank God!' she whispered. Then, 'Should I come back later?'

'No, go in and see for yourself. He's in Ward C.' Tom had promised a nurse that he would hurry back with Bill's pyjamas and a washbag. 'I have to run. Go on – go in.'

So Lizzie took a deep breath and continued on her way. The bullet had missed Bill's heart, she repeated to herself. Bill had pulled her to safety and was now clinging to life.

Ward C was at the end of a long, shiny corridor. Busy nurses paid Lizzie scant attention and she wasn't questioned as she went in through the swing doors into a large room with a high ceiling, cream walls and rows of beds down each side. Some were screened off and only two patients had visitors. She hesitated then looked round for a nurse.

'Can I help you, miss?' A porter with a squeaking trolley had followed her into the ward.

'Yes, I've come to see Bill Evans.'

The porter consulted a chart on the wall. 'Fourth bed on your left,' he told her.

So she ventured forward, her heart in her mouth. *Alive but still unconscious*, she reminded herself. And there Bill lay beneath immaculate hospital sheets, surrounded by metal stands with bottles containing mysterious liquids, connected to them by needles and rubber tubes. A temperature chart was clipped to the end of his bed. A tubular-steel chair was placed against the wall.

Lizzie moved it closer to Bill's bed, resolving to sit quietly for five minutes then leave. But when she gathered enough courage to look closely, distress almost brought her straight back on to her feet. His eyes were closed, his muscular arms and broad hands were placed clear of the sheets so as not to interfere with the tubes attaching him to the life-saving fluids. The handsome face was like a marble statue – quite still and lifeless, drained of colour.

It was hard to believe that a single bullet could reduce a man so strong and full of life and vitality to this. Bill was bold and carefree; he braved the waves, hauled in nets and washed down decks. It was impossible to believe that he lay here at death's door. Lizzie's legs trembled and she clasped her shaking hands together.

'Speak to him if you like,' a middle-aged nurse at a nearby bedside recommended crisply, offering the same advice as the first-aider in the ambulance the previous night. 'Sometimes hearing a voice they recognize brings them round.'

Lizzie took her tone from the nurse. 'Well, well – this is a fine mess.' She leaned forward to make sure of being heard. 'Look at the state of you, Bill Evans – and all because you put others first, as usual.'

His eyes stayed firmly shut.

'Carry on talking,' the nurse insisted, as Lizzie looked to her for guidance.

'You hear me?' she went on. 'You've got us all worried to death; Tom for a start. And me as well.'

Bill's eyelids flickered, the thick lashes casting shadows across his cheeks.

The nurse nodded encouragingly, replaced a thermometer in its glass then went about her business at the far end of the ward.

'I haven't had a wink of sleep since it happened,' Lizzie told Bill reproachfully. 'You're supposed to give first aid, not be on the receiving end. As for the blinking van, it barely got us to hospital. I thought I was going to have to give you a fireman's lift through the doors.'

Slowly Bill's eyelids fluttered open and he turned his head.

She laid a hand on his. 'What would I do without you to tell me what to do?' she murmured.

He opened his mouth to speak but no words emerged.

'I'd be lost; that's what.'

'Lizzie?' He tried to raise his head but it was too much effort.

'Yes, it's me. Lie still.'

Everything was blurred – walls and ceiling shifted and he couldn't focus on the blue-and-white shape beside his bed but he felt a soft touch and he recognized the voice. 'Lizzie?' he said again.

'Yes. Don't try to move.'

His last memory was of the town on fire – flames and smoke everywhere – and of Lizzie sitting in the driver's seat. Was that still happening? He couldn't smell smoke or cordite and it was daylight, so where was he?

'You're in hospital,' she told him. 'You're meant to lie still.' His grey eyes looked at her with dawning recognition. 'The doctors have worked miracles.'

He took a deep breath. 'How long have I been here?'

'A few hours – that's all. Shall I go and fetch a nurse?'

'No; stay.' He looked down at her small, slim hand resting on his. He was injured and had blank, dark hours that he couldn't recall. 'What happened?'

'A German plane – a Dornier – came at us, all guns blazing. Do you remember?'

Arcs of red bullets in the darkness, the sound of glass shattering. After that . . . nothing. Bill nodded slowly.

'You saved my life,' she told him, leaning forward and stroking his cheek.

The entrance to the public shelter on Gas Street had been damaged, along with the waterworks on the edge of town and a large grain mill overlooking the estuary. But by Thursday, true to form, the doughty citizens of Kelthorpe had picked themselves up and were going determinedly about their business. Traffic ran freely and goods trains arrived to bring coal in and carry timber out, according to the usual railway timetable. Most importantly, dockside trade continued as normal and the fishing boats went out at dawn as they had done for centuries.

On the Friday of that week, Pamela got ready for work at the Savoy. Dressed in a brand-new outfit of polka-dot-print cotton dress and white cardigan, she left number 21 hoping to cross paths with Fred on his way home from Anderson's and, sure enough, he stepped off a bus from the town centre just as she arrived at her stop (ten minutes early in order to maximize her chances). It was a bright, blustery day with light, puffy clouds flitting across the sky.

Fred's face lit up when he saw her and he greeted her with a kiss on the cheek. 'I have the night off. Shall I come to meet you after work?' he offered. 'Then I could walk you home through the park.'

Pamela agreed that he should. 'The film finishes at half nine.'

'I'll be there,' he promised. 'I must say, my day will end better than it began.'

'Why – what's happened?' She was curious because it was unusual for him to invite questions about his life at work.

'Nothing too serious – just some figures that don't add up, that's all.' He'd puzzled over them for the entire morning then shown them to Harold, who had quizzed George Bachelor about them – out of earshot, although Fred had been able to see from the foreman's surly expression that the enquiry had gone down badly. 'By the way, your father has invited us both to tea in Raby on Sunday.'

Pamela felt a small thrill of excitement at the news. 'Has Mummy agreed?'

'I assume so.' Earlier in the week, soon after Pamela's visit to the office, Harold had taken Fred to one side and asked him a direct question – were he and Pamela courting? Taken aback, at first Fred had gone on the defensive – why did Harold think that might be the case, et cetera.

'The spark between you is obvious, even to a dim-wit like me,' Harold had told him in his mild way. 'As her father I have a duty to look out for her.'

'Yes, sir; I appreciate that.' Fred had stopped pre-varicating. 'And yes, Pamela and I have grown fond of one another. I hope you don't object.'

'By no means.' Harold's round face had twinkled with pleasure. He'd gone home and reported back to Edith and Lilian. True to form, Edith had worried away at every aspect of the would-be suitor's charac-ter. What was his family background? Did Harold know anything about his past? Did Fred Miller strike him as a thoroughly decent young man?

Lilian, meanwhile, had rubbed her hands over the prospect of a first romantic dalliance for her niece. 'You can't wrap Pamela in cotton wool for ever,' she'd cautioned Edith.

'I suppose not,' Edith had conceded, but she'd con-tinued to fret.

'Sunday it is, then,' Pamela said as her bus appeared around the corner.

'And I'll see you at half past nine.' Fred watched his new sweetheart hop aboard the number 9 in a flounce of polka dots and a flash of white sandals. Events were moving faster than anticipated; perhaps because he and Pamela saw so much of each other, timing their breakfast appearances to coincide then getting together later in the day whenever they could. Wednesday had been her evening off from the cinema and they'd borrowed bikes from the Harrison girls and cycled up on to the moors. They'd stopped at Raynard's Folly and looking back Fred couldn't quite work out who'd made the first move; suffice it to say that there'd been a good deal of kissing until the sight of a thin crocodile of trekkers making their way up the hill in the fading daylight had put paid to their embraces. The downhill ride had been exhilarating. Then they'd returned their bikes to number 12 and he and Pamela had parted in Thora's hallway with chaste pecks; each to their own room and dreams of what might be to come.

Now, on Thursday evening, Fred had time to think things through. Ought he to put on the brakes? he wondered. After all, he'd been forced out of London and come this far north in order to start afresh. Could he afford a romantic entanglement that might complicate affairs if he had to move on in a rush a second time? But that would be a case of his head ruling his heart. He only had to visualize Pamela's face in close-up – the fascinating grey-green colour of her eyes, the dimple when she smiled and her soft lips – to let his feelings run away with him. It was a novel experience, similar to careering downhill on their bikes – fast and thrilling, with the distinct possibility that the brakes wouldn't work when they reached the bottom.

'Where are we going?' Connie asked George. Once again, Penrose had cut her working hours and given the Saturday matinee to a new girl, Dorothy Giles. George had showed up out of the blue, rat-a-tat-tatting on the door knocker of number 12 and inviting her to go on a jaunt with him.

'Not far,' he assured her once she was safely installed in the passenger seat of his Ford. 'Just round the corner, as a matter of fact.'

He whistled as he drove the short distance to Tennyson Street and stopped outside number 5.

'This is old Mr Ward's house.' Connie recognized it at once, as well as the house next to it, from which she and Tom had rescued Nancy Thomson and her two little girls. 'What are we doing here?'

'Come with me.' George looked swiftly up and down the length of the street before getting out of the car. A sharp shower had dampened the pavement but had eased off as he invited Connie to follow him up the short garden path.

She went reluctantly and was surprised to see George take a key from his jacket pocket and turn it in the lock. Before she could question him he'd opened the door and stepped into the house.

'Where did you get that key?' she demanded from the doorstep. She gazed down the dark hallway. 'And where's Mr Ward?'

'Didn't you know? He went to live with his daughter earlier this week.' George pulled her inside and slammed the door behind her. 'Don't dawdle out there.'

'What about the key?' Everything about this felt wrong, including the jaunty whistle that George kept up as he led the way along the narrow corridor.

'It's simple enough to change a lock, you know.' He popped the shiny key back into his pocket. 'Old man Ward left everything as it was – all the furniture, all of his clothes. It was careless of him. Anyone could break in and nab the lot.'

Connie peered into the back kitchen – there were no table or chairs and the cupboard doors hung open to reveal empty shelves. 'You didn't!' she gasped, running upstairs to find that there was not a stick of furniture to be seen.

'It wasn't worth much, worse luck,' he confessed. 'Except for a vase or two on the mantelpiece in the front room – oh, and a stash of five-pound notes hidden under the mattress. The daughter must have overlooked that in the rush to move him out.'

Dumbstruck, Connie pushed past George and made for the front door. She wanted nothing to do with the robbing of a helpless old man. But George was quick to follow and pin her against the wall. 'You don't think I'm the culprit, do you?'

Her breath came short because of the pressure of his forearm against her ribs. 'Who then?' she gasped.

'It's best not to ask.' Slowly releasing her, George watched her like a hawk. 'All that matters is that the house isn't lived in and there's a big, empty cellar that no one ever ventures into. Come and take a look.'

Steadying herself and pulling her jacket straight, Connie followed him down the stone steps into a dank cellar. She saw by the light of a torch that George swung around the room that this was where Mr Ward had stored stepladders and garden tools – all rotting and festooned with cobwebs. The usual row of meat hooks hung from the ceiling over a big stone keeping table piled high with cardboard boxes.

'How did those get there?' she asked.

His answer was simple and direct. 'I put them there.'

'And what's in them?'

'This and that.' George stood between Connie and the boxes. 'I wore my uniform and brought them here on the q.t. People don't think twice about a warden on patrol going about his business. The boxes will stay here until I can find a buyer in York or Leeds.'

'I see. This is a step up from the arrangement you had with John?' Carefully inserting his name into the conversation, she fished for more information.

Her new associate didn't take the bait. 'There's a lot more storage space, as you can see, and not so many prying eyes.'

Connie brushed aside a mixture of fear and mistrust that clung to her like the thick, dusty cobwebs. 'Your business is on the up, it seems. Won't you tell me what's in the boxes or is it top secret?'

Patting the tops of them, George shone his torch directly on to her face. 'This lot is mostly tobacco, cigarettes and rum on their way from the West Indies to the Royal Navy. The next lot will be vodka from Russia and whisky from Bonnie Scotland.'

'And my job would be – what?' Her steady voice belied her mounting dread.

George took his time over the details. 'To get the best price. Buyers can't resist a good-looking girl. You'll arrange to meet up in a pub – the busier the better – to discuss what each box is worth. You push the price as high as you can. How you do that is entirely up to you.' He lowered the torch beam and let it rest on her chest and then on her hips.

Connie held her nerve in the face of the none-too-subtle suggestion. 'And what's in it for me?'

'Fifteen per cent.' Cut and dried, no discussion. 'That's where your John went wrong, by the way. He argued over percentages. You have your head screwed on too tight to try that, I'm sure.'

'I see.' Scarcely able to breathe, she edged towards the stairs. 'Let's go up and get some fresh air.'

He swung the torch towards the door. 'After you.'

Connie went ahead, only taking a proper breath once she reached ground level.

'Well?' Once more, George shoved her against the wall, this time with less force and more insinuation. He leaned in with all his weight and turned her face towards him.

She met his gaze. 'Fifteen per cent isn't enough. Let's say twenty.'

He pressed against her. 'I admire a woman who drives a hard bargain. Twenty if you allow me certain benefits.'

His meaning was clear even before he forced his mouth against hers. She pushed him back with all her might and broke free. 'It's a deal. But the benefits don't apply until the money is safely in my pocket,' she insisted as she flung open the front door.

CHAPTER THIRTEEN

'Arnold, come down from there at once!' At the sight of her young cousin scaling the twisted metal staircase that rose from the ruins of the swimming baths, Connie gave a furious cry.

He swung like a monkey from girder to girder. Down below, his two pals hid behind a stack of charred, wooden beams to escape Connie's wrath.

'I said: come down!'

Standing beside Connie, Lizzie held her breath. The heaps of rubble bore no resemblance to the once-glorious building where she, Connie and more lately Pamela had laughed together and experienced so much fun. She sighed then forced her attention back to the present. Arnold was a scamp, right enough.

The sisters watched and waited until he'd swung himself to safety then descended what remained of the staircase. He seemed unrepentant as he scrambled over piles of bricks to rejoin his friends.

'All three of you, come here.' Connie wasn't ready to let them off the hook. 'You'll break your necks if you carry on like that. You see these barriers? They're telling you to keep out, as if you didn't know.'

The skinny urchins trudged towards Connie and

Lizzie. One wore a green jumper that was threadbare at the elbows and two sizes too small, and all three were dressed in baggy flannel shorts, wrinkled grey socks and dirty plimsolls.

'Don't tell Mam,' Arnold begged Lizzie. 'I'll get a big whack with the belt if you do.'

Connie intervened. 'There's no use trying to soft-soap Lizzie. If I see you mucking around on that bombsite one more time I'll have you scrubbing floors and washing windows down at the bakery every day from now until Christmas – do you hear me?'

Arnold nodded before quickly wheeling around, giving a shrill, devil-may-care whinny then galloping off down the street, cowboy-style, followed by his two young accomplices.

'Ready?' Lizzie suppressed a grin then sat astride her bike. It was a sunny morning and she and Connie planned to head south along the coast road towards White Sands Bay.

Connie followed Lizzie to the end of the street. She badly needed a couple of hours of carefree cycling before returning home to cook Sunday dinner.

Within ten minutes they were clear of the town and riding along a narrow lane with high hawthorn hedges on either side. A wind at their backs helped them to reach the top of a steep hill where the hedges finished and the road opened out to give them an uninterrupted sea view. Then it was downhill past a dairy farm with black-and-white cows in the surrounding fields and a strong farmyard smell, on again past stretches of newly planted wheat and glorious May blossom.

'Watch out for potholes!' Lizzie swerved on to the wrong side of the road.

Connie followed suit, then they both jammed on their brakes as a horse and cart approached. They ended up skidding into a ditch while the cart trundled on without the driver giving a backward glance.

'Charming!' Lizzie stood up and pulled her bike out of the ditch.

'Look at this mudguard.' Connie pulled a face and rattled the offending piece of metal. 'It's loose as anything.'

'Stand aside – let me see if I can fix it.' Lizzie quickly found the problem – a bent bracket and a loose bolt that she was able to tighten with the spanner she carried in her saddlebag. 'I went to see Bill again yesterday,' she mentioned mid-repair.

'Oh yes – how is he?' Connie retied her headscarf then brushed herself down.

'He's had an operation to remove pieces of glass from his chest. Luckily the bullet passed clean through the muscle.'

'How long will he have to stay in hospital?'

'Hard to tell. He's chafing at the bit to be let out.' Lizzie tested the mudguard then straightened up. 'You know what he's like.'

'The same as all men, I expect. They make terrible patients.' An awkwardness hung in the air, which Connie broke through with typical directness. 'Listen here, Lizzie. What does Bob think about you visiting Bill so often? That was the third time this week.'

'I don't tell him,' Lizzie confessed. 'It would only lead to another row.'

'Exactly.'

'What am I meant to do?' Lizzie spread her hands

helplessly. 'I go to see Bill because I've been worried to death about him and because seeing me helps him on the road to recovery.'

'Who says so?' Connie asked sharply.

'He does.' A silence hung in the air before Lizzie plunged on. 'We chat about everyday matters: the latest films or Bill's favourite tunes. He tells me about the places he's been to on his motorbike; last year he went on holiday to the west coast of Scotland, to the Isle of Skye. And there's no need to look at me like that,' she protested. 'There's nothing in it except friendship.'

Connie continued to stare until Lizzie sighed then walked up a nearby mound to gaze down at the waves pounding against dark rocks.

'All right, it could be more than friendship.'

'If it weren't for Bob?'

'Yes.' Lizzie covered her face with her hands. 'I'm all mixed up. What am I meant to do?'

'That depends.'

'On what?' Lizzie looked to Connie for answers that weren't forthcoming. 'I don't even know how I feel,' she went on. 'Perhaps I visit Bill out of guilt. This might never have happened if he hadn't thought about saving me. But it's more than that. We got on like a house on fire before this happened – he's so cheerful and easy-going.'

'Unlike someone we could mention?' Connie prompted.

'Yes, but it would break Bob's heart if I gave backword now. Imagine it – we've been sweethearts all these years. I've made promises. He relies on me. And what would his mother say if I broke it off?'

'Ah yes; Kathleen.' To Connie this seemed the least of Lizzie's worries. 'The thing is, Liz, do you even know how Bill feels towards you? Has he said anything?'

Lizzie shook her head. 'No, he wouldn't – not while I'm engaged to Bob.'

Connie picked up her bike and spun the back wheel then straightened the mudguard bracket a fraction more. 'From what I know of Bill, he's a decent chap – like his pal, Tom. They both enjoy a lark but they steer well clear of trouble.'

Lizzie sat astride her bike. 'So what are you saying – that I should do the right thing and stop visiting Bill?'

'For Bob's sake – yes. On the other hand, I've said it before: only you know how you truly feel.'

'Do I, though?' Lizzie wondered aloud. She pictured sitting on Bob's knee in the sunny kitchen window, kissing, cuddling and making plans, then remembered riding pillion on Bill's motorbike, her arms around his waist, a thrill of pure pleasure running through her.

They cycled on towards White Sands Bay. 'Take George Bachelor,' Connie said darkly as they rode side by side. 'Now he's a different kettle of fish.'

Sitting in front of the mirror in her attic room, Pamela had taken special care with her hair. She'd styled it with a side parting then put on an Alice band to hold it back from her face. Make-up had been out of the question if she wished to win her mother's approval. She'd chosen the most demure of her dresses: the pink-and-white one that had belonged to Connie.

Even so, as she and Fred approached her Aunty Lilian's cottage with five minutes to spare, the butterflies in her stomach fluttered frantically so she paused on the corner of the street to compose herself.

'Are you sure about this?' Fred, too, was nervous. Accepting the invitation to tea had been a serious step forward for them both.

'I am if you are,' she said. This would be the first time she'd taken a young man to meet her parents and she feared the worst. What if her mother was in one of her nit-picking moods? Would her sour-faced scrutiny make Fred run for cover or would he meet it head-on and win Edith over with his impeccable manners and clean-cut good looks?

He fiddled with the knot of his tie. 'They're expecting us. It would be rude to back out now.'

So they dragged their feet for the last few yards to Lilian's gate, where they found Harold waiting on the doorstep, his ruddy face wreathed in smiles.

'Here they are; bang on time,' he called over his shoulder. 'Come in, you two. Lilian has prepared a feast – sausage rolls, sandwiches, even a pork pie. Don't ask me how she does it. Come in, come in.'

Following Harold into the cramped parlour, Pamela and Fred were greeted by a table laid out with Lilian's best china and a vase of vibrant red tulips from her garden that sang out against the pure white of her linen tablecloth. It exceeded Harold's description: sandwiches piled high, the pork pie neatly sliced, sausage rolls still warm from the oven.

Once the guests were seated, Lilian appeared in her Sunday best: a lilac, cross-over blouse and dark purple skirt. She set a teapot down on the table then hugged Pamela and shook hands vigorously with Fred. 'Very nice to meet you, I'm sure. I'm Pamela's Aunty Lilian, the one who never stops talking. I expect she's told you about me. We'll wait for Edith – she'll be down in a minute.'

Despite Lilian's warm welcome, Pamela's stomach continued to churn.

'Now then, Fred.' Harold took up the reins. 'You'll be glad to know that your spot of sleuthing earlier this week has paid off: I mean those discrepancies you found in the invoices from last year. Mr Anderson – Hugh, as I think we can call him when we're not in the office – has amended the system so it can't happen again.' He turned to Pamela and Lilian. 'Excuse the work talk, ladies, but it took a sharp pair of eyes to pick it up.'

Fred accepted the praise with a modest smile then shot to his feet as the door opened and Pamela's mother came in.

Edith entered reluctantly. An hour earlier she'd tried to cry off with a headache but Lilian had scolded her and insisted that she get ready. 'But I have nothing to wear,' she'd complained. This excuse, too, had fallen on deaf ears, as had 'I'm not fit to be seen' and 'I really do feel unwell'. Now here she was in a plain grey dress and peach-coloured silk scarf, her hair pulled back severely from her heavily powdered face.

Harold stepped in to do the honours. 'Edith, dear; this is Fred.'

She hovered by the door, glancing uncertainly round the room until the visitor came forward to shake her hand. 'Please take my seat next to Pamela,' Fred insisted. 'I'm sure you two have plenty to catch up on.'

Edith acquiesced with a quiet, unsmiling thank you.

'Pamela, I've been singing Fred's praises to your mother,' Harold continued. 'I've told her how he pointed out my old-fashioned methods of bookkeeping in the nicest possible way. And now that I've got used to the tip-tap-tapping of his typewriter, we rub along splendidly.'

Pamela gave her father a grateful smile then turned to her mother. 'Fred has volunteered to work some evening shifts at the ARP Report and Control Centre in the town hall. He's surrounded by maps and charts, working out where to send rescue teams during an attack. Sometimes he has to decide whether or not to bring in the Home Guard to help.'

'It's the nerve centre of the whole Civil Defence operation,' Harold added. 'It takes brains to do what Fred does.'

As Pamela and Harold talked, Edith stole quick glances at the recipient of their praise. He certainly looked respectable and neat, which was a start. His sports jacket was made of good-quality tweed and his trousers were well pressed. He didn't look the brainy type, though he must be clever with figures if what Harold said was to be believed.

'That's quite enough about me.' Fred turned to their hostess, who had begun to pour the tea. 'How long have you lived in Raby?' he asked her.

'All my married life,' Lilian replied. 'I've been a widow for ten years. Alf and I didn't have any kiddies, worse luck. Still, Pamela came to stay with me for a few weeks after he passed away. She was only twelve at the time but she's always been a kind, caring girl. I think the world of her.'

Offering to hand out the cups, Fred was taken by surprise when Edith ordered Pamela to move so that he could sit beside her.

'You haven't been in the area for long, I understand?' she said with the air of suspicion that she bestowed on all outsiders.

'No, indeed. I came here from London.'

'Your parents were in the jewellery trade.' She took a sip of tea then reacted to Pamela's look of surprise. 'I made a point of finding out from his employer.'

'From Uncle Hugh?'

'Quite. He and I are on better terms of late and of course he looks into people's backgrounds before employing them. I made no bones about it; I said, "Hugh, what can you tell me about your new clerk?"'

'Mummy!' Pamela felt hot with embarrassment and avoided looking at Fred, who had retreated with an apprehensive expression to the far side of the room.

Edith waved away her objection. 'Don't worry – Hugh was the soul of discretion. I prised out of him only the basic facts: a few names and dates, and so on.'

'How is Hugh's wife?' Lilian saved the day with a brisk interruption and a gesture to Fred and Pamela that they should help themselves to sandwiches.

Edith went into chapter and verse about the nature of her sister-in-law's illness – a heart murmur and shortness of breath. 'Peggy's in White Sands nursing home at present. She never looked after herself properly, even when I knew her – she always stayed cooped up in the house instead of going outside into the fresh air.'

As Edith talked on, Pamela murmured an apology to Fred about her mother's inquisitiveness. He shrugged it off by saying that he had nothing to hide.

Edith noticed them in a huddle over the sausage rolls and broke off. 'Pamela, would you be a dear and bring me a slice of that pie? Only the smallest piece . . .'

'Let me.' Fred sprang forward eagerly. 'I was extremely sorry to hear about the loss of your Bechstein,' he sympathized with Edith, sitting beside her once more and taking charge of the conversation. 'They're fine instruments. Pamela tells me that you play very well.'

('Such lovely manners,' Edith remarked later to Harold and Lilian. 'And rather nice-looking, too.')

'It's a sad loss,' she said with a pained expression.

'And who is your favourite composer for the piano, if I may ask?'

Chopin and Brahms, Mendelssohn and Schumann – Clara, not Robert. The names fell thick and fast. Comparisons were made between Romantic and Classical; they both agreed that the supreme Beethoven came out on top by a mile.

'They're getting on like a house on fire.' Harold expressed amazement as he, Lilian and Pamela cleared away the dishes.

'That young man has got her wrapped around his little finger,' Lilian concurred.

Edith proved Lilian's point by keeping Fred at her side until seven o'clock, when Pamela insisted that they must be on their way.

'Time flies,' Edith said as she saw them off. She

211

had rare colour in her cheeks and a lively light in her eyes. 'Hurry home while it's still daylight. And come again, Fred. It's been delightful.'

He waited until they were out of sight before heaving a sigh of relief.

'I'm sorry – was it a terrible ordeal?' Pamela asked with a sinking heart.

'At first; yes.' He laughed and took her hand as they walked. 'But your mother's not too bad once you get her talking.'

The walk home took them along a coastal footpath that narrowed at times to single file. Light was fading as they made their way along the final stretch to Kelthorpe, with the restless sea crashing on to rocks below and threads of smoke from the town's chimneys spiralling into the clear sky.

'Let's stand for a minute.'

Fred's quiet suggestion made Pamela's heart lift as high as the gulls riding on air currents overhead. A breeze rustled through the silvery grasses at their feet.

He put his arm around her waist. In this space, in this moment, he felt exhilarated. The cares of the world were whisked away on the wind. Nothing was said for a long time until, concerned about the fading light and the steep descent into the town, she made as if to walk on.

'No,' he murmured. 'Stay here for a few more minutes.'

There was a catch in his voice; a hint of hidden sorrow. 'Don't be sad.' She leaned into him with both arms around his waist.

Fred kissed the top of her head. 'I'm not sad. I'm glad you're happy.'

'I am.' She looked up at him. 'Are you?'

'Right now? Yes, very.' Surrounded by sea and sky, holding Pamela close.

The wildness of their surroundings emboldened her. 'It sounds foolish, but I've never felt like this before.'

'It's not foolish.'

'I can't put it into words; my heart's too full.'

He kissed her again then tilted her face towards him. *Hold her tight. Don't let her go.*

The way down was rocky and in deep shadow. They really ought to walk on. 'Full to bursting,' she confessed. This was what poets wrote about, with the phrases she lacked: an overflowing of tenderness and yearning that until now she'd only read about. So what Pamela experienced emerged in three humble words, familiar yet foreign on her tongue. 'I love you.'

'And I love you.' Fred held her and kissed her. He feared it wouldn't last but for now it was enough.

'All quiet on the western front.' Bert used an old phrase to sum up his afternoon shift at the Gas Street post. He was handing over to Kenneth, ready to run through the list of evening trekkers with him, when Connie and Tom reported for duty.

'Ladies first.' Tom stood aside for Connie at the door. They'd bumped into each other at the gates to the Leisure Gardens then walked along Park Road together. He'd been his usual reticent self, leaving her to do the talking, and had been surprised to find her more subdued than usual. But when he'd asked her what was up she'd denied that anything was wrong.

'I'm just worn out,' she replied. 'Lizzie and I went on a long bike ride to White Sands Bay this morning.'

So for once, Tom had made the running, teasing her for her continued absence from choir practice and then giving her the latest news on Bill. 'Luckily he's strong as an ox,' he'd reported. 'The docs say that three out of four men who'd lost that much blood wouldn't have pulled through.'

By the time they reached the post Connie seemed back to her cheery self. 'We never got together for that second drink,' she reminded him as they stepped inside the old shoe mender's shop.

'The telephone box at the end of Maypole Street is out of order,' Bert reported to Kenneth in his methodical way after acknowledging Connie and Tom's arrival with a brief smile. 'And the Andrews family have been evacuated from number 50 – the house has been declared unsafe.'

Tom followed Connie into the storeroom at the back of the shop. 'We could meet up this coming Thursday if you're free – at the Red Lion on College Road. It's a step up from The Anchor.'

Tucking her torch and rattle into the slings on her belt before sliding her feet into her rubber boots, she accepted. 'You bet; I'll look forward to that.'

'Number 15 King Edward Street reported the loss of two gas masks.' Bert's gravelly voice reached them from the front of the shop. 'One adult's and one child's. I sent replacements with a messenger but I haven't had them checked for size yet.'

Kenneth noted down the information. 'They're no

good if they're not airtight. I'll send someone round right away.'

'Same here,' Tom replied to Connie as he reached for his helmet and gloves. 'Getting together will be the highlight of my week.' His low-key invitation had been met with an equally casual acceptance, which was fair enough. At least Connie hadn't said no.

'Who's on duty tonight?' Kenneth asked.

Bert listed half a dozen names, including Connie and Tom. 'George Bachelor was meant to be but he phoned in sick an hour ago.'

Overhearing this, Connie couldn't hide a sigh of relief. In the twenty-four hours since George had revealed his stash of contraband, she'd been caught on a painful hook of indecision that the morning bike ride with Lizzie hadn't completely banished. Though every nerve in her body screamed at her to walk away from George's illegal dealings, still she clung to her determination to find out the truth about John's death.

Tom couldn't help noticing her reaction. 'What's wrong? Has he stepped out of line again?'

Connie gave a dismissive shrug. 'You know George; he doesn't even see that there's a line.'

Their conversation was interrupted by fresh activity at the front counter.

The chief wardens greeted two newcomers with mild surprise. 'Aye, aye, Norman – to what do we owe the pleasure?' Kenneth asked.

'We'd like a word with George Bachelor,' a firm voice replied. 'It's official business, I'm afraid.'

Connie and Tom emerged from the storeroom to see two uniformed bobbies blocking the doorway.

'Why? What's he done?' Bert closed his notebook with a resigned air.

'We're keen to ask him a few questions, that's all.' The taller of the two policemen, a clean-shaven, burly sergeant, scanned the room.

Connie's heart lurched as she stepped from the storeroom into the middle of a nightmare.

'Well, he's not here.' Bert came out from behind the counter. 'He's poorly. I can give you his address if you like.'

'We know where he lives,' the sergeant replied as he fixed his gaze on Connie. 'We've already been to his house and there was no sign.'

'Are you sure? That doesn't add up.' Bert glanced over his shoulder at Kenneth, Connie and Tom.

'Connie Bailey?' Backed up by his constable, the sergeant took a step towards her.

The walls seemed to close in as she heard her name.

'Speak up!'

'Yes, that's me,' she answered faintly.

'We need a word with you, too.' He stood immovable as a rock in his dark-blue uniform, his eyes shaded by his helmet, the rest of his face expressionless.

'Steady on.' Bert's objection fell on deaf ears.

The constable asked him to step aside.

'What's this about?' Bert turned to Connie, who shook her head despairingly.

'There's been a report about theft of property from an empty house on Tennyson Street – number 5.' The sergeant's unyielding tone didn't alter as he observed Connie's mounting panic.

'You don't think . . . !' Bert's outrage stopped him from finishing his sentence. 'Connie – tell him!'

She shook her head again as the panic spread through her body.

Seeing the colour drain from her face, Tom sat her down on a stool.

'Walter Ward's daughter went back there early today to collect some of her father's things, only to find that the lock had been changed and looters had stripped the house bare. She ran straight down to the station to report it.'

Bert angrily shrugged off the constable. 'Are you mad? I know looting is rife, but Connie would never stoop to anything like that.'

'Dad, please,' she begged in an agony of shame, her heart thumping, her face running with cold sweat.

'We're not saying she did,' the sergeant continued. 'A witness at number 7 noticed George Bachelor and an accomplice emptying the place. They drove up with a furniture van so as not to arouse suspicion.'

Liar – dirty rotten liar! He swore he had nothing to do with it! A split second of anger against George was followed by a fresh accusation.

'The problem is, this same witness spotted Connie and Bachelor slipping into number 5 together yesterday – using a key, no less. Further investigation led us to a big haul of black-market goods stashed away in Mr Ward's cellar – cigarettes, rum, you name it.'

Connie sagged forward, her face in her hands. Tom crouched beside her and put his arm around her shoulder while Kenneth stepped forward to force Bert back behind the counter.

'Connie Bailey, you're under arrest,' the sergeant said calmly.

217

'Connie!' Bert's face was etched with disbelief.

With Tom's help, the junior policeman raised her from the stool.

'I'm sorry, Dad.' Sorry beyond words for the shock she had caused, sorry to drag the Harrison name into the mud, sorry that Tom should witness her fall from grace; above all, sick with shame at her involvement with George Bachelor, Connie was handcuffed then hurried on to the street and into the police car, head bowed, humiliated, with her life in ruins.

CHAPTER FOURTEEN

It was dark when Lizzie approached the police station on Gladstone Square. The streets of Kelthorpe were deserted, except for wardens on patrol and the occasional old man taking a dog for a walk. The blackout was in full swing. Silence reigned.

She gazed up at the dim blue lamp above the door. This was a building Lizzie had passed many times; it was nothing out of the ordinary, with its large sash windows and two steps up between stone pillars to a shiny, panelled door. However, she'd never been inside until now. Was it in order to walk straight in? she wondered.

As she hesitated, a car drew up and a young man in a lightweight trench coat and trilby hat got out. 'Can I help?' he asked, brushing past her then stopping in the doorway.

'Yes, where can I find Mrs Bailey – Connie Bailey?'

'Ah, yes; the woman we brought in for questioning earlier.' The man identified himself as a plain-clothes detective. 'And who might you be?'

'I'm her sister, Lizzie Harrison.'

'Wait here.' The detective opened the door and

called to the desk sergeant. 'What's the latest on the Bailey woman?'

'Who wants to know?'

'Her sister's here.'

'Send her in. Tell her she can take her off our hands.'

'You hear that?' The detective strode on along a wide corridor with his coat flapping open then disappeared through a door at the far end.

Lizzie followed him inside. A well-lit reception area was dominated by a high desk manned by the sergeant. He put down his pen to pick up a telephone, dial a number then bark into it. 'Bailey's sister is here.' He didn't bother to look in Lizzie's direction, simply continued to write in a large ledger next to the phone.

The wait seemed endless. A wall clock ticked, the detective in the trench coat reappeared and muttered something to the desk sergeant. Both men continued to ignore Lizzie. Then, just as she was losing hope that Connie would be released as promised, a young constable escorted the prisoner down the corridor.

'She's all yours,' he told Lizzie, handing Connie a paper bag containing her watch and wedding ring.

Connie's trembling fingers let the bag drop and Lizzie darted forward to catch it.

The detective rested one arm along the top of the desk and paid attention at last. 'She's been charged and released without bail,' he informed Lizzie. 'We're not sure how much she's taken in, though.'

'Charged with what?' Lizzie had listened in amazement to her father's jumbled account of events. What did he mean, the police had arrested Connie? What for, for heaven's sake? But as soon as Bert had mentioned George Bachelor's name, Lizzie had feared the worst. Something to do with looting and then something else about black-market goods. Still it hadn't made sense. Then, late in the evening, an ARP messenger had knocked on the door of number 12, sent from Gladstone Square, telling them that Connie could come home.

'At last they've come to their senses.' Bert had grasped the words 'come home' and clung to them like a drowning man.

But Lizzie had warned him not to get his hopes up. 'Charged with what?' she repeated now to the heartless young detective, who stared at her and Connie with contempt.

'Dealing in stolen goods.' It was all in a day's work, as far as he was concerned. Motives and excuses didn't matter to him, even if the suspect didn't fit the usual mould. Making the charge stick was what counted. 'Make sure she reports to the desk sergeant every forty-eight hours. Oh, and tell her not to book any holidays to Blackpool or Margate in the near future.'

Lizzie took Connie by the elbow and steered her out of the building. She marched her quickly across the square. 'Is it true?' she demanded. 'Did George drag you into this?'

Connie's eyes were wide and unblinking as she let herself be pulled along. She tripped over a kerb and almost fell.

'How many times did I warn you not to have anything to do with him?' Lizzie was furious. 'That man is a spiv through and through. Any fool can see that.'

Connie steadied herself against a lamp post. 'He

221

must have known the police were on to him – that's why he's vanished.'

Worse and worse! 'Oh, Connie; what a mess!'

'I've been an idiot.' It was only when they put her in a cell and turned the key that she began to realize what she'd done. In her imagination the word F-O-O-L had flashed up in big capital letters on the painted brick walls. *Fool, fool, fool.* 'I didn't steal anything but I did know what there was in Mr Ward's cellar – George showed me.'

'When?'

'Yesterday.'

Lizzie groaned. 'And you didn't go straight to the police and report him? Why not? No, don't tell me. You still thought you could trick him into giving the game away.' A warden came on to the square to carry out his patrol, so Lizzie dragged Connie out of sight down a deserted side street. 'What if there is no game, Con? What if John's death was an accident, pure and simple?'

Connie had no answer. The last few hours had scrambled the facts and she no longer knew what to believe. 'How has Dad taken it?' she asked as they made their way cautiously down the pitch-black street.

Lizzie's anger hadn't cooled. 'How do you think he's taken it? The police have arrested his daughter. His world has been turned upside down.'

Connie had to lean against the nearest wall until the sickening sensation in the pit of her stomach subsided.

'I left him with Aunty Vera. She's promised to keep an eye on him for a few days.'

'Does everybody and his aunt know?'

'What do you think?' News such as this spread like wildfire. Lizzie insisted that Connie walk on with her.

'I'll get the sack – you watch; Penrose will be glad to get rid of me. And I'll have to resign from the ARP.' Brick by brick the life that she'd built since John's death crumbled to dust. They skirted around the back of the burnt-out swimming baths then emerged on to Elliot Street.

Lizzie offered no words of comfort. Connie had been charged. Their dad was yet to learn the worst.

What have I done? Connie's feet dragged along the pavement. *All for the sake of a husband who belittled and bullied me and didn't care in the least what I thought or felt. What have I done?* The thoughts ran through her head, over and over, as she crept into the house and closed the door behind her.

Days crawled by. Lizzie took the brunt of running the bakery business while her father recovered from the shock of Connie's arrest. Bert took a few days off from warden duties, urged by his sister to take it easy until the initial scandal had died down.

'You know what they say – today's news is tomorrow's fish-and-chip paper.' Vera stepped in at number 12, providing Bert, Lizzie and Connie with hearty meals that no one felt like eating, making beds and hanging out washing. She avoided the question of Connie's guilt, which was on everyone's minds, and outstared the nosy parkers huddled in their doorways, gossiping for all they were worth. 'Show me a single person who hasn't fiddled their food coupons once in a while,' she declared as she plumped up Bert's pillows and straightened his sheets.

Bert said nothing but he wasn't daft; he knew there was a big difference between altering stamps in ration books to wangle an extra bag of sugar and the serious crime of which Connie was accused. Those boxes of smuggled goods had come straight off the ships at St Stephen's dock and been whisked away by the cartload for goodness knows how long. Even now the police were crawling all over Anderson's yard, investigating how Bachelor had got away with it. Of the man himself there was still no sign.

Closeted in the bedroom that she shared with Lizzie, Connie remained numb with shock. She'd predicted rightly that she would lose her job at the Savoy: Pamela called at the house on Monday evening, bearing a letter from the manager. Lizzie answered her knock and Connie opened her bedroom door to listen to their conversation.

'I'm sorry – I didn't want to do this but I couldn't get out of it,' Pamela began as she handed over the letter. 'Mr Penrose said I must deliver it by hand.'

Lizzie invited her in. 'Do you know what's in the letter?'

Pamela lowered her voice to a whisper. 'Services no longer required . . . terminated forthwith . . .'

Connie didn't need to hear more. She retreated into her room and fatalistically took her ARP uniform from its hanger, folding it neatly and removing the silver lapel badge inscribed with the letters 'ARP' under a royal crown. The sooner the uniform went back to the depot and was reissued to a new volunteer the better. With a hollow feeling, she went to the window to watch Pamela cross the street to number 21. What must her new friend think of her now?

On Tuesday she left the house to fulfil the conditions of her bail at the police station. Lizzie had offered to take time off to go with her but Connie had said no; the shame belonged to her alone. So she endured the twitching curtains and tutting tongues, the cool stare of the desk sergeant – a different one this time – and a humiliating chance encounter with Kenneth Browning, who had crossed Gladstone Square to avoid speaking to her. Guilty until proven innocent was how most people viewed her.

Heart sore, Connie hid from view through Wednesday and Thursday. Lizzie's time was taken up with bakery work – the van was back in action and deliveries took until late afternoon. In the evenings she carried out her duties as an ambulance driver. On Thursday Bert finished baking then went back to work at the sector post, despite Vera's protests. So, after a surreptitious visit to the police station to fulfil her bail conditions, Connie was in the house alone when there was a knock at the door.

She stayed in her bedroom, thinking that if she didn't answer the caller would eventually go away. But the knocking went on and when she parted the net curtains to see who was there, she saw Tom staring up at her. She gasped and stepped back quickly.

Tom stooped to shout through the letter box: 'Connie, open the door.'

Still she hesitated.

'I'm not going anywhere until you do.'

So she went down, unbolted the door an inch and spoke through the crack. 'Go away, Tom – please.'

He caught a glimpse of her pale face then said the

first daft thing that came into his head. 'I take it our date at the Red Lion is off?'

Connie gave a wan smile then opened the door. 'You'd better come in.'

'How about a cup of tea instead?' He waited for her to show him into the kitchen. The worry of the past few days had certainly taken its toll: Connie's long, wavy hair was tamed by a plain headscarf and her face was drawn, her expression guarded.

'I hope you haven't come to gloat,' she said, as she ran water into the kettle.

'Far from it; I wanted to know how you were.' He sat at the table without waiting to be asked. 'I was worried about you.'

Connie kept her back turned. 'That's good of you, but there's no need.'

He waited for her to finish with the tea things. 'You don't need to pretend with me,' he told her as she sat down opposite. 'We're friends, aren't we?'

She sighed and looked down at her hands.

'I miss you down at the sector post,' he went on. 'The place isn't the same without you.'

'I won't be coming back – I've handed in my uniform.'

'That's a pity. The coppers are still looking for George, by the way. Apparently he has relatives in York so that's where they're concentrating their search. York is a big place, though.' He waited in vain for Connie to respond. 'He's the one everyone blames. We all know you got dragged in without realizing.'

'Who's everyone?' She wished that her hands would stop shaking and that she could bring herself to look Tom in the eye.

'Me and Bill, for a start. We're both sure you couldn't have known what you were getting involved in.'

'I did, though.' She shook her head vigorously and forced herself to meet his gaze. 'I agreed to help George get rid of the stuff. There, that's the truth.'

'Crikey.' Tom gave a low whistle. 'I wasn't expecting that.'

'I'm full of surprises,' Connie said bitterly. 'There's a lot you don't know about me.'

He frowned. 'Bachelor must have forced you into it. You can't have done it of your own accord.'

Tom's faith in her touched a raw nerve. Her eyes filled with tears and she wiped them away with the back of her hand.

'Here.' Tom handed her a clean handkerchief.

'I've been a fool,' Connie admitted. 'I played along with him for reasons that you wouldn't understand.'

'Try me.' Tom thought back to the moment of her arrest: the panic in her eyes as she'd slumped forward on the stool. 'I'm doing my best to understand but I never got why a girl like you would have anything to do with George Bachelor.' Tom waited calmly for an explanation.

'I wouldn't have in the ordinary way of things.' Dash it – Tom was a loyal friend and he deserved to hear her reasons. 'Only, I'd known for a while that my John had been part of George's crooked set-up and after he died there were loose ends . . .' Connie trailed off with a helpless sigh.

Tom thought through the implications of what she'd said. 'All right; I can see why you might have had to keep mum when John was alive, but why afterwards?'

'Because I needed the answer to a question. You see, I was never happy about the way John died. They said on the yard that it was a straightforward accident and there was no need to involve the police. But I knew that he and George were in the middle of a disagreement when it happened and, idiot that I was, I wanted to trick George into giving himself away.'

'How do you mean?'

'Keep this to yourself.' Connie closed her eyes and swallowed hard. 'I've never said this out loud to anyone before – not even to Lizzie. I began to think; what if the argument was so bad that George had decided he wanted rid of John? In other words, when John stormed off in a rage into the area where Keith Nelson was operating, George could have – *should* have – warned him about the danger but he didn't.'

Taking in the news, Tom reached across the table to place his hand over Connie's. 'All right, I get the picture, but you'd need proof.'

'What if George had told John a deliberate lie – something that made him dash headlong into the prohibited area?'

'Such as?'

'I don't know – maybe he let slip that there was a stash of whisky or rum hidden there, which proved that he was double-crossing John. It made John desperate to get his hands on it. Maybe Keith was in on it too. Maybe they both wanted John out of the way.'

Tom gave a low whistle of surprise. 'That's a lot of maybes.'

'Yes, but George is capable of planning such a thing – I'm sure of it.'

'So you knew you were playing with fire?'

'That's exactly what Lizzie tried to tell me.' Tears fell again as she thought of the misery she'd caused.

He grasped her hand more tightly. 'I wish you'd told me earlier.'

'Why? What good would it have done?'

'I just wish I'd known, that's all. Maybe I could've helped.'

Everything was blurred – Tom's hand clasping hers, his sunburned face and earnest expression.

If ever there was a time for him to tell her what he felt it was now. 'I've seen how you operate when we're out on patrol,' he said gently. 'It was your idea to go into the swimming baths the other night – you risked everything to save a man's life. That's you to a T; brave as anything when it comes to carrying out your duty.'

She brushed aside his praise. 'Lizzie warned me not to get involved with George,' she repeated. 'But did I listen? No, I just steamed ahead like the idiot that I am.'

Tom released her hand. 'What I'm seeing now isn't the Connie Bailey I know; you seem to be giving in without a fight. I bet you haven't even told them down at the nick what you've just told me.'

'What would be the point? The police aren't interested in my reasons for getting involved with George; all that matters to them is that they have a witness in number 7 who saw me going into Mr Ward's house with him.'

'Number 7? That's where Eric Thomson lives.'

'Yes, until he was arrested for beating his wife.' Connie's brain had been too befuddled to make anything of this fact until now.

'He's out on bail.' Tom had kept abreast of events. 'The WVS found Nancy and the two little girls a permanent place to live, out of harm's way. Eric's trial is due next month.'

'So he's their witness?'

'Yes, and he has an axe to grind.' It was the single pinprick of light that Tom had picked up on so far. 'That's important.'

His earnest desire to help touched her deeply. 'Why are you so keen to get me off the hook?' she asked through trembling lips.

'Because I care about you, Connie; I always have.' There; it was out in the open for her to accept or reject. 'Anyway, it's not too late.'

'How . . . I mean why?'

'The real culprit has gone to ground but we'll flush him out, I swear.'

'No, I mean: why do you care?'

Tom moved round to her side of the table and raised her to her feet. He held her by the waist and brushed his broad thumb against her cheek. 'How can you ask me that?'

Connie caught his hand and held it against her face, like catching a wisp of hope, a straw in the wind.

'You don't have to fight this alone any more,' he vowed steadfastly. 'I'll stand by you and I won't ever let you down.'

Pamela's week ended in a flurry of arrangements. Tonight, Friday, she had planned to meet Fred after work and walk home through the Leisure Gardens; tomorrow they would ramble on the moor along a route that he had worked out with his usual attention to detail – following the public footpath to Raynard's Folly then cutting back towards the coast in the direction of Raby, where they would again have tea with Pamela's parents, before setting off along the coast path for home. Sunday was to be a day of rest when Pamela hoped to meet up with Lizzie, to hear the latest about Connie's dire situation.

'Connie won't come out of her room,' a worried Lizzie had warned Pamela when they'd crossed paths earlier in the week. 'She's refusing to see anyone. But come to number 12 on Sunday afternoon and we'll see if we can prise her out.'

Which left Friday morning for Pamela to tidy her room then spend an hour stitching the hem of a new dress she'd made from a pattern borrowed from Connie the previous weekend. She'd almost finished when she ran out of blue cotton thread and had to slip on her coat for a quick trip to the College Road haberdashery. As she dashed downstairs she was waylaid in the hallway by Mr Fielding, who was sober for once and blocked her exit with his considerable bulk.

'Now then, Miss Carr. What do you have to say about Herr Hess flying to Scotland for talks with the Duke of Hamilton?' he said out of the blue. 'Rather a rum do, don't you think?'

Pamela admitted that she knew nothing about the matter.

Fielding tutted. 'We must keep up to date with the news. Hess is in prison now, where he belongs. Meanwhile, our boys in the Med have reached Egypt at last. Things are looking up; yes, indeed.'

Not wishing to be rude, Pamela listened patiently

to her fellow lodger's patriotic slant on the latest events. It seemed Fielding kept up with many details that had escaped her attention; he gave her facts and figures about Merchant Navy convoys in the Mediterranean carrying supplies to back up a British desert offensive – fifty-seven tanks had been lost after one ship had struck a mine but over two hundred tanks and more than forty Hurricane fighters had made it through.

Eventually she stopped him in mid-flow. 'I'm sorry, Mr Fielding – I really must dash.'

Still he didn't move. 'You only have to listen to the news to know that Fritz is on the run. That's right, isn't it, Mrs Mason?'

Thora emerged from the breakfast room, feather duster in hand. She ignored Fielding's question and bent down to pick up the morning's post from the mat. Pamela squeezed past them both then retrieved a slip of paper that the landlady had overlooked. The paper was roughly six inches square and a muddy footprint partially obscured two words scrawled with a blunt pencil. Pamela made out the name 'Fred Miller'.

'What's that?' Thora held out her hand imperiously.

Who would write to Fred on a dirty piece of crumpled paper? Pamela wondered. She turned the paper over. 'TRAITOR!' One word was written in rough block capitals. Three heavy underlinings. A black swastika daubed underneath. She gasped and let the paper flutter to the floor.

'"Traitor!"' Thora picked it up and read it out loud. She turned it over and then over again. 'Well, I never,' she muttered thoughtfully as she stuffed the note into her apron pocket.

CHAPTER FIFTEEN

'What can it mean?' Pamela had knocked on Connie's door and refused to go away until at last she'd gained entrance to number 12. 'Who would write such a thing?'

It only took a second for Connie to realize that Pamela was distraught – she was gasping for breath and struggling to frame a sentence. Connie pulled her over the threshold. 'Slow down. Tell me what's happened.'

'Someone pushed a note through our letter box – for Fred. His name was on it.' Not knowing what else to do, Pamela had run over the road in a panic, desperately hoping that Connie would be at home.

Connie sat her down at the kitchen table. 'Who wrote it? What did it say?'

'It wasn't signed.'

'Here; drink this.' Connie brought her a glass of water. No explanation would be forthcoming until Pamela had calmed down. 'There's no rush. Just take your time.'

'It can't be true,' Pamela wailed as she sipped the water. 'Fred would never . . . It doesn't make sense.'

Ah, so Fred Miller wasn't as squeaky clean as he

appeared. He probably had another sweetheart tucked away on the other side of town and an anonymous note had landed on the mat and revealed the truth to poor Pamela. Connie's train of thought careered down an all-too-familiar track.

'Mrs Mason put it in her pocket. Mr Fielding saw it too.'

'Never mind about that. Sad to say, men don't always tell us the truth, especially when we're first getting to know them. But are you sure the note is genuine?'

'I'm not sure of anything.' Pamela shook her head helplessly then stared up at the rack suspended from the ceiling, where Bert's shirts and Lizzie and Connie's underthings hung to dry. 'I was on my way out to buy a reel of cotton.'

'And then this happened.' It was true what they said about the course of true love, Connie thought. It was never smooth. 'Let's suppose for a minute that you do have a rival for Fred's affections and that this other girl is jealous and so she wrote him a note to confront him. There's nothing to say that Fred feels anything for her, is there?'

Frown lines appeared on Pamela's smooth forehead. 'It didn't look like a girl's handwriting,' she objected.

Connie paused. 'Perhaps it was written in haste. She's probably already sorry she wrote it.'

Pamela scarcely took in what Connie said. 'I wish Mrs Mason hadn't kept it; then I could show you and you could judge for yourself.'

'Yes; why would Thora hang on to it? Fred's love life is none of her business.'

'The note isn't about his love life.' Connie's mistake began to dawn on Pamela. 'It wasn't anything to do with that.'

'What, then?'

'Let me show you. Do you have pen and paper?'

'Yes – here in the drawer.' Connie separated writing material from a tangle of string and parcel tape. 'Will a pencil do?'

Pamela controlled the trembling in her right hand to write down the single shameful word in heavy capital letters. 'TRAITOR!' Then she pushed the paper across the table for Connie to read.

'Goodness me! Was that it? Wasn't there anything else?'

'Nothing – only Fred's name scrawled on the other side. Oh, and a drawing of a German swastika.'

'Oh dear, but Fred works for the Civil Defence,' Connie said with a worried grimace. 'He's in the control room, right at the heart of things, coordinating our response, helping to save lives.'

'Yes, so how can he be a traitor?'

Connie pictured the room where Fred worked. There would be a row of telephonists seated at keyboards; there would be clerks and messengers, liaison officers from the police and fire brigade, a wall covered in charts and maps. Fred's job following any raid would be to compile detailed reports to be sent to the Ministry of Home Security. But just suppose those reports were to go astray and fall into enemy hands. 'You're sure there was no signature?' she asked as doubts clouded her brain.

'Quite sure.'

'So the note is written by someone who wants to

scare or threaten Fred,' Connie concluded. 'It can't be intended to warn the authorities; otherwise this person would have gone straight to the controller at the town hall.'

'It was written on a piece of scrap paper. There was a muddy footprint.' Pamela agreed that there was nothing official about it. 'What do you think I ought to do?'

'Well, you can't bury your head in the sand and pretend it never happened,' Connie decided. 'Thora and Fielding know about it.'

'But it's not true.' Pamela stood up and paced the floor. 'Fred wouldn't betray anyone.'

Connie wasn't convinced. It had to be admitted that Fred's recent arrival in Kelthorpe was something of a mystery. He'd found lodgings on Elliot Street and a job at Anderson's yard but his previous history was entirely unknown. No one had thought it unusual – during wartime people moved around the country a good deal. 'When do you next see him?' she asked.

'Tonight – after work.'

'Then you must tackle the problem head-on. Ask Fred the straight question: who would make such an accusation? Does he have any enemies or something in his past that might build up to this?'

Slowly Pamela absorbed the advice. As she turned to face Connie she brushed against the laundry hanging from the rack. 'Fred will say no,' she declared. 'And that will be that.'

'Let's hope so.' Connie gave an unconvincing smile. Experience told her that rumours, false or true, often burned slowly underground before the air got to them and set them ablaze.

Taking a deep breath, Pamela promised Connie that she would do as she'd suggested. 'Tonight,' she repeated. 'It's only fair he should know.'

Connie saw her to the door with a sinking heart. She looked out at the piles of rubble and twisted iron that had once been the municipal baths. Troubles came thick and fast to the residents of Elliot Street – bombs fell and buildings collapsed, crimes were committed and treason suspected. And now bruise-black clouds and rain. A heavy shower soaked Pamela as she rushed across the street, bareheaded and without her coat. Rain poured from gutters and bounced off the pavement, ran in streams by the side of the road and down drains that couldn't cope. 'Looters will be shot!' Through the downpour Connie read a new notice that had been placed at the entrance to the ruined baths. Scrap metal had gone up in value and thieves would steal anything they could lay their hands on. She groaned then closed the door and went back up to her room.

One last visit to the Queen Alexandra – Lizzie's mind was made up. After she'd finished her bread deliveries and before her evening shift with the ambulance team, she would drive to the hospital to see Bill, who was on the mend and would soon be discharged.

She'd made the decision as she'd lain awake the previous night, listening to Connie tossing and turning in her bed. It was time to stop daydreaming about what might have been with Bill and face up to reality. Their father needed her more than ever and though Lizzie still hadn't quite forgiven Connie for the shame she'd brought crashing down on the family's heads, it was clear she was suffering badly for her misdeeds. Staring up at the ceiling, listening to the muffled footsteps of wardens on patrol in the street below, Lizzie's thoughts had turned to Bob.

They'd seen each other only twice since her visit to his Easby home. There had been no more arguments about her work with the Civil Defence and Bob had made no mention of enlisting. Instead, they'd jogged along nicely, catching a film at the Savoy on one occasion and meeting for a picnic on the headland on the other. There'd been a development at work, Bob had told her as they'd eaten fish paste sandwiches and gazed out to sea. Keith Nelson was to take over from George Bachelor as foreman of the timber yard and Mr Anderson had given Bob his old job back. 'My wage has gone up again,' a smiling Bob had told Lizzie. 'That means I can save more and find us somewhere nice to live – either here in Kelthorpe or near my mother in Easby. Which would you rather?'

'Here in town,' Lizzie had replied quickly. Easby was a dead-end sort of place where nothing of interest went on – it had no cinema, no park and only two pubs to its name.

'Though rents are cheaper in Easby,' Bob had pointed out.

'It would be harder for me to get to work.' She'd seen this as her trump card.

'Maybe you won't want to carry on working after we're married.' Bob had sidled up until their shoulders had touched and he'd put his arm around her waist. 'With any luck, there'll soon be a baby for you to look after.'

Lizzie had thought of her fiancé as she'd lain in bed: his face shining with optimism, doing canny sums in his head as to how much money they would need to get by on. He'd built his whole future around her so why did her heart sink at the idea of marriage and babies? Was it normal to get cold feet prior to the event? She'd pictured their wedding day; her in a short white dress because of clothing rations, carrying a modest bouquet of lily of the valley, Bob in his best dark suit; the pair of them standing in the arched doorway of St Joseph's church, arms linked, smiling for the camera.

The black-and-white image froze in her mind and remained with her as she went through the hospital doors and walked along the long corridor to Ward C. She would be friendly with Bill and tell him how well he was looking and how glad she was that he was getting better. She would give him little titbits of news from the outside world, including the fact that Bob was looking for a place for them to live after they were married. *Draw a clear line, leave Bill in no doubt.*

She went into the ward to find him fully dressed and standing by his bed.

'That's good timing.' His face lit up when he saw her. 'They say I'm fit enough to be discharged. How about a lift home?'

'That's marvellous. And yes, of course; the van's parked by the door.'

A nurse appeared with a form for Bill to sign. 'Don't let him do too much,' she advised Lizzie. 'No running around a football pitch or chucking a cricket ball for a while.'

'Don't worry – I'll keep an eye on him.' Lizzie blushed at the nurse's assumption as Bill fastened a canvas holdall then shook hands with the patient in the bed next to him. All her good intentions melted to nothing as she saw him grin at the embarrassing mistake.

'Let's go.' He whisked her through the door and hurried her down the corridor.

'Slow down. You heard what the nurse said.'

'What for? I feel fit as a fiddle.' To prove it he strode on towards the van. 'I'll be back at the first-aid post before you know it.'

Lizzie took his bag from him with a reproachful look. 'You may have the constitution of an ox but remember you almost died from that bullet. You're meant to take it easy.'

'Yes, miss.' He sat beside her and waited for her to start the engine. 'By the way, have I said a proper thank you?'

She thought he meant for the lift home. 'It's nothing – saves you having to telephone for a taxi.'

'No; I meant for visiting me in my hour of need – for everything. It means a lot.' He turned his head to look directly at her. 'Thank you doesn't really cover it,' he admitted. 'I've looked forward to seeing you more than I ought, considering.'

Lizzie held her breath. Her hand was on the ignition key and when Bill reached out to touch it she didn't pull away.

'I've had a lot of time to think while I was lying there. And I realized something important.'

Lizzie opened her mouth to speak but no words came out.

'It's about you and me.' Sitting beside her in the enclosed cab, he grew tongue-tied. 'Maybe I'm making a big mistake. If I am, tell me to shut up.'

'No – I'm listening.'

His voice softened. 'I know you're engaged and this shouldn't be happening . . . But it is and I want to get it out into the open and to hell with the consequences. You and me, Lizzie; I need to know where we stand. Because if you don't feel anything for me . . . well, I'll go away with my tail between my legs and never bother you again. But if you do – if you wanted to be more than friends – I'd like to know.'

Lizzie struggled to reply. Her conscience fought to be heard yet Bill's touch and the intensity of his gaze overwhelmed her. 'I feel the same as you,' she whispered.

'More than friends?' he repeated, closing his hand over hers.

She had no power to deny him. He was sitting next to her and he was strong and almost well again, drawing her to him in a way she couldn't resist. So she nodded.

'I thought so,' he murmured as he leaned over to kiss her.

Their lips met with the softest of touches before Lizzie gave herself up to his embrace.

The rain continued on and off for the rest of the day. In the evening a decent crowd flocked to the Savoy to see Errol Flynn in *Footsteps in the Dark* – a routine murder yarn involving stolen diamonds and muddle-headed policemen. Pamela hadn't seen it but she overheard lukewarm comments as customers trickled out on to the rain-soaked streets.

'Dull as ditchwater,' a woman grumbled on her way out.

'A waste of money,' another added.

Pamela was uneasy as she handed over the day's takings to Mr Penrose then methodically gathered her belongings. Fred would no doubt be waiting for her outside the cinema and what she had to tell him was bound to cast a dark cloud over their walk home through the park.

'Thank you, Miss Carr.' The manager's tone of voice conveyed impatience – not 'thank you' so much as 'get a move on, if you please'.

So she picked up her umbrella and hurried out. At first Fred was nowhere to be seen but then she spied a familiar figure walking across the road to meet her, his hat pulled down over his forehead and his hands thrust deep into the pockets of his raincoat. She stepped out from under the cinema awning. 'There you are!' she exclaimed.

'Yes, here I am.' Fred smiled briefly then offered Pamela his arm.

She invited him under her umbrella and they walked on together in silence. 'We're like cats.' Her brief comment was an attempt to break the ice.

'With nine lives?' he asked.

'No; because we've learned to see in the dark.' Not a single light showed through the blackout and there were no street lamps to light their way. Fred's failure to respond to her small joke pushed her on into another inane remark – anything to delay addressing the issue of the note. 'How are things at work?'

'Very good,' he replied with a preoccupied air. 'The new foreman seems to know what he's doing. I've brought the bookkeeping methods further up to date.'

'And how's Father?'

'Well. He reminded me about the invitation to tea.'

'I expect Mother told him to.' Pamela swerved to avoid a puddle, almost poking Fred in the eye with her umbrella.

He ducked his head then picked up his pace.

Pamela hurried to catch up. 'Is something wrong?' she queried as they entered the Leisure Gardens.

Fred steered her up the hill towards the covered colonnade. 'I'm not sure. Fielding was acting strangely, that's all.'

Her heart skipped a beat as she closed her umbrella. 'In what way?'

'Not drunk, for once. He was on the landing when I got home from work so I called hello as usual. Instead of replying, he disappeared into his room and slammed the door – I've no idea why.'

'I may have the answer.' Pamela kept her voice calm although her heart was racing. 'You see, Mr Fielding saw a note that was pushed through our letter box this morning. It came without an envelope and it was addressed to you.'

Fred bristled at the idea of Fielding reading his mail but he tried to make light of the incident. 'Was it a reminder about late library books, by any chance?'

'I'm afraid not.' Better to get this over with than prolong it further. 'Someone is making a serious accusation against you. They wrote the word "traitor" on the piece of paper and drew a swastika.'

'I see.' He stopped in his tracks and stared at the

ground. Rain dribbled miserably through leaks in the flat roof then dripped from the Virginia creeper just coming into leaf. 'Do we know who this someone might be?'

Pamela had expected a less guarded reaction. 'No, but it's ridiculous,' she protested angrily. 'It must have been written by someone with a grudge – I can't imagine who.'

'Just the one word – "traitor"?' he checked. 'Where is the note now?'

'Mrs Mason put it in her pocket. If she has any sense she'll light the fire with it.' Wishing for all the world that she hadn't had to be the bearer of bad news, she bit her lip and waited.

'She probably won't do that,' Fred said with the same composure. He seemed to be working out the answer to a knotty problem. 'She may sit on it for a while before deciding what to do. If she confronts me directly I'll deny it, naturally. But if she takes it to the police they'll be obliged to follow it up.'

'The police?' Pamela echoed with growing dread.

He set off again without replying and looking straight ahead. 'No need to worry,' he assured her finally. 'The worst they can do is to take me off the control-room rota until the matter is cleared up. But that's jumping several steps ahead. Mrs Mason might simply destroy the note, as you say.'

It struck her as odd that Fred hadn't shown any surprise when she broke the news.

He continued to think aloud. 'Fielding is a different matter, though. The fellow is extremely jingoistic; I'm afraid that any mention of treachery will have been like a red rag to a bull.'

Once more Pamela had to run to keep up. 'Why would anyone do this to you?' she demanded.

'As you say; someone with a grudge.' He strode out of the colonnade into the heavy rain. 'It will blow over soon enough.' There was a suitcase under his bed packed with a change of clothes, ready for just such an emergency. 'I'm afraid the weather forecast for tomorrow is for more rain,' he mentioned, stopping suddenly and turning towards her.

It was as if shutters had come down; his face was a blank under the dark brim of his trilby.

Prepare for all eventualities. Check the train timetables. Leave no trace. 'We'll have to call off our ramble and tea with your parents, I'm afraid.'

'How does it feel to be home?' Tom went straight from swabbing decks to visit Bill in his harbourside cottage, rolling his damp cap then stuffing it into his pocket before stepping out of heavy drizzle into Bill's front room without waiting to be invited.

'It feels champion.' Bill cast an uneasy glance around the harbour before closing the door. 'I've no complaints about my treatment – the doctors and nurses were smashing. But I was bored stiff lying in a bed all day long.'

Tom flopped into a fireside chair, stretched out his long legs and glanced around the room. Everything was shipshape; life aboard cramped fishing boats had taught Bill the value of keeping a place tidy. A polished brass oil lamp stood on the windowsill and the linen antimacassars on the backs of the two fireside chairs were crisply pressed. There was a bookcase in one corner where maps were stored next to a few novels by Nevil Shute; a row of plaster flying ducks adorned the wall opposite. 'Better bored stiff than dead as a doornail,' he commented wryly as Bill went to the window and peered through the net curtains. 'Count yourself lucky the docs could stitch you back together. What's up – are you expecting someone?'

'Not really.' Bill pointed Tom to a chair then sat down opposite, easing his shoulder with a circular motion before admitting that the chest wound gave him a twinge every now and then. 'I'll be glad when the stitches are out and I can get back to normal.'

The two friends chatted easily. Bill mentioned a nurse called Sally at the Queen Alexandra who had kept him on his toes – a real sergeant major. The patient in the bed next to him had a tumour in his stomach the size of an orange but he had never once complained. Tom, in turn, told Bill about the part Connie had played in rescuing the fire watcher from the swimming-baths roof. 'You should have seen her climbing that metal staircase with flames everywhere and stuff crashing down from the ceiling; that girl doesn't know the meaning of the word fear.'

Bill got up and twitched at the curtain again. It was raining more heavily now as thick clouds rolled in off the sea. 'Those two Harrison sisters are quite something,' he agreed.

'But now Connie's in a right fix,' Tom confided. 'She got mixed up with George Bachelor and was seen going into a house with him. The thing is—'

'There was a stash of stolen goods in the house.' Bill didn't let him finish. 'I know – Lizzie told me.'

'When?'

'Yesterday. She drove me home from the hospital. She was in a state about it, if you must know.'

'And you were a handy shoulder to cry on?' Tom could see how it might have been; Lizzie upset about her sister, Bill turning on the sympathy tap. 'I hope you didn't lead her on. You know she's—'

'Engaged to Bob Waterhouse; yes, I bloody well know. No need to rub it in.' Bill stopped fidgeting with the curtain and went to sit down again. 'Just because they're engaged doesn't mean she can't talk to me, does it?'

'Whoa!' Tom raised both hands in a gesture of surrender. 'Sorry I spoke.'

'Lizzie's a free agent. We work together. Anyway, no one's seen hide nor hair of Bachelor, I take it?' Thinking that he heard light, quick footsteps approaching, Bill jumped up and went back to the window.

'As a matter of fact, I've been doing a bit of digging on that front.' Tom paused and frowned. 'Why are you up and down like a jack-in-the-box? What's going on?'

'Nothing.' There was a knock at the door and Bill rushed to open it. Tom caught a glimpse of a slightly built woman in a blue jacket. When she closed her umbrella he saw that it was Lizzie.

Bill acted like a boy caught scrumping apples with nowhere to run to. 'You'd better come in,' he mumbled to the visitor.

Tom sprang to his feet. 'I'd best be off.'

Lizzie had shaken the wet umbrella and taken one step into the room when she saw that Bill had company. 'I can come back later,' she offered breathlessly.

'No, don't go – not on my account.' Tom pulled his

cap from his pocket and set it firmly on his head. 'I was just going.'

Bill ran a hand through his hair. 'Stay, both of you.' He drew Lizzie into the room and kept hold of her hand. 'I invited her.' He gave Tom a long stare, daring him to challenge him.

Lizzie's face burned. Guilt caught her in its snare.

'That's why Bill was twitching at that curtain,' Tom realized. 'He's an idiot. I'd have come back later if I'd known.'

'It's not his fault. I was ten minutes early,' she confessed.

Still holding her hand, Bill muttered in her ear, 'We could say that you're here on a Florence Nightingale mission – the lady with the lamp – but I don't think Tom would wear it.'

'Damn right, he wouldn't.' Tom took off his cap and slapped it against his thigh. 'Hang it all, you two – you know you'll set tongues wagging from here to Scarborough if you go on like this.'

Lizzie squirmed and freed herself. 'Don't tell anyone,' she pleaded.

'Anyway, it's nobody's bloody business.' Bill let Tom know that the subject was *verboten*. He'd invited Lizzie to the house so that they could talk things through in private. Yesterday's kiss had brought to the surface feelings that had bubbled unseen for both of them ever since he'd led the first-aid class at St Joseph's. But no plans had been made and they'd acknowledged that the road ahead would be bumpy. 'I won't rush you,' Bill had promised. 'We'll take it one step at a time.'

'I feel torn,' she'd admitted in her direct way. 'Like

248

I'm standing on the edge of a cliff, looking down at waves crashing on to rocks.'

'You can turn and walk away if you like.' He'd tried to be as honest with her as she'd been with him. 'I'm not saying I wouldn't be disappointed but it's clear you don't owe me anything.'

What did one kiss mean? The question had tormented Lizzie all night and all through the day. Lips had touched; that was all. She was still engaged to Bob and the threads of her life were woven into his. How could she bear to unravel them and watch the weft and warp fly apart? And yet she'd come to Bill's house and stood in his front room, pleading with Tom to keep their secret.

'Don't worry; my lips are sealed.' Tom decided to make light of the situation by adopting a flippant tone. He backed towards the door. 'I'll be off – three's a crowd, as they say.'

'Hang on – what were you going to say about Bachelor?' Bill reminded him. 'You told me you'd done some digging, remember?'

'Yes, I promised Connie I would. It's not fair that he's left her to face the music so I've asked around. I know a few people on the timber yard but they all swore they'd no idea where Bachelor was.'

Relieved to focus on something other than her own agonizing doubts, Lizzie listened intently.

'Except for one of the secretaries in the office, Betty Holroyd,' Tom continued. 'She's convinced that she saw him in a pub in York – the Three Feathers. She was visiting her sister there and they had a night out in the city centre. Apparently, Bachelor was propping up the bar with a couple of shady-looking customers.'

'When?' Lizzie was alert to every word.

'Tuesday this week.'

'Was Betty sure it was him?'

'Pretty sure. She only saw his back view and Bachelor was wearing an overcoat and a trilby. Then who should walk in and go straight up to Bachelor but Keith Nelson, the new foreman at Anderson's. That's when it clicked with Betty – it really was who she thought it was.'

'Did she tell the police?' Bill realized this could be a big step forward.

Tom shook his head. 'Betty said her job was on the line if she did. Keith's been top dog with Hugh Anderson since Bachelor vanished.'

'But there's nothing to stop us from having a word with Nelson,' Bill pointed out. 'There'd be no need to drag Betty's name into it.'

Tom nodded. 'I was thinking along those lines myself. Connie says it's possible that Bachelor and Nelson are in cahoots.'

Lizzie wasn't so sure. 'We don't want to make the same mistake as she did.'

'How do you mean?' Bill asked.

'Connie knew about George's black-market racket.' Tom stepped in with a quick explanation. 'John Bailey was part of it, too. She decided to tackle it herself and look where it's landed her – up to her neck in it.'

The conversation stalled as each thought through the implications. It was likely that Keith Nelson would deny having been at the Three Feathers if challenged. And what if Betty had been mistaken about the chap at the bar? The more they considered it the more flimsy the case seemed to be.

However, Tom was reluctant to let it go. 'Has anyone got a better idea?' he challenged.

'Why not let me tell Connie the latest?' Lizzie suggested. 'She's the one in the middle of this. She ought to have the final say.'

It was agreed; Connie would decide.

'Tell her I'll do whatever she wants.' Tom opened the door to let in the sounds and smells of the busy harbourside – rain splashing on to cobbles, waves lapping at the stone jetty, voices calling from boat to shore, the tang of salt in the air. 'I mean it,' he assured Lizzie as he stepped outside. 'I swear I'll get to the bottom of this if it's the last thing I do.'

CHAPTER SIXTEEN

A hundred and thirty pairs of gloves, seventeen bottles of hair lotion and two fur coats had been looted from a department store in Leeds. Connie sat in her room reading a report in the *Evening Post*. The crime had been committed by two Civil Defence wardens, who had each been sentenced to five years in prison. The judge had condemned their actions for bringing the service into disrepute. 'Your job is to uphold the rule of law and to maintain public morale, and yet you saw fit to raid these premises in the midst of a prolonged aerial bombardment, abandoning your posts and in the process undoing the excellent reputation of your fellow wardens. It was a night when many of your comrades reacted bravely to an unprecedented attack . . .'

Connie pushed the newspaper to one side in disgust. Hair lotion, for goodness' sake! A gloomy, rain-soaked day crawled to an end and she'd spent it trapped inside the house, weighed down by a sense of foreboding that had nothing to do with German bombs. Daylight was fading when she heard a routine cry of 'Put that light out!' from a warden on patrol in Elliot Street: a painful reminder of her lost role and reputation. Then the turn of a key in the front door told her that Lizzie was home.

'Connie, are you there?' Lizzie called from the bottom of the stairs.

She went down slowly to find the kettle already on the hob and two cups set out on the kitchen table. 'Where have you been?' she asked listlessly as Lizzie spooned tea into the pot.

Lizzie examined Connie closely. She was barefoot and dressed in a plain fawn cardigan and a black skirt, her hair scraped back from her forehead. 'How long is it since you looked in a mirror?'

'What's the point? I asked you where you'd been.'

'To Bill's house, if you must know. He's out of hospital. I bumped into Tom while I was there.'

Connie's face showed a spark of interest that quickly faded.

Lizzie's heart softened at the glimpse of her sister's old vitality. 'Tom believes in you.' She put a firm emphasis on the first word.

'Which is more than you do.' Connie sat down heavily and pressed her fingertips to her aching forehead. Nothing had been the same between her and Lizzie since her arrest. Though they shared a bedroom it was as if there was a wall between them, built of bricks of silence that grew higher each day to the point where it seemed insurmountable. Connie couldn't blame Lizzie for being furious in the beginning but she'd hoped for more understanding as time went by. Instead of which, the barrier stayed in place.

'I didn't say I didn't believe in you.' Lizzie pushed Connie's cup towards her. 'I know you were full of good intentions that blew up in your face without warning. I did try to warn you, though.'

'I got it wrong, I admit. But I had no idea what George had stashed away in Mr Ward's cellar when I went into that house. You do believe that, don't you?'

Lizzie nodded. 'It's not me you have to convince – it's the police.'

'How?' Connie sighed deeply. 'Eric Thomson is against me and he'll swear black is white to get his own back. I've got no one to back me up.'

'Yes you have; you've got me.' Lizzie's response was slow and deliberate as she sat down next to Connie. She acted on a realization that had come to her as she'd made her last deliveries of the day; the coolness between them had gone on long enough and it was up to her to make the first move. 'You can use me as a witness. I'll go to the station with you and I'll give a statement.'

The flicker of hope burst back into life. 'Saying what?'

'The truth – that you suspected George of playing a part in John's death and were doing your best to prove it.'

The flame died and Connie shook her head. 'It's no good, Lizzie – they'd say you were making it up.'

'All right, so we should leave it to Tom?' Exasperated, Lizzie got to her feet. 'Sit back and let the man in shining armour ride up on his white charger; is that what we want?'

The taunt drew a startled response. 'In what way?'

'George has been spotted in York,' Lizzie went on rapidly. 'It seems he met up with Keith Nelson. Tom wants to follow it up with Keith. I said we should include you in whatever we decide to do next.'

'Keith Nelson was driving the crane when John had his accident.' Connie was sure of her facts; they had been clearly stated at the inquest and she'd played out the scene a hundred times in her head. 'He claimed he only spotted John after it was too late; the crane had already released its load. But I was never sure that Keith was telling the truth and now this!'

'So what do you say? Do we sit back and leave everything to Tom?' Lizzie chose her words carefully, hoping to jolt Connie out of her present apathy.

'You talk about "we"?' Connie looked imploringly at Lizzie, hardly daring to hope. 'Does that mean you've forgiven me?'

Lizzie slid her arm along the back of Connie's chair and poured out her feelings in a flow of words that took Connie by surprise. 'You're my big sister. All my life I've looked up to you. Wherever you led, I followed. And when Mum died, you were the one who looked after me, making sure that I wore socks that matched, brushing and plaiting my hair and giving me the last piece of chocolate when I begged for it. And so, yes; you've made a big mistake and I was angry, but I've come to realize that there's no point in us fighting, that I might have done the same thing in your position and that we must stick together, whatever happens.'

Slowly absorbing Lizzie's words, Connie felt an enormous sense of relief. 'Shoulder to shoulder,' she murmured.

'You bet your life,' Lizzie replied. 'So, are we ready for action?'

'Yes.' Connie scraped back her chair. Lizzie's repeated use of the word 'we' galvanized her into action and she stood to meet her sister's challenge. 'Say thank you to Tom; but we can deal with this ourselves.'

A bolder, more confident girl would have reacted differently. Pamela imagined how Connie would have responded when Fred had called off their ramble. She would have made an alternative indoors arrangement – a visit to a tea shop or the town art gallery, perhaps. Connie wouldn't have let it slide as Pamela had done.

She had slept badly and woken with a niggling anxiety about the note. Why hadn't Fred shown any surprise – or any emotion at all, for that matter? The ugly accusation symbolized by the crude drawing of a swastika hadn't provoked the expected reaction; instead, he'd retreated into himself and pulled out of their walk across the moors and the get-together with her parents, leaving her dangling. Getting dressed and giving herself a determined shake, Pamela had made what she could of the day by taking books out of the library then paying her usual WVS visit to patients at the Queen Alexandra. Afterwards she'd dawdled around the open-air market in Gladstone Square and heard newspaper vendors bawl out head-lines about the latest allied action in Egypt. Then, feeling damp, dull and miserable, she'd trudged home to Elliot Street.

She heard the shouting as she walked past the entrance to the old baths.

'I'll have you arrested and carted off to the Isle of

Man!' Fielding roared. 'You hear me, Miller, Muller, whatever your name is? You're a danger to this country, a risk to national security!'

Pamela halted outside her door. It stood ajar and she could hear every word of the insults that Fielding flung.

'You know what they do to enemy aliens? They arrest you under orders from Mr Churchill, no less, and they stick you in front of a tribunal. Before you know it you'll be locked up behind a barbed-wire fence and going nowhere.'

'What's going on?' Pamela pushed at the door to find her way blocked by her landlady.

Thora raised a warning finger. 'There's been another note.'

'If it was up to me I'd put you in front of a firing squad.' Further along the corridor Fielding continued to rant and Fred stood silent and pale, dressed in shirtsleeves and without a tie. He didn't react to Pamela's arrival.

'Lord knows how you wormed your way into the Report and Control Centre,' Fielding spat at him. 'But I know your game and so does Mrs Mason.'

'What does the note say?' Pamela pleaded with Thora, who shook her head and put a finger to her lips.

Fielding brandished a piece of paper in Pamela's direction then pushed it under Fred's nose. 'What does it say?' he screeched. 'Your lady friend wants to know what it says. Shall I read it to her or will you?'

'Now, now, Mr Fielding, there's no need for that.' Thora stepped forward to wrest the note from his grasp. 'It's time to calm down.'

'Not until the beggar has admitted it.' Fielding's red-rimmed eyes and unfocused gaze said it all – his fury was fuelled by drink and wouldn't be easily dampened. He thrust his forefinger into Fred's chest and jabbed repeatedly. 'Go on, tell her the truth. You're a Nazi spy.'

Fred didn't retaliate. With a resigned look he simply took two steps backwards towards the stairs.

'Mr Churchill warns us about the likes of you; fifth columnists – that's what he calls you Austrians and Germans living over here, doing Jerry's dirty work. We're to be on our guard.'

Pamela slipped past her landlady and laid a hand on Fielding's shoulder. 'Now look here . . .'

He fended her off with his elbow and caught her in the ribs. Fred lunged at him, throwing him off balance so that Fielding crashed heavily against the newel post.

'Now, now,' Thora repeated. 'Less of that, gentlemen, please.'

Fielding pushed himself upright. 'You stay right where you are,' he slurred. 'You hear me, Miller? Don't move an inch!'

'Where are you off to?' Thora demanded as Fielding launched himself towards the front door.

'To the nearest telephone box, to dial 999.'

Thora stepped in front of him and blocked his way with her bulky frame. 'That won't be necessary, Mr Fielding. There may be no smoke without fire, and Mr Miller may well be one of these fifth columnists, but I don't want to set the whole street gossiping, do I? No; the best thing is for Mr Miller to quietly pack up his things and leave without any bother.'

Fred turned and was halfway up the stairs before Pamela caught up with him and tugged at his arm. 'What on earth . . . ?'

Pressing his lips together, he shook his head.

'It's the best way,' Thora insisted to Fielding. 'If he's got any sense he'll catch the next train out of Kelthorpe, and good riddance. That's right, isn't it, Mr Miller?'

'But why?' Pamela ran down to plead with Thora.

With a sigh and taking her time, Thora straightened out the crumpled piece of paper. Then she showed Pamela the name scrawled in the same handwriting as before: 'Friedrich Muller'.

Pamela snatched the note from her and turned it over: 'Hang all traitors!' And underneath the words the swastika had been replaced by a crude drawing of a hangman's noose.

Inside the warm cocoon of Bill's cottage it was as if the rest of the world had ceased to exist. Lizzie had come to visit him again and they sat in the armchairs to either side of the fireplace, quietly absorbing the fact that they had taken another small step forward.

'Does it still feel like you're teetering on the brink?' he asked.

'Not so much,' she admitted. 'The worst bit will be breaking off with Bob. I still have to work out the best time and place.'

Bill stretched out his hand and felt her grasp it. 'Blame me,' he urged. 'Tell him I made the first move.'

'But you didn't.' Lizzie had resolved to be completely honest when the time came. 'Tomorrow's Sunday. I can drive to Bob's house in the morning.'

259

'Are you sure?' Bill pictured Lizzie screwing up her courage for the leap into the unknown. He saw her riding the air currents like a white gull, steering her way to safety. And he would be waiting down on the shoreline, ready to begin their new journey together.

'Yes. I've known for a while that I didn't feel the way I did when Bob and I first met. I tried to tell myself that it was normal – once the early shine comes off, every couple settles into a routine that's not so exciting.'

'How old were you?'

'When we started courting? I was fifteen and he was sixteen. Bob already had his job at Anderson's and he seemed a real man of the world to me. You don't mind me talking about him?'

'Why should I? You can say anything you want; I just like listening to you and looking at you.' Her openness fascinated Bill. Many of the girls he'd known had kept secrets and flirted to get what they wanted – a small gift of a Whitby jet brooch that they'd spotted in a shop window obtained by simpering looks and wistful sighs, or else praise squeezed out of him by none-too-subtle hints – is this dress too plain or too tight or too long? Does my hair look better pinned up or left loose? Not Lizzie – she never fished for compliments. She just shone effortlessly like a star.

'This may sound hard-hearted, but Bob seems more like a big brother to me now,' she went on. 'I know he would always look after me and keep me safe if I married him but there's a fine line between that and him taking charge of my life and making all the decisions for me.'

'You want adventure before you settle down,' Bill guessed. 'You'd like to sail the seven seas.'

Lizzie smiled. 'Not while there's a war on and there are ambulances to be driven. And not until we've got Connie out of the mess she's in. She's feeling better, by the way. We're planning a visit to Anderson's yard after work on Monday to see if we can find out anything useful about Keith Nelson's links with George Bachelor.'

Bill took in the information without commenting. 'But would you, though? Would you leave Kelthorpe and go roaming?'

She pictured long journeys to distant lands, to see the Egyptian pyramids and the sun-baked hillsides of Ceylon, where women wore brilliant turquoise saris as they picked tea, and the sky and sea were always blue. 'With you, I would,' she confessed.

Bill raised her to her feet and put his arms around her. She was small and slender, light as a feather. 'One thing I've learned this past week,' he murmured with his lips against her sweet-smelling hair, 'is that life is precious and we don't know how much of it we've got left – which is why we shouldn't waste a moment.'

They should seize the day. Lizzie tilted her head back, dizzy with the novelty of looking into Bill's eyes and breathing him in, of thrilling to his embrace.

Pamela waited in her room with the door wide open.

From the floor below she heard her landlady's firm voice persuading Fielding to go along with her plan.

'Remember, we don't want the police knocking at our door, do we now?'

Fielding mumbled an incomprehensible reply.

'They might want to search the house. And what would they say to all those bottles of whisky hidden under your bed, I wonder? They'd ask to see your ration book for a start.'

'I've got nothing to hide,' he protested weakly.

'That's as may be.' Thora hustled him along the landing into his room. 'But believe me, Mr Fielding, we'll be far better off just giving Mr Miller his marching orders and that'll be that. So you stay in there and have an early night. I'll see you in the morning.'

Pamela heard a door shut then footsteps retreating down to the ground floor. She sat on her bed in her coat and hat, with her umbrella by her side. The second she heard the click of Fred's door she would be ready to act.

At last she heard the sound she was waiting for. She rushed out on to her small landing and looked down the stairwell in time to see Fred wearing his fawn raincoat and carrying his small brown suitcase down the stairs. She stayed where she was until he'd lifted the latch on the front door and left the house then she dashed after him.

She ran to catch up with him before he reached the end of Elliot Street. He was looking straight ahead, walking quickly, head down and with his face hidden by the brim of his hat.

'I don't believe them!' she exclaimed. 'And it isn't fair – after all, you've always looked out for Mr Fielding, regardless. He ought to be grateful.'

Fred turned the corner without slowing his pace or turning his head. Why must she make this more difficult than it already was? The only way to get through it was not to feel anything, not to look back at what might have been. And yet the sound of Pamela's desperate voice was almost enough to break his resolution.

'I won't let you go like this.' A car with hooded lights passed slowly, followed by a man on a pushbike. The cyclist cast a curious glance in their direction. 'I think too much about you.'

'Please stop,' he begged.

'No – you know that I'm in love with you.'

Fred stopped under a street lamp to plead with her. 'You mustn't say that now.'

There was scarcely enough light to see his features. 'It's true. I've never loved anyone before but I love you.' She grew calm and sure. Even if Fred left Kelthorpe and disappeared out of her life for good, she would at least have spoken from the heart.

'Pamela.' He spoke her name but couldn't go on, recalling how shy and unsure she'd looked when she'd first arrived at the boarding house, how anxious she'd been when she'd introduced him to her formidable mother and how she had no idea how adorable she was with her heart-shaped face, grey-green eyes and cupid, kissable lips. Memories were the real traitors, robbing him of his purpose. *Move on, don't talk of love, get clean away.*

Fred strode on down the hill towards the Leisure Gardens. There was a train leaving for York in an hour – the last one of the day. He would stay two nights in a cheap hotel, then on Monday he would have his pick of destinations – Manchester, Glasgow, Birmingham – any big city where he could melt into the crowd and start again. Fred Miller, skilled in all types of clerical work and an expert typist.

'At least tell me I'm not mistaken.' Pamela kept pace with him as they entered the park. 'You may not love me any more but you are still fond of me. Be truthful.'

'How would that make it better?' he demanded with an angry sigh. 'How can I mend something that can't be mended – tell me?'

'I would know how you feel. I would have my memories.' Nothing else – no photographs, no letters, no reasons. But memories of a first love were more precious than any of these.

'Then yes; I wasn't lying. I am fond of you. And if you want to remember me, think of what we talked about; the books we liked, the opinions we shared.'

'I'll treasure every moment.' The path curved towards the boating pond and took them past the bandstand. 'Who wrote the notes?' Time was running out – she felt she must know everything.

'I honestly don't know – perhaps one of the men at Anderson's.' It was a pure guess and in one way it scarcely mattered. 'It must be someone with a grudge who had access to personal information.' The impossibility of wiping the slate clean struck Fred with fresh force and the urge to confide in Pamela overcame his weakening resolution. 'The fact is my family name was originally Muller: that part is true.'

Pale clouds were reflected in the black water of the pond, driven by a wind that brought with it a light, misty rain. Mystified, Pamela slowed him down and guided him to the shelter of the bandstand. 'Muller is a German name.'

'Yes. My parents changed it to Miller when they first came to England. I was fourteen at the time.'

'You were born in Germany? But your English is perfect.'

'We lived in Berlin. My mother was English. My father was German – a diamond cutter by trade. They quickly realized that the Third Reich was not a safe place for a Jewish boy to grow up in and so my mother decided that we must all move to London, change our names and start again. Only it wasn't so easy, even here in England. Fielding is right about one thing – we were classed as aliens and it says so on our identity cards.'

'Your poor parents.' To flee from Hitler and seek refuge in a country that didn't welcome them; to be forced to conceal their history in a desperate attempt to fit in.

'What is not true is how they died. It was the week *before* Black Saturday when the jewellery shop was destroyed – not by the Luftwaffe but by a mob of Mosley's fascists. When his Blackshirt followers learned of our Jewish origins they shattered our windows with stones and bricks then set fire to the place. We were cowering upstairs, listening to the angry cries and the sound of glass shattering – Mother and Father trapped at the front of the building, me at the rear where there was a fire escape. The flames were too fierce – I couldn't reach them.'

His sorrowful revelation took away her breath. There were no words of comfort; nothing that could possibly soften the inhumanity of such an act.

Fred leaned wretchedly against the banister of the bandstand. 'My mother's name before she was married was Vanessa Shaw; she was the kindest, gentlest of women, from a well-to-do family here in Yorkshire, and the best mother a son could wish for. She met my father soon after the Great War – in Paris, where the victors were busy sharing out the spoils of war. The two of them fell in love, got married and settled in Berlin, my father's home city.' He stopped then gave a hollow laugh. 'Nowhere was really home for them once Hitler rose to power.'

The scale of Fred's tragedy – the persecution of his parents, their flight to England and their horrific deaths at the hands of a fascist mob – dwarfed anything that Pamela had suffered. 'Is that why you fled to Kelthorpe: because your mother was a Yorkshire woman?'

'Yes. I hoped to put down roots.' He laughed again – a grating sound swallowed by the blackness of the night. 'But the past has caught up with me once more and I must move on.'

'Why must you?' Pamela watched the defeated slope of his shoulders as he stepped down on to the wet grass. She let him walk a few paces before she ran to overtake him. 'Why not make a stand – stay here and find out who has done this to you? It's not right that this person, whoever he or she is, should drive you out when you haven't done anything wrong.' Even to her ears the words sounded impossibly naive, almost childish. 'All right; I know that rumours are often enough to ruin a reputation, but you could choose to stay and fight. You wouldn't be alone – I would help you.'

'And where would I live and how would I earn my living while I cleared my name?' Fred mustered some last shreds of patience to explain the hopelessness of what Pamela proposed. 'Before you know it my name will be on a blacklist with every landlord and employer in town. I'll have no roof over my head and no money coming in.'

'You'll have me,' Pamela cried. 'Together we could fight to clear your name. But if you leave now I'll never see you again.' The thought was like a sharp blade thrust into her heart.

'It's for the best.' Ice-cold certainty made him sound unfeeling as he walked on through the park. 'You'll forget about me soon enough.'

Suddenly, before she could protest, a warning siren split the air – on-off, on-off: the intermittent warbling sound of a yellow alert. Fred and Pamela instinctively broke into a run, out between the park gates and on to College Road, joining dozens of others heading for the underground shelter there. Pamela was jostled and pushed aside by a burly man carrying a duffel bag. She slipped on the wet pavement and was pulled to her feet by Fred, who held on to her as others rushed by – a woman dragging along two small children, a young man in army uniform – urged to hurry by the warden stationed at the entrance to the shelter.

Searchlights were switched on. The siren continued to blare.

'Are you hurt?' Fred checked with Pamela.

She tested her weight on her left ankle then shook her head.

Beams from the searchlights raked the sky. Tom was the warden on duty at the sandbagged entrance, taking names and adding them to his list. A messenger sped up on his bike, mounting the pavement and weaving through the crowd to report to Tom that at least twenty German planes had been spotted on the report-centre radar.

Tom ushered the woman with the children down the stone steps as the yellow warning siren changed to continuous red. 'The steps are slippery,' he warned. 'Watch how you go.'

The man with the duffel bag refused at first to give his name and address. People behind yelled at him to get a move on. 'Henry ... Pitman, 15 Maypole Street.' The man plucked the information out of the air. The raid had caught him red-handed: he'd been with a woman who wasn't his wife and he needed to cover his tracks.

Tom made a note and allowed him to enter. Fred stood with Pamela until they reached the front of the queue while a second warden marched along the street, sounding his rattle loud enough to wake the dead.

Then the roar of mighty engines and a burst of anti-aircraft guns drowned out siren and rattle alike. The first incendiaries fell like fireflies on to the headland.

'Pamela Carr, 21 Elliot Street.' Gripping Fred's hand, she reminded Tom of her details.

'Thank you, Pamela – now hurry along.'

Without warning Fred prised his hand free. He swiftly turned and pushed his way through the crowd that had formed behind them.

A high explosive landed nearby, tearing a hole in the road, shattering a water main and creating a fountain whose cold spray drenched the shelter entrance.

Pamela was pushed from behind, down the stairs into a tiled area that split into two – one sign read

'Gentlemen', the other 'Ladies'. She tried to resist the crush by pressing herself against the wall. Breathless with fear, she looked back up the steps and called Fred's name.

'Fred!' He picked out her high, desperate voice through the rush of splashing water. More planes approached. He broke free of the crowd, wading through the stream to reach the end of the street. He turned the corner into the town square. At that moment the library took a direct hit. The roof caved in and then the walls and lastly the entrance, its pillars toppling like matchsticks. *Fred, come back!* Pamela's plea stayed with him as he walked on past the burning ruins, not once looking over his shoulder; on into chaos.

CHAPTER SEVENTEEN

A wind shook a cloud of white petals from the blossom trees as Lizzie drove to Easby. They drifted to the ground, mournful reminders of confetti sprinkled by well-wishers at the wedding she and Bob would never have.

This would be the cruellest, hardest thing she would ever have to do. *Bob doesn't deserve it*, she repeated over and over as she approached the square church tower at the top of the hill then slowly made her way down the main street. *I'm a terrible person; selfish through and through, seeking my own happiness at his expense.* Her mouth was dry and her hands gripped the steering wheel. She was within seconds of turning the van around and driving back to Kelthorpe, but as luck would have it Kathleen was on her way home from church and she flagged Lizzie down.

'Thanks, love – this saves me having to walk on my bad ankle. It's still giving me trouble every now and then.' Bob's mother sighed as she settled into the passenger seat. 'Bob didn't say you were coming. If he had I'd have baked scones.'

'He doesn't know,' Lizzie said quietly. She pressed the clutch and moved down a gear.

Kathleen noticed that Lizzie wasn't wearing her ring. 'Have you two had another barney? Bob's not still going on about joining the navy, is he?'

Lizzie shook her head.

'So what's it about this time?'

'I'd rather not say.' The street seemed narrower and more winding than ever, with glimpses of the steel-grey sea between the houses and clouds hanging low over the horizon.

'Then I'll mind my own business.' A resolute Kathleen clutched her handbag and stared straight ahead.

Lizzie parked the van at the entrance to the alleyway leading into the courtyard where Bob and Kathleen lived. Kathleen invented an excuse and told Lizzie to go on without her. 'The vicar's asked me to deliver today's collection money to the church warden,' she explained.

So Lizzie walked alone down the narrow alley then across the shadowed yard. Bob's door was ajar, the cat sat on the doorstep – all was as she'd known it. And all was about to be transformed.

Bob appeared in the doorway, dressed in dark trousers and a matching waistcoat. His shirtsleeves were rolled to the elbow and his hair was uncombed. He waited for Lizzie to approach, one hand in his trouser pocket, leaning a shoulder against the door jamb.

She hesitated. Something in his attitude told her that he'd already guessed why she'd come. 'Can we go inside?' she asked.

Bob stepped aside. He followed her into the front room, where she stood with her back to the fireplace. 'Don't!' he said abruptly before she could open her mouth.

'Don't what?'

'Say anything. I don't want to hear it.'

'Bob, please!' Lizzie felt as if her legs were about to give way.

He pulled out his packet of cigarettes then thought better of it and cast it to one side. The packet skittered across the mantelpiece then fell to the floor. 'I know why you're here, Lizzie. I'm not stupid. You want us to break off.'

'It's for the best.'

'Best for who?' Spitting out the bitter words, he strode to the window and turned his back. 'I don't understand – what have I done wrong?'

'You haven't done anything wrong. It's me; I just don't feel the same as I did.' The phrases fell lamely from her lips.

'This is Connie's doing, isn't it?'

The needle was stuck in the same old groove. Lizzie flicked the suggestion aside. 'It's me, not Connie.'

'So what made you change your mind all of a sudden?' She'd said yes to marrying him, for Christ's sake. She couldn't just back out for no good reason.

'I've changed.'

'Changed – how? It's the bloody volunteering; that's what's done it. Until then we were fine.'

'No; I just see things differently. I'm not ready to settle down.'

'Right.' Bob clenched his jaw and stooped to pick up the cigarettes. 'That's the first I've heard of it.'

'Own up, Bob – you must have realized we were drifting apart.'

'No,' he insisted, in a deliberate attempt to make this as bloody hard as possible for her. 'This is a bombshell, as far as I'm concerned.' He lit a cigarette and inhaled deeply.

Lizzie's heart was wrung dry. 'I'm sorry. I really am.'

No wedding, no house, no babies. Sorry just wasn't enough. 'I know what's brought this on.' He narrowed his eyes and blew smoke down his nose. 'Or should I say *who*? Don't tell me – let me guess. His initials wouldn't be B. E., by any chance?'

Lizzie reached for the mantelpiece to steady herself. She stayed silent.

'You don't deny it? Bill Evans is standing by, ready to hop into my shoes – it's true, isn't it?'

Lizzie nodded slowly. She'd promised herself that she would not lie. 'But it would have happened anyway. I'm just not ready to get married.'

'Not to me, anyway.' Anger burned through the hurt. 'That's what you're saying: that you don't love me but you do love him. Don't treat me like an idiot; at least do me that favour.' Bill Evans with his fancy, fast motorbike and his ever-ready smile was the culprit here. Bob had been right not to trust him. He'd never liked him, not even when they were at school and Bill had been captain of the cricket team, lording it over the smaller, skinnier kids. 'I'll knock his bloody brains out,' he threatened.

'It's my choice, my decision,' Lizzie insisted. 'No one else's.'

'And that's it, is it?' How many years was it? Seven years of their lives thrown away in a second, smashed to smithereens, blown up in his face.

'Please don't hate me.' Lizzie drew a small blue box containing her engagement ring from her pocket.

She placed it in the centre of the mantelpiece. There was nothing else to say.

But as she moved towards the door, the cat glided into the room, soon followed by Kathleen, who moved close to the window where Bob still stood. She understood everything in a flash – it was written on Bob's glowering expression, veiled by a cloud of blue smoke, and on Lizzie's deathly pale face.

'You make yourself scarce – he'll be all right,' she promised Lizzie quietly and calmly.

Bob stubbed out his cigarette. *Bloody Bill Evans, the hero – getting shot in the chest as he saved Lizzie's life*. There was not a cat in hell's chance of competing with that.

'You go,' Kathleen insisted to Lizzie. 'I'll look after him.'

So a grateful Lizzie slipped from the house and out of Bob's life for ever.

'Where's your sister?' Bert came downstairs to find Connie cooking him a breakfast of bacon and egg.

'She's gone to Easby to see Bob.' Connie didn't provide a reason, though she knew it well enough.

'I wanted to ask her if she knew where my blue socks were.' Bert cast a vague eye down at his bare feet and then around the kitchen as if the socks were hiding from him.

'They're in your top drawer. I put them there myself.'

He shuffled off then reappeared complete with socks and slippers. The last week seemed to have aged him – his shoulders were stooped and his face was thinner. He still couldn't look Connie in the eye.

She put his plate on the table with a pronounced

flourish. 'Breakfast is served.' If only he would glance at her – just offer the briefest sign – the slightest hope that he, like Lizzie, might one day forgive her. But no; nothing.

Bert ate slowly. 'Vera tells me that Lizzie's been visiting young Bill Evans.'

Connie gave a small start.

'Don't stand there gawping. Kelthorpe's a small town.'

'What did Aunty Vera say, exactly?'

'Just that. Do you know owt about it?'

'Yes, but you'd better ask Lizzie to her face.'

'I never thought Bob was right for her.' Bert astounded Connie for a second time. 'But I hope she doesn't string him along for too long – that wouldn't be fair.'

Connie added a slice of fried bread to his plate. This was the first conversation she and her father had entered into all week and she was determined to push on. 'Lizzie knows that. But listen, Dad; has Aunty Vera said anything about me and my predicament?'

Bert sighed and tried to push his plate away but Connie pushed it back. 'Waste not, want not,' she insisted. 'Well, has she?'

'Vera hasn't broached the subject and neither has anyone else; not in my hearing. Anyway, what's it matter what anyone else thinks? It's my opinion that counts.'

'Well?' Connie sat down next to him, her stomach tightening as she waited for the verdict that mattered most.

'I think that you're sorry you let us down,' Bert said without looking up.

275

'I am, Dad – believe me.'

'I'm disappointed in you, I can't deny it.'

Connie's cheeks flamed. If only he would be angry instead. She could cope better with that.

'I want to know why you did it.' All week he'd failed to understand why Connie had fallen in with Bachelor in the first place. 'Why?'

'It's complicated. But I never looted anything, Dad – I swear I wouldn't do that. And I hope to prove it.'

He turned his head to look at her. 'Good,' he said. 'What about the stuff in the cellar?'

'That's the complicated part,' she admitted. 'All I can say is that I was hoping to prove that there's a connection between George's smuggling and John's death. I believe that George knows more about it than he let on at the inquest.'

Bert took his time to think this one through. 'So you took him on at his own nasty game and came unstuck?'

'Yes.' Thank goodness; her father had stripped it back to the bare bones. Connie could have thrown her arms around his neck and wept.

'You rushed at things like a bull in a china shop, as usual,' Bert continued. 'Always in a hurry – dashing up the aisle with a man who was nowhere near good enough for you; decent-looking but never someone you could rely on.'

'Good grief!' It hit Connie like a ton of bricks that her father had known this all along. 'Why on earth didn't you say something? No, don't answer that – you sat tight and hoped I'd find out for myself before it was too late.'

'Aye and you'd never have listened anyway. And that's partly my fault for bringing you up the way I did, without your mother's steadying hand. I always egged you on to do anything you set your mind to and not to let anyone stand in your way.'

She recaptured a clear memory of him standing waist-deep in the swimming-pool water, arms spread wide, looking up at her and crying, 'That's it, Con; head first. Ready, steady, dive!'

'That was my mistake,' Bert admitted. 'I ought to have taught you that sometimes it pays to think twice.'

'Like Lizzie – she usually looks before she leaps,' Connie pointed out.

'Yes, you're different in that way.'

'So how can it be your fault? You treated us both the same. It's how we're born that counts.'

'Maybe.' He set down his knife and fork and rested his elbows on the table. 'So, what now?'

'So we can hope that the police track George down and get the truth out of him – that I didn't do any looting and that I hadn't actually touched any of the smuggled goods.'

'There's fat chance of that,' Bert muttered. 'What else?'

'Lizzie and I think that Keith Nelson, the new foreman at Anderson's, is an easier nut to crack. He might tell us more.'

Bert frowned. 'And who'll do the cracking – not you, I hope?'

'Not by myself,' she promised. 'As I say, Lizzie will help me and Tom Rose is standing by.'

Bert gave a satisfied nod. 'Tom knows what he's doing,' he concluded.

'I know he does, Dad.' Smiling at her father's under-stated seal of approval, Connie took his plate to the sink and rinsed it under the tap. 'Tom is one in a million. And thank goodness he's on my side.'

Still in a daze after losing Fred and spending the night in the College Road shelter, Pamela had emerged as dawn broke and returned to Elliot Street, where she'd holed up in her room and wept non-stop. She'd lain on her bed fully clothed, muffling the sound of her crying by pressing her face into the pillow, and had stayed there all morning. There'd been a knock on her door that she'd refused to answer followed by a conversation between Mrs Mason and Mr Fielding on the landing below.

'She's in there but she won't open up.' Thora hadn't bothered to lower her voice.

'She's as bad as him, if you ask me.' Fielding had stomped up and down the narrow corridor. 'You can bet your life she knew what Muller was up to.'

Pamela had pulled the pillow over her head to block them out. It had been midday before she'd emerged from under the bedclothes, hollow from hunger and despair. Why had Fred abandoned her? If he'd gone into the shelter with her they would have talked through the night, working out a way to prove his innocence. *He's no traitor!* This is what she would have said to anyone who challenged her. *Leave him alone. He's a good, kind, honest man who's been through a lot worse than you or me.*

Instead, he'd wrenched his hand free and vanished. She'd struggled back up the stone steps, only to be told by Tom that she must stay underground. The street had been flooded; incendiaries had lit up the sky. 'Go back down!' Tom had blocked her exit. A thunderous explosion from the direction of the town square had almost split her eardrums.

Fred hadn't cared if he lived or died. He'd chosen to walk away.

Sobbing quietly, Pamela had put on her coat then crept downstairs. Thora had intercepted her in the hallway. 'You're wrong – Fred Miller isn't a traitor!' Pamela had shouted without waiting for a reply. Having slammed the door, she'd stood for a while wondering what to do and where to go until a taxi had dropped off a passenger at the corner of Maypole Street and she'd flagged the driver down. 'Take me to Raby, please.' The words had spilled from her lips without forethought. 'Number 32 Valley Mount.' Raby and Aunty Lilian – a safe haven.

'That'll be one shilling and threepence,' the driver told her when they reached their destination.

Lilian rushed down the path as Pamela fumbled in her purse. She helped her out of the taxi then bundled her into the house.

Harold came down the stairs, full of concern. 'What's up? What's going on?'

'I have no idea. Look at her – she's been crying her eyes out.' Lilian led Pamela into the front room, where she sat her down on the settee.

What could have upset his daughter to this extent? Harold's mind flew over the possibilities: from lovers' tiff to the ultimate tragedy of Fred having lost his life in last night's air raid. He looked helplessly at Lilian.

'Don't just stand there,' his sister told him, 'make the girl a cup of tea.'

As if tea solved everything! Still, Harold did as he was bidden.

Lilian sat beside Pamela and stroked strands of damp hair from her cheek. 'Can you tell us what's going on?'

'Fred.' Unable to raise her voice above a whisper and feeling the tears well up once more, Pamela fell silent.

'Well?' Lilian prompted gently.

'They said terrible things about him,' Pamela murmured through dry sobs. 'There were notes . . .'

'There, there. What kind of notes?' Lilian stroked her hair.

'They found out he wasn't born in England.' Pamela's explanation was dragged out one slow word at a time.

'Is that so?' Lilian looked up in alarm as Edith came in from the back garden, wearing an apron and carrying secateurs. Not a hair was out of place and her face was rouged and powdered, ready to face any eventuality.

'They say he's a traitor but he isn't.' Pamela twisted the handkerchief that Lilian had given her.

'Of course he isn't.' Edith put down the secateurs with a no-nonsense rap. 'What a ridiculous thing to say. Fred Miller is no more a traitor to this country than I am. Move out of the way, Lilian. Let my talk to my daughter.'

Pamela braced herself for sharp barbs of criticism as she felt her mother take her aunt's place on the settee.

'Look at me.' Edith tilted Pamela's chin upwards. She spoke firmly but with genuine concern. 'Where is Fred now?'

'I don't know. He was supposed to come into the shelter with me but he didn't.'

'Why not?'

'Because his past has caught up with him – that's how he put it. Because he's half German.'

'Of course he is.' Edith's fingertips brushed Pamela's cheek. 'His family fled from the Nazis. I know all about it.'

Lilian retreated to the kitchen. 'Blow me!' she breathed to Harold, otherwise speechless as she arranged teacups on a tray.

'*How* do you know?' Back in the front room, with early-afternoon sunlight streaming through the window, Pamela's eyes grew wide with astonishment.

'I talked to your Uncle Hugh, remember. He told me that Fred's employment record is clearly stamped with the words "Enemy Alien". It was discussed at his interview for the clerk's job. Given his family background, Fred was deemed a Category C, which means no risk to national security. Hugh liked Fred's honesty and gave him the job.'

'When did you find out?' Pamela drew a deep breath.

'Before you two came here to tea. I like to be prepared.' Edith recalled how her nerves had almost got the better of her as usual. 'I wasn't feeling at all well that day but I was intrigued. In the event, I was glad I'd made the effort. I saw in a second that you were head over heels in love with him.'

'I was. I am.' Pamela's sorrowful sigh filled the small room.

Edith squeezed her hand. 'Believe it or not, I remember how that feels.' From the kitchen she heard the light tinkle of teaspoons being set in saucers.

'And now he's gone and I don't know where to.'

'But listen to this.' A practical plan had occurred to Edith and she explained carefully to a distraught Pamela. 'Fred will have to ask Hugh for his employment record when he applies for another job. There will be a forwarding address.'

Pamela grasped at the straw. 'That's right; there will.'

'We may have to be patient,' Edith warned. 'It might not happen straight away.'

Or at all. Pamela couldn't dismiss the deep dread that Fred hadn't survived last night's raid. But she held her chin up and clung on to the faint hope that her mother offered. 'You're certain that Uncle Hugh will be willing to show us the new contact address?'

'You mean: please stay in his good books for your sake?' Edith gave a tight smile. 'Don't worry on that score; it's the Treaty of Versailles written anew.'

'You two really have made up?'

Edith straightened the creases in her apron then patted Pamela's knee. 'To the extent that he's offered your father and me permanent use of the annexe at Sunrise. Of course, there's no sea view but beggars can't be choosers. We intend to move in as soon as we can.'

'Connie didn't say outright that we couldn't.' Tom sat with Bill on a bench overlooking the harbour. There was an idle, Sunday feel about the place; no market bustle or the call of weary trawlermen, only the lapping of waves against the jetty and the strut of large grey gulls with orange feet and razor-sharp bills across the otherwise deserted cobbles.

Bill was dubious about Tom's latest proposal. 'But did she say that we could?'

'Could what?' Lizzie had cycled from Elliot Street and arrived unannounced. Fresh air had helped ease the burden of her morning's tête-à-tête with Bob and she no longer felt that she was the worst woman in all of England. In fact, she was eager to tell Bill that the deed was done. However, Tom's presence would force her to save the news until later.

'Pay Eric Thomson a visit,' Tom explained. 'She's stopped me from having a word with Keith Nelson but nothing was said about the Thomson chap.'

'Sit down – there's room for a little one.' Bill made space for Lizzie at the end of the bench. 'What do you say to Tom's latest plan?'

'I'm not sure. Do either of you know Eric Thomson?'

'Not as such.' Thomson was a well-known figure around the town's public houses. He was a sullen lone drinker who would sit for hours at the bar without saying a word, only returning home to Tennyson Street when the landlord called time. 'He calls in at The Anchor most Fridays,' Bill added.

'He's the only witness in Connie's case,' Tom pointed out. 'He'll take the oath and swear blind that he saw her going into the Wards' place with Bachelor.'

Lizzie frowned uneasily. 'I hear that he's a brute.'

'And a liar.' Tom let his exasperation show. 'I swore I'd help Connie to get out of this fix. If you two can suggest a better idea than getting Thomson to change his story, I'd like to hear it.'

'It's too risky,' Bill decided after glancing at Lizzie's worried expression.

'It is,' she agreed. 'And anyway, that part is true.'

Tom stood up then strode to the water's edge. 'We're getting nowhere. The coppers are no nearer to finding George and you're living in cloud cuckoo land if you and Connie expect to get anything useful out of Keith Nelson. Put yourself in his shoes – if you'd been in touch with George would you admit it to Connie of all people? I damn well wouldn't.' Shaking his head angrily, he took his cap from his jacket pocket and rammed it on his head.

'Hang on; where are you off to?' Forgetting his injury, Bill stood up too quickly and felt a stabbing pain in his chest. He winced and sat down again.

It was up to Lizzie to calm Tom down. 'Think,' she pleaded. 'We have to make the police investigate it properly – tell them Connie was the one who rescued Thomson's wife and daughters after he'd locked them in the house during an air raid. That's bound to make him an unreliable witness.'

'That makes sense,' Tom admitted. 'But doing nothing feels wrong.' He felt as if he was fighting with his hands tied behind his back.

'Then why not do *something*?' Lizzie had left Connie at a loose end. Their dad was out for the afternoon, helping Vera plant peas in her allotment. 'Connie's stuck at home on her own, twiddling her thumbs.'

Clever! Bill admired the way Lizzie had steered Tom away from the brink of hasty action.

'She'd be glad to see you, I'm sure.'

'Right you are.' No sooner said than Tom squared his shoulders and hurried off along the quay.

Bill opened the door to his cottage and invited her in. *I love you, Lizzie Harrison!*

She brushed against him as she stepped inside. *I love you too.*

Neither needed to speak – it shone out of their eyes like sunlight.

CHAPTER EIGHTEEN

Connie answered the door to Tom with freshly washed hair and a face free of make-up. She invited him into the front room with apologies about the mess – jade-green fabric was draped across a chair and paper pattern pieces were scattered across the floor. The sewing machine was set up in the alcove next to the fireplace. 'To what do I owe the pleasure?'

'Do I need a reason to be here?' He looked around for somewhere to sit and, not finding a free seat, stood awkwardly in the middle of the room.

She swept the fabric from the chair and plumped up the cushion for him. 'One of these days you'll visit me and the place will be spick and span,' she promised.

Tom picked his way between the pattern pieces and sat down. 'Lizzie mentioned you were at home.'

'Did she now?' Connie tucked her blouse into the waistband of her trousers then checked her hair in the mirror above the mantelpiece. 'Where did you run into her? Was it at Bill's house, by any chance?'

'It was close by,' Tom admitted.

She raised her finely arched eyebrows and he returned the look with a brief, non-committal toss of his head.

'I'm saying nothing – it's none of my business.'

'Lizzie broke off with Bob earlier today.' Connie picked up a pair of scissors and a tape measure from the rug. 'I expect she wanted to let Bill know.'

Retrieving a packet of sewing pins from under his thigh, Tom handed them to her.

'Oh, Lord – I hope they didn't skewer you.' She put the pins on the shelf above the machine.

He laughed. 'No harm done.' Connie's movements fascinated him – she stooped and stretched, gathered and turned with unselfconscious grace. He could sit and look at her all day if she would let him. 'It was a rough old night last night,' he reported. 'I was stationed outside the College Road shelter when all hell broke loose.'

'Worse than usual?' For Connie, stuck at home during the raid, the night had been a unique kind of torment. She'd longed to be on patrol, in the thick of things and lending a hand wherever she was needed. Instead, she'd been confined to the cellar, pacing the floor out of frustration and listening helplessly to muffled explosions.

'I'd say so. The library and the railway station copped it this time. There were a couple of near misses at the hospital as well. Oh, and I had to stop Pamela Carr from chasing after the new clerk at Anderson's – what's his name?'

'Fred Miller.'

'That's him. He turned tail and bolted instead of following her into the shelter. She cried her eyes out, poor girl.'

'Fred is her first sweetheart.' Connie parted the net curtains and looked out of the window for signs of life at number 21. The blackout blind was still pulled down at a first-floor window and the front door was firmly shut. Later she would make time to walk across the street to find out more. 'I had high hopes for them.'

Tom came and stood beside her. 'Have you been doing a spot of matchmaking?'

Connie shrugged. It occurred to her, not for the first time, that Tom was like an oak tree: sturdy and strong, able to withstand any kind of rough weather. Standing next to him was like sheltering under one of its branches until the storm had passed.

'It must run in the family – remember; it was your sister who sent me here.'

'Wouldn't you have come of your own accord?' she asked teasingly.

'You know me – I sometimes need a nudge.'

'This kind of a nudge?' Impulsively she put her arms around his neck. 'Or this?' The kiss was soft and inviting.

Tom kissed her back. He marvelled at everything: the scent of Connie's shampoo, her smooth skin, the weight of her arms on his shoulders. How long had he wanted this? How many days, weeks, months had he waited for this moment? 'Are you sure?' he murmured.

She replied with another kiss. *Never more certain.*

So he held her and felt his doubts float away. He had Connie in his arms; it was a dream come true. When she pulled back and held him at arm's length, he saw soft desire in her eyes. 'Sure?' he said again.

Connie nodded and led him up the stairs. They went into her bedroom and, still holding his hand, she closed the curtains then he lifted her and laid her on her bed – the untidy one of the two with the crumpled pink eiderdown and a damp towel flung across it. The imprint of her head was on the pillow.

She drew him down; felt his weight, his strength, let her mind float free. Her mouth responded to the kisses he showered on her face and lips. Here was love – the genuine article. At last.

Cranes were at work on Monday morning, clearing debris around what was left of the library and the railway station. A rescue team sent by the WAAF salvaged a Dornier from the grounds of the Queen Alexandra, attracting the interest of boys on their way to the nearby grammar school. They watched wide-eyed as the battered enemy aircraft was winched into the air minus one of its wings and with the Perspex hood ripped clean off. Two of the boldest boys ignored the 'Do Not Touch' sign, scrambling over the rubble for a closer look until one of the winch operators leaned out of her cab and told them to bugger off. Other women heaved on ropes and used spanners and wrenches to demolish what was left of the aircraft.

Back in the town square, a bonfire was made of thousands of library books damaged beyond repair. The few that could be salvaged were carried away in a council van. A rescue squad was present to cut off an underground mains supply – their helmets covered with special oilskin hoods. They worked with rubber-handled axes as a safeguard against electrocution. Meanwhile, an ambulance stood by with its engine idling.

Of all the buildings in Kelthorpe, the site that had been most badly damaged by Saturday's raid was the railway station. It had been built of red brick at the height of the Victorian era and its impressive gabled entrance had greeted travellers for more than five decades. Inside had been a ticket office and a waiting room and beyond that two long platforms linked by a pedestrian bridge. Three high-explosive bombs had torn up the steel rails and demolished most of the buildings. The station clock still hung on creaking hinges from its iron bracket, its round, white face smashed. A green metal turnstile lay on its side on what remained of a platform.

The decision had been made on the Sunday to employ a special team from the ARP Engineer Services. They brought in ten men under a foreman, whose job it was to check the damage then organize where jacks and blocks and tackles should be placed to raise girders and sections of sheet metal. Searchlights were set up overnight and cutting equipment was used. At one in the morning two bodies were discovered under rubble on the tracks and the emergency mortuary service was brought in to remove the crushed corpses.

Fred lay nearby, trapped beneath bricks and plaster. He'd been standing outside the deserted ticket office when a deafening blast had lifted him off his feet and flung him backwards through the door of the office. He'd landed under a sturdy wooden counter that had protected him from tons of falling debris. Covered in brick dust, he'd curled into a ball with his hands over his head then waited for what felt like hours but must only have been minutes.

Trapped. An eerie silence had followed. In total darkness Fred had explored the space with his fingertips – he seemed to be in a cramped hole just large enough for him to stretch out his legs and high enough for him to turn on to his back. Any movement had caused small pieces of rubble to rattle down so he'd kept as still as possible. There had been no telling how many tons of demolished bricks were piled on top of him or how long it would be before his air pocket was exhausted. And so he'd waited for rescue. And waited until his mouth had grown parched and his cold limbs had stiffened. He'd listened and hoped, lost hope then listened again.

The first noise from above was the faint sound of trickling water. Fred heard it drip and land close to his head. He reached out and paddled his fingers in a small puddle. With difficulty he was able to scoop water into his palm then wet his lips. Where had it come from? A burst main, perhaps. But then again the water might have been pumped in by a fire-service crew, sent to tackle the station's smouldering remains. Yes; that was it! And if the fire service had arrived on the scene, other rescue teams must certainly follow. In his coffin-shaped hole, with every nerve in his body stretched to breaking point, Fred strained to hear voices. Meanwhile, fine debris sifted through overhead cracks and the trickle of water increased to a steady flow.

The filing system in Hugh Anderson's office was poorly organized. Papers had been shoved into cabinets without any thought to alphabetical order or date and it took Hugh some time to discover the document that Harold and Pamela had requested.

'Fred's folder must be here somewhere.' He sifted through old letters of application dating back several years. A small, thin man, he had many of his sister Edith's attributes, including a tendency to worry and be thrown by any disruption to his routine. This morning, for instance, he'd reacted badly to a telephone call from her while he was having breakfast.

'Does it have to be this morning?' he'd snapped down the phone. 'Can't it wait?'

Edith had insisted. 'Poor Pamela is distressed about Fred's disappearance. The least you can do is let her and Harold look through his employment record for clues to where he might have gone.'

'Fred is an excellent clerk,' Hugh had conceded. 'I'd be sorry to lose him.'

'Then you must help her to find out where he went and persuade him to return to his job. Harold and Pamela will be waiting for you when you arrive at your office.'

And sure enough, they had knocked at his door at eight thirty and Harold had assured Hugh that he would make up for any lost time, explaining that Fred had been falsely accused of unpatriotic activity and hounded out of his lodging house.

'We can't have that,' Hugh had declared, immediately making up his mind to assist.

Pamela watched anxiously as her uncle sorted through piles of paperwork. Expensively dressed in a double-breasted suit and with a gold tiepin set off against a dark red tie, his thick white hair rose from a high forehead and was held in place by Brylcreem. He had a prominent nose and a small, grey moustache.

'Damn it, the file can't have vanished into thin air.' Slamming one drawer shut then opening another, Hugh went on searching. 'Look here, Harold, we need to create a new system as soon as possible; bring some order into the chaos. Fred would be the man for that, don't you know.'

Harold bit his tongue. Over the years he'd made countless suggestions as to how Hugh could bring more efficiency into his office but all his ideas had fallen on deaf ears. In fact, Hugh had a poor head for detail and the business had slipped under his leadership – hence the inconsistencies that Fred had discovered in the accounting system. And when it came to the crunch, Hugh's poor leadership had played its part in allowing a channel for smuggled goods to be created; a better manager of men would never have appointed George Bachelor as foreman, for instance.

'Ah, here it is.' Hugh pulled a buff-coloured folder from a pile of papers on top of one of the cabinets.

Pamela took a jerky step forward. A clue; any clue at all! Once more she felt the tug on her arm as Fred had snatched his hand away. She'd seen only the back of his head as he'd pushed past Tom Rose without turning round. Sirens and rattles, incendiaries lighting up the inky sky. 'Go down! Go down!' Alone, without the man she loved.

Hugh handed Harold the file. 'You see: "Enemy Alien. Category C" – quite clearly stamped on the front. Fred was open about his background when he applied for the position.'

'Who else might have seen this?' Harold asked as he examined the contents.

Hugh sat down at his desk. 'My secretary, naturally. The cleaner, the caretaker – any number of people.'

'Here's a London address.' Harold showed Pamela

Fred's original letter of application. 'And here's a letter of recommendation from a Mr Robert Lawson with another address.'

Hugh gave her a pencil and paper to scribble them down. 'Surely Fred wouldn't return to London. Did he have any relatives elsewhere in the country that you know of?'

She shook her head. 'None that I know of.'

'Any other connections that might help?'

'No.'

'But at least we have a name – Mr Robert Lawson. We'll write to him to see if he has further information about Fred's background,' Harold promised as he handed back the file. 'We'll do it tonight.'

Hugh patted it thoughtfully. A gold signet ring on his little finger glinted in the light. 'If I put myself in Fred's shoes, what would I do? Number one: the sirens are sounding so I take my sweetheart to the nearest shelter and make sure she's safe.'

Pamela felt a surge of hope suffuse her body. Perhaps her uncle's fresh perspective would offer a new lead.

'Number two: my intention is to get as far away from my current persecutor as possible and as quickly as possible. How would I do that? The answer is obvious – I would go straight to the railway station.'

'But there were no trains running out of Kelthorpe on Saturday night,' Harold objected. 'Not once the sirens started. And none since – the station took a direct hit; both lines were destroyed.'

For a heart-stopping moment Pamela feared that she might have to sit down. Her thoughts whirled. Why hadn't she thought of this? Fred must have left her and run straight to the station – along College Road, past the library and on through Gladstone Square, as bombs had continued to rain down. Her uncle was right – Fred's one thought would have been to escape from the town.

Hugh saw her grasp the edge of his desk and quickly offered her his chair.

She drew air into her lungs. 'No – thank you.' Her heart told her she must go straight there; there wasn't a moment to lose. It was a sixth sense, a sudden certainty that this was where Fred would be found.

'Pamela – wait!' Harold was too slow to stop her as she ran from the office, down the stairs and out into the yard.

'Let her go.' Hugh put out a hand to prevent his brother-in-law from following.

The two men stood at the window and watched Pamela's slight figure disappear from sight.

'All you can do is wait,' Hugh advised. 'And be there to support her, whatever the outcome.'

Water trickled in from above. Fred lay in three inches of cold water and the level was slowly rising. Vibrations from machinery that had started work to clear the rubble overhead caused chunks of debris to fall and trap his legs. There was pain but he scarcely noticed it. He heard voices but couldn't decipher what was said. Then the machinery stopped and the voices ceased.

'Help!' he cried out at the top of his voice.

Silence and no movement.

'Help!'

Silence again, followed by an order to turn off the hoses. The flow of water dislodged several bricks so that the wood panel above his head shifted then slid at a steep angle, trapping him further. Now he could move only one arm and his head.

'Help – man trapped down here!' Grit fell on Fred's wet face and into his mouth as he yelled for all he was worth.

'You hear that?' a muffled voice queried. Then, 'Turn off the bloody hose, damn you!'

Fred listened to bricks shifting, loosening and grinding together. There was increased activity, the same authoritative voice issuing orders. 'That's right – steady as you go. Not like that, you idiot! Slowly; one brick at a time.'

Dirty water trickled into Fred's mouth and he spat it out. They'd better reach him fast or it would be too late – those hoses pumped out hundreds of gallons per minute. The wooden panel shifted again, pressing down on his chest and making it hard to breathe. Then he saw it – a chink of daylight – directly above his head, then another and then fingers curling round a brick and slowly easing it clear. Light flooded in and blinded him. He spat again then protected his face with his free hand. 'Go easy,' he pleaded.

A face appeared in the gap. 'All right, son – I see you.' The man called over his shoulder for the rest of his team to stop work. 'I'll get you out double quick,' he promised Fred.

But time expanded. Each brick took an age to shift and every time the patch of sky surrounding the rescue leader's helmet increased in size more dust and debris fell. At last the man cleared the final brick and was able to lift the wooden panel that had saved Fred's life. He could breathe again.

Gentle hands – he didn't know how many – reached down and lifted him clear of the black water in which he'd lain. There were more white helmets against a blue sky. Dazzled, Fred closed his eyes and groaned.

A first-aider gave him water then quickly examined him for injuries and covered him with a blanket. Then he called for stretcher bearers.

'He was bloody lucky,' the first-aider muttered to the leader of the rescue team as he pulled a brown label out of his haversack and prepared to write. 'A few scratches and possibly a broken ankle, that's all. We need a name.'

'What's your name, son?' The team leader was an older man wearing anti-spark goggles and oxygen apparatus. He bent over the patient to hear his reply.

'His name's Fred – Fred Miller.' Pamela spoke for him. She'd run all the way from Anderson's to the station without stopping once. Her lungs ached from the effort, but she'd arrived in time to see the auxiliary firemen turn off their hoses. She'd heard the order to remove the bricks by hand, one at a time, and she'd held her breath as a rescue worker slowly raised a wooden panel.

'Stay back.' The gruff order had come from a fireman but she'd ignored it and the thin spirals of smoke drifting skywards. She'd scrambled over bricks and concrete and here she was, reaching for Fred's hand as he was placed on the stretcher.

Turning his head, he saw her and grasped her hand. 'My love, I'm sorry.' Faint words spoken through cracked lips.

'Fred Miller.' The first-aider wrote the name in capital letters then attached the label to Fred's lapel.

'Hush,' she murmured.

The stretcher bearers lifted the patient and carried him over mounds of rubble towards the waiting ambulance. And Pamela didn't let go of his hand.

As foreman at Anderson's yard, it was Keith Nelson's job to supervise the final delivery of the day: a load of timber from Sweden, off a Ministry of War cargo ship, the SS *Andromeda*. With Bob Waterhouse in charge of the remaining crane, the operation had gone smoothly. The yard was now quiet and Keith was carrying out one last check when the boss himself put in an appearance.

'All well?' Hugh asked his new foreman.

'Yes, sir.' Hugh was on his guard; Mr Anderson didn't usually like to get his hands dirty – or, more specifically, to get cinder dust on his highly polished shoes – by coming down from his office and crossing the yard.

Hugh cast a quick look around. The crew of the *Andromeda* were busy with ropes, cables and capstans, waiting for the harbourmaster to guide them out to sea. Timber was neatly stacked, the tall crane idle. 'Paperwork in order?'

'Yes, sir.'

'Very well. Visitors at the gate,' Hugh said in the curt manner that he reserved for employees, wrongly believing that it increased his air of authority.

'For me, sir?' Once more Keith was surprised.

'Yes, for you.' Betty had already clocked off, otherwise he would have sent her down with the message. Hugh had been about to leave for home and a glass of whisky before dinner when the gatekeeper had telephoned his office. 'A Mrs Connie Bailey and a Miss Lizzie Harrison,' he added, buttoning his overcoat and walking to his car.

'Right you are.' Keith hurried to the gate. Though he'd never met Lizzie, the name was familiar to him as Bob's fiancée. And everyone knew that Connie Bailey was John's widow. Since her arrest, tongues had wagged non-stop. But what the women wanted with him was a mystery.

'Is that him?' Lizzie saw Keith emerge from behind the cutting shed and nudged Connie with her elbow. He was shorter than she'd expected, with curly brown hair, a jutting jaw and the jaunty but pugnacious air of a middleweight boxer.

'Yes, that's him.' Connie stepped aside for a shiny black Bentley to glide by.

They waited for Keith to clock off inside the gatekeeper's booth.

'Now then, girls,' he began warily as he joined them outside the tall iron gates. He regarded them through narrowed eyes. 'What can I do for you?'

Lizzie had warned Connie not to jump in with two left feet – 'Keep quiet while I do the talking' – so she began by apologizing. 'We're sorry to bother you, especially after a hard day's work.'

Keith gestured for them to walk with him along the dock. He stopped in the shadow of SS *Andromeda* to light a cigarette. 'Is this to do with George?'

'As a matter of fact, it is.' Feeling Connie grow tense, Lizzie hurried the conversation forward. 'We've come to you because we thought you might help us.'

Keith gave an impatient snort before replying, 'Cut to the chase.'

299

'Very well.' Lizzie looked him in the eye. 'Did you meet George Bachelor in the Three Feathers in York?'

'The answer is yes, I did. But it wasn't planned; I just happened to be in York seeing a lady friend. And who should I run into but the Scarlet Pimpernel himself.'

Lizzie ignored Connie's sceptical sigh. 'You hadn't arranged to meet him?'

'Why should I?' Keith retorted. 'We're not bosom buddies – far from it.' He studied Connie's glowering expression with wry amusement.

'Pull the other one!' Connie couldn't contain herself any longer. 'You don't expect us to believe that.'

'Believe what you like.' He shrugged and was about to walk away when Lizzie put out a hand to stop him.

'No, wait. How come you and George don't get along?'

'He's a bloody big-headed so-and-so, that's why. He struts around like he owns the place.'

Resentment oozed out of every pore – Lizzie had no doubt that Keith was sincere. 'Carry on – we're listening,' she urged.

'It was Bachelor's gift of the gab that snatched the foreman's job out from under me two years back. I was first in line until he came along.'

As the cargo ship's whistle sounded and the anchor was winched up with a loud grinding noise and the rattle of heavy chains, Connie found herself forced into a drastic rethink.

Lizzie, too, was taken aback but she managed to hold to her train of thought. 'What did you say when you ran into him in the Three Feathers?'

Keith flicked ash from his cigarette. 'Not much. His two mates did most of the talking.'

'Saying what, exactly?' Connie spoke against the churn of propellers as the ship edged away from the quay.

'That it would be bad for my health if I mentioned seeing George.' Keith's flippant tone disguised the seriousness of the threat. Finding himself outnumbered, he'd promised to keep his mouth shut then hurried out of the pub, breaking into a cold sweat and looking over his shoulder to make sure no one had followed him.

'Then what?' Lizzie demanded.

'Then I slept on it. Next day at work I saw Betty giving me funny looks.'

'Who's Betty?' Connie fired her question before Keith had finished his sentence.

'Mr Anderson's secretary. She came up to me in the canteen and, blow me down, she said she'd caught sight of me in the Three Feathers the night before. I invented a big fat whopper – told her it wasn't me; it must have been my double.'

'Was she taken in?' Connie asked.

'What do you think?'

'You don't look like a man who would scare easily,' Connie challenged.

Keith flicked his cigarette stub over the edge of the dock. 'You never saw George's two heavyweights.' He picked a shred of tobacco from the tip of his tongue. 'Anyway, after my chat with the lovely Betty I decided my best option was to drop in at the police station after all.'

Connie glanced uncertainly at Lizzie, who stepped

301

in with the next question. 'Why the sudden change of heart?'

'I told you; I hated Bachelor's guts. Besides, I knew the cops would come after me if Betty let on that I'd been seen with him. The sergeant at the station wrote it all down; a sighting of the main suspect in the Three Feathers at half past nine on Tuesday the thirteenth of May.'

The turn of events stunned Connie and Lizzie, who both stood open-mouthed.

Enjoying their astonishment, Keith finished with a flourish. 'They're hot on his tail as we speak. I call that quits between George Bachelor and me, don't you?'

Connie frowned. 'Is that God's honest truth?'

'Cross my heart,' Keith said with a grin. 'But while we're at it, why not ask me about the row between George and your John on the day he died – the one that didn't get investigated at the inquest?'

'What was it about?' Connie's voice was faint.

'Money.' Keith confirmed Connie's suspicions. 'I heard them going at it hammer and tongs right here on this quay. John said George owed him fifty quid for the latest . . . consignment – that was the word he used. George told him to bugger off. There was a scuffle. They didn't see me and I left them to it. I went straight back to work. The next thing I know, George is in the yard, standing on a pile of timber with a split lip and blood pouring from his mouth. He's waving his arms like a lunatic and yelling at the top of his voice but a ship is coming in to dock, engines grinding and making a heck of a racket. I'm doing my best to mind my own business, dropping a load of logs in an area that had been roped off.'

'At this point could you hear what George was saying?' Lizzie asked as she took hold of Connie's shaking hand.

'Sorry – not a clue.' Keith turned down the corners of his mouth. 'Next thing I know, George loses his balance and slides out of sight. Bob Waterhouse is on the other side of the yard, jumping out of his cab and sprinting towards me – to warn me, as it turns out. Too late; I've already released the logs.' He stopped, closed his eyes and sighed. 'I'm sorry, Connie. That's what happened, without a word of a lie.'

It was as if someone had smashed a mirror and shattered the silvery reflection. Having convinced herself during months of stewing over details that John's death had been no accident but a conspiracy to murder, Connie now had to pick up the razor-sharp fragments and reassemble them. George Bachelor hadn't plotted John's death with Keith Nelson after all. It had been two dishonest men – George and John – arguing over money, plain and simple. Fury had banished common sense. John had lost his head and stormed off, blind to danger. Perhaps George had even tried to warn him. Keith had known nothing at all. At the inquest he'd been called to the witness stand and told the truth, the whole truth and nothing but the truth.

CHAPTER NINETEEN

A stern nurse made Pamela stand in the corridor while Fred was admitted to Ward A of the Queen Alexandra hospital. 'Wait here,' she instructed with scarcely a glance. Her starched white cap and crisply ironed blue uniform gave her a commanding air that brooked no argument as she hurried away.

Pamela watched the red second hand on the clock at the end of the corridor jerk around the dial. She breathed in smells of disinfectant, floor polish and fresh paint, pressing against the wall as porters wheeled wide beds and squeaky trolleys in and out of wards. Bespectacled doctors in unbuttoned white coats with stethoscopes strung around their necks discussed blood transfusions and dosages of medication with primly efficient nurses. Still Pamela waited, trying not to dwell on the hours that Fred had spent in the dark, trapped under tons of rubble, fearing that every breath might be his last.

She didn't care how long she had to wait – through the night, if necessary. All that mattered was that the ARP rescue team had pulled him out and he was alive.

'Pamela Carr?' A younger, more sympathetic nurse emerged from the ward.

She nodded and held her breath.

'You can come in now.' The junior nurse held open the door.

Pamela entered a large room with two rows of neatly made beds. She hesitated, waiting for direction.

'Fifth bed on your left,' the nurse informed her on her way out, letting the door swing closed behind her.

All heads turned expectantly towards the visitor then turned away disconsolately – all except Fred's; his gaze was fixed on her as she approached.

'I'm sorry.' He repeated the words he'd spoken when the rescue team had pulled him free of the rubble.

She sat by his bed and sighed. His face was unmarked, though his eyes were sunken and dark. A wire cage had been placed under the blanket to protect his left leg. 'Never mind that; what do the doctors say?'

'Pamela, forgive me,' he begged. 'I'm so sorry.'

'What for?' Tears of relief filled her eyes as she cradled his hand between hers. There was grime under his nails where he'd scrabbled at the earth and his knuckles were scraped from banging his fist against the wooden panel in an attempt to be heard.

'For leaving you in the lurch.' Countless times during his ordeal Fred had relived the moment on the steps of the shelter when he'd let go of her hand. 'I abandoned you – it was a coward's way out.'

'That's not the way I look at it.' She was desperate to ease his guilt. 'Far from being a coward, you helped me to the shelter and made sure I was safe. I call that brave.'

'But I ran away.' *In a panic, without thinking of you, thinking only of myself.*

Pamela refused to let Fred take the blame. 'I understand why you had to get away from men like Fielding and whoever wrote those hateful notes. They're ignorant, small-minded people who wanted to make your life a misery; but we won't let them win.'

Closing his eyes, Fred heard the passion in her voice. Was it strong enough to cancel out the years of flight and concealment that his family had undergone, to overcome the mindless hatred that he'd endured? A swastika and a noose – the notes had contained the most potent of threats, and the very thought of them made him tremble anew.

'My dearest,' she continued, 'we'll face this together. Nothing can separate us as long as we carry on loving one another.'

'Loving,' he echoed, opening his eyes. The word was like a soft breeze blowing through the dark chambers of his heart. Until now he'd guarded against love as a weakness, but as he gazed at the slight, grave, beautiful girl sitting at his hospital bedside, for the first time he saw it as a source of strength. 'I'll stay here in Kelthorpe with you,' he vowed, raising his head from the pillow to kiss her hands. 'I promise never to run away again.'

A doctor accompanied by two juniors came into the ward and hovered over a patient in the far corner. A muttered consultation occurred before screens were wheeled into place. A newspaper slid from the bed of another patient on to the polished floor. Someone else called out for a nurse.

'Let me speak to Uncle Hugh.' With a heart full to bursting, Pamela made eager plans. 'He understands your situation so I'm sure that your job will be waiting for you when you're better. My father will hold the fort while you're away. As for finding you somewhere to live—'

Fred stopped her. 'I may have a broken ankle but I'm not helpless,' he assured her. 'I can do that for myself.'

'Yes; of course.' She blushed and was about to let go of his hand but he grasped it more tightly.

'I'm hoping they'll let me out of here tomorrow with a pair of crutches, once they've checked me for concussion and so on. I don't suppose the rescue team retrieved my suitcase, by any chance? It had my belongings in it.'

Pamela shook her head. 'They'd be ruined anyway – you'll need new clothes.'

'I left a few things at Elliot Street – trousers and a jacket that I couldn't fit into my case.'

'That's good – it means I won't have to go to the next WVS jumble sale to kit you out.' The idea of well-groomed, dapper Fred wearing cast-off clothes made them both smile.

'You'll fetch them for me?' Mundane matters helped Fred to emerge from the shock of being buried alive. He would never forget the moments of gut-wrenching panic as the bomb had exploded or the thunderous shower of bricks and steel tumbling down on his head, but he would push the memory to the back of his mind where it would lurk with the flames and smoke following the Blackshirts' raid on his father's shop. A new life with Pamela beckoned and he would use all his strength of will to contain and control those close encounters with death.

'First thing tomorrow morning,' she promised.

With tears in his eyes Fred let his head sink back on to the pillow. 'Thank you.' *For being there when they raised me Lazarus-like from the rubble, for standing by me, for loving me.*

'That'll be one shilling and three pence, please.' Connie charged Dorothy Giles, the new usherette at the Savoy, for two loaves of bread and three teacakes. The ring of the cash register was almost as familiar to her as breathing and yet, as she pressed the keys and the drawer sprang open for her to insert the money and dispense the change, she felt uneasy. She was sure that Dorothy's unblinking scrutiny was tinged with contempt but the change was pocketed without a word and out she went.

Connie sighed and looked at the clock on the wall. Ten o'clock. Bert was busy in the bakery and Lizzie was due back from her first delivery of the morning. Connie's time behind the counter had never passed so slowly.

'Hello, love.' The shop bell rang and her Aunty Vera entered.

At last: a friendly face. 'What can I get you?'

'The usual brown loaf, please.' Vera delved into her worn purse for some coins. 'It's good to see you out and about. I've been worried about you.'

'This is my first morning back at work,' Connie admitted. 'Lizzie said it was like falling off your horse – the sooner you get back in the saddle the better.'

'She has a wise head on young shoulders, that one.' Vera handed over her money and took the loaf that Connie had wrapped in tissue paper. 'Talk of the devil,' she added with a wink as Lizzie breezed into the

308

shop. 'By the way, I've been meaning to ask – are the coppers any nearer to nabbing George Bachelor?'

'We haven't heard anything more, worse luck.' Lizzie spoke for Connie. The day was fine and warm so she'd been driving the van with the windows open. Her hair was tousled and her cheeks flushed. She wore a blue-and-white-checked blouse with the sleeves rolled up and a pair of dark-blue slacks. 'We had an idea that the new foreman at Anderson's might be able to tell us a bit more on that score but it turned out to be a dead end.'

'How's Arnold?' Connie broke in, wishing to change the subject as she spied another customer crossing the street. 'Still leading you a merry dance?'

Vera nodded. 'The little tyke tried to smuggle Scruffy up to Raynard's Folly again last night.'

The shop bell rang and as Vera departed, the new customer entered. It was Thora Mason, dressed in a grey coat and a shiny, helmet-shaped hat that had the look of armour plating. She ignored Lizzie as she skewered Connie with her gimlet gaze. 'I didn't expect to see you here,' she barked. 'I thought you'd gone to ground.'

'No, as you see; I'm back.' Connie put her hands in her apron pockets and stood her ground.

'They're not letting you out on warden patrol, I hope?'

Lizzie ducked under the counter with a disgusted grunt then disappeared into the back room. She didn't trust herself to keep a civil tongue when confronted by their troublemaking neighbour.

'By "they" you mean the Civil Defence, I suppose?' Connie swallowed a rising sense of humiliation. 'As a matter of fact, I've handed over my uniform until the business with George Bachelor is sorted out. But then I'll be back out on patrol, don't you worry.'

'Doing your bit for king and country.' Thora's tone was sarcastic. 'By the by, you've heard about the fifth columnist I was harbouring at number 21 – without my knowledge, I hasten to add.'

Recalling Pamela's distraught visit earlier in the week, Connie quickly made sense of Thora's enigmatic remark. 'If you're talking about the note sent to Fred Miller, I'd take that with a pinch of salt – unless there's any evidence to prove it.' She faltered under Thora's triumphant gaze.

'Plenty!' Thora assured her. 'His name is Friedrich Muller, not Fred Miller. It turns out he's a German spy.'

'Good Lord!' Connie gasped.

'Poor Pamela!' Lizzie had returned in time to hear the tail end of Thora's accusation. 'She must be beside herself.'

'That's not the end of it,' Thora crowed. 'After I turfed the nasty little turncoat out of the house he went straight to the railway station and got himself buried under rubble during Saturday's air raid. Apparently the rescue team dug down and pulled him out. I don't know why they bothered – I'd have left him there to rot.'

'Oh dear; how has Pamela taken it?' Once more Connie resolved to call on her friend as soon as she was able.

Thora viewed the situation in her customary black-and-white way. She snorted loudly. 'Miss Carr is sticking by him, thinking the sun shines out of his backside. If you ask me, that makes her as bad as him—'

'No one did ask you.' Connie cut her off mid-sentence as Lizzie flounced off again. 'Now, Thora; what can I do for you? Is it your usual Hovis?'

'Yes, and I'll have two of those sausage rolls, if you please – one for me and one for Mr Fielding. They'll do nicely for our tea.'

'I'll come with you,' Lizzie decided.

It was early on Tuesday evening when Connie acted on her resolution to visit Pamela. She'd told Lizzie of her intention and quickly agreed that two offers of support were better than one.

'I did know something about this,' Connie confessed as she and Lizzie crossed the street. 'Pamela popped in the other day and told me what had happened. She was having none of it – determined to believe that Fred was innocent.'

'Blinded by love, maybe?' Lizzie knocked on the door then stood back.

'Yes, and I ought to be the first to say that Fred *is* innocent until proved guilty.' Still harbouring doubts, Connie glanced up to see movement at a first-floor window. 'I can't bear this curtain twitching – it gets on my nerves.'

Lizzie grew impatient. 'Come on; someone answer the door.'

At last it opened a crack and a bleary-eyed Fielding peered out.

'We've come to see Pamela,' Connie told him without preliminaries.

'Not here.' He moved to slam the door in their faces but Connie stuck her foot in the gap.

'Can you tell us where she is?'

'Holed up with the German quisling, for all I know,' he grunted, pushing in vain and squashing Connie's foot in the process.

'No, she isn't.' From her attic room Pamela had heard Fielding shuffling downstairs to answer the door. 'She's here!'

Connie gave the door a hefty shove with her shoulder and forced Fielding backwards, allowing Pamela to slide past him into the street.

'Let's go for a walk in the Leisure Gardens,' she suggested to Connie and Lizzie. 'It's my night off so I've got plenty of time.'

Puzzled, the sisters adapted to Pamela's sprightly pace. She was clear-eyed and walked with her head held high, wearing a new summer jacket over her green dress.

'We thought you'd be the picture of misery,' Connie challenged. 'Not like the cat that got the cream. What's happened?'

As they entered the park, Pamela linked arms with them both and swept them up the hill, past the bandstand towards the sun colonnade. 'I'm in love,' she confessed with a wide, bright smile.

'We know that,' Lizzie objected.

'Fred loves me back,' she told them proudly.

'Now, *that* we didn't know.' Connie was aware that it was a long way up to cloud nine and she feared a bumpy descent for their naive young friend.

'He's found new lodgings,' Pamela continued blithely. 'Thanks to Uncle Hugh, Fred will move into a terraced house on the seafront, not far from Sun-rise. Uncle Hugh has vouched for him and the land-lord has agreed not to take any notice of the silly gossip that's been circulating.'

'Has he now?' For once Connie took her time to mull things over. 'You say that Fred is bona fide and Hugh Anderson is backing him?'

Pamela nodded. 'He knew all along that Fred's family had been forced out of Berlin by Hitler and that his parents had paid the very worst price for being Jewish—'

'Steady on!' Lizzie interrupted with a loud gasp. 'Jewish, you say?'

'Yes; what's wrong with that? Uncle Hugh says that Fred is the best clerk he's ever had.' It had taken little persuasion for Fred to accept help from his employer, even though he'd told Pamela that he was injured but not helpless. It turned out that the room on the seafront would be perfect for him; within walking distance of St Stephen's dock and a stone's throw from where Pamela's parents would be living. He hoped with all his heart that the stain on his reputa-tion would fade once the malicious accusation was accepted as false; meanwhile, he would grow a thicker skin and hold his head high. At any rate, that was the plan.

Connie stopped at the entrance to the colonnade. 'That's certainly a turn-up for the books.'

'You can say that again.' Lizzie gave Pamela's arm an affectionate squeeze. 'And the main thing is Fred is able stay here in Kelthorpe.'

'I know – isn't it marvellous?' With sparkling eyes and a definite bounce in her step, Pamela paraded

with Lizzie and Connie along the length of the colonnade. 'I intend to find new lodgings for myself
once I've helped Mum and Dad to move into the
annexe at Sunrise.'

'I don't blame you,' Lizzie said with a brief frown.
'Thora Mason is hard to stomach at the best of times.
And as for Fielding . . .'

Connie thought back to the days when she'd lived
next door to the Carrs on Musgrave Street and she'd
viewed Pamela as a little mouse who was scared of her
own shadow. Now suddenly it seemed as if she could
conquer the world. 'Have you ever thought of volunteering as a warden?' she ventured as they turned
and retraced their steps.

'Oh dear, here we go again!' Lizzie's comical lam-
ent echoed along the colonnade. 'Connie can't help
herself – she's always looking to swell the ranks.'

'As a matter of fact, I have considered it.' Pamela's
answer surprised them both. 'The problem is, my job
at the Savoy means my evenings aren't free.'

'It wouldn't have to be full-time.' Connie steam-
rollered the objection. 'You could cut back your
hours at the cinema and volunteer two or three
nights a week.'

'Yes, but Mr Penrose . . .' Pamela pulled a face as
she imagined the fussy little manager's reaction.

'Hang Mr Penrose!' Connie exclaimed with vigour.
'I can just see you in your bluette uniform with your
ski cap perched at an angle, looking adorable and
patrolling the streets with your torch and rattle.'

'You know what – so can I.' Lizzie struck up a
marching rhythm – left, right, left. 'I can see us all –
me driving my ambulance; you, Pamela, with your

"Put that light out!" and Connie at the Gas Street station, back where she belongs.'

Riding the shared wave of optimism, Connie showed Lizzie and Pamela her crossed fingers. 'Now all that's left is to get the police to drop the charge against me.'

'Watch out, George Bachelor; we're on the warpath!' Lizzie sang out. Her voice rang with confidence.

And the three girls marched on under the Virginia creeper, out of the colonnade and into the park, where the sun was setting in a warm flare of crimson, and ducks squabbled noisily at the edge of the pond.

It was Lizzie and Bill's first time out as a couple – a Saturday night when most of Kelthorpe was set on ignoring wartime deprivations and the ever-present threat of another air raid. They filled the pubs and took evening strolls in the Leisure Gardens or along the prom; a flow of cooped-up couples and families leaving their houses to enjoy the mild spring air.

Emerging from his harbourside cottage, Bill offered Lizzie his arm. She'd been nervous when she'd knocked on his door, wearing a pale-blue dress with sleeves fashioned as a short cape, draping over her shoulders and reaching midway to her elbows. The skirt had flared out as she turned quickly to see who might be watching her.

He'd invited her in while he finished getting ready. 'I don't care who knows about us,' he'd declared, fastening his tie then accepting her help to put on his jacket. He wasn't really a collar-and-tie man so he'd checked with her that the knot was done right.

She'd taken a deep breath, adjusted the knot and

agreed that stepping out together was the next big move. 'Be prepared for tongues to wag,' she'd warned him.

Now here they were, walking slowly around the headland towards the prom where they'd arranged to meet up with Connie and Tom. And in fact, Kelthorpe seemed not to know or care that Lizzie had broken off her engagement and found herself a new sweetheart. Children whizzed by on roller skates, old men sat and nattered on benches looking out to sea, girls sat on railings, their shapely legs crossed and revealing lacy petticoats as the breeze tugged at their skirts.

'See; the world carries on as normal,' Bill assured Lizzie. Wanting to show her off, he stopped occasionally to talk to fellow fishermen. They discussed tides and weather forecasts, drifters and trawlers, mines and submarines, and the ineffectiveness of the old Lewis guns that had been installed on some of the trawlers to ward off enemy attack. Lizzie paid scant attention and instead concentrated on the sparkling horizon, watching in awe as the sinking sun turned the blue sky pink.

'When will you be back in business?' one old trawlerman asked Bill, his face wrinkled and leathery, eyelids drooping under bushy white eyebrows.

'As soon as I've had the stitches out.' Bill hated being idle and was impatient to be back at sea. 'Tom's doing the job of two men while I sit on my backside. The good thing is I can start teaching first-aid classes again even while I'm laid up.'

'That'll keep you out of mischief,' the old sea dog said with a knowing wink in Lizzie's direction.

They strolled on until they came to steps leading down from the promenade on to the beach; their prearranged meeting place with Tom and Connie. It was opposite the burned-out shell of the Royal that nestled against the limestone headland rising almost vertically behind it.

'What kept you?' Connie demanded with her usual impatience as soon as she spotted Lizzie and Bill. 'We've been here ages.'

'Blame me.' Bill offered his apologies before they walked on together – the two men slightly ahead while Connie and Lizzie lagged behind.

'Well?' Connie nudged Lizzie with her elbow and tilted her head towards Bill.

'So far, so good.' Lizzie held up her crossed fingers.

'See!' Connie had told her not to mind what others thought. 'Your love life is nobody's business except yours. If anyone tries to poke their nose in where it's not wanted tell them to get lost.'

'How about you two?' Lizzie pointed in Tom's direction.

'Hunky-dory.' Connie hadn't needed to go into details with Lizzie about her time in the bedroom with Tom – Lizzie had simply guessed. Call it sixth sense, call it sisterly intuition or whatever you liked; Lizzie had simply known what had happened the second she'd set eyes on Connie. It didn't need to be discussed.

'Bill and I may not be moving full steam ahead as fast as you two, but the fact is we're two pairs of love-birds, billing and cooing,' she joked as they rushed to catch up with Tom and Bill.

A hundred yards further along the promenade the

foursome stopped outside a smart pub called the Harbourmaster's Inn.

'Shall we try a different watering hole for a change?' Tom held open the door for the girls and Bill.

Inside they found a large, red-carpeted room with a long, sleek bar and bucket-shaped lounge chairs arranged around shiny tables close to large, plate-glass windows. Connie and Lizzie made for an empty table while Tom and Bill went to order drinks at the bar.

'We've gone up in the world.' Connie settled into a plush crimson chair, straightening her smart slacks before neatly crossing her ankles. She wore a short-sleeved, off-the-shoulder white blouse that comple-mented a healthy, early-summer tan.

Lizzie agreed that the Harbourmaster's was sev-eral steps up from The Anchor then bemoaned the fact that Connie's skin bronzed more easily than hers. 'Why is that?' she said with a sigh. 'It really isn't fair.'

Then suddenly she froze. Connie turned her head to follow Lizzie's startled gaze. Who should have walked in but Bob. And who was he with? Why, none other than Hugh Anderson's secretary, Betty Holroyd.

The pair didn't spot them. Betty stood in the door-way, self-absorbed and fussing with her windswept hair. She wore a striking apple-green halter-neck dress with high-heeled black shoes. The neckline plunged daringly, attracting glances from many of the men in the room. Bob's back was turned to Lizzie and Connie as he escorted Betty across the room.

'Well, I never!' Connie's brown eyes were open wide and she moved to the edge of her seat, ready for a quick exit if Lizzie so chose.

Lizzie swallowed hard. Bob's hand was on Betty's bare shoulder as he guided her towards a vacant table. It was when he turned to make his way to the bar that he saw Lizzie, ducked his head then quickly raised it again. Their eyes met.

Lizzie stared. Unabashed, Bob acknowledged her with a nod of his head.

Seven years were erased in an instant – like a page torn out of an exercise book, crumpled and thrown into the waste-paper basket to reveal a pristine new surface beneath.

'Stay or go?' Connie used shorthand to decipher Lizzie's wishes.

'Stay,' Lizzie decided. Her mind was cool and clear. She noted that Bob, in a rapid kick-start to his stalled life, had opted for a totally different type: Betty was blonde where she was dark, sophisticated and chic where she, Lizzie, had a natural, take-me-as-you-find-me glow.

While Bob went to the bar, Betty took out a powder compact and peered into its small, round mirror. Satisfied with what she saw, she soon returned the compact to her handbag.

Tom and Bill arrived with the drinks. 'Is anything the matter?' Bill asked as he sat down next to Lizzie. 'You look as if you've seen a ghost.' He turned his head in time to see Bob carrying drinks to Betty's table. 'Ah!'

'Don't worry – he has a perfect right.' Lizzie sipped from her glass.

'Good; now you have no need to feel guilty.' Connie immediately looked on the bright side. 'Not that either of you should feel bad anyway,' she gabbled to Bill, her tongue running away with her. 'You're ten times more suited to one another than Bob and Lizzie ever were. And you're better-looking than him by far.'

'Connie, love.' Tom put his hand over hers. 'When you're in a hole, it's best to stop digging.'

'Right.' She blushed and laughed. 'It's true, though,' she said sotto voce to no one in particular, making them all laugh with her.

Betty and Bob left after one drink. No further glances were exchanged. A new chapter had begun.

'Now that we've got you two sorted,' Tom said as he sipped at his second pint of bitter, 'we should do the same for Connie. Yes, I know it's proving a harder one to solve,' he went on, 'but Bill, you and I did talk about getting Eric Thomson to change his story – do you remember?'

'Of course I do. You said we shouldn't cross swords without checking with Connie first.'

Lizzie intervened. 'Never mind that, Bill Evans. You're not to cross swords with anyone, you hear? Not until that wound has completely healed.'

'Anyway, what would be the point?' From what she knew about Thomson, Connie felt sure that he wouldn't budge. 'Personally, I'm banking on the police following the York lead and finding George – once they charge him he'll have to put his hand on the Bible and swear that I played a part in looting number 5 as well as selling on his damned contraband. Even he might not have the gall to say that black is white.'

Tom shook his head doubtfully.

'Seriously, Connie's right.' Lizzie was keen to avoid any more dashing in where angels feared to tread.

'Maybe.' Reluctantly Bill sided with the girls. 'There's

no telling what Thomson would do if we cornered him.'

They drank in silence for a while, gazing out as the gold disc of the sun slipped slowly behind the watery horizon – a full circle kissed the perfectly flat line dividing sky from sea then became a semicircle until finally only a sliver of glowing light remained.

'Time to make a move?' Bill was the first to his feet, soon followed by Lizzie. They led the way out on to the almost deserted seafront and the four of them were strolling back around the headland towards the old town when the quiet air was split by the blare of an intermittent siren.

Connie reacted as if she'd been stung. 'Yellow alert!'

'Here we go again,' Lizzie groaned. The promenade emptied fast. A few people turned tail and ran in the direction of the North Street shelter at the far end of the prom, scattering like ants under a giant boot, but Lizzie's group kept on towards the harbour. If yellow turned to red they would all be able to seek refuge in the communal College Road shelter just beyond.

The sound of the siren filled their heads but as yet there were no searchlights raking the dark grey sky, no frantic messengers pedalling by, no wardens setting up their cry. And so far no deadly drone of engines approaching from the east.

They'd reached the harbour when the siren suddenly stopped.

'False alarm!' A boy on a bike rode by, spreading the latest word. 'False alarm, everyone!'

Bill stopped outside his door, unsure whether or not to trust the latest twist. They all looked beyond the harbour to scan the oil-dark sea and listen intently. Tom decided that he would check in at the Gas Street station just in case his services were needed while Lizzie said she would wait with Bill in his cottage. Connie was happy to go as far as Gas Street with Tom then make her own way home from there. So the two couples parted company.

'Trust Jerry to ruin a good night out,' Tom grumbled as he and Connie hurried along King Edward Street.

'Except that he didn't, thank heavens.' She was relieved that the warning had come to nothing. As they approached Tennyson Street she slowed down.

'Would you rather make a detour?' Tom asked.

'No; I'm fine.' She shrugged off the cold shiver that had run up and down her spine. Old habits die hard, and as they progressed down the street she found herself checking blackout blinds and felt a spurt of anger when she saw that a light shone clear as day from the upstairs window of number 7. The front door stood wide open.

'Trust Eric Thomson,' Connie muttered. It seemed that their paths might cross after all.

'Wait here while I take a quick look,' Tom instructed her.

Connie's unease grew as she watched him approach the door.

'Put that light out!' Tom yelled through the door into the dark passageway.

There was no response and as Tom called again then entered the building Connie noticed that the door to number 5 was also ajar.

She stood for a moment, unsure. Should she call

for Tom to come back out or should she investigate without him? The street was empty. A few cars were parked at the kerbside and a bike had been abandoned in the middle of the footpath. Had Mr Ward's daughter been back here? It seemed unlikely; George Bachelor and his accomplice had stripped the house bare. Had a gang of kids somehow managed to gain entry? Or had Eric Thomson left his own house and come snooping next door to see what he could scrounge – stray coins wedged between floorboards, even a pound note?

Yes, that must be it. Connie set off up the short path. Her intention was to pull the door shut to prevent Thomson from bursting out once he realized he'd been caught red-handed. The same shiver passed along her spine. She had to step over the threshold to reach the door handle.

There was a short, vicious cry – like the snarl of a dog – and Connie felt herself being pulled off balance then flung down the passage as the door slammed behind her. She landed heavily on bare floorboards, heard the snarl again and put up an arm to shield her head. Before she could cry out for help, she was yanked to her feet and a hand was clamped around her mouth.

'If you make a sound you're dead.'

The assailant was no taller than her but he was strong, standing behind her and wrapping an arm around her chest. He smelled of tobacco and stale beer.

Connie kicked back at him and caught him on the shins. She bit the flesh at the base of the thumb on the hand that covered her mouth. It was no good – the man's grip tightened.

Then there was the grating sound of footsteps on stone – a second man was mounting the cellar steps. In desperation Connie used her elbows to jab at her attacker's ribs. A torch went on, aimed from the top of the cellar steps directly at her face. She blinked in the sudden yellow glare.

'The bitch bit me,' her attacker complained.

'All right, Eric – keep your hair on.'

'She bloody bit me!' Thomson thrust Connie from him.

'Tut-tut,' the second man said, catching her as she stumbled. 'Do you hear that siren, Connie?'

This time there was no yellow warning; the air raid siren went straight to continuous red alert. Connie tried to pull free. Though she couldn't see him in the thick, musty darkness of the corridor, the mocking voice could only belong to one man – her arch enemy, George Bachelor.

'Fritz is gunning for us,' Bachelor warned, shoving Connie back towards Thomson then holding open the cellar door. 'It looks as though we'll have to sit it out until morning; just the three of us.'

CHAPTER TWENTY

Tom's mission was to turn off the light in Eric Thomson's bedroom. Without a torch he had to feel his way up the stairs, stumbling over boots, discarded clothes and other obstacles, doing his best to ignore the stench of stale urine that greeted him as he entered the room. The chamber pot had overflowed on to the threadbare rug and he saw that bedclothes had been carelessly cast aside so that one corner of a sheet was draped over the stinking wet patch, soaking up the mess. He gave a grunt of disgust as he flicked off the light then felt his way back downstairs.

He'd reached the bottom before remembering that he ought to have pulled down the blackout blind so he reluctantly retraced his steps and completed his task. *This place is a pigsty.* He noticed beer bottles under the bed next to plates of congealed food. Holding his breath until he reached the front door, he only inhaled again as he walked out on to the pavement expecting to see Connie.

At that moment a shrill, ear-splitting red alert broke the silence. The false alarm had proved to be wrong; enemy bombers were close by. All along Tennyson Street people burst out of their houses; a woman carrying a baby stumbled against a parked car in her haste. Tom ran to help her up. The baby cried but was unhurt. The mother's eyes were dark with terror. From the house next to hers two young lads supported a third smaller boy hobbling along with a plaster cast on his leg. They seemed not to know which way to turn.

'Head for Maypole Street!' Tom yelled at them. 'That's your nearest shelter.'

The siren continued to blare and the dark street filled with anxious residents. 'Trust this to happen on the one night I choose not to go trekking,' an elderly woman grumbled. She clutched a knitted shawl around her shoulders and shuffled along in carpet slippers. 'I'm too old for this lark.'

Tom took her arm. He helped her to negotiate her way around an abandoned pram and a large heap of rubble from a previous raid that blocked the pavement. Then a man in shirtsleeves rushed towards them. 'Come with me, Mum – this way.' He thanked Tom then hurried the old lady towards Maypole Street.

Tom paused. Connie should have been waiting for him outside Thomson's house but there'd been no sign of her. Had she got caught up in the panic and run for shelter like everyone else? No, more likely she'd sprung into action at the sound of the siren; it was second nature for her to offer assistance. So he backtracked towards number 7, going against the flow of people running for shelter. 'Connie?' He stood on the spot where he'd last seen her and called her name.

No reply. The street was emptying fast. Silence except for the wailing siren. Tom looked up at the sky – heavy clouds obscured the moon and deadened any sound of approaching planes. His heart pounded as he realized they would have to fly in low, probably from the east, materializing out of nowhere with a sudden roar. By then it would be too late to seek shelter.

'Connie!' Tom called a second time, his voice more urgent than before.

The first Messerschmitts came from the west, not the east – three of them flying at under a thousand feet, dropping their bombs on Kelthorpe's defence-less streets. Houses collapsed in an instant; their roofs fell in and their walls caved inwards. A church spire toppled. Machine guns blazed; bullets shattered windows and tore up gardens. The engine shed behind the ruined railway station went up in flames.

Tom saw an incendiary land fifty yards from where he stood. He seized a fire bucket and sprinted towards it but the bomb exploded before he could reach it and in a great whoosh of air he was lifted off his feet and propelled backwards across the street, thudding to the ground where he lay, face down and motionless.

'Surprised to see me?' George Bachelor regarded Connie with amusement.

She lay sprawled across the floor in a damp corner of the cellar with Eric Thomson's foot pressing hard into the small of her back. A dim bulb gave enough light for her to see George leaning against the edge of the stone keeping table, calmly smoking a cigarette. By twisting her head she saw that Thomson was drinking beer from a bottle as he kept her pinned down.

'The scene of the crime, eh?' George gestured

327

around the cellar with its rusty meat hooks hanging from the ceiling and worm-eaten stepladders propped against the wall. There was a crate of beer at the foot of the steps. 'Only, the spoils are long gone, worse luck.'

Connie knew better than to resist. Thomson had knocked her down with brutal force and stamped on her hand as she'd raised it to protect herself. Her face was grazed from impact with the rough floor.

'All that evidence against us,' George mused. 'I wonder where it is now.'

Living on the run had done nothing to dent his sneering confidence. His appearance was as slick as ever – the same stylishly cut wavy hair, tailored jacket and polished shoes. He wore a gold signet ring on his little finger that Connie had never noticed before.

'According to Eric here, the boys in blue took the rum et cetera away for safekeeping,' he went on. 'That's what they call it but I wouldn't be surprised if a lot of it went missing between here and the Gladstone Square nick. And who can blame our boys in blue? Anyway, I must say, it's useful to have a sharp pair of eyes on the job. Eric never misses a trick.'

Connie groaned as the pressure on her back increased. It had become difficult to breathe and she feared she might black out.

'The trouble is, he can be heavy-handed at times,' George observed. 'But sometimes you need muscle power to get things done.'

She groaned again.

'You're wondering how come I persuaded Eric to join our little enterprise, aren't you?'

Connie wasn't wondering anything of the sort

but she was forced to endure George's boastful explanation.

'It wasn't easy; after all, you were the snooping so-and-so who reported him for keeping his better half locked up during the air raid. Now the poor devil has no one to clean and cook for him. But let's just say I talked him round.' Finishing the cigarette, George flicked it to the floor.

She flinched as red sparks flew close to her face.

'Oh, Connie,' George sighed. 'Don't look so surprised. It pays to forge new alliances, especially with your enemies. Yes, Eric's evidence against us was inconvenient, but what's done is done. Can't you see that it's far better to have him on our side than against us?'

She squirmed sideways, only to be pinned down more firmly by Thomson's foot.

'Think how differently things could have turned out. All you had to do was play the game according to my rules – the way Eric is now and the way John did until he got greedy.' Bachelor walked slowly around the table then ground out the glowing butt with the tip of his pointed shoe. His foot came within inches of her face as he ordered Thomson to stand back. Then he raised Connie to her feet, gripping her by the elbow and thrusting her against the table. His sneer disappeared and he spoke with vicious intensity. 'You didn't fool me, not for one second. I knew what you were up to right from the start.'

She shook her head. 'That's not true. You'd never have risked bringing me down here and showing me the boxes.'

'Well, let's say I had my suspicions and that was my

way of finding out which side you were on. And maybe I thought that even if you weren't convinced in the beginning, I could eventually bend you to my way of thinking – I usually can.'

His face was close enough for her to smell a mixture of cologne and nicotine. 'Not this time,' she said through gritted teeth.

He shrugged then stroked the side of her face before running his fingers through her hair until she jerked her head away. 'That's as maybe; but you should be flattered – I thought that you, Connie Bailey, were worth a long shot.'

'Why did you come back?' she demanded, her flesh quivering under his lascivious gaze. 'There's nothing for you here.'

Thrusting his hands into his pockets as if to resist temptation, he strolled around the table, kicking away the bottle that Thomson had discarded. It rolled noisily into a corner to join two others. 'Now that's where you're wrong,' he countered. 'I had a tip-off from Eric that old man Ward was rumoured to have a lot more cash stashed away besides the wad of notes we found under the mattress – a classic case of Scrooge not wanting anyone to know how much he was worth. We were about to roll up our sleeves and take a proper look up chimneys and under floorboards when you barged in.'

His big-headed way of talking infuriated Connie but she knew she must keep quiet. Thomson's fuse when drunk was notoriously short. One word from George and he would lay into her with fists and feet.

'And now this.' George rolled his eyes towards the cellar ceiling and the deadened sound of bombs exploding. 'How's it feel, Connie, to be stuck down here with us with all that going on outside?'

'Lousy, if you must know.' She put her fingertips to her bleeding cheek. Her breath came shallow and she felt light-headed. But she refused to give the two men the satisfaction of seeing her faint.

'Here.' George pulled a clean handkerchief from his top pocket. 'Couldn't you reconsider?' he wheedled. 'Think about it – you're already up to your neck; what's to stop us picking up where we left off? I could ask Eric to say sorry and make him promise to behave.'

She clamped the handkerchief to her cheek and looked fearfully from one to the other – George smiling without meaning it, Thomson scowling as he lurked in the corner.

'There's still money in this smuggling lark and some of it's yours for the taking. Think of the dresses, the shoes, the handbags. Oh, and if you're worried about your court case, Eric can alter his statement if we ask him nicely. That would get us both off the hook.'

Connie took a deep breath, dabbing at her cheek and playing for time. Was it her imagination or were the filthy, dank walls actually closing in on her? George's renewed offer made her sick to the stomach and her sense of self-preservation began to slip away.

He gave his mirthless laugh. 'Aha, that's got you thinking, Mrs Bailey! What do you say, Eric? Shall we leave Connie wrestling with her conscience and do what we came here to do?'

'Oh no you don't!' Furious, she reached the bottom of the cellar steps before them and blocked their exit. 'You're mad if you think for one moment that

I'll reconsider, as you call it. I was a fool to let you come anywhere near me in the first place. You're poison, pure and simple. As for this brute—' Too slow to ward off Thomson's charge, she felt him butt her in the chest. It was a hard blow and she lost her balance and fell backwards.

George clicked his tongue disapprovingly against the roof of his mouth as he stepped over her. 'Well, you can't say I didn't try. Eric, you're a witness to that.'

Ignoring the fresh pain, Connie sprang up and flailed with her fists as Thomson lunged again. She gave an angry cry as he grabbed her wrists and dragged her across the room.

'Stay here and keep an eye on her.' George took the steps two at a time and opened the cellar door to the deafening crash and boom of bombs exploding nearby. 'You're not going anywhere, Mrs Bailey,' he called over his shoulder. 'Not until we've knocked some sense into you. Eric will see to that.'

There was no telling how long Tom had lain unconscious. When he came round, Tennyson Street was deserted and a nearby house was ablaze. Acrid, black smoke billowed towards him, filling his lungs and causing him to cough and choke. Too weak to stand, he started to slither away from the fire. He seemed to go at a snail's pace, head hanging, using his elbows to push himself forward, his chest racked by further bursts of harsh coughing. He'd almost reached the end of the street when a large high explosive fell on King Edward Street and the vibration brought down debris from damaged houses to Tom's right. He covered his head and waited for the dislodged bricks to stop falling. Then a rescue squad trundled into view in an open-topped lorry. There were six men on board, all wearing gas masks and protective gloves, and when, in a flare of light from yet another incendiary, they spotted Tom crawling towards them, two jumped down and raced to help him.

'It's all right, pal; we've got you,' a muffled voice said as they hooked their arms under Tom's armpits and hauled him to his feet. They dragged him to the lorry, where a third member of the rescue squad gave him water from a metal bottle then wrapped a blanket around his shoulders and checked his injuries. Nothing broken, he confirmed; just a few superficial cuts.

'Get a move on back there.' There were reports of people trapped in a cellar on Maypole Street and the team leader was keen to reach their destination.

'Hop on the back,' the first-aider told Tom. 'We'll drop you off at the nearest shelter.'

But Tom shook his head. 'I'm looking for someone,' he gasped, his face streaked with soot and dirt, his bruised limbs aching. 'I can't leave without her.'

'You're Tom Rose, aren't you?' A member of the squad leaned over the side of the truck. 'He's a warden at the Gas Street post. He knows what he's doing.'

'You're sure you're all right?' the first-aider checked, leaving Tom the water bottle and handing over his own gas mask. 'I've got a spare in the cab,' he explained.

Tom nodded. Slowly he slung the mask around his neck and stood up. His legs were like jelly and his throat was scorched so he made his way to a nearby garden wall where he sat to drink more water and catch his breath. 'You carry on,' he insisted, his voice deadened as he raised the mask to cover his nose and mouth.

So the men jumped back in the rescue lorry and it drove off through the smoke, its rear lights blinking red in the gloom, leaving Tom to recover and get his bearings. He worked out that the house where fire still raged was number 13. The roof was gone and tongues of flame flickered from the upstairs windows but as yet the fire hadn't reached ground level or the mains services – if it did there was a fair chance of a gas explosion.

Where the hell was Connie? Tom's head was starting to clear and he backtracked over events. He'd been inside number 7 for three or four minutes at the most. When he came out she hadn't been where he'd left her – of that he was sure. After that it was a muddle – the siren, the eruption of activity; residents running, bombs starting to fall. He remembered the stuttering sound of Jerry's machine guns as the first three Messerschmitts flew in from the west followed by booming explosions that continued still. The enemy was flinging everything they had at Kelthorpe; dozens more planes had followed and were circling the town, carefully choosing their targets. Search-lights picked up some of the low-flying fighter planes; the daring tip-and-run raiders whose 500-kilogram bombs often did the worst damage because they were so accurate. One of the flashy blighters coming in at 1,000 feet was hit by the anti-aircraft boys on the beach. The Junkers exploded in mid-air in a spectacular burst of sparks and white flame, the fragments cascading on to the headland.

Connie, where are you? Fear on her behalf fuelled Tom's next move. He heaved himself upright and walked unsteadily towards number 7. *Take it from when and where you last saw her, work it out – knowing her, where would she go? What would she do when the red alert sounded?*

The fire at number 13 blazed fiercely. Roof timbers cracked and collapsed, showering sparks on to the ground.

She wouldn't run; of that he grew more and more certain. *Think back.* 'Trust Eric Thomson.' He could hear the irritation in Connie's voice when she'd spotted the blatant breach of blackout rules. 'Wait here . . .' Tom had said before swinging open the gate to number 7 and marching up the path. He'd glanced sideways and noticed in passing that the door to old Mr Ward's house was also open. A jolt like an electric charge ran through Tom's body. *Of course; Connie went to shut it!*

It hit him with complete certainty that this is what she would have done. Though the old man's house was empty she would have wanted to find a way to secure the building. She'd ventured inside and when the bombing had started she'd stayed in there for some unknown reason. And that – the reason – was what he intended to discover. Still groggy and breathing with difficulty, Tom approached the door to number 5.

Loathing filled Connie's entire body. Thomson was slouched in a corner. He sucked at a bottle and watched her every move. He had small, piggy eyes and slobbery, unshaven chops, glugging greedily at the beer, breathing heavily as he tossed away a fourth empty bottle. It smashed as it landed and he staggered slightly, wiping his mouth with the back of his hand.

The brute was drunk! He had to lean against the stone table to right himself and as he did so his foot came up against a heavy metal object hidden underneath.

'What are you staring at?' he snarled.

Connie didn't reply. *Drunk and incapable. The filthy pig.*

Thomson shoved the object out of his way with the side of his foot – a battered tin box containing a rusty saw and some other tools.

Connie's eyes widened.

'I said, what are you staring at?'

'Nothing.' She circled the table, coming as close as she dared to the box.

But Thomson didn't back off. He swayed and gave a nasty, leering smile. 'Don't think you can get round me.'

She took a step backwards as if to heed the warning. He slurred his words and his actions were slow and clumsy – he was no match for her if only she could get near those damned tools.

'I know your game.' He swore then wiped the spittle from his mouth. 'You think you can win me over. It might've worked on Bachelor but not on me. You're not my type.'

No; you prefer a small, skinny woman who you can knock about. The furious words were on the tip of her tongue. Without taking her eyes off Thomson she gestured towards the crate of bottles in the corner. 'I'm parched. You'll let me have a drink, won't you?'

'Not bloody likely.' He lurched away from the tool box to defend the contents of his crate.

Now was the moment! Connie darted forward and seized the first thing that came to hand – a heavy pickaxe. She wielded it above her head with two hands, poised to strike.

Thomson backed away. He tripped against the crate, fell to the floor and cut his hand on a shard of broken glass. Swearing savagely, he shuffled backwards on his backside as Connie advanced.

'I could and I should!' she muttered savagely. 'You deserve it.'

He scrabbled sideways, blood pouring from the cut.

One blow from the pickaxe and that would be the end of him. The gorge rose in Connie's throat and threatened to choke her. One single blow.

But she couldn't do it. Instead of bringing the weapon down, she reversed the pickaxe so the blade pointed backwards and she used the blunt end to whack Thomson once in the ribs.

There was a sharp crack and he howled and curled into a ball.

While he rolled in agony, Connie dropped the axe and fled from the cellar – straight into George's arms.

He caught her at the top of the stone steps. There was no leering smile now. His eyes were cruel, his grip around her neck tight as a vice. 'What have you done?' he said in a dry, grating voice.

Down in the cellar, Thomson continued to yelp and howl.

Connie brought her knee up sharply to catch George in the groin. He released his stranglehold and bent double. But the corridor was narrow and he blocked her way, shoving his shoulder hard into her abdomen and winding her as he rose to his full height.

Then the front door burst open. Tom took in the scene: George towering over Connie, whose face was cut and whose arms were wrapped around her body as if in pain; George advancing towards her, about to grab her by the throat.

Tom saw red. Finding new strength, he tore off his gas mask and pounced on Connie's attacker. Hooking an arm around his neck, he throttled him as he dragged him backwards. But George managed to dig in his heels and jerk his body forward, tugging Tom over his hunched back as if they were two fighters slugging it out in a wrestling ring then dumping him with a loud thud at Connie's feet.

She crouched to help Tom up and in the time it took to get him back on his feet, George had turned tail and run for the door. They followed, just in time to see him sprint towards his car. His figure was a black silhouette against the flames that had by now spread from number 13 to the neighbouring house. Yanking at the door, he slid into the driver's seat and started the engine.

'That's it – we'll never catch him,' Connie groaned. Weariness overwhelmed her – she was ready to admit defeat.

But Tom ignored her and sprinted towards Bachelor's car. He jumped on to the running board and clung to the wing mirror as the car pulled away then swerved around a deep hole in the road before braking hard as it approached an overturned van that blocked the road. Connie heard a squeal of brakes and saw Tom lose his grip and slide to the ground.

He landed on his feet and managed to dodge the door that was flung open in his face. There was a scuffle as Tom tried to prevent Bachelor from fleeing on foot. Connie raced to join them, in time to see the glint of a blade in George's right hand. The knife flashed and Tom ducked. It flashed again and missed its target a second time, then George wheeled away in fury and sprinted hard down the hill towards King Edward Street and the harbour beyond.

Connie checked that Tom was unhurt.

'I'm fine; let's go!' Bachelor had a head start of some twenty yards but he was on foot and he would have to contend with Jerry as well as Connie and Tom. The sky lit up with more incendiaries – sparks of white light illuminated a second deep crater at the bottom of the hill. Bachelor's progress came to a sudden halt. He was forced to divert down an alleyway. His footsteps rang out then stopped as he realized that the alley ended in a small, cobbled courtyard littered with upturned dustbins and broken furniture.

'Wait!' Connie stepped in front of Tom to prevent him from following the fugitive down the alley. 'It's a dead end. He'll have to turn around.'

Sure enough, Bachelor reappeared, wielding the lethal-looking knife, forcing them to back off by jabbing it at Connie and slashing it close to her face. His eyes glittered and his lips were stretched taut to show his teeth.

Tom pulled her out of danger, allowing Bachelor a vital split second to run again – down into the crater and out the far side then across King Edward Street to the harbourside, where he hesitated and looked over his shoulder to see that he was still being pursued.

Then he turned towards the dock area that he knew so well.

Heaving air into their lungs, Connie and Tom watched their quarry head purposefully towards Anderson's. Part of the high fence was down, destroyed by an incendiary, and a fire burned at the edge of the yard. Bachelor headed for the gap in the fence, his athletic figure silhouetted against the flames as he vaulted over stacks of logs then ran alongside the office building and round the back of the cutting shed.

'He reckons he can shake us off.' Tom knew there were a dozen places where Bachelor could hide. 'He plans to lie low until we give up and go away.'

'We won't give up,' Connie vowed.

They followed Bachelor into the yard, scrambling over timber and skirting the cutting shed in the hope of gaining a fresh sighting.

'There he is!' Tom pointed towards the base of the crane stationed at the far end of the timber yard.

Bachelor disappeared again, this time behind a smaller shed where goods were checked in and papers signed. The shed faced directly on to the dockside, with access on to the narrow quay.

Connie and Tom reached the crane in time to see George enter the shed. A sudden, massive explosion on the nearside of the headland shot a red fireball high into the black sky, lighting up the whole dockside – cranes, stacks of timber, sheds, ships at anchor, tenders and trawlers, tugs and rowing boats – and raining rocks and earth into the sea. They flung themselves to the ground and covered their heads. When the rocks had stopped falling they looked up again and saw that the shed where Bachelor had taken refuge had been flattened.

Connie's heart jolted then recovered. Was that the end?

Tom gestured for them to move slowly forward towards the wrecked shed. Three searchlights lit the headland. Their beams cast faint light on St Stephen's dock and Connie watched in horror as Bachelor clawed aside splintered planks and emerged from the ruins of the shed. He had survived. He limped towards the quayside, swaying and staggering as he went. Straight ahead of him was a Royal Navy Patrol Service vessel, a minesweeper used to escort convoys across the North Sea. It towered over him, its smooth grey bulk tethered to the dock by thick cables. Bachelor staggered blindly forward until his foot caught in one of the cables. He toppled, arms flailing as he disappeared over the edge of the quay. There was no cry.

Connie and Tom were sick with dread as they scrambled over debris. They reached the edge and lay on their stomachs to peer down the dizzying drop to the black water below. There was no sign of the fallen man. Water slapped against the ship's hull. The air stank of diesel and rank, rotting seaweed. Seconds dragged on into minutes.

'He's gone,' Tom muttered, helping Connie to her feet. The water had closed over George's head and he had sunk without trace.

She had no feeling of relief or triumph, no sense that Bachelor had got what he deserved; nothing except dark shock. A man had drowned – that was all she knew.

CHAPTER TWENTY-ONE

Pamela watched her mother fold her new silk scarf with swift, precise movements then place it in a drawer on top of two others. She disliked rayon, which she regarded as inauthentic. No; she preferred to replace the scarves lost in the Musgrave Street fire with the genuine article because silk, though expensive, lasted a lifetime provided you took proper care.

'Don't just stand there,' Edith chided. 'Make yourself useful by unpacking your father's suitcase.'

So Pamela took out two white shirts and hung them in the wardrobe. 'It's very good of Uncle Hugh to let you live here,' she commented, glancing through the open French doors at her uncle and father standing on Sunrise's manicured lawn. Both were smoking – Hugh a cigar and Harold a cigarette – and looking out to sea, their backs turned to the bungalow annexe where Pamela was helping Edith to settle in.

'Hugh is doing his best to make amends.' Edith didn't exude gratitude; to her mind, her brother's conciliatory move was long overdue. Nevertheless, the new situation was satisfactory – the furniture in the modern, airy bungalow was to her taste and there was a promise to build her a greenhouse in a corner of the large, shared garden and in due course to buy her a new piano.

'Do you think Dad will be happy here?' Pamela unpacked his socks, ties and handkerchiefs and stored them under Edith's direction.

'What an odd question.' Edith cocked her head to one side to consider her answer. 'He'll be happy that I'm happy,' she decided. Then, 'Your father has always kept his feelings well hidden – like most men, I suppose. He's seldom angry or hasty, which has been a blessing, but on the other hand I rarely see him jump for joy.' Even in the dim and distant past, when Harold had first courted her and she'd consented to be his sweetheart, he hadn't worn his heart on his sleeve. Perhaps that was what had appealed to Edith – Harold's steady, unshowy loyalty in contrast to her father's fiery, unpredictable temper.

Out on the lawn, Hugh and Harold parted company and Harold walked briskly towards the bungalow.

'Are your ears burning?' Pamela asked as he came into the room.

'No; why should they be?'

'We were talking about you; that's why.' Edith arranged her brush, comb and vanity mirror on the dressing table. 'Pamela is worried that you won't be happy here.'

'Oh goodness; never mind about me.' True to form, Harold brushed the question aside. 'I was just talking to Hugh and he assures me that the company can absorb the cost of rebuilding the shed and the fence after last night's raid. All being well, there'll be no interruption to our day-to-day business.'

'You see?' Edith murmured slyly to Pamela.

'And the police have identified the body of the chap they pulled out of St Stephen's dock this morning. It's George Bachelor, our old foreman.'

'Good riddance to bad rubbish.' Edith's sharp retort startled Pamela. 'Don't look at me like that. I thought you'd be the first to agree, since he's the one who dragged the Bailey woman's name through the mud before vanishing into thin air. I pay attention to these things, I'll have you know.' She shook out the creases in a pale pink blouse before hanging it next to Harold's shirts. 'Including the fatherly interest that Hugh takes in your young man, by the way.'

Pamela turned to her father for an explanation.

'Fred's wages will go up by ten shillings a week when he comes back to work,' Harold told her in his mild, even manner. 'Talking of ears burning . . .' He nodded towards the big house, where Fred had arrived and stood in conversation with Hugh.

Pamela gave a small cry of delight. 'Can I – do you mind?' she asked Edith as she flung ties on to the bed then quickly checked her reflection in the dressing-table mirror.

'Be gone!' her mother commanded.

Edith and Harold watched their daughter practically skip across the lawn. 'Those two will be engaged before we know it,' she predicted quietly.

'They're made for each other,' he said with a wistful smile as he slid his arm around his wife's waist.

Pamela had a hundred questions for Fred as they slowly made their way along the promenade. How were his new lodgings? Hopefully they were a big improvement on Elliot Street. Was his ankle still painful? Was he getting used to his crutches? Ought they to sit and rest in the nearest shelter?

Fred was glad to sit down. 'I have to keep this plaster cast on for six weeks,' he complained, putting his crutches to one side. 'But I've assured Mr Anderson that it won't stop me from going into work tomorrow – or manning the desk at the Report and Control Centre on Tuesday, for that matter.'

'That's the spirit.' Pamela couldn't help sighing as she gazed down at the activity on the beach, where a demolition team prepared to take sledgehammers to what was left of a concrete pillbox damaged in last night's raid. The sea beyond was choppy and brownish-grey under a misty sky.

She was dressed only in a thin, short-sleeved jumper so Fred unbuttoned his overcoat and invited her to snuggle close. 'There'll be an end to the bombing some day,' he promised her. *And to the persecution and the hate.* 'It can't go on for ever.'

'You're right.' She relaxed into the warmth of his body, resting her head on his shoulder and wrapping her arms around his waist, revelling in the quiet moment until the gang set to work and the pounding of their hammers startled the gulls perched on the roof of the wrought-iron shelter. The birds screeched and flapped away.

Fred kissed the top of Pamela's head. 'Will your father be all right with me now that he knows my background?'

'Perfectly,' she insisted.

'And your mother?'

'Likewise.' Pamela hugged him more tightly. 'As

you know, her bark is worse than her bite. Anyway, she fully approves of you, my dear.'

'That's good.' He kissed her again, tilting her head and brushing her forehead with his lips. 'But it won't all be plain sailing – you know that?' There were men like Fielding and the anonymous note-writer around every corner, fuelled by jingoism and ignorance. 'The first big test of nerve will be when I walk into the control centre again.'

She imagined hostile stares and muttered comments, cold shoulders and rudely turned backs. 'You don't have to do it if you don't want to. Someone else could take your place and no one would blame you.'

Fred's mind was made up – there was to be no more running away. '*I* would – I would blame me.'

So Pamela held him and they gazed out to sea, watching for a break in the clouds and a glimpse of blue to brighten their way.

Shock clung to Connie throughout the night, long after the air raid had ended and Tom had brought her home to Elliot Street. She'd lain in bed with the clammy sensation that a blanket soaked in seawater covered her face, making it impossible to breathe. She'd tossed and turned under Lizzie's watchful eye until eventually dawn light had crept into the sky and the girls had ventured downstairs to the kitchen, where Lizzie made tea then coaxed an account of the previous night's events out of her.

'I loathed George for what he was and what he did to me but I didn't wish him dead,' Connie began in a faltering voice. Her body ached from the blows that Thomson had inflicted and there was a large bruise in the small of her back. 'I wanted him to come clean, that's all.'

'He'd never have done that.' Lizzie patted her sister's hand. 'And from what Tom told us about last night, you weren't to blame in any way.'

'George believed he was above the law.' Connie would never forget Bachelor's habitual swagger – head up, chest out – it was etched in her memory, as was his grotesque emergence from the ruined shed; a Frankenstein figure clawing his way on to the quayside. She brushed a strand of hair from her grazed face then clasped her hands over the top of her head, as if to contain the whirlwind inside her brain.

'You must try not to look back.' Easier said than done, Lizzie knew. 'Remember – he was his own worst enemy.'

The gap between the patrol vessel and the quay had been no more than three feet wide. The drop at low tide had been as much as thirty. Bachelor must have hit his head against the ship's hull as he'd plummeted, possibly knocking him unconscious. It had been pitch-black as she and Tom had stared down into the oily water, waiting in vain for him to resurface. Dorniers and Junkers had circled overhead, releasing the last of their bombs.

The door opened and Bert came into the room. He'd spent the night fully dressed, sitting on a chair in his bedroom, unable to sleep. Hearing voices, he'd come downstairs to join his girls.

'There's tea in the pot,' Lizzie told him.

They sat together, saying little but comforted by each other's presence until there was a sharp knock on the door and Bert went to answer it. He came back with a bobby in tow: a tall, well-built young man who seemed too big to fit comfortably into the cramped space.

The policeman took off his helmet and tucked it under his arm. 'We've received information about an incident at St Stephen's dock late last night,' he informed them without preliminaries. 'A man was reported to have fallen to his death.'

Connie stiffened and flashed a frightened look at Lizzie.

'Who made the report?' Bert asked, as ever the voice of reason.

'Tom Rose. He says he was a witness.'

'And have they found a body?' Connie's father didn't beat about the bush – best to get this over and done with as quickly as possible.

The officer nodded. 'The harbourmaster identified it as George Bachelor. My sergeant sent me to inform you.'

Bert gave a small grunt of satisfaction while Connie drew a long, shuddering breath.

'There could well be a silver lining,' the well-intentioned young constable went on. 'With luck, Bachelor's death might mean that the sarge loses interest in the contraband case – with Bachelor being the main suspect and all.'

Lizzie was quick to jump in. 'That's right; plus, there'll be no one to argue with your version of events, Connie: that George tricked you into viewing the stuff in the cellar and that you never had any intention of getting involved in his shady business.'

'Quite right,' Bert confirmed quietly.

The constable nodded in agreement. 'Fingers crossed, you're off the hook.'

With another short grunt, Bert slapped the table with the palm of his hand.

But there was more. 'Oh, and we've arrested Eric Thomson for holding you prisoner at number 5 Tennyson Street,' the bobby continued. 'You've got Mr Rose to thank for that as well.'

Connie's hands shook as she absorbed the news. Tom must have done this after bringing her home and all she could think was that she must find him and thank him.

As a grateful Bert saw the policeman to the door, Connie told Lizzie her plan. 'I'll get changed then go to Tom's lodgings.' She winced as she stood up – her back had stiffened up and the bruises on her arms and legs hurt when she moved.

'You'll do no such thing,' Lizzie objected. 'You need to rest.'

'But I have to see him.' Despite her resolution, Connie sank on to the hard wooden chair and groaned.

'I'll get him to come to you,' Lizzie promised. 'For the time being you're going back to bed.'

Lizzie fussed, Bert backed her up and Connie gave in. It was two in the afternoon and Connie was fast in an exhausted, dreamless sleep when, true to her word, Lizzie collected Tom from his lodgings and drove him to Elliot Street.

'You have a visitor,' she told Connie as she shook her gently awake. 'Get dressed and come downstairs.'

A weak sun shone through the thin curtains as Connie struggled into her blouse and slacks then ran a comb through her hair. She looked a mess – her

349

face was ashen and there were dark circles under her eyes. A livid graze ran from the top of her cheek to the corner of her mouth.

Downstairs, Bert showed Tom into the front room. They talked of the aftermath of last night's raid, skirting round the subject of Connie's violent encounter with Thomson and Bachelor. When Bert heard Connie's footsteps on the stairs he quickly made himself scarce.

'I look a sight.' Connie hovered in the doorway.

Tom sprang to his feet and had to stop himself from embracing her – she looked so pale and frail he felt he might snap her in two. 'Here – have this chair.'

She ignored it and went to the window to stare out at the familiar Sunday afternoon scene. A small girl went by on a tricycle, followed by a black-and-white dog. An old man stood under a lamp post, shaking his stick and calling the dog back. The dog ignored its master and trotted out of sight. Connie started to cry.

'Don't,' Tom said gently. He stood beside her, their shoulders touching. 'Everything will be all right.'

'I know.' The tears fell regardless.

'You'll set me off.' Tom felt for a handkerchief then turned her head towards him and dabbed at the tears. 'Your poor face.'

Connie's fingers encircled his wrist. 'Will there be a scar?'

'No, it'll heal.' He meant more than the graze. 'You'll soon be your old self.'

'You came back,' she murmured. She'd been trapped in the house with George and Thomson – alone and terrified.

'Of course I did.'

'Thank you.' She murmured the words, her lips against his cheek.

'I love you, Connie Bailey – you know I do.'

'Yes. I love you, too.' Her whirling fears settled and she smiled up at him through her tears. Nothing felt more certain or more right.

Lizzie waited for Bill in St Joseph's school playground. She'd driven through the war-ravaged streets to offer him a lift home after his Monday evening first-aid class.

'I wasn't expecting to see you,' were his first words after he'd locked up. The class had gone well – he told Lizzie that he'd had two new volunteers, one of whom had asked him to keep her attendance a secret for now because her friends and family didn't yet know that she'd volunteered. The other was Betty Holroyd from Anderson's yard. 'I reckon Betty fancies herself in a warden's uniform.'

Lizzie suppressed a smile. 'I wonder what Bob had to say about that.'

Bill shrugged as he posted the key through the caretaker's letter box. 'I didn't get the impression that Betty would care. Anyway, she might not stick at it – to tell you the truth, she didn't seem too interested in bandages and splints.'

'It was probably the teacher she had her eye on.' Lizzie had no doubt – Bill was a catch in anyone's book – and she laughed out loud.

'Cheeky!' He swiped her playfully on the arm. The action tugged at his stitches and he grimaced.

'It serves you right.' She led the way to the van. 'Where to, your lordship?'

Bill glanced up at a cloudless sky. The first stars had begun to twinkle and for once there was hardly any breeze. 'Anywhere you like.'

'Somewhere nice and quiet.' Lizzie knew the perfect spot along the coast road to the north – a promontory with a spectacular view of the sea.

So they set off in the gathering dusk, glad to leave behind the bombsites and smouldering ruins, catching sight of a straggling line of nightly trekkers on the outskirts of town, on their way to the folly with knapsacks on their backs and blanket rolls under their arms.

'When will the bombing end?' Lizzie asked with an apprehensive glance at the eastern horizon. Conditions were clear enough tonight to tempt Jerry back for yet another go at poor old Kelthorpe.

There was no way of knowing. 'We keep calm and carry on,' Bill insisted. 'We drive our ambulances, give first aid and make the best of a bad job.'

The road climbed steeply, following the curve of the coastline until they reached the deserted spot that Lizzie had in mind. She parked the van on a patch of gravel then walked towards a lookout point where the local council had built a small concrete pedestal and installed a brass telescope with a slot for pennies and a collection box underneath. Bill delved into his pocket and produced two coins. He inserted one then invited Lizzie to take the first look.

She swung the telescope along the empty horizon. 'Ships? I see no ships!' she reported gaily.

Bill nudged her to one side. He directed the telescope on to the rocks below the promontory to watch the white foam of the breaking waves. 'Did you know there's a smugglers' cave down there?'

'Pull the other one,' she retorted.

'It's a well-known fact – the smugglers used the cave to avoid the excise men.'

'Oh, stop. I've heard more than enough about contraband lately, thank you very much.' It was Lizzie's turn to shoulder Bill aside.

'Sorry – I wasn't thinking.' Tom had brought Bill up to date with events surrounding George Bachelor's gruesome death. He'd reported that Connie was badly shaken but not seriously hurt.

There was a click and the shutter slid across the lens. 'Another penny, please.'

Bill stood close behind her to insert the coin. 'What can you see?'

'"We joined the navy to see the world and what did we see? We saw the sea."' She chirruped the Irving Berlin lyrics.

Bill encircled her waist and swayed her from side to side. The gentlest of breezes had sprung up and brushed her soft hair against his face. He breathed in the Lizzie smell of talcum powder against warm skin. 'What else?'

'A ship – no, two – no, three!' In fact, a small convoy sailed out of Kelthorpe harbour.

She handed over the telescope to Bill, who identified the vessels as British merchant ships escorted by Royal Navy frigates.

At the second click they stepped down from the pedestal and contented themselves with standing arm in arm to watch the progress of the convoy.

'It's a big, wide world.' Lizzie was wistful. 'Kelthorpe is a tiny spot on an enormous globe.'

'Canada,' Bill confided. 'That's a place I'd like to see.'

'Why Canada?'

'I don't know – because it's new. There's a lot to explore over there. Or Australia.'

Lizzie came down in favour of Canada because of the mountains. 'And the lakes and the pine trees and the snow.'

'Canada it is, then.'

One day, when the war was over and he and Lizzie had saved enough money, they would sail the Atlantic to reach its frozen shores.

Early on a Friday evening at the beginning of June, Pamela knocked on Lizzie and Connie's door. She adjusted her cap as she waited on the doorstep.

'Blimey!' Connie opened the door wide and was astonished by what she saw. 'Lizzie, take a look at this!'

'Coming.' Lizzie grabbed her key from the kitchen table. She and Connie had been gossiping so they were late setting off for their evening shifts. Whoever was at the door would have to be sent on their way. But it was Pamela, shiny and neat in a warden's uniform, complete with ski cap and gleaming silver badge. 'Goodness!' Lizzie exclaimed.

Pamela beamed brightly as she clicked her heels together and stood to attention. 'Junior Warden Carr reporting for duty.'

Amazed, Connie and Lizzie stepped out on to the street. They inspected Pamela's smart blue battledress – the pointed flaps on the neat top pockets, one with the letters 'CD' embroidered in gold, the gold stripe on her arm, the natty ski cap and the shiny black brogues. All was brand new – the very latest issue to replace the old ARP bluette overalls. 'When? How? Where?' they gasped.

'I volunteered.' Pamela glowed with pride. 'You suggested it, Connie, but I kept it a secret while I did my training – elementary first aid and so on.'

'With Bill?' Lizzie asked.

'Yes. I was the only girl in the class except for Betty Holroyd and she dropped out after the second session.'

Lizzie grinned to herself but said nothing.

'We covered anti-gas measures with Mr Harrison and how to deal with incendiaries. I got my special badge for resuscitation.'

'Well done, you.' Connie was genuinely impressed.

'This is my first night on duty.' Making the tough choice to volunteer was Pamela's proudest achievement to date. She'd discussed it with Fred and he'd supported her, although she would have done it even without his backing; this was something she'd thought through carefully – weighing the dangers against the challenges – and she signed up for herself and for her country.

Somehow the uniform made Pamela look even younger than she was. '"The air raid warden is chosen as a responsible and reliable member of the public who will undertake to advise and help his fellow citizens in all the risks and calamities which might follow from an air attack."' Connie wore a huge grin as she quoted word for word from the ARP Handbook. 'And yet they're happy to let a mere child loose with a torch and a stirrup pump.'

Pamela pulled her Card of Appointment from her top pocket and began to read. '"Town of Kelthorpe:

Air Raid Precautions. This is to certify that Miss P. Carr has been duly appointed . . ."' She stopped and thrust the card under Lizzie and Connie's noses. 'Signed by the Chief Constable, no less.'

'Good for you!' Lizzie hugged their plucky friend then dragged her towards the van with Connie close on their heels. 'Where are you based? Can we give you a lift?'

'I'm at the Gas Street post.' Pamela felt herself bundled into the passenger seat.

'Snap!' Connie jumped in and sat on Pamela's lap. 'Praise be – the sector warden has let me resume duties!' A call to action at last; back where she belonged.

Climbing into the driver's seat, Lizzie started the engine. It was a fine evening. Wisps of white cloud trailed across a blue sky and black crows soared on air currents above the rows of chimney pots, blown this way and that by a blustery wind.

It was the first night back on duty for Connie and a new beginning for all three girls. No one could predict when grey war clouds would gather to block out this sun-drenched moment but they would stand by with torch and rattle and with first-aid kit and stretcher. Lizzie's ambulance would carry the injured to hospital and 'Put that light out!' would ring through the streets of Kelthorpe once more.

ACKNOWLEDGEMENTS

A huge thank you to my wonderful editor, Francesca Best, for her support and encouragement, and to the equally wonderful Transworld team.

I owe an enormous debt of gratitude to those women, now in their eighties and nineties, who survived the Blitz and who generously shared their memories with me. Thank you.

The adventures of the Air Raid Girls continue in:

The Air Raid Girls at Christmas

Catch up with **Connie**, **Lizzie** and **Pamela** as they prepare for Christmas in the midst of wartime.

Available for preorder now.
Ebook and paperback out in autumn 2021.

The Spitfire Girls

Book 1 in *The Spitfire Girls* series

'Anything to Anywhere!'

That's the motto of the Air
Transport Auxiliary, the brave
team of female pilots who fly
fighter planes between bases
at the height of the Second
World War.

Mary is a driver for the ATA
and although she yearns to fly
a Spitfire, she fears her humble
background will hold her back.
After all, glamorous **Angela** is
set to be the next 'Atta Girl' on
recruitment posters. **Bobbie**
learned to fly in her father's private plane and **Jean** was
taught the Queen's English at grammar school before
joining the squad. Dedicated and resilient, the three girls
rule the skies: weathering storms and dodging enemy
fire. Mary can only dream of joining them – until she
gets the push she needs to overcome her self-doubt.

Thrown together, the girls form a tight bond as they face
the perils of their job. But they soon find that affairs of the
heart can be just as dangerous as attacks from the skies.

**With all the fear and uncertainty ahead – can their
friendship see them through the tests of war?**

Available now

The Spitfire Girls Fly for Victory

Book 2 in *The Spitfire Girls* series

Bobbie Fraser, **Mary Holland** and **Jean Thornton** are Atta Girls – part of the Air Transport Auxiliary team flying planes between bases. Taking to the air in anything they're given, their work is dangerous but their courage always comes through.

Now there's a new girl joining the ranks – Canadian **Viv Robertson**, who is bright, brash and brave. But will Viv settle into her new home with the other girls?

And when life on the ground leaves them as vulnerable as in the skies, can they stick together through the tough times ahead and ultimately fly to victory?

Available now

Christmas with the Spitfire Girls

Book 3 in *The Spitfire Girls* series

Yorkshire 1944: all they want this year is a truly happy Christmas . . .

The end of the war feels tantalizingly close, but Air Transport Auxiliary girls **Bobbie**, **Viv** and **Mary** have plenty more flights in their beloved Spitfires – battling everything from snow to enemy fire on their journeys.

Risking their lives doing their bit for their country, this Christmas they're determined to have some festive fun. But as they set about bringing good tidings for all, a stern and mysterious new flyer in the form of **Peggy** arrives. What secret is Peggy hiding?

Mary has a wedding to plan before her fiancé is sent away, but she then makes a devastating discovery so shameful she can't tell the other girls. Bobbie's beau issues an ultimatum, and Viv is wondering whether she wants a man at all . . .

With the big day around the corner and hope of peace on the horizon, can the girls find joy and love this Christmas after so many years of war?

Available now

The Land Girls at Christmas

Book 1 in *The Land Girls* series

'Calling All Women!'

It's 1941 and as the Second
World War rages on, girls from
all over the country are
signing up to the Women's
Land Army. Renowned for
their camaraderie and spirit, it
is these brave women who step
in to take on the gruelling
farm work from the men
conscripted into the armed
forces.

When Yorkshire mill girl **Una**
joins the cause, she wonders
how she'll adapt to country life. Luckily she's quickly
befriended by more experienced Land Girls **Brenda** and
Grace. But as Christmas draws ever nearer, the girls'
resolve is tested as scandals and secrets are revealed,
lovers risk being torn apart, and even patriotic loyalties
are called into question . . .

**With only a week to go until the festivities, can the
strain of wartime still allow for the magic of Christmas?**

Available now